The Suspect

Judy Baer

BETHANY HOUSE PUBLISHERS
MINNEAPOLIS, MINNESOTA 55438

Hear the miner's mother, at eighty-two still scrubbing the doorstep and tending her son, who says, "Life is so very sweet . . . I still find it sweet."

Hear the artist Goya, whose drawing of an old, old man—painted at eighty with desperately failing eyesight—bore the triumphant inscription "I am still learning."

Hear the Montessori teacher—vivacious, amused, alert—who says, "I'm nearly ninety-one and I'm arthritic from the top of my head to my toes . . ." but "I see well, so I read. Thankfully, I read. Oh, books, how I love you!"

Hear the student, age seventy-two, who is busy getting his Ph.D. in psychology and who says, "I have more projects than I can do in the next fifty years. I don't have time to die."

Hear the writer Colette who, though she spent her last years in pain on her divan-bed, set out—and lived out—these plans for her seventh decade:

"I am planning to live a little longer, to go on suffering in an honorable fashion, which is to say without noisy protest and without rancor . . . to laugh all to myself about things in secret, and also to laugh openly when I have reason to, [and] to love whoever loves me. . . ."

And hear Lady Thelma, ninety, who awakens every morning full of plans and who says that, although she's "terrifically old . . . there are still things that I have to do—a lot more things. Are you listening up there?"

I must mention one more woman, a memorable woman, a psychoanalyst and teacher, a lover of movies and books and museums and good laughs, who kept throughout her life that very sweetest of all hungers—her curiosity—and whose overriding interest in life was people.

The feeling was mutual.

Indeed, on her eightieth birthday, an Eightieth Birthday Committee was formed to accommodate all who wished to honor her day, and it took five separate parties—as it might

for some queen of the Orient—to celebrate.

But she never queened it over anyone—she was always the active listener, perched at the edge of her chair with encouraging "ahs," and in her wise and benign and utterly unsentimental presence people grew bigger.

"She didn't praise my work—she helped me tell myself I'd done well," said one of her students. And a former patient recalled that "instead of being my comforting mother, she tried to teach me how to mother myself." A friend of hers, attempting to describe the special magic that I and others instantly sensed in her presence, explained, "She always made you feel that you were being given something. No one ever left her empty-handed."

I met her only once—a small, fragile lady, attending a lecture in a wheelchair. She was struggling to breathe, and vividly alive. Within the brief time that we talked, I fell under her spell, I fell in love, I needed to know her. And I thought, I'll drive to her house tomorrow and leave a rose at her door, and maybe she'll like that, maybe she'll let me know her.

She died before I had a chance to know her.

But among the many legacies this lady left behind is a dream she told to a friend, who shared it with me. And much like poetry, it captures her essence in a few compelling images.

In the dream she sits at a table. She is dining with some friends. She is eating, eating with pleasure, from her plate and theirs. But before she has finished her dinner, a waiter starts clearing the dishes away. She protestingly raises her hand. She wants to stop him.

But then she reconsiders. And she slowly drops her hand. She'll let him clear—she will not tell him no. Her meal isn't finished, the food still tastes good and she'd certainly like to have more. But she's had enough, and she's ready to let the rest go.

This is the dream of a woman wholly in life until she died, the dream I would like to dream at the end of my days. This is a dream that tells me life can gently be set aside when it's lived to the full—not only in spring but in winter.

There is not, however, one "right" way of living old age to the full. People age well in many different modes. And sometimes quite opposite roads can lead to what sociologists call high life satisfaction.

Good aging is seen, for instance, among the so-called "reorganizers," who continue to fight the shrinkage of their world, maintaining a highly active life by replacing—with new relationships and new projects—whatever it is that the coming of age has taken from them.

But good aging can also be seen among the so-called "focused" types, who display only medium levels of activity, replacing a broader spectrum of involvements and concerns with one or two special interests such as gardening or homemaking or grandchildren.

And good aging can also be seen among the so-called "disengaged"—inner-directed but certainly not self-absorbed—who accept and adapt to their shrinking world and who find great satisfaction in contemplative, withdrawn, low-activity lives.

There are those whose good old age consists of gazing with serenity at the troubled, imperfect world which they inhabit, in contrast to, say, the Gray Panthers, who are enjoying their old age by fighting "for social initiative, for freedom, justice and peace for all persons everywhere." There also are those who pride themselves on maintaining their manners and morals in the face of some of age's cruelest blows, and those who in their last decades give up the poses and deceptions of a lifetime.

Old age can be active or disengaged, feisty or serene, a keeping up of our front or a dropping of masks, a consolidation of what we know and what we've done before, or a new—even unconventional—exploration. Consider, for instance, Jenny Joseph's "Warning":

> *When I am an old woman I shall wear purple*
> *With a red hat which doesn't go, and doesn't suit me,*
> *And I shall spend my pension on brandy and summer gloves*
> *And satin sandals, and say we've no money for butter.*
> *I shall sit down on the pavement when I'm tired*
> *And gobble up samples in shops and press alarm bells*
> *And run my stick along the public railings*
> *And make up for the sobriety of my youth.*
> *I shall go out in my slippers in the rain*
> *And pick the flowers in other people's gardens*
> *And learn to spit.*

Less rebellious old ladies may prefer to rock in their rocking chairs. That too, of course, can make for a good old age.

It is easier to grow old if we are neither bored nor boring, if we have people and projects we care about, if we are open and flexible and mature enough to submit—when we need to submit—to immutable losses. The process, begun in infancy, of loving and letting go can help prepare us for these final losses. But stripped—as age does strip us—of some of what we love in ourselves, we may find that a good old age demands a capacity for what is called "ego transcendence."

A capacity to feel pleasure in the pleasures of other people.

A capacity for concern about events not directly related to our self-interest.

A capacity to invest ourselves (though we won't be around to see it) in tomorrow's world.

Ego transcendence allows us, while perceiving our-

selves as finite, to connect to the future through people or through ideas, surpassing our personal limits by means of some legacy we can leave to the next generation. As grandparents, teachers, mentors, social reformers, collectors of art—or creators of art—we can touch those who will be there when we are gone. This endeavor to leave a trace—intellectual, spiritual, material, even physical—is a constructive way of dealing with the grief we are feeling over the loss of ourself.

An investment in the future through the leaving of a legacy can help enhance the quality of old age. But so does a stronger emphasis on the pleasures of the moment and a capacity to live in the here and now. In a good growing old we can stop obsessing about time running out and learn to fully inhabit the time we are in, acquiring what Butler calls "a sense of presentness or elementality," and what Fisher calls that reward of age "when the sound of a child's laugh, or the catch of sunlight on a flower petal is as poignant as ever was a girl's voice to an adolescent ear, or the tap of a golf-ball into its cup to a balding banker's."

When the present and future have value to us, old age can be enhanced. But of course the past is of vast importance too. Through memory we can be sustained by the "great sights" of our own history, by a "vanished geography" we can always walk through. We also can engage in what Butler terms "the life review"—a taking stock, a summing up, a final integration of our past.

In examining the past we are engaged in the central task which Erikson assigns to the eighth age of man. And if this examination is not to lead to disgust and despair but to "integrity," we will have to accept our "one and only life cycle," call it our own and—imperfections and all—find meaning and value in it.

We will have to accept, says Erikson, "the fact that one's life is one's own responsibility."

* * *

Old age is our responsibility too.

Indeed, it has been argued that healthy-enough older people should not be exempt from the judgments of the world, and that if they are boring, garrulous, self-centered, vapid, querulous or obsessed with the state of their belly and their bowels, we sometimes ought to say to them, "Shape up!"—or as Ronald Blythe rather coolly puts it, "How can you expect us to be interested in this minimal you, with your mean days and little grumbles?"

Butler adds that the old should not be treated as if age made them moral eunuchs. He says that they still can do harm, and still atone. He says that the old remain capable of cruelty and greed and assorted misdeeds and that it "denigrates their humanness" to exempt them from responsibility and guilt.

He also says that the old "have made—and continue to make—their own contribution to their own fate." These contributions to the specific character of an old age may begin in childhood.

For in our daily experience we see evidence of the elderly becoming ever more clearly what they have been. And the way we too may age—be it self-pityingly or bitterly or gallantly—has been in large measure prepared for earlier on. All of us have met those types whom Fisher calls "bright souls"—merry, lively, serene both in youth and old age. But because the greatest stresses of life are likely to occur in our later years, and because disturbing traits are very likely to be accentuated by stress, the mean may get meaner, the fearful may get more afraid and the apathetic may sink into near-paralysis.

Many students of aging agree that the core of our personality tends to remain rather constant through our life, concluding that we are, in old age, the person we've always

been . . . except maybe more so. In a study of *Personality and Patterns of Aging*, the authors found that, confronted with "a wide range of social and biological changes," the aging person

> continues to exercise choice and to select from the environment in accordance with his own long-established needs. He ages according to a pattern that has a long history and that maintains itself, with adaptation, to the end of life. . . . There is considerable evidence that, in normal men and women, there is no sharp discontinuity of personality with age, but instead an increasing consistency. Those characteristics that have been central to the personality seem to become even more clearly delineated. . . .

But although our present is shaped by our past, personality changes are possible, even unto the seventh, eighth, ninth decade. We are never a "finished product"—we refine and we rearrange and we revise. Normal development doesn't end, and over the course of our life, important new tasks—or crises—will arise. We can change in old age because every stage of our life, including our last one, affords new opportunities for change.

"All is uncharted and uncertain," writes octogenarian Florida Scott-Maxwell; "we seem to lead the way into the unknown. It can feel as though all our lives we have been caught in absurdly small personalities and circumstances and beliefs. Our accustomed shell cracks here, cracks there, and that tiresomely rigid person we supposed to be ourselves stretches, expands. . . ."

Among the great expanders of our time is the world-famous baby doctor Benjamin Spock, a vigorous octogenarian who has traveled quite a way from his conservative WASP New England Republican origins. Furthermore, although he probably ceased to believe early on that Calvin Coolidge was our greatest President, all of Spock's astonishing life

changes have taken place in his sixties and seventies.

For during those years the highly respected author of *Baby and Child Care*, a book whose sales figures are currently over 30 million and whose reassuring good sense had won him the affection and gratitude of mothers all over the world, put his reputation, repose, comfort and income on the line because his conscience told him that he had to. Morally outraged by the Vietnam war, Spock became increasingly involved in the antiwar movement of the 1960s, marching in demonstrations, being arrested for civil disobedience and, in 1968, indicted, tried and convicted for conspiracy to aid and abet draft resistance. (Subsequently, however, a higher court not only overturned the conviction but directed an order of acquittal.)

The consequences of his political activism, Spock tells me, were sometimes painful, for many of those who had formerly been so admiring reviled him as a commie, a traitor and worse. But once he became convinced of the moral correctness of his position, there was no turning back, he explains, because "You can't say to people, 'Well, I think I've done enough,' or 'I'm getting scared,' or 'I might lose some sales on *Baby and Child Care*.'"

Not turning back, Spock ran for President on the People's Party ticket in 1972, and for Vice President in 1976. He also became a feminist, his consciousness raised by critics like Gloria Steinem, who admonished him for being "a major oppressor of women, in the same category as Sigmund Freud." Spock jokes that "I tried to get what satisfaction I could from being linked that closely with Sigmund Freud," but he took her and other criticisms of his sexism to heart and is now a staunch defender of women's rights.

Another major change in the 1970s was ending his marriage to his wife, Jane, a marriage which had lasted for almost half a century. And yet, when I ask Spock if he ever

feels guilty about leaving his wife, he answers without hesitation that he does not, explaining that the divorce had been preceded by five years of therapy in an effort to resolve their marital differences.

"I'm a fantastically guilt-ridden person, a person who feels guilty about ... everything," Spock says. But it was precisely because of his gift for guilt that he was compelled to try particularly hard and long—too long, he now believes—to repair the marriage. Like his political activism, his decision to divorce was well thought out—intellectual, not emotional—and once made, not subject to second thoughts and agonizing. Divorcing Jane, he felt then and he feels now, was "the right thing."

In 1976 Benjamin Spock took a new wife, a feisty woman—forty years younger than he—named Mary Morgan, who introduced him to his first body massage and his first Jacuzzi and his first (initially "very difficult") experience as stepfather to a teenaged girl. Spock says he fell for Mary because she was "energetic, vivacious, determined and beautiful—and I liked her enthusiasm for me, I ate it up." With her heavy Arkansas drawl (she calls him "Bin"), sassy ways and insistent physicality, she isn't much like the sixty-five-year-old lady with the Vassar in her voice whom, he suspects, his sons expected him to marry. But Mary is—in addition to cuddly—a shrewd, highly competent woman who now arranges the details of Spock's professional life, who worries about him and takes care of him—and who gives him the adoration he adores. The differences between them are the normal tensions of marriage; they aren't due, Spock says, to the difference in age. And in response to my question he describes himself, judiciously, as "a happily married man—with reservations."

The Spocks live part of the time in Arkansas and part of the time on two sailboats—one in the Virgin Islands, one in Maine—with Spock continuing to speak out on po-

litical issues and to engage in an occasional act of civil disobedience, while writing a column on child care for *Redbook* magazine. In addition, he is currently receiving individual therapy, couples therapy and group therapy because, he ruefully tells me, two wives, two sons and several therapists have informed him over the years that he is a man who is out of touch with his feelings.

Meanwhile, however, he doesn't seem all that worried about it. Indeed, he seems like a man who is feeling pretty damn good about himself. He says that there is a photograph taken of him at age one which may help explain why.

In this photo he is sitting in a little-boy-sized chair, elegantly turned out in a hat, a dress, a fancy coat with scalloped collar, neat white socks and sparkling Mary Jane shoes. His feet don't quite touch the ground but his hands are firmly planted on the arms of his chair. And on his handsome and amiable face is a smile, a smile of confident expectation, the smile of a child who knows, Spock says, "that the world is his oyster."

It is clear that he still believes that the world is his oyster. And why not? He has come to his eighties with his intelligence, passions, health and good looks intact. In any room he enters he is more than likely to be the most noticeable (six feet four and slim, with perfect posture), the most charming (great hugger, great kisser, great storyteller), the most cheerful (twinkling blue eyes, ready laughter) and the most sheerly attractive person present. He is an ardent sailor, an enthusiastic early-morning rower, an accomplished late-into-the-night dancer. He is also, he says, the beneficiary of good genes ("I think that the fact that I'm spry at eighty is partly that my mother lived to be ninety-three") and of a lifelong optimism which derives from the fact that his mother—harsh and critical though she could be—"gave me a feeling of being very well loved."

Spock describes himself as a man who has grown

"younger in spirit as the decades have gone on," as well as less judgmental, less hard-driving, less reserved and far more demonstrative. He says, "I can recognize that I'm old, and I'm not embarrassed that I'm old, but I don't—I never do—*feel* old." He concedes, however, that he "can't expect to have the same perkiness and vigor at ninety that I've managed to maintain at eighty. You've got to begin sliding sooner or later." His concern when the slide starts, he says, is to not be pathetic, is to remain dignified, is— and he is kidding but also not kidding—"to be particularly careful to look at my suits to make sure there's no spots on them, and to be particularly concerned when I come out of the bathroom in public that I've zipped up my zipper."

As for death, he says it doesn't worry him—"probably," he adds with a grin, "because I'm not in touch with my feelings." But, he hastens to promise, he'll keep trying to get in touch with them—"I'm going to keep trying, right up until the end."

Our earlier life history is important in determining our capacity to change and grow in old age. But age itself may also call forth new strengths and new capabilities that weren't available at previous stages. There may be more wisdom, more freedom, more perspective and more toughness. There may be more candor with others, more self-honesty. There also may be a shift in the way we perceive the hard times in our life—a shift from "tragedy" to "irony."

By tragedy I mean a perception that leaves no room for other possibilities. Tragedy is all-encompassing and all black. There is no yesterday. There is no tomorrow. There is no hope. There is no consolation. There is only absolutely rotten, totally irreparable now. Irony sees the same event written a little smaller. Its blackness doesn't fill the entire

screen. Irony offers a context in which we are able to tell ourselves that things could be worse. It also offers a context in which we even might imagine that things could get better. This shift in perception from tragedy to irony may be the special gift of our late years, helping us to deal with our accumulating losses and sometimes also helping us to grow.

With flexibility and perhaps a touch of irony, we can continue to change and grow in old age. But we also can change and grow in old age—though Sigmund Freud said otherwise—through psychoanalysis and psychotherapy.

Certainly psychotherapy can ease the emotional problems that the coming of age may initiate or intensify: anxiety, hypochondria, paranoia and—most prevalent—depression. But in addition to the relief that psychotherapy can provide, psychological work with the old can effect sweeping change, bringing vital transformations through a process Pollock calls "mourning-liberation." He writes:

> The basic insight is that parts of self that once were, or that one hoped might be, are no longer possible. With the working out of the mourning for a changed self, lost others, unfulfilled hopes and aspirations, as well as feelings about other reality losses and changes, there is an increasing ability to face reality as it is and as it can be. "Liberation" from the past and the unattainable occurs. New sublimations, interests and activities appear. There can be new relationships. . . . Past truly can become past, distinguished from present and future. Affects of serenity, joy, pleasure and excitement come into being.

Psychoanalysts report that psychoanalysis with the elderly has helped their patients retrieve their sense of self-worth; has helped them to forgive others—and themselves; has helped them find new adaptations when old age has rendered their past adaptations unworkable; has even helped a woman in her mid-seventies to become orgastic for the first time! In this same report we encounter a woman who—sixty years after the fact—was able to get over the anger she felt at the death of her mother, becoming free thereafter

to write, to stabilize her marriage and to accept the prospect of her own mortality. We also encounter a man who, ending a six-year analysis at age sixty-five, experiences a vital new sense of aliveness. And although he died at age seventy, he felt that in his final eleven years he was happier than he had ever been in his life.

Why, a seventy-six-year-old woman was asked, are you seeking therapy at *your* age? Reflecting both her losses and hopes, she answered, unforgettably, "Doctor, all I've got left is my future."

Some of the old sit waiting, Blythe tells us, for Meals on Wheels or death—whichever comes first. Some of the old, like my friend the seventy-two-year-old Ph.D. candidate, have so many projects they'll never have time to die. Some speak of death, some think of death, some suffer enough to long for death, and others will deny and deny and deny, successfully persuading themselves that death will make an exception in their case.

But there seems to be no evidence that the old are especially haunted by fears of death. Indeed, they may be less frightened of it than the young. Furthermore, the conditions of their dying—it often is said—are of greater concern to them than is death itself.

Nevertheless, it is true, as Sophocles poignantly observes in a play he wrote at the age of eighty-nine, that

> *Though he has watched a decent age pass by,*
> *A man will sometimes still desire the world.*

And it is also true that in dying and death—whatever the dying is like, whatever the death means—we come face-to-face with the ultimate separation.

19 ~

The ABC of Dying

> A person spends years coming into his own, developing
> his talent, his unique gifts, perfecting his discriminations
> about the world, broadening and sharpening his appe-
> tite, learning to bear the disappointments of life, be-
> coming mature, seasoned—finally a unique creature in
> nature, standing with some dignity and nobility and
> transcending the animal condition; no longer driven, no
> longer a complete reflex, not stamped out of any mold.
> And then the real tragedy...: that it takes sixty years
> of incredible suffering and effort to make such an in-
> dividual, and then he is good only for dying.
>
> —ERNEST BECKER

*W*hen I was a little girl I used to close my
eyes at night and imagine the world going on and on forever.
I'd imagine, with absolute terror, the world going on and
on forever—and me not there. Freud writes that we are
incapable of imagining our own death, but I am here to tell
you that's not true. Please God, I used to pray, I know you
can't take death away. But couldn't you just arrange for
me to stop thinking about it?

Whether or not fear of death is, in fact, a universal fear, it
is surely a feeling that most of us cannot abide. Consciously
or unconsciously, we push death thoughts away. We live a

342

life in which death is denied. This doesn't mean we deny the fact that all men and women, including ourselves, are mortal. Nor does this mean we avoid the articles, seminars, TV programs which feature the now chic subject of Dying and Death. What it means is that, despite all the talk, we go about our lives with the fact of our finitude held at emotional bay. Denial of death means never allowing ourselves to confront the anxiety summoned by visions of this last separation.

You may be asking, What's so bad about that?

For how can we live as fully conscious animals, the only creatures on earth that *know* they will die? How can we, in the chilling words of Ernest Becker's great book *The Denial of Death*, endure the awareness that we are "food for worms"? Our denial of death makes it easier to walk through our days and our nights unmindful of the abyss beneath our feet. But denial of death will also, as Freud and others convincingly argue, impoverish our lives.

Because we consume too much psychological energy fending off our thoughts—and fears—of death.

Because we replace death fears with other anxieties.

Because death is so interwoven with life that we close off parts of life when we shun thoughts of death.

And because the emotional knowledge that we surely will die someday can heighten and fine-tune our sense of the present moment.

"Death is the mother of beauty," writes the poet Wallace Stevens.

"Life without death is meaningless . . . a picture without a frame," says the "black holes" physicist John A. Wheeler.

"And if one is not able to die, is he really able to live?" asks the famed theologian Paul Tillich.

And novelist Muriel Spark, in her disturbing-the-peace book on death—*Memento Mori*—has one of her characters speak the following lines:

"If I had my life over again, I should form the habit of nightly composing myself to thoughts of death. I would practice, as it were, the remembrance of death. There is no other practice which so intensifies life. Death . . . should be part of the full expectancy of life. Without an ever-present sense of death life is insipid. You might as well live on the whites of eggs."

In the spring of 1970, within six shocking weeks, my good friend's teen-age daughter died of an embolism, my husband's best friend died of cancer at age thirty-nine and my mother's heart failed just short of her sixty-third birthday. I lost my fear of flying that spring—I'll fly on anything now—for I had become reacquainted with mortality and I recognized that even if I stayed grounded all of my life I still would die. And as Jodi's death and Gersh's death and my mother's death and the death that would someday be mine suffused me with anxiety and confusion, what I wanted was someone to teach me what to do with it all.

To teach me how to know death and go on with life.

To teach me how to love life and not fear death.

To teach me, before it was time for me to take the final exam, the ABC of dying.

For awareness of our mortality may heighten our love of life without making death—our personal death—acceptable. Looking death straight in the eye, we may hate it a lot. And although our sense of finitude may be the mother of beauty, the frame of the picture and even the yolk of the egg, it may make a mockery of our works and our days.

By assaulting our feelings of personal significance.

By rendering all of our enterprises meaningless.

By tainting our deepest and dearest attachments with transience.

By taunting us with the question Why were we born if it wasn't forever? By taunting us with the question Why is there death?

Some philosophers tell us that there can be no birth without death, that procreation must preclude immortality, that the earth could not sustain both reproduction and eternally living beings, that we need to clear out and make room for the new generations. Some theologians tell us that Adam and Eve could only be capable of seeing, and of choosing between, good and evil by eating of the forbidden fruit and thus giving up immortality for knowledge, for moral choice, for becoming human. Ecclesiastes tells us that "to every thing there is a season," including a "time to be born, and a time to die." And, pursuing a rather less speculative response to the question Why death? some scientists have theorized that our cells have a maximum life span, that human beings are genetically programmed to die.

There are various other responses, but to those who find death unacceptable, all justifications are unacceptable too. They view death as an evil, as a curse laid on their lives. And some of them—rejecting the scientists' view—maintain that death is not "natural" but an ill that will eventually be cured. Indeed, there are people who actually do arrange with cryonics companies to be deep-frozen at death and later thawed, while others are persuaded that through megadoses of nutrients they can extend their lives . . . perhaps to eternity. It is possible that some of those striving for physical immortality are spurred by their love of life and their vast faith in science. But I suspect that most of them are spurred by their vast terror—their terror of death.

Indeed, it is hard for most of us to contemplate our death without being scared of it.

We are scared of annihilation and of non-being. We are scared of going into the unknown. We are scared of an afterlife where we may have to pay for our sins. We are

scared of being helplessly alone. There are many, it is said, who fear the agonies of a last illness, whose fear is of dying—not of being dead. But it also has been said that we carry within us, all of our life, a dread of abandonment.

Our earliest separations, it is argued, have given us all our first, bitter foretaste of death.

And our later encounters with death—with death down the road or with death knocking at our door—revive the terrors of those first separations.

There is no more rending account of one man's anguished confrontation with his mortality than Leo Tolstoy's "The Death of Ivan Ilych," where an ailing man comes to realize that "something terrible, new and more important than anything before in his life was taking place. . . ."

He comes to realize that he is dying.

"My God! My God! . . . I'm dying . . . it may happen this moment. There was light and now there is darkness. I was here and now I'm going there! . . . There will be nothing. . . . Can this be dying? No, I don't want to!"

A chill comes over Ivan Ilych, his hands tremble, his breathing ceases and he feels only the throbbing of his heart. Choked with anger and misery, he thinks, "It is impossible that all men have been doomed to suffer this awful horror!"

More specifically, he thinks that it is impossible for *him* to suffer this horror.

The syllogism he had learnt from Kiesewetter's Logic: "Caius is a man, men are mortal, therefore Caius is mortal," had always seemed to him correct as applied to Caius, but certainly not as applied to himself. That Caius—man in the abstract—was mortal, was perfectly correct, but he was not Caius, not an abstract man, but a creature quite separate from all others. He had been little Vanya, with a mamma and a papa . . . and with all the joys, griefs and delights of childhood, boyhood and youth. What did Caius

know of the smell of that striped leather ball Vanya had been so fond of? Had Caius kissed his mother's hand like that, and did the silk of her dress rustle so for Caius? . . . Had Caius been in love like that? Could Caius preside at a session as he did? "Caius really was mortal, and it was right for him to die; but for me, little Vanya, Ivan Ilych, with all my thoughts and emotions, it's altogether a different matter."

Although Ivan Ilych says, "It cannot be that I ought to die. That would be too terrible," he also understands that death is near. *It* arrives in the midst of his working day, to "stand before him and look at him." He is petrified. It joins him in his study, where he is "alone with *It*: face to face with *It*." He shudders with fear.

He ponders the question "Why, and for what purpose, is there all this horror?"

"Agony, death . . ." he asks himself. "What for?"

Ivan Ilych's family and friends cannot relieve his anguished aloneness, for none of them speak—or will let him speak—of his dying. Indeed, they not only avoid all mention of this gruesome subject; they pretend to his face that he isn't dying at all.

> This deception tortured him—their not wishing to admit what they all knew and what he knew, but wanting to lie to him concerning his terrible condition, and wishing and forcing him to participate in that lie. Those lies—lies enacted over him on the eve of his death and destined to degrade this awful, solemn act . . .—were a terrible agony for Ivan Ilych. And strangely enough, many times . . . he had been within a hairbreadth of calling out to them: "Stop lying! You know and I know that I am dying. Then at least stop lying about it!"

Such taboos against speaking of death, such lies and deceptions surrounding death, have been vigorously challenged in recent years, with books like Elisabeth Kübler-Ross's highly influential *On Death and Dying* urg-

ing us to open up a dialogue with those who are terminally ill. Psychiatrist Kübler-Ross describes the enormous relief provided to dying patients when they are invited to share their fears and their needs. And she argues that such dialogues can ease their journey toward death, a journey she sees divided into five stages:

Denial, she says, is the first response to the news of a fatal illness: "There must be some mistake! This cannot be!"

Anger (at the doctors, at fate) and envy (of the undying) come next—the classic question here is, "Why me?"

Bargaining is the third response, an attempt to postpone the inevitable, promises made in exchange for a longer run—though the woman who swears she'll be willing to die if she can just live long enough to see her son married, may then renege on the bargain with: "Now don't forget I have *another* son."

Depression, the fourth of these stages, is a sorrowing over past losses and a sorrowing over the great loss yet to come. And the need of the dying engaged in a preparatory mourning of their own death is for someone to sit with their sadness and let them be sad.

Acceptance, the final stage, "should not be mistaken," says Kübler-Ross, "for a happy phase." It is "almost void of feelings"; it seems to be, she says, a time when the struggle is done. She concludes that when the dying have been given some assistance in working their way through all of the previous stages, they will no longer be depressed or scared or envious or angry or unreconciled, but will contemplate their coming end "with a certain degree of quiet expectation."

Does everyone pass—should everyone pass—through these five stages of dying? Critics of Kübler-Ross say no, and no. Not everyone wants to look at his death; some people do best if they cling, till the end, to denial. Some

people, raging and raging "against the dying of the light," will go out the way Dylan Thomas said we should go—and what he said was, "Do not go gentle...." Nor do all of those who arrive at an acceptance of their death arrive there via the stages that she describes. And some critics fear that a "right" way to die, a Kübler-Ross right way to die, may be mindlessly imposed upon the dying.

Dr. Edwin Shneidman, who has also worked extensively with the dying, writes that "my own experiences have led me to radically different conclusions" from those of Kübler-Ross. He continues:

> ... I reject the notion that human beings, as they die, are somehow marched in lock step through a series of stages of the dying process. On the contrary ... the emotional states, the psychological mechanisms of defense, the needs and drives, are as variegated in the dying as they are in the nondying.... They include such reactions as stoicism, rage, guilt, terror, cringing, fear, surrender, heroism, dependency, ennui, need for control, fight for autonomy and dignity, and denial.

He also, challenging Kübler-Ross's view that acceptance occurs in the last stage of dying, argues that this is not necessarily so. He writes that there is no "natural law ... that an individual has to achieve a state of psychoanalytic grace or any other kind of closure before death sets its seal. The cold fact is that most people die too soon or too late, with loose threads and fragments of life's agenda uncompleted."

But however correct the criticism of Kübler-Ross's five stages, her critics seem to agree with her central theme: that only by drawing close to the dying, only by not fleeing death, can we discover what each Ivan Ilych needs. That need may be for silence, for talk, for the freedom to weep or rage, for the touching of hands in wordless communication. That need may be, and often is, to be allowed to be a baby again. We can make ourselves available to be

used as they wish to use us, but we cannot teach the dying how to die. If we are there, however, and if we are paying careful attention, they will teach us.

In 1984, I watched three women I loved very dearly die of cancer. All of them in their fifties, all of them vitally in life, they—all of them in cruel prematurity—died. One faced her fate straight on—she knew she was dying, she talked about death, she calmly accepted it. One, knowing death was near and wishing to choose her moment of dying, hoarded her pills and committed suicide. And one, the blond-haired, blue-eyed interloper I'd known since birth—my sister Lois—fought against her death, until the moment she closed her eyes, with awesome ferocity.

Lois—the great rival of my childhood, the tagalong pest I had come so deeply to love—has died of cancer in the autumn of this awful year, just as I sit down to write this chapter. She died in her bed at home, and, watching her during those last hours, I believe that she died free of pain and free of fear. But as long as she was conscious, she maintained her defiance of death—she was out to beat it.

For although Lois knew very well indeed that she had a fatal illness, she didn't intend to let it push her around. So she wrote her will, settled her affairs, held some discussions with her husband and children and then—having thoroughly dealt with the administrative details—she turned from death and concentrated on life. Furthermore, she concentrated not on mere survival but on enjoying whatever there was to be enjoyed, refusing to let the limits imposed by her steadily failing body intrude upon her pleasures or her relationships.

When tennis—her great passion—was no longer pos-

sible, she bit her lip and put her racquet away, directing her athlete's body toward more sedentary activities, becoming a vigorous knitter, reader, writer. In the last few months of her illness, with her energies further depleted, her weight at ninety-five pounds, her eyesight dim, she planned new adaptations—could she, perhaps, learn a foreign language on cassettes? In the last week of her life she sent me her recipe for Chinese spicy noodles (a dried noodle in the envelope, to make sure that I purchased the right kind), and through the blur of her heavy-duty pain killers still remembered to ask about *my* health. She never became obsessed with herself—even in that last week—obsessed with her sickness, her suffering, her fate. And she never, until the coma of her final day of life, broke her connections with the people she loved.

Nor did she say goodbye, because she wasn't planning to leave; she was planning—or at least trying her damnedest—to live. "Some of us do survive," she once told me, "and why not focus on hope instead of despair?" And for most of the hard four years during which she battled her spreading cancer, she focused on hope.

Now make no mistake: My sister was neither a martyr nor a saint. She had her times of terror and despair, times when she couldn't do anything because her body was wracked with nausea and pain, times when she bitched and wept and moaned and asked—only part in jest—"What did I do? What did I do to deserve this?" But most of the time she didn't cry, and she didn't brood about dying. She was fighting to live, and she was fighting to win. She believed until the end that if a person really tried, the human spirit could triumph over biology. And although she didn't beat death, we watched her play—she really did play—a championship game.

There are people like Lois at every age and with all kinds of fatal ailments who hang on to hope, who fight to

stay alive, trusting in will, in spirit, in remissions, in brand-new miracle drugs or—in miracles. "Don't they know they can't make it?" we may wonder, having heard the grim statistics. But they have heard them too, and what they do is tell us, and themselves, "I'm not a statistic."

In videotapes about a thirty-nine-year-old doctor pain-fully dying of cancer, he—and his wife and a brother and doctors and clergymen—describe his harrowing struggle to stay alive. In his final weeks, refusing to quit, he insisted on being fed through a vein in his neck and as the pains worsened he grew so dependent upon narcotic drugs that he underwent—observers agreed—a personality change. Some doctors have said that by his insistence on taking command of his case, this man prolonged his life "unnec-essarily." But just before he died, when asked by his wife if his fight for survival had been worth it, he answered with an unequivocal "Yes."

My friend Ruth did it differently. Knowing the game was lost, knowing that only pain and death lay ahead, she ar-ranged a last, perfect evening for her and her loving, be-loved husband and then—when he left for work the next day—took an overdose. With her artist's esthetic sense and her lifelong need to maintain control, Ruth wouldn't permit the cancer to have its way with her—to ravage her further (she was a beautiful woman), to impose further suffering (she had suffered enormously), to strip her (as she feared she'd be stripped) of herself.

In all the endeavors of her hard and sometimes tragic life, Ruth had been feisty and brave, she had been a fighter. Red hair streaming and green eyes ablaze, she had stood up against brutal losses—and prevailed. But faced with this illness after the last chemotherapy treatments had failed and she'd been sent home to wait for a difficult death, she

preferred to select the time and place of the meeting. And although I know that suicide may be viewed as a crime or a sin, or cowardly, or weak, or pathological, I believe that Ruthie's suicide—the suicide of my sorrowing, suffering friend—was an act of courage and consummate rationality.

Perhaps Ruth's suicide is what psychoanalyst K. R. Eissler has called a revolt against death, a way that "the condemned cheats the executioner." But it also is a suicide which strikes me as healthy, not sick, as right, not wrong. Let me hasten to declare that I believe that most suicides are, indeed, pathological and that most of the would-be suicides need to be helped to live, not permitted to die. I also believe, however, that under certain special conditions, self-murder can be a sane and legitimate option— the best response available to the horrors of terminal illness, or to the dependencies and deteriorations of age.

But whatever we think of such suicides, people are committing them. In 1982, for instance, for every 100,000 men the suicide rates were 28.3 for ages sixty-five to sixty-nine, 43.7 for ages seventy-five to seventy-nine and 50.2 for eighty-five plus. In these—and indeed in every age category— the suicide rates per 100,000 *women* were lower, sometimes astoundingly lower: 7.3 for ages sixty-five to sixty-nine, 6.3 for ages seventy-five to seventy-nine and 3.9 for eighty-five plus!

Sometimes very old couples, their competencies failing, may make the poignant decision to die together rather than be separated or rendered helpless by their growing infirmities. Thus Cecil and Julia Saunders—ages eighty-five and eighty-one respectively—ate hot dogs and beans for lunch, drove their Chevy to a quiet place, rolled up the windows, put cotton in their ears, after which Cecil fired twice into his waiting wife's heart, then aimed the gun at his own heart and fired. The suicide note which they left was addressed to their children:

This we know will be a terrible shock & embarrassment. But as we see it, it is one solution to the problem of growing old. We greatly appreciate your willingness to try to take care of us.

After being married for 60 years it only makes sense for us to leave this world together because we loved each other so much.

Don't grieve, because we had a very good life and saw our two children turn out to be such fine persons.

Love Moth & Fath

As for the terminally ill, there is a growing interest in self-arranged termination. The wish not to suffer, to stay in charge, to be remembered by loved ones the way they were motivates some to choose the hour of their death. And while our instincts may prompt us to hasten to reach out a rescuing hand and cry, "Don't do it," while we are aware that many who wish to die today may want to live if they'll but wait a week, while we are concerned with the often traumatic effects on the family of a suicide, we also—like one writer—must ponder: "Who knows how he may be tempted? It is his case; it may be thine."

Now certainly there are people who would never opt for suicide but who nonetheless greet death with open arms, who look upon their death as a release, as a relief, as deliverance, surcease. Death is not their enemy. Death becomes a friend. It offers the chance to lay their burden down, whether the burden they yearn to lay down is the agony of a last illness; the helplessness, uselessness, loneliness of old age; the sufferings, at any age, attendant upon an unendurable loss; or the struggle of trying to live in a world which assails us, as Mark Twain writes, with "care, grief [and] perplexity." The reason, Twain explains in an autobiography which recounts many terrible losses, that "annihilation has no terrors for me" is

because I have already tried it before I was born—a hundred million years—and I have suffered more in an hour, in this life,

than I remember to have suffered in the whole hundred million years put together. There was a peace, a serenity, an absence of all sense of responsibility, an absence of worry, an absence of care, grief, perplexity; and the presence of a deep content and unbroken satisfaction in that hundred million years of holiday which I look back upon with a tender longing and with a grateful desire to resume, when the opportunity comes.

This "tender longing" for death, this grateful welcoming of death is one of many versions of acceptance. For there is also resigned acceptance ("Men must endure their going hence, even as their coming hither"), practical acceptance ("When I catch myself resenting not being immortal, I pull myself up short by asking whether I should really like the prospect of having to make out an annual income tax return for an infinite number of years ahead"), joyful acceptance ("Without regret for father, mother, sister,/Or any memory of this world below,/My soul in joy embraces her redeemer"), democratic acceptance ("Thou shalt lie down/With patriarchs of the infant world—with kings,/The powerful of the earth—the wise, the good,/Fair forms, and hoary seers of ages past,/All in one mighty sepulchre") and what I think might be called creative acceptance.

This is the kind of acceptance that my friend Carol displayed toward her death. An acceptance, without bitterness, of her fate. An acceptance of herself as a highly valued, uniquely valuable human being. An acceptance which permitted her, during the autumn afternoons of her dying, to speak with equal interest about the music that she wished to have played at her funeral and how to cook a terrific ratatouille.

With no belief in an afterlife and zero expectations of a reprieve, and with—like Ruth and Lois—some terrible times, some of the time, with physical pain, she spent her last weeks in her bedroom saying goodbye to her family and friends, and waiting—with astonishing calm—to die. She invited all of us to engage with her in some no-nonsense

talk of her mortality, but death wasn't the only subject she had on her mind. She wanted to talk about us, about the coming election, about the latest gossip, and she continued to offer her funny and wise and utterly irreverent comments on . . . everything. No, she wasn't relentlessly gallant; there were times when she needed to cry about all the sweetness that she was leaving behind. And once she summed up her feelings about her premature departure by quoting this verse of Robert Louis Stevenson:

> *And does it not seem hard to you,*
> *When all the sky is clear and blue,*
> *And I should like so much to play,*
> *To have to go to bed by day?*

It did seem hard, but as Carol became increasingly acquainted with her death, she also accepted going to bed by day.

During one of our visits Carol said to me, "I've never died before," then added, "so I don't know how to do it."

But having watched the dying of this serene, undespairing, most remarkable woman, I want to tell you all, Oh, yes, she did.

What do we know about who dies how? Not an enormous amount, though it often is said that accomplishment makes it easier, that those who have achieved what they set out to do in life die more contentedly than those who have not. Philosopher Walter Kaufmann, in maintaining that satisfaction with our accomplishments "makes all the difference in facing death," illustrates his argument with the following poem by Friedrich Holderlin:

> *A single summer grant me, great powers, and*
> *A single autumn for fully ripened song*
> *That, sated with the sweetness of my*

> *Playing, my heart may more willingly die.*
> *The soul that, living, did not attain its divine*
> *Right cannot repose in the nether world.*
> *But once what I am bent on, what is*
> *Holy, my poetry, is accomplished,*
> *Be welcome then, stillness of the shadows' world!*
> *I shall be satisfied though my lyre will not*
> *Accompany me down there. Once I*
> *Lived like the gods, and more is not needed.*

Kaufmann argues that if we achieve—"in the face of death, in the race with death"—a project that is truly, uniquely our own, our "heart may more willingly die" because we have, in some sense, triumphed over death. In a similar vein Hattie Rosenthal observes in her "Psychotherapy for the Dying" that it "is the person who is convinced that he has lived a full life who is ready to die, and who develops comparatively little anxiety."

In many discussions of who dies how it also is maintained that we die in character, die the way we live: That the spunky die with spunk. That the stoics submit unprotestingly to this final necessity. That those who deny reality will continue, till their death day, to deny it. That those who overzealously guard their desperately won independence will feel ashamed and shattered by their dying's dependencies. That those for whom separation has always been a terror-filled walk into the darkness will find this last separation the ultimate terror.

But there is also the observation that our dying may sometimes provide a new opportunity, that dying may sometimes permit—yes!—growth and change, that dying may precipitate a further stage of emotional development that had—until now—been well beyond our capacities. Eissler writes that "the knowledge or the vague feeling that the end is approaching may enable some persons to step aside, so to speak, and view themselves and significant sectors of their lives with humility and also with insight

into the futility of so much that is taken too seriously so long as the world is near and man is passionately living *in* it." He says that this final stage can dissolve certain deeply entrenched ways of being, permitting what he calls "a last step forward."

This concept of a "last step forward" helps me understand how Lois, who had always been viewed as the "weak one" in our family, became, in her dying, so brave and so strong—such a fighter. It also helps explain the "perfect death" that is described by Lily Pincus, the death of her up to that moment very dependent, anxiety-ridden mother-in-law:

Who after a stroke, awoke, sat up and asked to see all the people in the house, then serenely bid each one a loving goodbye. Who then calmly closed her eyes, saying, "Now let me sleep." And who, when a doctor arrived to jolt her out of her final sleep with an injection, roused herself just long enough to persuade him to let her be, to let her die peacefully.

"What hidden strengths," asks Pincus, "in this delicate, frightened woman, who throughout her life had avoided facing anything difficult and who had never been able to make a decision, had enabled her not only to die in this way, but to ensure that her final sleep remained undisturbed?" Her answer, like Eissler's, is that approaching death may bring about remarkable, utterly unforeseen transformations.

Eissler goes so far as to argue that the experiencing of our dying can be the "crowning" achievement of our life. He writes:

The full awareness of each step that leads closer to death, the unconscious experience of one's own death up to the last second which permits awareness and consciousness, would be the crown-

ing triumph of an individually lived life. It would be taken as the only way man ought to die if individuality were really accepted as the only adequate form of living and if life in all its manifestations were integrated, which would of course include death and the sorrows of the terminal pathway.

But not all of us are going to have the chance to reflect on our dying while we are dying. Accidents and ailments will take some of us instantaneously, unaware. Nor, in fact, do all of us have the *wish* to reflect on our dying while we are dying. Many of us, indeed, would psychologically rather not be there when it happens. According to Philippe Ariès, in his study of death throughout history, the concept of the "good death" has been redefined, so that instead of its being a conscious, expected, ritualized departure, as once it was, a good death today "corresponds exactly to what used to be the accursed death": Sudden death. The death that strikes without warning. The death that takes us quietly in our sleep.

Contrasted with a slow dying, often alone, in a hospital bed—plugged into tubes and machines and subject to bureaucratic failures and sometimes worse—sudden death may strike us as a great blessing, as a very good death indeed. But perhaps new approaches to the dying process—I am thinking, in particular, of the growing hospice movement, which provides compassionate care and relief from pain without artificial extension of life—may again redefine the good death as one in which there is time to experience our dying.

But whether or not we have the chance to experience our dying, whether or not our dying becomes a "last step forward," an instrument of growth, we can—long before we arrive at the month, the week, the day, the hour of our death—enrich our life by remembering that we will die.

Now many believe, like La Rochefoucauld, that even the brave and clever should always "avoid looking it [death] straight in the face." Perhaps we can only do so if death does not mean the end of everything that we are. Perhaps we can only do so if we are able to set our own death within some context of after-death continuity.

Indeed, it has been argued that there is—in all of us— a need for connections that last beyond our own lifetime, a need to feel that our finite self is part of a larger something that endures. There are various contexts in which we may experience, or struggle toward, this connection. And each of these contexts can offer us an image of what it seems fair to call . . . immortality.

Our most familiar image of immortality is religious, with an indestructible soul and a life after death, with the promise that our last separation will lead to eternal reunion, with the assurance that all will not be lost, but found. However, as Robert J. Lifton points out in his brilliant discussion of modes of immortality, not every religion rests its case on a literal afterlife or an immortal soul. Rather, he writes, what is more universal to the religious experience is a sense of connection with a spiritual *power*: A power "derived from a more-than-natural source." A power in which we share and which protects us. A power through which we may be reborn—spiritually, symbolically—into a realm of "death-transcending truths."

Freud argues that such religious beliefs are illusions built up by man to make his helplessness in this world endurable. He writes that just as children depend on their parents to protect them, so anxious adults depend on gods and God. He says we create religion to "exorcise the terrors" of nature and to make up for the sufferings civilization imposes. And he says that we use religion to reconcile ourselves to fate's cruelty, "particularly as it is shown in death."

But religion isn't the only context in which we can sum-

mon up for ourselves images of after-death continuity. We can agree with Robert Lifton that death brings about "biological and psychic annihilation," while also agreeing with him that death does not therefore have to mean the absolute end. There are other ways of imagining how some part of us might endure—beyond our death, beyond annihilation. There are other ways of imagining immortalizing connections and continuities.

Living on through nature, for instance—through oceans, mountains, trees, recurring seasons—serves some of us as an image of immortality. We die, but the earth goes on and on and on. Furthermore, in returning to earth, as the poem "Thanatopsis" describes, we are literally part of that endless continuity:

> ...*Earth, that nourished thee, shall claim*
> *Thy growth, to be resolved to earth again,*
> *And, lost each human trace, surrendering up*
> *Thine individual being, shalt thou go*
> *To mix forever with the elements...*

For others among us, immortality resides in those works and acts which have some impact on future generations—in the causes we fight (sometimes die) for, in the discoveries we make, in what we construct or teach or invent or create. Here the Emperor Hadrian, vividly drawn in Marguerite Yourcenar's novel, ponders—as he approaches death—the relation between his endeavors and immortality:

Life is atrocious, we know. But precisely because I expect little of the human condition, man's periods of felicity, his partial progress, his efforts to begin over again and continue, all seem to me like so many prodigies which nearly compensate for the monstrous mass of ills and defeats, of indifference and error. Catastrophe and ruin will come; disorder will triumph, but order will too, from time to time.... Not all our books will perish, nor our statues, if broken, lie unrepaired; other domes and other pediments will arise from our domes and pediments; some few men will think and work and feel as we have done, and I venture to count upon such contin-

uators, placed irregularly throughout the centuries, and upon this kind of intermittent immortality.

There are people who surely can count on living on through their civilization-changing works—the Hadrians and Homers, the Michelangelos and Voltaires and Einsteins (and Hitlers). But we need not appear in the history books nor engage in world-shaking enterprises to view what we do as having continuing impact. Our everyday works and our private acts may yield significant consequences that ripple and ripple and ripple down through time.

And then there is the image of biological continuity, the image of living on through our children and theirs, or a broader—"biosocial"—image of living on through our nation, our race or mankind. Some of us do perceive ourselves as a link in a chain of life which stretches, unbroken, from the past to the future, connecting us never-endingly to the lives that have been and will come, offering us—as long as man lasts—immortality.

But beyond the four images thus far described of after-death continuity are direct, intense experiences of transcendence—experiences that re-echo our old ecstatic merger with mother, experiences of oneness in which boundaries and time and death itself disappear. These unbounded oneness experiences may occur, as we have seen, through sexual passion, drugs, art, nature, God. They give us a sense of "an indissoluble bond . . . with the external world as a whole," a sense that "we cannot fall out of this world."

Not every adult, however, can experience this oneness. "I cannot discover," Freud writes, "this 'oceanic' feeling in myself." Nor will everyone find—in religion or nature or man's works or the bio- (social or logical) connection—visions of immortality that make it easier to look on death. Simone de Beauvoir says, "Whether you think of it as heavenly or as earthly, if you love life immortality is no

consolation for death." Woody Allen makes the same point: "I don't want to gain immortality through my work. I want to gain immortality by not dying." And the fatally ill young man who is asked if he can take comfort in knowing that his friend will weep for him when he is gone, gives his friend an answer that clearly rejects such abstract versions of immortality: "Not unless I be aware and hear you weeping."

Some people insist that any hope of after-death continuity—even without other worlds or immortal souls—is always denial of death, is nothing more than a defense against anxiety. Lifton, however, argues that a sense of immortality is "a corollary of the knowledge of death . . . ," of the knowledge that, despite our connections to the future and past, our existence is finite.

Our existence is finite. The self that we have created through so many years of effort and suffering will die. And sustained though we may be by the idea, the hope, the certainty that some portion of us will eternally endure, we also must acknowledge that this "I" who breathes and loves and works and knows itself will be forever and ever and ever . . . obliterated.

So whether or not we live with images of continuity— of immortality—we also will have to live with a sense of transience, aware that no matter how passionately we love whatever we love, we don't have the power to make either it, or us, stay. Centuries of poets have addressed themselves to the brevity of existence and what their exquisite images have to say is that all is vanity, that we have but an hour to strut upon the stage, that the days of wine and roses vanish swiftly, that we must die. The poets have also offered us—in every voice, in every emotional tone—the words in which the dying say goodbye. And as I consider

my finitude, and plan what I ardently hope is well ahead,
I turn to this poem by Louis MacNeice for the words I
would most wish to say at my last leaving:

> The sunlight on the garden
> Hardens and grows cold,
> We cannot cage the minute
> Within its nets of gold,
> When all is told
> We cannot beg for pardon.
>
> Our freedom as free lances
> Advances towards its end;
> The earth compels, upon it
> Sonnets and birds descend;
> And soon, my friend,
> We shall have no time for dances.
>
> The sky was good for flying
> Defying the church bells
> And every evil iron
> Siren and what it tells:
> The earth compels,
> We are dying, Egypt, dying.
>
> And not expecting pardon,
> Hardened in heart anew,
> But glad to have sat under
> Thunder and rain with you,
> And grateful too
> For sunlight on the garden.

20 ❧

Reconnections

But as she has grown, her smile has widened with a touch of fear and her glance has taken on depth. Now she is aware of some of the losses you incur by being here—the extraordinary rent you have to pay as long as you stay.

—ANNIE DILLARD

My youngest son is waiting to hear from the college of his choice. He'll be leaving home. My mother, my sister, too many dear friends are dead. I'm taking calcium pills to save my middle-aged bones from osteoporosis. I'm living on Lean Cuisine in a last-ditch effort to defeat my middle-aged spread. And although my husband and I have maintained our imperfect connection for twenty-five rich full years, the bombs of divorce and widowhood are falling all around us. We live with loss.

Both in my life and this book I have tried to talk about loss in a number of different languages: The scholarly and the vernacular. The subjective and the objective. The private and the public. The funny and the sad. I have found illumination and consolation in the theories of psychoanalysis, in the vivid, compressed intensities of poems, in the fictional realities of Emma Bovary, Alex Portnoy, Ivan Ilych and in the as-told-to-me secrets of strangers and friends. I have found them, too, in the subterranean ex-

ploration of my own experience. Here's what I've learned:

I've learned that in the course of our life we leave and are left and let go of much that we love. Losing is the price we pay for living. It is also the source of much of our growth and gain. Making our way from birth to death, we also have to make our way through the pain of giving up and giving up and giving up some portion of what we cherish.

We have to deal with our necessary losses.

We should understand how these losses are linked to our gains.

For in leaving the blurred-boundary bliss of mother-child oneness, we become a conscious, unique and separate self, exchanging the illusion of absolute shelter and absolute safety for the triumphant anxieties of standing alone.

And in bowing to the forbidden and the impossible, we become a moral, responsible, adult self, discovering—within the limitations imposed by necessity—our freedoms and choices.

And in giving up our impossible expectations, we become a lovingly connected self, renouncing ideal visions of perfect friendship, marriage, children, family life for the sweet imperfections of all-too-human relationships.

And in confronting the many losses that are brought by time and death, we become a mourning and adapting self, finding at every stage—until we draw our final breath—opportunities for creative transformations.

In thinking about development as a lifelong series of necessary losses—of necessary losses and subsequent gains—I am constantly struck by the fact that in human experience opposites frequently converge. I have found that little can be understood in terms of "eithers" and "ors." I have found that the answer to the question "Is it *this* or *that*?" is often "Both."

That we love and we hate the same person.

That the same person—us, for instance, is both good and bad.

That although we are driven by forces that are beyond our control and awareness, we are also the active authors of our fate.

And that, although the course of our life is marked with repetition and continuity, it also is remarkably open to change.

For yes, it is true that as long as we live we may keep repeating the patterns established in childhood. It is true that the present is powerfully shaped by the past. But it also is true that the circumstances of every stage of development can shake up and revise the old arrangements. And it's true that insight at any age can free us from singing the same sad songs again.

Thus, although our early experiences are decisive, some of these decisions can be reversed. We can't understand our history in terms of continuity *or* change. We must include both.

And we can't understand our history unless we recognize that it is comprised of both outer and inner realities. For what we call our "experiences" include not only what happens to us out there, but how we interpret what happens to us out there. A kiss is *not* just a kiss—it may feel like sweet intimacy; it may feel like outrageous intrusion. It may even be only a fantasy in our mind. Each of us has an inner response to the outer events of our life. We must include both.

Another set of paired opposites which tend to merge in real life are nature and nurture. For what we come into the world with—our innate qualities, our "constitutional givens"—interacts with the nurture we receive. We cannot view development in terms of either environment or heredity. We must include both.

As for our losses and gains, we have seen how often they are inextricably mixed. There is plenty we have to give up in order to grow. For we cannot deeply love anything without becoming vulnerable to loss. And we cannot become separate people, responsible people, connected people, reflective people without some losing and leaving and letting go.

Notes and Elaborations

CHAPTER ONE   THE HIGH COST OF SEPARATION

page 10 Separation from mother:
Anna Freud, the noted child psychoanalyst and her colleague Dorothy Burlingham directed three nurseries, the Hamstead Nurseries, in England during World War II, recording with exquisite and poignant detail the reactions of young children separated from their families. In *War and Children* Miss Freud writes: "The war acquires comparatively little significance for children so long as it only threatens their lives, disturbs their material comfort or cuts their food rations. It becomes enormously significant the moment it breaks up family life and uproots the first emotional attachments of the child within the family group. London children, therefore, were on the whole much less upset by bombing than by evacuation to the country as a protection against it" (p. 37). She also notes that separation is painful even when the mothers concerned "are not 'good mothers' in the ordinary sense of the word. . . . It is a known fact that children will cling even to mothers who are continually cross and sometimes cruel to them. The attachment of the small child to its mother seems to a large degree independent of her personal qualities . . ." (p. 45).

page 10 "There is no such thing":
Winnicott, *Collected Papers*, "Anxiety Associated with Insecurity," p. 99.

page 11 may be permanent:
British psychoanalyst John Bowlby's three-volume work on attachment and loss (see note below) is a pioneering study of the nature of human attachment and the effects on young children of temporary and permanent separation. In *Loss* he presents material supporting

369

the view that "there is a tendency to underestimate how distressing and disabling loss usually is and for how long the distress, and often the disablement, commonly last." He lays emphasis "on the long duration of grief, on the difficulties of recovering from its effects, and on the adverse consequences for personality functioning that loss so often brings" (p. 8).

page 13 separation anxiety:
Studies of separation reactions can be found in Bowlby's three volumes—*Attachment, Separation, Loss*—and in Heinicke and Westheimer's *Brief Separations*. My usage of separation anxiety comes from the discussion of its two meanings in *Brief Separations*, pp. 327–328.

page 14 time accelerates with the years:
See Goldstein, Freud, Solnit, *Beyond the Best Interests of the Child*, for a discussion of the child's sense of time (pp. 40–42).

page 14 "the frustration and longing":
See Bowlby, *Loss*, p. 10. He is quoting James Robertson, who worked with Bowlby on studies of children and separation.

page 15 a typical sequence of responses:
Discussions of protest, despair and detachment can be found in Bowlby, *Separation*, pp. 26–27 and *Loss*, pp. 19–22.

page 15 "assured himself and anybody":
A. Freud and Burlingham, *War and Children*, pp. 99–100.

page 16 This response is called detachment:
In *Loss*, Bowlby writes that detachment—which sometimes alternates with tenacious clinging—is "regularly seen whenever a child between the ages of about six months and three years has spent a week or more out of his mother's care and without being cared for by a specially assigned substitute" (p. 20).

page 16 "it's like a scar on your brain":
Fraiberg, *Every Child's Birthright*, p. 160.

page 19 "stomach love":
The phrase is from A. Freud and Burlingham's *War and Children*, p. 190. The Freudian view of love's origins must be understood within the context of Sigmund Freud's dual-instinct theory, which proposes that human beings are impelled by two basic instinctual drives: the sexual and the aggressive. In Freud's usage, sex encompasses many component instincts which only at puberty are organized into the genital sexuality we usually think of as sex. Component instincts, however, are present from birth and are first manifested as oral drives for which the infant seeks gratification through sucking and eating. Thus it is the sexual drive, in its oral form, which initially impels the

infant toward his mother. The gratification of this instinct becomes
the basis, in Freud's view, for love. In *Standard Edition*, Vol. 23, "An
Outline of Psychoanalysis," Freud writes: "A child's first erotic object
is the mother's breast that nourishes it; love has its origin in attachment
to the satisfied need for nourishment" (p. 188). For further discussion,
see Freud's *Standard Edition*, Vol. 7, "Three Essays on the Theory
of Sexuality." A. Freud and Burlingham's *Infants Without Families*
provides a brief summary of this view of the origins of love (p. 23).

page 19 "The love of others":
Suttie, *The Origins of Love and Hate*, p. 30. Suttie, anticipating Bowlby,
relates love to the animal instinct of self-preservation. But he
says that what distinguishes man from other animals is the "extreme
degree to which the definite, stereotyped, specific instincts of 'self-
preservation' of his pre-human ancestors are 'melted down' . . . into a
dependent love-for-mother . . ." (p. 20).

   In recent years, many "object relations" theorists have also challenged the stomach-love point of view. Pointing to the importance of
the early mother-child relationship, they have argued that Freud's
dual-instinct theory doesn't give that relationship the centrality it de-
serves. Thus British analyst W. R. D. Fairbairn, for instance, in his
book *An Object Relations Theory of the Personality*, rejects the dual-
instinct theory and argues instead that the baby's primary need is not
to gratify oral sexual drives but to seek relationships. In psychoanalytic parlance the bloodless word "object" actually means
human object. And so, when Fairbairn proposes that the infant is
object-seeking from the start, he simply is saying that first comes the
need for attachment, that babies are seeking a mother, not a meal.
(He also holds the view that aggression is not a basic instinct but a
reaction to experiences of frustration in the pursuit of that attachment.)

   There are some interesting efforts at reconciliation between object-
relations theory and Freud's dual-instinct theory in Modell's "The Ego
and the Id: Fifty Years Later," *The International Journal of Psycho-
Analysis*, Vol. 26, Part 1, pp. 57–68, and Loewald's "Instinct Theory,
Object Relations and Psychic Structure Formation," *Journal of the
American Psychoanalytic Association*, Vol. 26, No. 3, pp. 493–506.
And for more on the British object-relations theorists, see Sutherland's
review in the *Journal of the American Psychoanalytic Association*,
Vol. 28, No. 4, pp. 829–860.

page 20 "attachment behavior":
Bowlby's *Attachment* presents this view of the mother-infant bond,
using extensive material from animal studies.

page 20 breaking that crucial bond:
There is much compelling evidence, for instance, in studies of the
institution-raised child, about the dangers of nonconnection. A classic
work on this subject is Rene Spitz's "Hospitalism," *The Psycho-*

analytic Study of the Child, Vol. 1. Dr. Spitz, an internationally famous psychoanalyst, spent many years conducting analytic research in child development. His hospitalism study found severe developmental retardation in infants reared in an institution with no mother and no mother substitute, but only "one-eighth" of a nurse. Spitz concludes that we must "take into consideration in our institutions, in our charitable activities, in our social legislation, the overwhelming and unique importance of an adequate and satisfactory mother-child relationship during the first year . . ." (p. 72).

page 20 foster home:
If a reliable mother-child bond is essential for healthy human development, we must be appalled by those current adoption procedures where a child is shunted from foster home to foster home—interminably—before the hearings and paperwork are complete. According to *Foster Care 1984: A Report on the Implementation of the Recommendations of the Mayor's Task Force on Foster Care*, p. 58, the average waiting time from foster care to final adoption in New York City is now an unbelievable six years—six years of tenuous and frequently broken connections.

page 20 hospital stay:
See James Robertson's "A Two Year Old Goes to Hospital," a documentary film which movingly demonstrates the impact of separation on a hospitalized child. See also my article on the emotional implications of hospitalization for children and the changes in hospital policy that are helping to allay separation fears: Viorst, "The Hospital That Has Patience for Its Patients: A Look at Children's Hospital in Washington, D.C.," *Redbook*, February 1977, pp. 48–54.

page 20 working mothers:
The Division of Employment and Unemployment Analysis of the Bureau of Labor Statistics says that as of March 1983, 50.5 percent of women with children under six were in the labor force. This is a total of 7.6 million women.

page 21 "In the years":
Fraiberg, *Every Child's Birthright*, p. 111. This view has been challenged by Harvard psychologist Jerome Kagan, who offers evidence that infants in full-time day care can in fact flourish, developing with neither intellectual nor emotional impairment, and with no harm done to the mother-child attachment. His is the kind of study which women who must, or wish to, work will find consoling. But it cannot be embraced without taking note of a number of highly significant ifs:
   —if the caretaker is sensitive, warm, responsive and constant—not one of several interchangeable caretakers.
   —if the infant-caretaker ratio is small—three to one.
   —if the mother is reliably present, before and after day care, in the child's life.

—and if the day care begins before or after the age of maximum separation anxiety.

This material is presented in *Infancy*, by Kagan, Richard B. Kearsley and Philip R. Zelazo. The authors studied 33 Chinese and Caucasian children from working- and middle-class families in the Boston area who were enrolled in an experimental full-time day-care center starting at age three and a half months to five and a half months and continuing until age 29 months. Comparing these children to a home-reared control group, the authors conclude that responsible day care does not hold hidden psychological or intellectual dangers. They remind the reader, however, that "we are evaluating how children grow under surrogate care conditions that are, according to current theoretical views, similar to home rearing" (p. 176).

page 22 early childhood losses make us sensitive:
With some modifications and additions, Bowlby's *Separation* and *Loss* form the basis of my discussion in this chapter of anxiety, depression and defense in adult functioning.

page 23 "a rock...feels no pain":
From the Simon and Garfunkel song "I Am a Rock."

page 23 "when my mother left me":
Marilynne Robinson, *Housekeeping*, p. 214.

page 23 "gigantic and multiple":
Ibid., p. 195.

CHAPTER TWO   THE ULTIMATE CONNECTION

page 24 "harmonious interpenetrating mix-up":
Balint, *The Basic Fault*, p. 66.

page 24 "I'm in the milk":
Maurice Sendak, *In the Night Kitchen*, unpaged.

page 24 Our original bliss connection:
Analyst Otto Rank offers us the concept of the womb as paradise, the "blessed primal condition," in *The Trauma of Birth*, p. 113. He argues that every anxiety can be traced to the anxiety of birth and that "every pleasure has as its final aim the reestablishment of the intrauterine primal pleasure" (p. 17). Although we cannot bear our separation from paradise, says Rank, the memory of primal anxiety—the anxiety of birth—prevents us from turning back to a womblike state. Rather we are "urged forward to seek for Paradise in the world formed in the image of the mother, instead of seeking it in the past, and, in so far as this fails, to look for it in the sublime wish compensations of religion, art and philosophy" (p. 190). Indeed Rank seems to ascribe all human activity, both normal and pathological, to our reactions to the primal

birth situation, though in his later writings he shifts the emphasis from physical to psychological birth.

page 25 "for which deep down":
Mahler, Pine, Bergman, *The Psychological Birth of the Human Infant*, p. 227. Analyst Margaret Mahler postulates two developmental stages which occur between our literal birth and our "psychological birth," some five months later. She calls the earliest stage of extrauterine life the *normal autistic phase*, during which we are utterly unaware, according to Mahler, of the existence of any other human presence. This normal autistic phase is followed by the *normal symbiotic phase*, which begins in the second month when our shut-tight universe expands and we merge with our mother to form "a dual unity within one common boundary" (p. 44). Symbiosis is brought to an end by the "psychological birth of the human infant," a step-by-step process of separation-individuation which will be discussed in the next chapter.

Mahler's formulation and description of a universal symbiotic phase during the second to fifth months of life are based on studies begun in the late 1950s of normal infant-mother pairs. Mahler concedes that she and her colleagues are relying on their carefully observant "psychoanalytic eye" but cannot ultimately prove the correctness of the inferences they have made about the inner world of preverbal infants. But the book's conclusions about symbiosis and separation-individuation, and the wealth of clinical vignettes that accompany them, support her contention that her formulations are plausible and useful.

Further clues to the nonverbal workings of the mind can be obtained through patients who have regressed to the symbiotic phase or who have continued to function symbiotically at later stages of development. See Mahler's book *On Human Symbiosis and the Vicissitudes of Individuation*, Vol. I.

page 26 "Afterwards, the compromise":
Kumin, *Our Ground Time Here Will Be Brief*, "After Love," p. 182.

page 26 "the perfect compromise":
Bak, "Being in Love and Object Loss," *The International Journal of Psycho-Analysis*, Vol. 54, Part 1, p. 7. In a similar vein, analyst Jacobson writes in *The Self and the Object World* that the desire "to reestablish that lost unit . . . probably never ceases to play a part in our emotional life. Even normally, the experience of physical merging and of an 'identity' of pleasure in the sexual act may harbor elements of happiness derived from the feeling of return to the lost, original union with the mother" (p. 39).

page 26 "further and further":
Lawrence, *Lady Chatterley's Lover*, p. 208.

page 27 "as if the opposites":
W. James, *The Varieties of Religious Experience*, p. 306.

page 27 "to return from the solitude":
Ibid., p. 311. James is quoting the German idealist Malwida von Meysenburg.

page 27 "I am two":
Mr. Allen confirms having made this statement but neither I nor his office have been able to establish where it originally appeared.

page 27 "one vast world-encircling harmony":
James, *The Varieties of Religious Experience*, p. 311. James is quoting the German idealist Malwida von Meysenburg.

page 27 "pure moments":
Dillard, *Pilgrim at Tinker Creek*, p. 82. A friend of mine described a similar experience of oneness upon viewing Rembrandt's painting "The Night Watch," when "time stopped, the museum I was standing in disappeared, I was inside the painting."

page 28 "when she [the soul]":
James, *The Varieties of Religious Experience*, p. 321. James is quoting Saint Teresa.

page 28 "the me, and the we":
Ibid., p. 329. James is quoting Sufi Gulshan-Raz.

page 28 "Ecstatically, I merged":
Silverman, Lachmann, Milich, *The Search for Oneness*, p. 247.

pages 28–29 "thinking crazily":
This case is cited in Silverman, Lachmann, Milich, *The Search for Oneness*, p. 5.

page 29 "I am not I":
Rank, *The Trauma of Birth*, p. 177. Rank, by the way, is quoting an ecstatic Islamic mystic, not a psychotic child. Clearly there are striking similarities between the psychotic and the spiritual union.

page 29 Consider Mrs. C:
The case of Mrs. A.C. is discussed by analyst George Pollock in "On Symbiosis and Symbiotic Neurosis," *The International Journal of Psycho-Analysis*, Vol. 45, Part 1, pp. 1–30.

page 30 "Probably the greatest reason":
Searles, *Countertransference*, p. 42.

pages 30–31 "I have always felt":
Smith, "The Golden Fantasy: A Regressive Reaction to Separation Anxiety," *The International Journal of Psycho-Analysis*, Vol. 58, Part 3, p. 314. Smith's paper, pp. 311–324, provides examples of the golden fantasy, including the vignette of the spoon-fed lady.

page 31 "regression in the service of the ego":
The term was coined by analyst Ernst Kris. See his *Selected Papers*

of Ernst Kris, "Some Problems of War Propaganda," where he writes: "The antithesis of regression and ego control, of irrational and rational behavior, is a dangerous simplification. No such exclusion exists. To put it in the negative: He who cannot *pro tempore* relax, let loose the reins and indulge in regression, is according to generally accepted clinical standards ill. Regression is not always opposed to ego control; it can take place, as it were, in the service of the ego" (p. 448).

page 31 "To merge in order":
Rose's statement is quoted in Silverman, Lachmann, Milich's *The Search for Oneness*, p. 6. Rose argues that there is great growth-promoting value in our ability, throughout life, to "temporarily suspend the distinction between self and others and thus momentarily experience a state of mind similar to the early unity with mother" (pp. 5–6).

page 31 The Search for Oneness:
The next several paragraphs are summaries of material drawn from Silverman, Lachmann, Milich, *The Search for Oneness*. See the book for further details on experiments with subliminal *Mommy and I Are One* messages.

page 33 "No one":
Searles, *Countertransference*, p. 176.

page 34 "an incurable wound":
Nacht and Viderman, "The Pre-Object Universe in the Transference Situation," *The International Journal of Psycho-Analysis*, Vol. 41, Parts 4–5, p. 387.

page 34 "The force behind":
Robinson, *Housekeeping*, p. 192.

CHAPTER THREE   STANDING ALONE

page 36 "something at the root":
This line and the verse that begins the chapter are from Richard Wilbur's poem "Seed Leaves," *The Norton Anthology of Poetry*, Allison et al., eds., pp. 1201–1202.

page 36 "psychological birth":
The Psychological Birth of the Human Infant by Mahler, Pine and Bergman is the basis for the separation-individuation material in this chapter. Additional information is provided by two papers: "The Separation-Individuation Process and Identity Formation," pp. 395–406, and "Object Constancy, Individuality, and Internalization," pp. 407–423, both by Mahler and John B. McDevitt, found in *The Course of Life*, Vol. 1, Greenspan and Pollock, eds. In these groundbreaking studies, separation and individuation are presented as two different

but intertwined lines of development, with separation meaning the child's achievement of an inner—intrapsychic—sense of separateness from his mother, and individuation meaning the child's acquisition of the specific qualities that makes him an individual. Mahler's four subphases of separation-individuation are differentiation (from five to nine months), practicing (from nine to fifteen months), rapprochement (from fifteen to twenty-four months) and consolidation of individuality and the beginning of emotional object constancy (from twenty-four to thirty-six months).

page 36 "hatched":

Mahler writes that "we came to recognize at some point during the differentiation subphase a certain new look of alertness, persistence and goal-directedness. We have taken this look to be a behavioral manifestation of hatching and have loosely said that an infant with this look "has hatched" (p. 54). This and all further notes for this chapter referring to Mahler are from *The Psychological Birth of the Human Infant.*

page 37 "emotional refueling":

Mahler credits Furer with the term "emotional refueling" and notes: "It is easy to observe how the wilting and fatigued infant 'perks up' in the shortest time following such contact; then he quickly goes on with his explorations and once again becomes absorbed in his pleasure in functioning" (p. 69).

page 37 a love affair with the world:

Mahler credits analyst Phyllis Greenacre with the phrase "love affair with the world" (p. 70).

page 37 "I celebrate myself":

Walt Whitman, "Song of Myself," *The Norton Anthology of Poetry*, Allison et al., eds., pp. 816–820.

page 38 At eighteen or so months:

At this stage our mind becomes capable of creating symbols and manipulating images. We can picture a separate me and a separate mother, a mother who therefore isn't the ever available appendage that we had thought her to be. The concept of a mother who is separate from oneself and who, when absent from view, possesses an independent existence elsewhere, is what Piaget calls "object permanence."

page 42 split in two:

This discussion of splitting is derived from Kernberg's *Object Relations Theory and Clinical Psychoanalysis.* He postulates that our early interpersonal relationships are reproduced internally as images—as an inner image of ourself (a self-image) and of our mother (an object-image) along with the emotional atmosphere (good or bad) under which a particular experience (feeding, playing, whatever) occurs. In taking in these experiences we split the good and bad. Loving, pleasing baby-

mother contacts are grouped together as good internal images, while painful rejecting contacts become bad internal images. Splitting, he writes, begins as a normal inability of the immature mind to integrate, but by three or four months it becomes an active defense mechanism. The defense is against the danger that our aggression (either strong innate aggression or intense aggression produced by early frustration) will spoil or destroy what we love. Splitting gradually disappears in the third year but if we continue to have great anxiety about our aggression, we may perpetuate splitting into adult life.

page 43 object constancy:
Our earliest mother memory is "recognition memory"—confronted with her face, we know her face. Later, when we have physical or psychological need of her, we can summon up her image in her absence. At fifteen to eighteen months we can evoke our mother's image—"evocative memory"—without any special stimulus or need, with evocative memory linked to our grasp of the concept "object permanence"—the independent existence of absent others. However, writes Mahler, the concept of "emotional object constancy" implies something more than all of the above. "It also implies the unifying of the 'good' and 'bad' object into one whole representation" so that ". . . the love object will not be rejected or exchanged for another if it can no longer provide satisfactions; and in that state, the object is still longed for, and not rejected (hated) as unsatisfactory simply because it is absent" (p. 110). Selma Fraiberg, though putting object constancy at an earlier age, offers a full and fascinating discussion of the subject in a paper entitled "Libidinal Object Constancy and Mental Representation," found in *The Psychoanalytic Study of the Child*, Vol. 24.

page 43 holding environment:
Winnicott has written a great deal about the maternal "holding environment," a concept he has named and discusses in eloquent and highly accessible language. See his *Collected Papers*, "The Depressive Position in Normal Emotional Development," and *The Maturational Processes and the Facilitating Environment*, "The Capacity to be Alone."

CHAPTER FOUR   THE PRIVATE "I"

page 46 a model of the mind:
Freud's three-part division of the mind, his structural theory of the mind, is first set forth in the *Standard Edition*, Vol. 19, "The Ego and the Id." Heinz Hartmann later used "self" to refer to the entire person—body and mind—and located the representation of that self in the system ego.

page 46 an image of "psychic self":
The formation of a self involves, among other achievements: Knowing

where our body ends and the world begins. Being able to organize memories, establish inner images of outer reality and have some sense of what that reality is. Tolerating our mixed emotions. Acquiring a healthy and stable narcissism. And forming identifications with our parents. See McDevitt and Mahler's "Object Constancy, Individuality and Internalization," *The Course of Life*, Vol. 1, Greenspan and Pollock, eds., pp. 407–423.

page 46 identification is one of the central processes:
My material on identification was drawn from Edith Jacobson's *The Self and the Object World*, Roy Schafer's *Aspects of Internalization*, Otto Kernberg's *Object Relations Theory and Clinical Psychoanalysis*, and John McDevitt's "The Role of Internalization in the Development of Object Relations during the Separation-Individuation Phase," from the *Journal of the American Psychoanalytic Association*, Vol. 27, No. 2, pp. 327–343.

page 47 "I am a part":
The line is from Tennyson's poem "Ulysses," *The Norton Anthology of Poetry*, Allison et al., pp. 757–758.

page 49 "Not that I would not":
James, *The Principles of Psychology*, pp. 309–310.

page 50 "toy with his own":
This material is drawn from Farber's article "On Jealousy" in *Commentary*, October 1973, pp. 50–58. The specific material quoted can be found on p. 56 and p. 57.

page 50 "two me's":
Bowlby, *Loss*, p. 227.

pages 50–51 "who glittered when he walked":
These quotations are from the poem "Richard Cory" by Edwin Arlington Robinson, *Contemporary Trends*, Nelson and Cargill, eds., p. 669.

page 51 The true self:
This section is based on Winnicott's discussion of the true self and false self, found in *The Maturational Processes and the Facilitating Environment*, "Ego Distortion in Terms of True and False Self."

page 52 The as-if personality:
This section is based on Deutsch's discussion of the as-if personality found in *Neuroses and Character Types*, "Some Forms of Emotional Disturbance and Their Relationship to Schizophrenia." The quoted material appears on p. 265.

page 52 The borderline personality:
Otto Kernberg's *Borderline Conditions and Pathological Narcissism* provides a full discussion of the borderline personality. See also the

third edition of the *Diagnostic and Statistical Manual of Mental Disorders*, the American Psychiatric Association, code 301.83.

page 53 "actively cutting off":
Kernberg, *Borderline Conditions and Pathological Narcissism*, p. 165.

page 54 Freud said that the love:
See Freud's discussion in the *Standard Edition*, Vol. 14, "On Narcissism: An Introduction."

page 54 Narcissism, says Kohut:
My discussion of narcissism is based primarily on the fascinating and somewhat controversial theories of Heinz Kohut as presented in his two books, *The Analysis of the Self* and *The Restoration of the Self*. Kohut describes two separate side-by-side lines of development, one leading to love of others (object love) and one leading to higher, healthy forms of self-love (narcissism). In Kohut's view, the development of narcissism begins with a state of primary narcissism, when self and mother form a perfect oneness, and continues after separation with the child trying to restore that lost perfection by creating (a) an exhibitionistic "grandiose self" on which all power and goodness can be concentrated, and (b) an "idealized parent imago," in whose great power and goodness he can participate.

In time, says Kohut, these two poles of self will be modified into realistic ambitions and ideals and we will possess a steady but not excessive narcissism. But first we must pass through a normal phase during which our parents function as parts of ourself, as "self-objects," to confirm and support our grandiosity and idealizations. This developmental phase begins approximately at the period between the end of symbiosis and the early stages of separation-individuation (*Kohut, The Analysis of the Self*, p. 220).

page 54 to function as that mirror:
When the parent (usually the mother) functions as a "mirroring self-object" who enjoys and admires her child, the child receives confirmation of "his tentatively established, yet still vulnerable, creative-productive-active self" (Kohut, *The Restoration of the Self*, p. 76).

page 55 to function as that ideal:
When the parent (usually the father) functions as an "idealized self-object" who permits and enjoys his child's idealization of him and merger with him, the child feels enlarged and augmented (Kohut, *The Restoration of the Self*, p. 185).

page 55 And supplied with these vital ingredients:
Kohut writes that while traces of ambitions and ideals are beginning to be acquired in early infancy, most of our grandiosity consolidates into core ambitions around the second, third and fourth years, while most of our core ideals are acquired in later childhood, around the

fourth, fifth and sixth years (Kohut, *The Restoration of the Self*, p. 179). Kohut also notes that if there is failure in the development of either our grandiose or idealizing aspect we can compensate by the especially strong development of one or the other aspect. We have, therefore, two chances to make good—"self disturbances of pathological degree result only from the failure of both of these developmental opportunities" (Kohut, *The Restoration of the Self*, p. 185).

page 55 missing pieces of self:
Our relationships with others, says Kohut, can be understood in terms of whether we are actually loving them as others or loving them as parts of ourself, as self-objects. However, he writes, "I have no hesitation in claiming that there is no mature love in which the love object is not also a self-object. . . . There is no love relationship without mutual (self-esteem enhancing) mirroring and idealization" (Kohut, *The Restoration of the Self*, p. 122).

page 56 "not loved or admired":
Kohut, *The Analysis of the Self*, p. 45.

page 56 A composite portrait:
This composite draws from Kohut's writings, Kernberg's *Borderline Conditions and Pathological Narcissism* and Christopher Lasch's elegant, highly readable *The Culture of Narcissism*.

page 57 "considers himself to be":
Don Marquis, *archy and mehitabel*, p. 82.

page 57 "The question was raised":
Kohut, *The Analysis of the Self*, p. 149.

page 57 The trouble with grandiosity:
Kernberg, *Borderline Conditions and Pathological Narcissism*, discusses this vulnerability, pp. 310-311.

page 58 "All her substitute":
Miller, *Prisoners of Childhood*, p. 42.

pages 58-59 "the total involvement":
Johnson, "A Temple of Last Resorts: Youth and Shared Narcissisms," p. 42. Her discussion of narcissism and cults is found in *The Narcissistic Condition*, Marie Coleman Nelson, ed.

pages 59-60 "I painted a picture":
Cynthia Macdonald, "Accomplishments," *A Geography of Poets*, Edward Field, ed., pp. 332-333.

page 60 Such narcissistic parents:
Miller's *Prisoners of Childhood* discusses narcissistic parents.

page 60 the pathological narcissist:
According to Kohut, people may deal with defects in their self by

developing "defensive structures" to cover the damaged parts and "compensatory structures" to strengthen the healthy parts (Kohut, *The Restoration of the Self*, p. 3).

page 61 a sense of identity:
Useful discussions of identity can be found in Heinz Lichtenstein's "The Dilemma of Human Identity: Notes on Self-Transformation, Self-Objectivation and Metamorphosis," the *Journal of the American Psychoanalytic Association*, Vol. 11, No. 1, pp. 173–223; Hans Loewald's "On the Therapeutic Action of Psychoanalysis," *International Journal of Psycho-Analysis*, Vol. 41, Part 1, pp. 16–33; "Problems of Identity," panel, David Rubinfine, reporter, *Journal of the American Psychoanalytic Association*, Vol. 6 No. 1, pp. 131–142; and Erik Erikson's *Identity: Youth and Crisis*.

page 62 Our mother helps us fulfill:
See Loewald, "On the Therapeutic Action of Psychoanalysis," *The International Journal of Psycho-Analysis*, Vol. 41, Part 1, pp. 16–33. This paper discusses the mother's crucial role as her baby's organizer or mediator: "The bodily handling of and concern with the child, the manner in which the child is fed, touched, cleaned, the way it is looked at, talked to, called by name, recognized and rerecognized—all these and many other ways of communicating with the child, and communicating to him his identity, sameness, unity and individuality, shape and mould him so that he can begin to identify himself, to feel and recognize himself as one and as separate from others yet with others. The child begins to experience himself as a centered unit by being centered upon" (p. 20).

CHAPTER FIVE   LESSONS IN LOVE

page 63 Our mother loves without limits:
In "Love for the Mother and Mother-Love," *International Journal of Psycho-Analysis*, Vol. 30, pp. 251–259, Alice Balint discusses unconditional love.

page 64 if a mother is good enough:
In *Collected Papers*, "Mind and Its Relation to the Psyche-Soma," Winnicott writes: "*The ordinary good mother is good enough.* If she is *good enough* the infant becomes able to allow for her deficiencies by mental activity.... The mental activity of the infant turns a *good-enough* environment into a perfect environment...." (p. 245).

page 64 the wish to undo that separation:
The wish to undo separation by being in love is discussed by Robert Bak in "Being in Love and Object Loss," *International Journal of Psycho-Analysis*, Vol. 54, Part 1, pp. 1–7.

page 64 "The more I give":
The line is from Shakespeare's *Romeo and Juliet*, Act 2, Scene 2.

page 65 "Infantile love follows":
Fromm, *The Art of Loving*, pp. 40–41.

page 65 "With the exception":
S. Freud, *Standard Edition*, Vol. 14, "Thoughts for the Times on War and Death," p. 298.

page 66 "Ah, I have loved":
The quoted material is from Racine's *Andromache*, Act Two.

page 66 Winnicott lists eighteen reasons:
The list appears in Winnicott's *Collected Papers*, "Hate in the Countertransference," p. 201.

page 66 "it contains a denial":
Ibid., p. 202.

pages 66–67 "He will just do nothing at all":
This poem appears in Karl Menninger's *Love Against Hate*, pp. 19–20, credited to *The New Yorker*, July 1, 1939.

page 67 "We'll eat you up":
The phrase quoted from Maurice Sendak's *Where the Wild Things Are*, unpaged.

page 67 "It is indeed foreign":
S. Freud, *Standard Edition*, Vol. 14, "Thoughts for the Times on War and Death," p. 299.

page 67 we are all still murderers:
Ibid., p. 297. "And so, if we are to be judged by our unconscious wishful impulses, we ourselves are, like primaeval man, a gang of murderers."

page 68 the daimonic:
For May's discussion of the daimonic see his *Love and Will*, Chapters 5 and 6.

page 68 "the urge in every being":
Ibid., p. 122.

page 68 "If my devils":
Ibid., p. 121.

page 68 Liv Ullmann:
These paragraphs are based on my interview with Liv Ullmann, supplemented by material from her book *Changing*, pp. 96–97.

page 69 "This nasty stuff":
Many argue, however, that the aggressive drive isn't exclusively "nasty

stuff." Although Freud presented aggression as a destructive force linked to the death instinct, others talk about constructive aggression as well: the urge for mastery, for achievement, for power, for obstacles to overcome. There is a good survey of current thinking about aggression in Justin Krent's "Some Thoughts on Aggression," *Journal of the American Psychoanalytic Association*, Vol. 26, No. 1, pp. 185–232.

page 70 our "second other":
The phrase and much useful material on early fathering can be found in Stanley Greenspan's "'The Second Other'—The Role of the Father in Early Personality Formation and in the Dyadic-Phallic Phase of Development," found in *Anthology on Fatherhood*, S. Cath, A. Gurwitt, J. Ross, eds.

page 70 "the father's role":
Michael Yogman, "Development of the Father-Infant Relationship," *Theory and Research in Behavioral Pediatrics*, Vol. 1, Fitzgerald, Lester, Yogman, eds., p. 221. In this fascinating chapter, Yogman reviews historical, cross-cultural, phylogenetic and anthropological studies of the father-infant relationship, seeking to understand paternity in *biological* terms as well as psychological ones. He also reviews recent studies of the father-infant relationship from birth to two years of age. Some of his major points include:

—With the recent increased interest by and involvement of fathers in child care there has been a legitimization, in the last ten years, of father-infant research. Earlier studies of attachment focused almost entirely on the mother in the infant's first year of life.

—Infants are biologically adapted to elicit caregiving from adults and thus insure their survival. They can elicit this care from both male and female adults.

—Interactions between fathers and infants are characterized by accentuated shifts from peaks of maximal attention to valleys of minimal attention. Interactions between mothers and infants are characterized by more gradual and modulated shifts.

—Fathers do not evoke a more excited response in babies because they are more novel. There are qualitative differences in care even when they are the primary caretaker.

—Mothers spend more time with their babies than fathers do; the studies Yogman cites "have been based on the assumption that the quality of the father-infant relationship is more important than the quantity, given some yet-to-be-defined lower limit" (p. 256).

—Fathers as well as mothers undergo psychological changes during pregnancy (and even some physical ones) and experience parenthood as a psychosocial crisis—generativity versus self-absorption, in Erikson's terms.

page 70 "provide conclusive evidence":
Ibid., p. 253.

page 71 "qualitatively different":
Ibid., p. 259.

page 71 the "biological component":
Ibid., p. 270.

page 71 "We're not very happy today":
Greene, *Good Morning, Merry Sunshine*, pp. 102–103.

page 72 "no known society":
Alice Rossi, "A Biosocial Perspective on Parenting," *Daedalus*, Spring 1977, pp. 1–31. The statement appears on p. 5.

page 72 "A biosocial perspective":
Ibid., p. 4.

page 72 This isn't meant to suggest that fathers aren't important:
For further discussion of the father's role see: Cath, Gurwitt, Ross, *Father and Child*; John Munder Ross's "Fathering: A Review of Some Psychoanalytic Contributions on Paternity," *The International Journal of Psycho-Analysis*, Vol. 60, Part 3, pp. 317–327; J. O. Wisdom's "The Role of the Father in the Mind of Parents, in Psychoanalytic Theory and in the Life of the Infant," *The International Review of Psychoanalysis*, Vol. 3, Part 2, pp. 231–239; "The Role of the Father in the Preoedipal Years," reported by Robert Prall, *Journal of the American Psychoanalytic Association*, Vol. 26, No. 1, pp. 143–161; and *The Role of the Father in Child Development*, Michael Lamb, ed.

pages 73–74 Liv Ullmann:
These paragraphs are based on my interview with Liv Ullmann supplemented by material from her book *Changing*, pp. 11–12.

page 75 the repetition compulsion:
The compulsion to repeat is first discussed by Freud in *Standard Edition*, Vol. 12, "Remembering, Repeating and Working-Through." He notes that events we cannot remember are reproduced as actions and that this "repetition is a transference of the forgotten past . . ." onto the present (p. 151). In *Standard Edition*, Vol. 18, "Beyond the Pleasure Principle," Freud asserts the universality of the repetition compulsion and relates it to the death instinct (see note "the death instinct," p. 79, below). Anna Freud clarifies the relationship between the repetition compulsion and transference in *The Ego and the Mechanisms of Defense*: "By transference we mean all those impulses . . . which are not newly created . . . but have their source in early—indeed, the very earliest—object relations and are now merely revived under the influence of the repetition compulsion" (p. 18). She also notes (p. 19) that the repetition compulsion extends not only to former impulses but also to former defensive measures against them.

page 76 For many men the denial of dependency:
Analyst Otto Kernberg describes a promiscuous patient of his, a smart

and successful man in his early thirties, who found himself again and again engaged in short-lived sexual encounters: pursuing women, taking them to bed, and then moving on before he could form a relationship. His mother had chronically frustrated him, withdrawing from him both physically and emotionally. She possessed such treasures, he felt, but she would not share them. He remembered trying to cling to her while she coldly rejected his love and his demands upon her. And through his promiscuity, he enacted one version of that early history, taking a woman's treasures and—by loving and leaving—denying how much he needed her. (See *Object-Relations Theory and Clinical Psychoanalysis*, pp. 191–195.)

page 77 "Out of boredom":
K. Snow, *Willo*, pp. 96–97.

page 77 Benjamin Spock:
This material is based on my interviews with Dr. Spock and Mary Morgan in 1983.

pages 77–78 the woman described by Freud:
S. Freud, *Standard Edition*, Vol. 18, "Beyond the Pleasure Principle," p. 22.

page 78 the woman who disdained her parents' . . . marriage:
Miller describes this case in her book *Prisoners of Childhood*, pp. 60–61.

page 79 "pursued by a malignant fate":
S. Freud, *Standard Edition*, Vol. 18, "Beyond the Pleasure Principle," p. 21.

page 79 transference love:
In Freud's *Standard Edition*, Vol. 12, "Observations on Transference-Love," he notes that "love consists of new editions of old traits and that it repeats infantile reactions. But this is the essential character of being in love. There is no such state which does not reproduce infantile prototypes" (p. 168).

page 79 the death instinct:
Freud presents his controversial theory of the death instinct in *Standard Edition*, Vol. 18, "Beyond the Pleasure Principle," and develops it in subsequent publications. Taking the sexual and aggressive instincts back one step, he establishes the ultimate polarity—the life instinct and the death instinct. The life instinct—Eros—is the sexual drive operating in us to preserve life, reproduce it, bring it together. The death instinct—sometimes called Thanatos—is the aggressive drive operating in us to destroy through killing and through dying.

Freud attributes the urge to restore an earlier state of things, manifested as the repetition compulsion, to the death instinct, which seeks to return to the "quiescence of the inorganic world" (p. 62). However, many analysts hold that all behavior (and not just that which is at-

tributed to the death instinct) is in part under the sway of the repetition compulsion. Furthermore, many analysts who accept Freud's sex-aggression duality reject the concept of a death instinct.

page 79 to undo—rewrite—the past:
In *Standard Edition*, Vol. 20, "Inhibitions, Symptoms and Anxiety," Freud offers this explanation for the compulsion to repeat. He writes: "When anything has not happened in the desired way, it is undone by being repeated in a different way" (p. 120).

page 79 "Only connect!":
Forster, *Howards End*, p. 186.

page 80 we try to love:
In *Love and Will* May describes four kinds of love: *libido, eros, philia* and *caritas* (p. 37).

page 80 "Man is gifted":
Fromm, *The Art of Loving*, p. 8.

CHAPTER SIX WHEN ARE YOU TAKING THAT NEW KID BACK TO THE HOSPITAL?

page 84 "I thought. That question":
Hayward, *Haywire*, pp. 123-124.

page 85 "A small child":
S. Freud, *Standard Edition*, Vol. 15, "Introductory Lectures on Psycho-Analysis, Parts I and II," p. 204.

page 86 Symbiosis was strictly mama and me:
I am arguing here that every child experiences himself as his mother's only child during the symbiotic phase and thus all children (not only the oldest) suffer the loss of an exclusive mother-child relationship. (This is not to deny, of course, the unique displacement of the oldest child who in fact as well as in symbiotic delusion has had his mother to himself.)

page 86 "And the Lord had respect":
Holy Bible, Genesis.

page 87 inside our head:
Levy's *Studies in Sibling Rivalry* gives us a glimpse of some of these murderous sibling fantasies. He presents cases based on a series of play-technique experiments in which children with younger siblings were shown a mother doll, a nursing baby doll and an older brother or sister doll and invited to express the feelings of the older doll-sibling. The children responded by crushing, piercing, hammering, smashing and tearing apart the baby doll nursing at the mother doll's breast.

page 87 "extreme jealousy and competitiveness":
A. Freud, *Normality and Pathology in Childhood*, p. 176.

page 87 threatens vast anxiety:
In *Standard Edition*, Vol. 20, "Inhibitions, Symptoms and Anxiety," pp. 77–175, Freud states that human beings develop automatic anxiety when confronted with situations so overwhelming that they are rendered helpless. In the course of development we learn to anticipate these overwhelming situations—these traumatic situations—and to experience a diminished form of anxiety—signal anxiety—*before* the trauma occurs. Signal anxiety, then, is an internal warning signal whose function is to mobilize our defenses so that we can avert traumatic situations.

page 87 our dangerous and now unwanted impulse:
These dangerous and unwanted impulses stem from the part of our psyche called the id—seat of our unconscious primitive wishes. But another part of our psyche, the ego, is perpetually engaged in unconscious defensive operations against our id, providing us with both the warning of danger (through signal anxiety) and the means of protecting ourselves from the dangers (through our defense mechanisms).

page 87 a feared or actual loss:
In *Standard Edition*, Vol. 20, "Inhibitions, Symptoms and Anxiety," Freud describes a series of typical danger situations where the anxiety that threatens us is attendant upon an unendurable loss: The loss of the person we love. The loss of that loved person's love. The loss of some beloved body part—i.e., castration. And the loss of the loving approval of our conscience, of our own internal judge. Each of these danger situations corresponds to a particular developmental phase, and each is liable to precipitate a traumatic experience. Freud says that the original danger situation—the prototype of absolute helplessness in the face of overwhelming stimuli—is birth.

page 87 our common everyday mechanisms of defense:
See A. Freud's *The Ego and the Mechanisms of Defense*, and Brenner's lucid discussion of defense in *An Elementary Textbook of Psychoanalysis*, pp. 79–96. Different theorists differ about what they would include on their list of "mechanisms of defense." They agree, however, that defenses sometimes lead to healthy adaptation and sometimes to neurotic symptoms. For instance, a person who regularly uses isolation as a defense may become cut off from his emotional life, feeling nothing very much about anything. Or a person who relies on projection may, by attributing all of his hostile feelings to others, become a paranoid who believes "they're all out to get me." On the other hand, identification may lead to self-enrichment through the acquisition of valuable characteristics, reaction formation may sometimes help establish useful and humane qualities, and sublimation, at its best, may produce great art.

page 89 almost anything can serve as a defense mechanism:
In *An Elementary Textbook of Psychoanalysis*, Brenner states that "the ego can and does use all the processes of normal ego formation and ego function for defensive purposes at one time or another" (p. 80).

page 89 "de-identification":
For a discussion of de-identification and split-parent identification, see "Sibling Deidentification and Split-Parent Identification: A Family Tetrad," by Frances Fuchs Schachter, pp. 123–151, in *Sibling Relationships: Their Nature and Significance Across the Lifespan*, Michael E. Lamb and Brian Sutton-Smith, eds.

page 90 Each could even feel superior:
Ibid. Schachter notes that these feelings of superiority suggest that de-identification may be a muted way of maintaining the benefits of sibling rivalry while minimizing the costs.

page 90 half of a whole human being:
An interesting problem with role polarization is discussed in "A Survey of Learning Difficulties in Children" by Gerald Pearson, *The Psychoanalytic Study of the Child*, Vol. 7. Pearson describes a thirteen-year-old girl who was interested in her school work to the exclusion of all else, in marked contrast to her older sister who was an indifferent student, a party girl, intensely sociable, etc. "Learning, for her, became a way of establishing her individuality, a way of expressing her rivalry with her sister, a way of obtaining her parents' love in a field that would not arouse her sister's jealousy and a method of avoiding her sister's jealous hostility" (p. 345).

pages 90–91 "My mother used to characterize Margo":
Fishel, *Sisters*, p. 108.

page 91 "he will become a fighting child":
Adler, *Problems of Neurosis*, p. 98.

page 92 interesting work on adult sibling rivalry:
H. Ross and J. Milgram, "Important Variables in Adult Sibling Relationships: A Qualitative Study," *Sibling Relationships: Their Nature and Significance Across the Lifespan*, Lamb and Sutton-Smith, eds. Ross and Milgram describe three types of adult sibling rivalry: simple sibling rivalry, which involves one sib's resentment of another's greater strengths in one or more areas; reciprocal sibling rivalry, with each sib having certain strengths and weaknesses and resenting the strengths the other sib possesses; and sex-linked sibling rivalry, where the privileges granted for being a male or a female are resented—sometimes for a lifetime—by the one who isn't getting them.
    Why the secrecy about this rivalry? Ross and Milgram speculate that it may have to do, first, with the fear that an admission of rivalrous

feelings is akin to an admission of maladjustment. There may also be a concern that such disclosure would do permanent damage to the relationship. "Furthermore," they write, "to reveal feelings of rivalry to a brother or sister who is perceived as being stronger or as having the upper hand in the relationship increases one's vulnerability in an already unsafe situation" (pp. 236–237).

page 93 Henry and . . . William James:
The quoted material about and from Henry and William can be found in Edel's *Henry James*, Vol. 5, p. 295, p. 301, p. 300 and p. 298. Edel perceives them as a Jacob and Esau battling over their birthright.

page 93 Olivia de Havilland and Joan Fontaine:
From Joan Fontaine's autobiography, *No Bed of Roses*, "were not encouraged . . ." p. 102; "Now what had I done . . ." pp. 145–146.

page 94 Billy Carter . . . Jimmy Carter:
The material on the Carter brothers comes from Bank and Kahn, *The Sibling Bond*, pp. 229–231.

page 94 "for the favor of parents":
Cited in Arnstein, *Brothers and Sisters/Sisters and Brothers*, p. 3.

page 94 "is always breathing down my neck":
Ibid., pp. 3–4.

page 95 "I later discovered":
Ibid., p. 4.

page 96 "The nature and quality":
S. Freud, *Standard Edition*, Vol. 13, "Some Reflections on Schoolboy Psychology," p. 243.

page 96 "she had been the younger":
This case is discussed in Josephine Hilgard's "Sibling Rivalry and Social Heredity," *Psychiatry*, Vol. 14, No. 4, pp. 375–385. The quoted material appears on p. 380.

page 97 "My mom says I'm her sugarplum":
Viorst, *If I Were in Charge of the World, and Other Worries*, "Some Things Don't Make Any Sense At All," p. 8.

page 97 family order of birth:
Theories abound, and often conflict, on the relationship of order of birth to personality, but there seems to be agreement on some of the advantages and disadvantages of being the firstborn child. See Bank and Kahn, *The Sibling Bond*, for discussion of firstborn advantages and disadvantages, pp. 205–206, and for references to birth-order research, pp. 6–7. For the first serious effort to correlate birth order and personality, see Adler, *Problems of Neurosis*, Chapter 7. Arnstein's *Brothers and Sisters/Sisters and Brothers* mentions a study

which showed that a majority of the members of Congress in a randomly selected sample were firstborns, but so were 31 out of a sample of 35 stripteasers. "It was suggested that both . . . have marked needs for recognition, attention and appreciation. Certainly both expose themselves in one way or another to public view" (p. 87).

page 97 "Apparently his mother":
Frisch, *I'm Not Stiller*, pp. 285–286.

page 98 "rotten bad influence":
E. O'Neill, *Long Day's Journey into Night*, p. 165.

page 99 Hansels and Gretels:
Hansels and Gretels are discussed in *The Sibling Bond*, Bank and Kahn, Chapter 5. The Jerome quotes can be found on p. 117. The authors point out that the development of these intense loyalties requires the presence of some loving figure in early life.

page 101 "one can conceive of rivalry":
Cicirelli discusses the sibling tie in "Sibling Influence Throughout the Lifespan," from *Sibling Relationships: Their Nature and Significance Across the Lifespan*, Lamb and Sutton-Smith, eds. The quoted material appears on p. 278.

page 101 "Sisters, while they are growing up":
Mead, *Blackberry Winter*, p. 70.

CHAPTER SEVEN   PASSIONATE TRIANGLES

page 104 from mouth to anus to genitals:
The first full discussion of sexuality in children is found in Freud, *Standard Edition*, Vol. 7, "Three Essays on the Theory of Sexuality." Freud describes the stages of psychosexual development and the successively central erogenous zones as follows:

From zero to one and a half years old—the oral phase—the zone is the mouth, and sucking and biting the pleasure.

From one and a half to three years old—the anal phase—the zone is the anus, and expelling and holding the pleasure.

From three to five or six years old—the phallic phase—the zone is the genital organs, and masturbation the pleasure.

And after a phase of relative calm, called latency, we enter—at puberty—into the genital phase.

The oral, anal and phallic phases of childhood described by Freud overlap and never completely vanish. Instead they become component parts of adult genital sexuality. In addition, there are other manifestations of the sexual instinct in childhood—a wish to look, a wish to exhibit, urethral erotism (sensual pleasure connected with urinating and the urethra) and sensual pleasure connected with hearing or smell-

ing. Some of these, to varying degrees, may also become part of adult sexuality. A strong and persistent emotional investment in infantile modes (sucking, for instance) or objects (mother, for instance) of sexual gratification is called a fixation. A turning back to an earlier mode or object of gratification is called a regression.

page 104 "decisive encounters":
Erikson, *Childhood and Society*, p. 71. He also notes that "the optimum total situation implied in the baby's readiness to get what is given is his mutual regulation with a mother who will permit him to develop and co-ordinate his means of getting as she develops and co-ordinates her means of giving. There is a high premium of libidinal pleasure on this co-ordination . . ." (pp. 75–76). For further discussion, see his chapter on "The Theory of Infantile Sexuality."

While Erikson—in his amplification of Freud's psychosexual stages—emphasizes the links between erogenous zones and interpersonal relationships, Kernberg—in his amplification—focuses on *internalized* object relations (the mental representations of relationships). He states in *Object Relations Theory and Clinical Psychoanalysis* that "internalized object relations are a major organizer of instinctual development in man" (p. 186).

page 105 It was Sigmund Freud who discovered and described the Oedipus complex:
Freud's writings on the Oedipus complex include, all from the *Standard Edition*, "The Interpretation of Dreams" (Vol. 4), "Introductory Lectures on Psycho-Analysis" (Vol. 16), "The Ego and the Id," "The Dissolution of the Oedipus Complex" and "Some Psychical Consequences of the Anatomical Distinction Between the Sexes" (Vol. 19).

When Freud talks about incestuous wishes, he is talking about a child's unconscious wish to engage in sexual activities with his or her parent, though the fantasies of exactly what these sexual activities are may be quite inaccurate and bizarre. When Freud talks about murderous wishes, he is talking about a child's unconscious wish to kill his or her parent, though a child may not know that death is a permanent state.

The destiny of Oedipus moves us, writes Freud in "The Interpretation of Dreams," "only because it might have been ours—because the oracle laid the same curse upon us before our birth as upon him. It is the fate of all of us, perhaps, to direct our first sexual impulse towards our mother and our first hatred and our first murderous wish against our father" (p. 262).

pages 105–6 our unconscious fear of damage:
This damage, according to Freud, is—for a boy—castration, untechnically defined as the loss of his beloved sex organ, his penis. (His observation that there actually are certain human beings who lack a penis persuades him that the loss of his is possible.) For a girl this

fear of damage is much more vaguely defined by Freud and his fol-
lowers. (Fear of genital injury through intercourse with her father is
one suggestion.)

page 107 "an injured third party":
Freud, *Standard Edition*, Vol. 11, "A Special Type of Choice of Object
Made By Men," p. 166.

page 107 "that the injured third party":
Ibid., p. 169.

page 108 Hamlet's famous procrastination as oedipal:
E. Jones, *Hamlet and Oedipus*. The quoted material appears on p. 51
and p. 100. Freud makes the same point in "The Interpretation of
Dreams" when he writes: "Hamlet is able to do anything—except
take vengeance on the man who did away with his father and took
that father's place with his mother, the man who shows him the repressed wishes of his own childhood realized" (p. 265).

page 109 Or whether we're ready to deal with them:
There are many adults, and many patients in therapy, whose emotional
life has not reached the level of oedipal conflict. Instead of being
concerned with triangular issues of sexual love and competition, they
are still struggling with whether they and others exist as whole and
separate selves, with whether or not they can survive separateness
or with a narcissistic perception of others as nothing more than ex-
tensions of themself.

page 109 "The forces of conscience":
Freud, *Standard Edition*, Vol. 14, "Some Character-Types Met with
in Psycho-Analytic Work," p. 331. See also an excellent article on the
success neurosis by Bryce Nelson called "Self-Sabotage in Careers—
A Common Trap," *The New York Times*, February 15, 1983.

The success neurosis, by the way, can be generated in love as well
as in work. Oedipal victors—people who symbolically (or actually)
succeed in winning the sexually yearned-for parent—may also suffer
from a success neurosis.

page 111 the negative Oedipus complex:
Freud's writings on the negative Oedipus complex include, in the
Standard Edition, Vol. 19, "The Ego and the Id," "The Dissolution
of the Oedipus Complex" and "Some Psychical Consequences of the
Anatomical Distinction Between the Sexes."

Some writings seem to suggest that the negative Oedipus complex
is a more well-defined phase—preceding the positive Oedipus complex—in girls than in boys. Boys do, however, have strong negative
oedipal wishes to take their mother's place with their father. They
relinquish this wish for the same reason they ultimately relinquish
their sexual wish for their mother—castration anxiety. "For both of

them entail . . . the loss of his penis—the masculine [way of obtaining satisfaction] . . . as a resulting punishment and the feminine one as a precondition" ("The Dissolution of the Oedipus Complex," p. 176).

page 111 Little girls must submit their first love to a sex change:
See Freud, *Standard Edition*, Vol. 21, "Female Sexuality," where he writes that "a woman's strong dependence on her father merely takes over the heritage of an equally strong attachment to her mother. . . ." (p. 227). See also J. Lampl-De Groot's "The Evolution of the Oedipus Complex in Women," *The International Journal of Psycho-Analysis*, Vol. 9 (pp. 332–345). These papers argue that little girls give up their mother as a sex object because they blame her for making them incomplete—i.e., for failing to give them a penis, which they covet and envy. Thus, while castration concerns put an *end* to the boy's positive Oedipus complex, they *are the beginning* of a girl's positive Oedipus complex, turning her angrily against her mother and sending her to her father with fantasies that through him she will receive a penis substitute—a baby. Many analysts today reject penis envy as a reason for the girl's shift from mother to father, though—as we will see in the next chapter—penis envy (along with womb envy and other kinds of envy) may play an important part in our mental life.

page 112 significantly reflect our human environment:
In *The Collected Papers of Otto Fenichel*, "Specific Forms of the Oedipus Complex," Fenichel discusses the influence of various environmental factors on oedipal conflicts.

For instance, he notes that our brothers and our sisters "are, above all, objects of jealousy, and, according to the individual circumstances, they may either increase the hatred directed in the Oedipus complex against one parent or they may deflect it and so diminish it" (p. 212). However, he says they can serve as love objects too.

He also makes the point that the Oedipus complex in children "is in part stimulated also by the corresponding attitude in their parents: the father loves the daughter and the mother the son. This unconscious sexual attachment to the children becomes specially strong wherever the parents' real sexual gratification leaves them unsatisfied" (p. 212).

Further material on environmental factors can be found in Lidz's *Hamlet's Enemy*, Chapter 17, "The Oedipal Transition: An Existential Interpretation." See also Peter Neubauer's "The One-Parent Child and His Oedipal Development" in *The Psychoanalytic Study of the Child*, Vol. 15.

page 112 "just a case of the kid":
Personal communication from Dr. Louis Breger.

page 112 "transitional space":
This discussion of the family, transitional space and incest comes from Dr. Winer's paper "Incest" (unpublished).

page 113 "After her mother died":
Fitzgerald, *Tender Is the Night*, p. 129.

page 113 "rigidness of her shocked body":
Morrison, *The Bluest Eye*, p. 128.

page 114 "I have blotted out":
Fields, *Like Father, Like Daughter*, pp. 161–162.

page 114 "incestuous fantasies may be realized":
Winer, "Incest" (unpublished).

page 114 motherly incest fantasies:
Feldman, "On Romance," *Bulletin of the Philadelphia Association for Psychoanalysis*, Vol. 19, No. 3, pp. 153–157.

page 115 the child doesn't wind up walking away with the parent:
In her book *The Magic Years*, Selma Fraiberg talks about the ways in which "we create the feeling in the child that his parents' relationship . . . must be respected. A child, dearly loved as he is, may not intrude upon this intimate relationship, cannot share the intimacies of his parents' lives, and cannot obtain the exclusive love of a parent. If the child has fantasies about marrying the parent of his choice, fantasies about a more intimate and exclusive love, the fantasy remains a fantasy, for we do nothing to encourage it, and without encouragement the fantasy will be given up" (p. 225).

page 115 At dinner a four-year-old girl:
Sweet, "The Electra Complex," *Ms.*, May 1984, pp. 148–149. The quoted material appears on p. 149.

page 116 One woman, who lived with a man she loved:
Fenichel describes this case in *The Collected Papers of Otto Fenichel*, "Specific Forms of the Oedipus Complex," pp. 213–214.

page 117 Linda Bird Francke's "The Sons of Divorce":
Francke's survey of studies on the impact of divorce on boys, "The Sons of Divorce," appeared in *The New York Times Magazine*, May 22, 1983, pp. 40–41, 54–57. Her article is the source of the quotations from Dr. Livingston and the three "divorced" sons.

page 118 We will struggle with oedipal conflicts all our life:
Loewald makes this point in a beautiful paper called "The Waning of the Oedipus Complex," *Journal of the American Psychoanalytic Association*, Vol. 27, No. 4. He writes that "no matter how resolutely the ego turns away from it and what the relative proportions of repression, sublimation, 'destruction' might be, in adolescence the Oedipus complex rears its head again, and it does during later periods in life. . . . It repeatedly requires repression, internalization, transformation, sublimation, in short, some forms of mastery in the course of life" (p. 753).

page 119 an inner law-enforcement agency:
The taking in of our parents' moral standards provides us with an inner ally in our struggle to repudiate our dangerous oedipal wishes. This inner ally, our superego, is thus—in Freud's words—the "heir" of the Oedipus complex.

page 119 the Oedipus complex "has taken its name from failure":
Mead's statement on oedipal failure and success appears in *Male and Female*, p. 108.

page 119 "Aha! a traitor in the camp":
Ibid., pp. 108–109. In a footnote Mead provides the complete text of Eugene Field's poem "To a Usurper."

CHAPTER EIGHT ANATOMY AND DESTINY

page 121 our wish to do so may be "one of the deepest tendencies":
See Lawrence Kubie's "The Drive to Become Both Sexes," *The Psychoanalytic Quarterly*, Vol. 43, No. 3, pp. 349–426. The passage quoted appears on p. 370.

page 121 Orlando:
See Virginia Woolf's novel *Orlando*.

page 122 gender identity:
According to analyst Robert Stoller, gender identity is fairly irreversibly established between eighteen months and three years. His research persuasively challenges Freud's theory that while males have a primary masculinity, a little girl's femininity is a later development which occurs after the traumatic discovery that she lacks a penis. Rejecting the notion of a primary femininity, Freud describes the little girl as masculine in her sexuality until the recognition of the differences between boys and girls, which—he says—leads to feelings of being castrated, and penis envy. As a result of this penis envy, her self-love is mortified, she renounces masturbatory satisfaction (because her equipment—her clitoris—is so inferior), she blames her mother for failing to equip her properly and she perceives her, and all penisless women, as debased. At this point she turns from her mother to her father, a shift that initiates the female Oedipus complex and also initiates the development of femininity.

Stoller, in "A Different View of Oedipal Conflict," *The Course of Life*, Vol. 1, Greenspan and Pollock, eds., argues for a primary femininity—an early "unquestioned, unconflicted, egosyntonic acceptance of oneself as female" (p. 595). In another paper, "Primary Femininity," *Journal of the American Psychoanalytic Association*, Vol. 24, No. 5, he discusses "core gender identity," which he defines as "the sense we have of our sex—of maleness in males and female-

ness in females" (p. 61). It is around this core that our gender identity, a broader term including masculinity and femininity and various sex-linked roles and relationships, gradually forms. Stoller says core gender identity is the result of five factors: (1) a biological "force"—the effect of sex hormones on the fetus; (2) sex assignment at birth; (3) parental attitudes toward the sex assignment, reflected back onto the infant; (4) "biopsychic" phenomena—the effects of patterns of handling, conditioning, imprinting; (5) bodily sensations, especially from the genitals.

James Kleeman, same journal, notes in his paper "Freud's Views on Early Female Sexuality in the Light of Direct Child Observation" that an important key to early gender identity is the child's conscious and not-so-conscious labeling of him or her self as a boy or a girl. This labeling "serves as the primary and basic organizer for subsequent gender experience" (p. 15).

page 123 three feminist writers:
Viorst, "Are Men and Women Different?" *Redbook*, November 1978. See pp. 46–50 for responses from Gould, Steinem, Jong, etc.

page 123 Sigmund Freud would have answered:
Freud, *Standard Edition*, Vol. 22, "New Introductory Lectures on Psycho-Analysis," offers this characterization of women in his lecture on "Femininity."

page 124 "certainly incomplete and fragmentary":
Ibid., p. 135.

page 124 Two Stanford psychologists:
Maccoby and Jacklin summarize and comment on patterns of difference and similarity in Chapter 10 of *The Psychology of Sex Differences*, pp. 349–374.

page 125 "I think hormones":
Viorst, "Are Men and Women Different?" *Redbook*, November 1978, p. 48.

page 126 "Here it was—The Cinderella Complex":
Dowling, *The Cinderella Complex*, p. 64. There is also a stirring exposition of this theme in Vivian Gornick's "Toward a Definition of the Female Sensibility" in *The Village Voice*, May 31, 1973.
She writes: "The subjection of women, in my view, lies most deeply in the ingrained conviction—shared by both men and women—that for women marriage is the pivotal experience. It is this conviction, primarily, that reduces and ultimately destroys in women that flow of psychic energy that is fed in men from birth by the anxious knowledge given them that one is alone in this world; that one is never taken care of; that life is a naked battle between fear and desire, and that fear is kept in abeyance only through the recurrent urge of desire;

that desire is whetted only if it is reinforced by the capacity to experience oneself; that the capacity to experience oneself is everything."

She continues: "It is the re-creation in women of the experiencing self that is the business of contemporary feminism: the absence of that self is the slave that must be squeezed out drop by drop. Vast internal changes must occur in women. . . . A new kind of journey into the interior must be taken, one in which the terms of internal conflict are re-defined. It is a journey of unimaginable pain and loneliness, this journey, a battle all the way, one in which the same inch of emotional ground must be fought for over and over again, alone and without allies, the only soldier in the army the struggling self. But on the other side lies freedom: self-possession" (pp. 21–22).

page 127 "mature dependence":
The phrase is Fairbairn's, from *Psychoanalytic Studies of the Personality*. He notes that he prefers the term "mature dependence" to "independence" because "a capacity for relationships necessarily implies dependence of some sort" (p. 145).

page 128 "male and female voices":
Gilligan, *In a Different Voice*, p. 156.

page 128 women's concern with relationships:
In Gilligan's thought-provoking *In a Different Voice* she refers to a study on adult fantasies of power showing that "women are more concerned than men with both sides of an interdependent relationship" and "quicker to recognize their own interdependence." The study also found that "while men represent powerful activity as assertion and aggression, women in contrast portray acts of nurturance as acts of strength" (pp. 167–168).

page 128 "By yourself":
Ibid., p. 160.

page 128 "What I had to learn":
Scarf, *Unfinished Business*, p. 89.

page 128 "We are never so defenseless":
Freud, *Standard Edition*, Vol. 21, "Civilization and Its Discontents," p. 82.

page 128 depression when important love relationships are through:
See Maggie Scarf's fine book, *Unfinished Business*, which relates depression in women to "the loss of an important, self-defining, powerful and binding emotional relationship" (p. 86). Scarf reports that depression is suffered by an estimated three to six times as many women as men.

In further support of her point, see Erik Erikson's *Identity: Youth and Crisis*, where his clinical experience leads him to conclude: "Emp-

tiness is the female form of perdition. . . . To be left, for her, means to be left empty, to be drained of the blood of the body, the warmth of the heart, the sap of life" (p. 278).

page 129 they do *do it differently:*
In Mead's *Male and Female,* for instance, she notes that in a two-sex world "we find that there are certain biological regularities" (p. 147). These include the fact that the mother nurses both boys and girls, which means that "the female child's earliest experience is one of closeness to her own nature" while the little boy must "begin to differentiate himself from the person closest to him" (p. 148). Mead adds, however, that this biological regularity would vanish if men shared equally in child care, a point that is eloquently elaborated on in Dorothy Dinnerstein's difficult and elegant book, *The Mermaid and the Minotaur.*

For a full discussion of the developmental differences between boys and girls in establishing their gender identity, see Tyson, "A Developmental Line of Gender Identity, Gender Role and Choice of Love Object," *Journal of the American Psychoanalytic Association,* Vol. 30, No. 1, pp. 61–86.

page 129 Boys, to be boys:
See Stoller and Herdt, "The Development of Masculinity: A Cross-Cultural Contribution," in the *Journal of the American Psychoanalytic Association,* Vol. 30, No. 1. Here the authors hypothesize that the earliest stage of masculine development is a "protofemininity, a condition induced through the merging that occurs in the mother-infant symbiosis." To develop masculinity, the boy must erect an inner barrier, a protective shield against the urge "to maintain the blissful sense of being one with mother" (pp. 32–33).

page 130 "until it seemed we were one":
L. Michaels, *The Men's Club,* p. 161.

page 132 "This renunciation":
L. Altman, "Some Vicissitudes of Love," *Journal of the American Psychoanalytic Association,* Vol. 25, No. 1, p. 48.

page 132 For a girl to give up her mother:
In "Some Thoughts on the Nature of Woman," *Bulletin of the Philadelphia Association for Psychoanalysis,* Vol. 20, Louis Kaplan writes: "Penis envy then does not arise from the chance observation that her brother or her father are better endowed but rather from the realization that they can and she can't achieve ultimate reunion with mother" (p. 324).

page 132 "to be discontent":
This Webster dictionary definition of envy is used by Daniel Jaffe to explore womb envy in "The Masculine Envy of Woman's Procreative

Function," *Journal of the American Psychoanalytic Association*, Vol. 16, No. 3, pp. 521–548.

page 132 "source of all comforts":
Hanna Segal, *Introduction to the Work of Melanie Klein*, p. 40. See Chapter Four of her book for further discussion of breast envy.

page 133 creating new life:
There is an interesting discussion of creativity and gender in Greenacre's book *Emotional Growth*, Vol. 2, "Woman as Artist." And Mead notes in *Male and Female* that it is civilization's problem to define a role for men that will give them a sense of "irreversible achievement" comparable to that which women achieve through childbearing (p. 160).

page 133 And some puberty rites:
Bettelheim, *Symbolic Wounds*. The quoted material is found respectively on p. 262 and p. 264.

page 134 Felix Boehm wrote of the male's intense envy:
Boehm, "The Femininity-Complex in Men," *The International Journal of Psycho-Analysis*, Vol. 11, Part 4, pp. 444–469. The quoted material is found respectively on p. 456 and p. 457.

page 134 "remember that every son":
Piercy, *Circles on the Water*, "Doing It Differently," p. 113.

page 135 working woman's version of penis envy:
See Applegarth's "Some Observation on Work Inhibitions in Women," *Journal of the American Psychoanalytic Association*, Vol. 24, No. 5, pp. 251–268.

page 135 In a recent study:
Carol Tavris, with Dr. Alice Baumgartner, reports on this study in "How Would Your Life Be Different If You'd Been Born a Boy?" *Redbook*, February 1983, pp. 92–95. Dr. Baumgartner and her colleagues at the University of Colorado's Institute for Equality in Education surveyed nearly 2,000 schoolchildren in Colorado and found that both sexes still think that boys have it better.

page 136 that "something" a penis has come to represent:
One analyst says, "My experience with women patients has shown me that penis envy is not an end in itself, but rather the expression of a desire to triumph over the . . . mother through the possession of the organ the mother lacks. . . ." (Chasseguet-Smirgel, "Freud and Female Sexuality: The Consideration of Some Blind Spots in the Exploration of the 'Dark Continent,'" *The International Journal of Psycho-Analysis*, Vol. 57, Part 3, p. 285.)

Another analyst says that penis envy may sometimes be "the wish to have something personally satisfying to lessen dependence on men. . . ." (Moore, B., "Freud and Female Sexuality: A Current View,"

from above-mentioned journal, p. 296.)

See also Grossman and Stewart, "Penis Envy: From Childhood Wish to Developmental Metaphor," *Journal of the American Psychoanalytic Association*, Vol. 24, No. 5, pp. 193–212.

page 136 "cut short of something":
In Freud's *Standard Edition*, Vol. 14, "Some Character-Types Met With in Psycho-Analytic Work," he wrote about men and women who secretly feel that life has done them wrong and who therefore feel entitled to special treatment and exemptions. He says that we all have our buried, or maybe not so buried, grievances and that "we all demand reparation for early wounds to our narcissism, our self-love." But some people, says Freud, people whom he labeled "the exceptions," actually live as if they are exceptions: Demanding special treatment. Believing that the rules don't apply to them. And some people—women!—he says, because they feel "undeservedly cut short of something and unfairly treated" believe themselves deserving of exemptions from "many of the importunities of life" (p. 315). His point seems to be that women think that they ought to be spared because they have suffered enough, that the absence of a penis makes women feel entitled to claim special treatment.

page 136 Thus the discovery:
According to all the latest research—and contrary to Freud's assumptions—penis envy, along with castration anxiety and a wish for a baby, can occur well before the oedipal phase.

page 137 castration anxiety:
In "Comments on Penis Envy and Orgasm in Women," *The Psychoanalytic Study of the Child*, Vol. 32, K. R. Eissler compares male and female psychosexual processes and concludes that, because of male castration anxiety, men have a harder developmental task than women do. While a woman "runs the risk of being plagued for the rest of her life by envy . . . a man may have to expect to be haunted by the anxiety that he will be deprived of his penis. It stands to reason that envy is far more easy to bear and far less painful than such a terrible anxiety" (p. 65).

page 137 "Daddy, I love you!":
Tyson, "A Developmental Line of Gender Identity, Gender Role and Choice of Love Object," *Journal of the American Psychoanalytic Association*, Vol. 30, No. 1, p. 69.

page 138 we identify with our other parent too:
Analyst Albert Solnit notes: "It is the child's bisexuality that enables him to identify with both parents, to acquire a maternal as well as a *paternal* psychological capacity. . . ." See "Psychoanalytic Perspectives on Children One—Three Years of Age," *The Course of Life*, Vol. 1, Greenspan and Pollock, eds. (p. 512).

page 138 "The potter who works with clay":
Mead, "Male and Female," p. 19.

CHAPTER NINE   GOOD AS GUILT

page 140 the price we pay for civilization:
In his *Standard Edition*, Vol. 21, "Civilization and Its Discontents,"
Freud discusses the limits we must place upon ourselves in order to
live as civilized members of a society. He says that it is his intention
"to represent the sense of guilt as the most important problem in the
development of civilization and to show that the price we pay for our
advance in civilization is a loss of happiness through the heightening
of the sense of guilt" (p. 134).

page 140 True guilt:
Whether or not we have feelings of guilt before we have a conscience
or superego (I am using the words interchangeably) has been the
subject of much psychoanalytic debate, the answers to which depend
on how broadly or narrowly the concept of guilt is defined. In "Civilization and Its Discontents," see note above, Freud takes both positions, saying (p. 136) that guilt is in existence before conscience,
after having said (p. 125) that it is not until the establishment of the
superego "that we should speak of . . . a sense of guilt." In "On the
Concept of Superego," *The Psychoanalytic Study of the Child*, Vol.
15, analyst Joseph Sandler supports this second view, writing that
what we are displaying in the preoedipal years is an "undergraduate
superego which only works under the supervision of the parents. . . .
It has not yet gained a license for independent practice. . . ." Thus, he
argues, when this undergraduate superego sends us a warning signal
of impending punishment or loss of love, that signal "does not yet
deserve the name of guilt, though the affective state it produces in
the ego may be identical with that which we refer to as guilt, later in
the child's development" (pp. 152–153).

page 140 our parents installed in our mind:
It has been observed, however, that sometimes the child of lenient or
tolerant parents develops a very harsh and punitive superego. Why?
Because some children have more innate aggression than others and
because in the process of controlling this aggression they turn a portion
of it back against themselves. Nevertheless, as Freud notes in "Civilization and Its Discontents," see the first note for this chapter, a
severe upbringing "does also exert a strong influence on the formation
of the child's superego. What it amounts to is that in the formation
of the superego . . . innate constitutional factors and influences from
the real environment act in combination" (p. 130).

page 140 the stages of our moral reasoning:
Kohlberg's six stages of moral thought are divided into three major

levels—preconventional, conventional and postconventional or autonomous—and there are two stages within each level. (See Kohlberg and Gilligan's "The Adolescent as a Philosopher: The Discovery of the Self in a Postconventional World," *Daedalus*, pp. 1066-1068.)

Kohlberg's work builds on Piaget, who describes the following sequence of logical and cognitive development from the egocentrism of infancy—where thought is tied to action—to the capacity for abstract thought: Ages 0 to two, the era of sensori-motor intelligence; ages two to five, the era of symbolic, intuitive or prelogical thought; ages six to ten, the era of concrete operational thought; and ages eleven to adult, the era of formal-operational thought. (See p. 1063 of abovementioned paper.)

Kohlberg relates the stage of our moral reasoning to the level of cognitive development we attain—though he notes that "cognitive maturity is a necessary but not a sufficient condition for moral judgment maturity" (p. 1071, same paper). Underscoring this relationship between cognitive and moral development, some researchers observe that guilt requires the ability to mentally reverse an act and consider alternative possibilities. They note that this ability belongs to the concrete-operational level of thought, which—they further note—is achieved around the end of the oedipal phase.

Both Kohlberg and Piaget see the stages they describe as an unvariable progression from less to more complex, although not everyone reaches Piaget's cognitive stage of formal operational thought or Kohlberg's fifth or sixth moral stages.

For full discussions of these ideas, see Kohlberg and Gilligan's paper, pp. 1051-1086. See also Kohlberg and Kramer, "Continuities and Discontinuities in Childhood and Adult Moral Development," *Human Development* 12, pp. 93-120. An excellent synthesis of theories of conscience formation and cognitive and moral development can be found in Chapter 8 of Louis Breger's *From Instinct to Identity*.

page 141 inner *submission to human law:*
Just to remind you: According to Freud, the superego comes into existence as a way of resolving the Oedipus complex. Impelled by the fear of castration (or, in girls, some less specific injury) and the fear of losing our parents' love, we become like our parents in repudiating our wishes to kill one parent and to possess the other one sexually. These primal prohibitions are the foundation of our superego, our conscience.

Thus the superego is regarded as a structure in the human personality which comes into being at a certain stage in our development. Our preoedipal experiences, however, strongly influence the character of our superego and many of the elements that go into the formation of our superego—called "superego precursors"—are present in the preoedipal years.

The superego which emerges in the fifth or sixth year, however,

does not become stable until age nine or ten, does not become independent of outside authority until the end of adolescence and may be subject to some alteration throughout life.

Freud also asserted, by the way, that the female superego is weaker, less inexorable, less impersonal than the male's because the threat to female anatomy, being less drastic than the threat of castration, is less likely to motivate her to as full a resolution of her Oedipus complex. Carol Gilligan's *In a Different Voice* also finds differences between male and female moral reasoning—with women emphasizing connectedness and care and men emphasizing personal integrity. But, she argues, one is not superior to the other. Rather, they represent two modes of experience and interpretation which together could enable us to "arrive at a more complex rendition of human experience" (p. 174).

page 142 This excessive punishing guilt:
The more primitive parts of our mind still believe in talion law, which demands that a criminal's punishment be the same injury he inflicted on his victim—"an eye for an eye, a tooth for a tooth." Some of us guilt-ridden people, however, may go even further than talion law by insisting on imposing upon ourself capital punishments for misdemeanors.

page 142 A rabbi:
H. Kushner, *When Bad Things Happen to Good People*, p. 91.

page 143 "But the neurotic conscience":
Fraiberg, *The Magic Years*, p. 247.

page 144 "I think, in general":
Dr. Louis Breger, personal communication.

page 144 "Can't smoke, hardly drink":
Roth, *Portnoy's Complaint*, pp. 124–125.

page 145 "Ellie and Marvin":
J. Viorst, *How Did I Get to Be Forty and Other Atrocities*, "Secret Meetings," pp. 26–27.

page 147 "In such instances":
Freud, *Standard Edition*, Vol. 19, "The Economic Problem of Masochism," p. 166. See also, from the same volume, "The Ego and the Id," pp. 49–50, for more on the unconscious sense of guilt.

page 147 deficiencies in our capacity for guilt:
In his *Standard Edition*, Vol. 22, "New Introductory Lectures on Psycho-Analysis," Freud writes: "Following a well-known pronouncement of Kant's which couples the conscience within us with the starry Heavens, a pious man might well be tempted to honour these two things as the masterpieces of creation. The stars are indeed magnifi-

cent, but as regards conscience God has done an uneven and careless piece of work, for a large majority of men have brought along with them only a modest amount of it, or scarcely enough to be worth mentioning" (p. 61).

page 148 to punish, not to prevent:
Jacobson refers, in her book *The Self and the Object World*, to "the type of patients who constantly act out impulsively and then pay for their sins with depressive conditions and the destructive results of their actions; persons whose superego is punitive but, in spite of this, never serves either as a moral preventive or as a moral incentive. Fundamentally, their moral conflict appears to survive and to remain unchanged from one depression and one impulsive action to the next" (p. 134).

page 148 to expiate unconscious guilt:
Freud, *Standard Edition*, Vol. 14, "Some Character-Types Met With in Psycho-Analytic Work," writes about people who "might justly be described as criminals from a sense of guilt," whose misdeeds do not precede, but follow, their feelings of guilt and whose guilty acts actually serve to relieve their oppressive and free-floating guilt feelings because now the "guilt was at least attached to something" (p. 332).

page 148 psychopathic personalities:
In a troubling and fascinating book, *The Mask of Sanity*, Hervey Cleckley presents case after case of these psychopathic personalities. Although the book is marred by freewheeling assaults on a variety of ideas and people, it is a riveting account of a group of men and women who seem to have no sense of guilt or remorse, conscious or unconscious.

page 149 In a famous experiment:
The experiment is described in Milgram's book *Obedience to Authority*. The quotes appear on p. 10 and p. 5.

page 150 The philosopher Martin Buber:
Buber, "Guilt and Guilt Feelings," *Psychiatry*, Vol. 20, No. 2, p. 119, p. 118, p. 121, p. 128.

page 151 our conscience also contains our ego ideal:
In his *Standard Edition*, Vol. 22, "New Introductory Lectures on Psycho-Analysis," Freud writes that another important function of the superego is as "the vehicle of the ego ideal, by which the ego measures itself . . . and whose demand for ever greater perfection it strives to fulfill" (pp. 64–65). See also Schafer, "The Loving and Beloved Superego in Freud's Structural Theory," *The Psychoanalytic Study of the Child*, Vol. 15, pp. 163–188.

page 151 our lost narcissism lives on—in our ego ideal:
In Hartmann and Lowenstein's "Notes on the Superego," *The Psy-*

choanalytic Study of the Child, Vol. 17, the authors write that "the ego ideal can be considered a rescue operation for narcissism" (p. 61). And in *The Self and the Object World* Jacobson writes that by means of the ego ideal, "the superego, this unique human acquisition, becomes the one area in the psychic organization where . . . the child's grandiose wishful fantasies can find a safe refuge and can be maintained forever to the profit of the ego" (p. 94).

Jacobson also notes that because the ego ideal has a "double face," because it is a unification of idealized parents and idealized self, it also gratifies "the infantile longing . . . to be one with the love object. Even our never-ending struggle for oneness between ego and ego ideal reflects the enduring persistence of this desire" (p. 96). Joseph Sandler, in his "On the Concept of Superego," *The Psychoanalytic Study of the Child*, Vol. 15, makes a similar point when, speaking of the superego, he writes that "although it is often the agent of pain and destruction, its existence appears to be brought about by the child's attempt to transform paradise lost into paradise regained" (p. 159).

CHAPTER TEN   CHILDHOOD'S END

page 153 "I'm getting sick of this":
One version of this wonderful story, attributed to *The New Yorker*, appears in Fraiberg's *The Magic Years*, p. 250.

page 154 Freud labeled "latency":
Freud's *Standard Edition*, Vol. 7, "Three Essays on the Theory of Sexuality," introduced the concept of latency back in 1905. Much of the material on which I am basing the latency section of this chapter comes from a series of recent papers found in *The Course of Life*, Vol. 2, Greenspan and Pollock, eds.

In these discussions latency is seen, not as an absence of sexuality, but as a stage of relative calm between two more intense phases of sexual development. There is some debate about whether this relative calm is due to diminished instinctual urges or to increased coping mechanisms, but whatever the reason, our ego—at latency—seems to have more power vis-a-vis our id. During latency our sexual (and aggressive) urges are partly repressed (pushed out of consciousness) and partly sublimated (redirected) toward other activities—scholarly, social and athletic. In addition to the defenses of repression and sublimination, there is also the defense of reaction-formation where, by replacing unacceptable impulses with their opposites, we develop socially acceptable virtues, like—for example—cleanliness and modesty.

Interesting sidelight: Most of us come to latency having forgotten large portions of our pre-latency life—a family vacation, a former neighbor, a once extremely beloved baby-sitter. The reason is that,

in repressing the passions of our oedipal stage, we repress the events surrounding those passions, too. And although we cannot obliterate them, we can bury them so deep that they are unavailable to our consciousness. The result is a universal condition called infantile amnesia, the loss of a part of ourself, the loss of our past. It is the psychological equivalent, you might say, of throwing out the baby with the bath water.

page 154 our latency phase may be linked to a biological clock:
It has been argued that the changes in neurobiological and cognitive development which occur at around age seven provide latency with many of its characteristics. These changes include the refinement of perceptual and motor skills; a maturing of our time and space orientation; the brain's development of feedback systems allowing for longer attention spans; and the development of the brain's frontal lobe, which seems to have a bearing on socialization. Among the cognitive changes of this period is the ability to perform what Piaget calls concrete operations, which permits us—among other things—to form categories and to see a sameness despite apparent differences. These operations help us proceed from an egocentric to a more objective view by enabling us to see that what we know about Y can also apply to Z, thus helping us put ourself in another's shoes. As I discussed in a backnote for Chapter 9 (page 402), researchers have found a correlation between logical and moral reasoning. For a full discussion of the cognitive and physiological underpinnings of latency, see Shapiro and Perry's "Latency Revisited," *The Psychoanalytic Study of the Child*, Vol. 31, pp. 79–105.

page 154 trouble taking on these tasks:
Learning difficulties, behavior difficulties, troubles with peer relationships, school phobias and homesickness are characteristic problems of latency children. So, because of the harshness of our new superego, is a hypersensitivity to criticism and an unreasonable demand on ourself for perfection. Indeed, at this age, we often project our harsh conscience onto somebody else and complain of a teacher or parent, "She's always picking on me," when in fact the person who is always picking on us is no one but us. A successful latency requires some modification of the strictness of our conscience and a capacity to live, at least some of the time, by the spirit instead of the letter of the law.

page 155 that parents are fallible:
In addition to realistically perceiving our parents as fallible and imperfect, many of us at latency develop a fantasy known as the "family romance." In this typical latency fantasy we imagine that we have been adopted, that we are not our parents' biological child and that our true biological parents are far more exalted, aristocratic people.

In other words, though mom and dad are clods, I am by birth and blood a prince or princess.

page 155 "Eight Ages of Man":
In Erikson's *Childhood and Society*, his chapter entitled "Eight Ages of Man" describes a stage-by-stage series of critical points in human psychosocial development when there are "moments of decision between progress and regression, integration and retardation" (pp. 270–271). The issues to be determined at each of these ages are: basic trust versus basic mistrust, autonomy versus shame and doubt, initiative versus guilt, industry versus inferiority, identity versus role confusion, intimacy versus isolation, generativity versus stagnation and ego integrity versus despair.

Erikson notes that what he is speaking of here are not absolute achievements but "favorable ratios" of positive to negative, with the negatives remaining a "dynamic counterpart" throughout our life (p. 274).

pages 155–56 "sooner or later, become dissatisfied":
Erikson, *Identity: Youth and Crisis*, p. 123.

page 156 Joseph Conrad:
In Conrad's *Heart of Darkness* Marlow says: "I don't like work,—no man does—but I like what is in the work,—the chance to find yourself. Your own reality—for yourself, not for others—what no other man can ever know" (p. 41).

page 156 flame-kindling grownup:
In Erikson's *Identity: Youth and Crisis* he writes: "Again and again in interviews with especially gifted and inspired people, one is told spontaneously and with a special glow that *one* teacher can be credited with having kindled the flame of hidden talent" (p. 125).

page 157 "And as I was green and carefree":
Thomas, "Fern Hill," *The Norton Anthology of Poetry*, Allison et al., eds., pp. 1166–1167.

page 158 "transition from barrenness to fertility":
The phrase is derived from Kestenberg's paper "Eleven, Twelve, Thirteen: Years of Transition from the Barrenness of Childhood to the Fertility of Adolescence" in *The Course of Life*, Vol. 2, Greenspan and Pollock, eds.

page 159 "My mother's always talking":
Blume, *Are You There God? It's Me, Margaret*, p. 25.

page 159 "Are you there God?":
Ibid., p. 37.

pages 159–60 "that extended period of rage":
Roth, *Portnoy's Complaint*, pp. 40–41.

page 160 "that the assumption of responsibility":
Growing up as a form of homicide is discussed by analyst Hans Loewald in "The Waning of the Oedipus Complex," *Journal of the American Psychoanalytic Association*, Vol. 27, No. 4, pp. 751–775. The quoted material appears on p. 757. Later Loewald notes that "Parricide, if the child convincingly develops as an individual, is more than symbolic. . . . Not to shrink from blunt language, in our role as children of our parents, by genuine emancipation we do kill something vital in them—not all in one blow and not in all respects, but contributing to their dying" (p. 764). See also Modell's discussion of separation guilt in "On Having the Right to a Life: An Aspect of the Superego's Development," *The International Journal of Psycho-Analysis*, Vol. 46, part 3, pp. 323–331.

page 161 Zapped by hormones:
Girls generally mature two years before boys, though there are both early and late bloomers of both sexes. For most girls the onset of menstruation (menarche) has occurred by age fourteen. A good discussion of physical changes at puberty and the psychological reactions to them can be found in Morris Sklansky's "The Pubescent Years: Eleven to Fourteen," in *The Course of Life*, Vol. 2, Greenspan and Pollock, eds., pp. 265–292.

pages 161–62 "If you are a girl":
Ephron, *Teenage Romance*, p. 115.

page 162 "to be different":
Esman quoting Schoenfeld in "Mid-Adolescence—Foundations for Later Psychopathology," in *The Course of Life*, Vol. 2, Greenspan and Pollock, eds., p. 421.

page 162 anorexia nervosa:
It has been found that girls suffering from anorexia nervosa have a near-delusional perception of themselves—even when down to skin and bones—as too fat, that "fat" is sometimes equated unconsciously with "pregnant" and that sexual features like breasts or menstruation may be a source of powerful shame and guilt. All these elements may intermingle with earlier disturbances in separation-individuation, and with an actual inability to recognize the body signal of "hunger," and with a fearful need to control a body which—in the spurts and explosions of puberty—seems to have gone utterly out of control. See Bruch's "The Sleeping Beauty: Escape From Change," in *The Course of Life*, Vol. 2, Greenspan and Pollock, eds., pp. 431–444.

page 163 so restless and twitchy and awkward:
"The rapidity of the growth spurt is in itself disturbing to the body image and may explain the physical awkwardness of some adolescents." See Sklansky, "The Pubescent Years: Eleven to Fourteen," in *The Course of Life*, Vol. 2, Greenspan and Pollock, eds., p. 272.

page 163 sex on the brain:
"Pubescence is usually followed by an onset or increase in genital masturbation." Ibid., p. 269.

page 163 agony to ecstasy:
Adolescents "... are subject to the variations in mood which result from unstable self-definition. Compensatory grandiosity in fantasy and behavior alternates with periods of low self-esteem and a sense of fragility." Ibid., p. 276.

page 163 capable of abstract logical thinking:
Jean Piaget writes that "the great novelty that characterizes adolescent thought and that starts around the age of 11 to 12, but does not reach its point of equilibrium until the age of 14 or 15—this novelty consists in detaching the concrete logic from the objects themselves, so that it can function on verbal or symbolic statements without other support. ... The great novelty that results consists in the possibility of manipulating ideas in themselves and no longer in merely manipulating objects." See Piaget's "The Intellectual Development of the Adolescent," in *Adolescence: Psychosocial Perspectives*, Caplan and Lebovici, eds., p. 23.

page 163 parents as merely fallible:
"For most adolescents this deidealization is in the service of ego development and autonomy.... That the deidealization serves an intrapsychic growth process, rather than being simply an accurate assessment of the reality of the parent, is evident from the frequent exaggeration of their faults and the amount of affect that accompanies the faultfinding. Of course, parents naturally do not react amiably to this process...." See Sklansky, "The Pubescent Years: Eleven to Fourteen," in *The Course of Life*, Vol. 2, Greenspan and Pollock, eds., p. 277.

pages 163–64 "that is normal for an adolescent":
Anna Freud, "Adolescence," *The Psychoanalytic Study of the Child*, Vol. 13, p. 275. While this paper (pp. 255–278) asserts the universality of turmoil in adolescence, a study of a group of normal adolescents whose progression through adolescence was apparently untumultuous is described by Offer in his paper "Adolescent Development: A Normative Perspective," *The Course of Life*, Vol. 2, Greenspan and Pollock, eds., pp. 357–372. However, it seems widely agreed that some turmoil is inevitable and universal, whether or not it is accompanied by overt disruptions.

page 164 the sexual stew of adolescence:
The intensification of sexual urges at puberty reactivates the old oedipal triangle, with young adolescents experiencing erotic fantasies and feelings about their parents which are sometimes quite conscious and explicit, evoking anxiety or shame or guilt. (Because of these re-

awakened oedipal stirrings, for instance, adolescent girls do not feel comfortable being hugged by daddy or sitting on his lap, while adolescent boys feel a similar uneasiness with their mothers.) However, in contrast to the earlier resolution of oedipal struggles, when sexual impulses were more or less repressed, adolescents must manage the tricky task of renouncing incestuous sexual wishes without renouncing sexual wishes in general.

page 164 "develop the prerequisites":
Erikson, *Identity: Youth and Crisis*, p. 91.

page 165 toning down of our conscience's harshness:
Analyst Aaron Esman writes that "adolescence affords an opportunity for the reshaping of the ego ideal and a readjustment of the superego." The ego ideal, he says, is "more closely attuned to current reality, closer to consciousness and normally less peremptory in nature . . ." while the superego "loses its categorical all or nothing quality. . . ." From "Mid-Adolescence—Foundations for Later Psychopathology," *The Course of Life*, Vol. 2, Greenspan and Pollock, eds., p. 427.

page 166 There is a course to adolescence:
Different researchers may place some of these struggles at different points in the stages of adolescence, but all seem to agree that dealing with pubertal changes is the focus of the first stage of adolescence and that separation is a pervasive issue.

page 167 "an intensity of grief":
In Martha Wolfenstein's "How Is Mourning Possible?" found in *The Psychoanalytic Study of the Child*, Vol. 21, pp. 93–123, she quotes Jacobson on the intensity of grief in adolescence (p. 114) and A. E. Housman's poem about the land of lost content (p. 115).

page 167 College-bound Roger:
Dr. Cheryl Kurash, in her paper "The Transition to College: A Study of Separation-Individuation in Late Adolescence" (unpublished), divides this transition into three subphases: anticipatory, leavetaking, and settling in. During the anticipatory subphase, she writes, "adolescents renew their efforts to further distance themselves from their parents. . . . Perhaps most notable is the increased expression of aggression toward both parents" (pp. 71–72).

page 168 "All through senior year":
Ibid., p. 1.

page 168 depression, breakdowns, suicide:
This is not to say that such adolescent problems are always the result of separation difficulties. See Noshpitz's "Disturbances in Early Adolescent Development," *The Course of Life*, Vol. 2, Greenspan and Pollock, eds., pp. 309–356, for an excellent review of the developmental problems of adolescence.

page 168 the rate of suicide:
The suicide statistics are from the National Center for Health Statistics.

page 168 "Don't ever tell anybody":
Salinger, *The Catcher in the Rye*, p. 214.

page 169 Henry David Thoreau:
See Edel, *Stuff of Sleep and Dreams*, "The Mystery of Walden Pond," pp. 47–65. The "buckle on your knapsack" and "methinks" material appears on p. 54, and Edel's comment about "Thoreau, shut up in his childhood" appears on p. 62.

page 169 "Adolescent individuation":
Blos, *On Adolescence*, p. 12.

page 170 "I keep picturing":
Salinger, *The Catcher in the Rye*, p. 173.

page 171 "warn of the utterly destructive consequences":
Bettelheim, *Freud and Man's Soul*, p. 25.

page 171 "There is no guilt, my man":
MacLeish, *J. B.*, p. 123.

page 172 "The two Greek goddesses":
Blos, *On Adolescence*, p. 195.

CHAPTER ELEVEN   DREAMS AND REALITIES

page 175 dearest megalomaniacal dreams:
Blos, in his book *On Adolescence*, writes: "Adolescent individuation . . . brings some of the dearest megalomaniacal dreams of childhood to an irrevocable end. They must now be relegated entirely to fantasy: their fulfillments can never again be considered seriously" (p. 12).

page 175 they press themselves upon us in sneaky ways:
According to psychoanalytic theory, conflicts over repressed impulses may result in neurotic symptoms; and slips of the tongue, lapses of memory, accidents and other similar mishaps do not occur by chance but are intentional acts unconsciously motivated. (For instance, a mishap like spilling the borscht may occur when a hostile impulse— get that rival!—escapes from repression.) See, in the *Standard Edition*, "Introductory Lectures on Psycho-Analysis," Freud's discussion of The Paths to the Formation of Symptoms (Vol. 16) and Parapraxes (Vol. 15).

page 179 the omnipotence of thoughts:
In Freud's *Standard Edition*, Vol. 17, "The Uncanny," he discusses "the old, animistic conception of the universe" characterized "by the

subject's narcissistic overvaluation of his own mental processes; by the belief in the omnipotence of thoughts. . . ." He says that "each one of us has been through a phase of individual development corresponding to this animistic stage in primitive man, that none of us has passed through it without preserving certain residues and traces of it" (p. 240).

page 179 "It is as though":
Ibid., p. 248.

page 181 the vibrant, secret language of our unconscious:
This language is different from, and alien to, the orderly ways we consciously use our mind. It relies on what is called "primary-process thinking." This is the mode of "thought" we use before we learn to think with logic and reason, before we achieve the capacity for grown-up "secondary-process thinking." There is a beautiful description of primary-process thinking in Ann and Barry Ulanov's book *Religion and the Unconscious*, pp. 26–32. See also Brenner's lucid book for the general reader, *An Elementary Textbook of Psychoanalysis*, pp. 45–53. But the original discussion of primary-process thinking is found in Freud's *Standard Edition*, Vols. 4 and 5. "The Interpretation of Dreams," a dazzling exploration into the mysteries of unconscious mental functioning.

page 181 "My mother was speaking":
Altman, *The Dream in Psychoanalysis*, p. 10, provides this fine example of condensation.

page 181 "I was standing":
Ibid., p. 13, provides this example of displacement.

page 181 A woman dreams of a German officer:
Psychoanalyst Justin Frank (private communication) provided this example.

page 182 This dream that we recall:
In "The Interpretation of Dreams" (see note above, "the vibrant . . . unconscious"), Freud discusses the process by which our unconscious dream thoughts and wishes (the *latent content*) are transformed into the dream we recall upon waking (the *manifest content*).

Freud also says that dreams are given their shape by two forces, one of which constructs a wish and the other of which censors the expression of that wish. The bizarre and distorted qualities of the manifest dream are thus reflections of its primary-process nature, of the secondary revision and of the further distortions imposed on it by its need to be acceptable to the dream censorship.

page 182 Hugo's dream:
Altman presents and discusses Hugo's dream in *The Dream in Psychoanalysis*, pp. 126–128.

page 182 Freud says every dream contains a wish:
Although the forbidden wishes of our childhood arise from the part of our psyche called the id, a dream is not *merely* the expression of id wishes, for even during dreaming our ego's intentions and our superego's constraints make themselves felt, insist on having their say. Our dreams, then, are a compromise that is reached between these three conflicting forces—id, ego, and superego.

It also should be noted that many students of dreams today are less singleminded than Freud about perceiving the dream's *only* function as wish fulfillment. Erikson writes, for instance, that dreams "not only fulfill naked wishes of sexual license, of unlimited dominance and of unrestricted destructiveness;... they also lift the dreamer's isolation, appease his conscience and preserve his identity, each in specific and instructive ways" (p. 55, reference follows). For material on post-Freudian dream theory, see Erikson's "The Dream Specimen of Psychoanalysis," *Journal of the American Psychoanalytic Association*, Vol. 2, No. 1, pp. 5–56; Rycroft's *The Innocence of Dreams*; and *The Dream in Clinical Practice*, Joseph Natterson, ed. In this last volume, however, Samuel Eisenstein notes in his "The Dream in Psychoanalysis" that most analysts still subscribe to Freud's view of "the central role of wish fulfillment in the dream" (p. 362).

page 183 waking or sleeping fantasies:
Freud writes eloquently of fantasy—which his translators spell "phantasy"—in *Standard Edition*, Vol. 16, "Introductory Lectures on Psycho-Analysis (Part 3)." He states: "Every desire takes before long the form of picturing its own fulfillment; there is no doubt that dwelling upon imaginary wish-fulfillments brings satisfaction with it.... The creation of the mental realm of phantasy finds a perfect parallel in the establishment of 'reservations' or 'nature reserves' in places where the requirements of agriculture, communications and industry threaten to bring about changes in the original face of the earth.... A nature reserve preserves its original state.... Everything, including what is useless and even what is noxious, can grow and proliferate there as it pleases. The mental realm of phantasy is just such a reservation withdrawn from the reality principle."

Freud notes that while the "best-known productions of phantasy are the so-called 'day-dreams,'" the "night-dream is at bottom nothing other than a day-dream that has been made utilizable owing to the liberation of the instinctual impulses at night, and that has been distorted by the form assumed by mental activity at night." He also notes "that there are unconscious [as well as conscious] daydreams" (pp. 372–373).

page 183 "healthy adult":
My description of the "healthy adult" draws heavily from McGlashan and Miller's "The Goals of Psychoanalysis and Psychoanalytic Psy-

chotherapy," *Archives of General Psychiatry*, Vol. 39, pp. 377–388. The authors note that many of the aims discussed in their paper "are synonymous with general mental health and emotional maturity" (p. 378).

page 184 "reality testing":
A discussion of reality-testing can be found in Freud's *Standard Edition*, Vol. 14, "A Metapsychological Supplement to the Theory of Dreams," pp. 230–234.

CHAPTER TWELVE   CONVENIENCE FRIENDS...

page 188 the curse of ambivalence:
In Freud's *Standard Edition*, Vol. 13, "Totem and Taboo," he writes: "In almost every case where there is an intense emotional attachment to a particular person we find that behind the tender love there is a concealed hostility in the unconscious. This is the classical example, the prototype, of the ambivalence of human emotions. This ambivalence is present to a greater or less amount in the innate disposition of everyone" (p. 60). In the same volume, "Some Reflections on Schoolboy Psychology," Freud writes that ambivalent feelings in later life have their origins in early childhood, when the child's love/hate feelings toward his parents and siblings become fixed. "All those whom he gets to know later become substitute figures for these first objects of his feelings.... His later acquaintances are thus obliged to take over a kind of emotional heritage" (p. 243).

page 188 Dinah, wife and mother:
Robb Forman Dew, *Dale Loves Sophie to Death*, p. 132, p. 131, p. 134.

page 189 Freud argued that all love relationships:
In Freud's *Standard Edition*, Vol. 18, "Group Psychology and the Analysis of the Ego," he writes: "The nucleus of what we mean by love naturally consists . . . in sexual love with sexual union as its aim. But we do not separate from this . . . on the one hand, self-love, and on the other, love for parents and children, friendship and love for humanity. . . . Our justification lies in the fact that psycho-analytic research has taught us that all these tendencies are an expression of the same instinctual impulses; in relations between the sexes these impulses force their way toward sexual union, but in other circumstances they are diverted from the aim or are prevented from reaching it" (p. 90).

pages 189–90 "no individual is limited":
Freud, *Standard Edition*, Vol. 23, "An Outline of Psychoanalysis," p. 188. Some of Freud's other discussions of bisexuality appear in *Stan-*

dard Edition, Vol. 7, "Three Essays on the Theory of Sexuality," pp. 141–148, and Vol. 21, "Civilization and Its Discontents," pp. 105–106 (footnote). A footnote in Vol. 19, "The Ego and the Id," points out that in writing about bisexuality to his friend Wilhelm Fliess, Freud commented: "I am accustoming myself to regarding every sexual act as an event between four individuals" (p. 33).

page 191 having "sexual feelings toward someone of the same sex":
Group for the Advancement of Psychiatry, *Friends and Lovers in the College Years*, p. 88. For a discussion of homosexual relationships, see Chapter 7.

page 191 "There need not be":
Shere Hite, *The Hite Report*, p. 365.

page 191 "much as pink":
Leo Rangell, "On Friendship," *Journal of the American Psychoanalytic Association*, Vol. 11, No. 1, p. 5. Rangell is quoting Hart, who has this to say about Freud's discussion of friendship: "Friendliness and friendship are referred to as if they were dilute editions of love, much as pink is regarded as a dilution of red."

page 191 "differ from one's main relationship":
James McMahon, "Intimacy Among Friends and Lovers," *Intimacy*, Fisher and Stricker, eds., p. 302.

page 192 "no man or woman can be all things to another":
Ibid., p. 304. See also anthropologist Robert Brain's *Friends and Lovers*, where he, too, vigorously denies "that the needs of a man and a woman for love and friendship can be satisfied by one single partnership.... The man who drinks with his friends every night often loves them as much as he loves his wife—in a different way. And his wife loves her friend next door, who comes in and watches television with her every afternoon" (pp. 262–263).

page 192 "If I told my wife":
Wagenvoord and Bailey (producers), *Men: A Book for Women*, p. 277.

page 193 men friends to be less open and intimate:
In Robert Bell's *Worlds of Friendship* he writes: "The evidence clearly indicates that female patterns of friendship are much more revealing and intimate than those found among men" (p. 62). In his interviews with 101 women and 65 men, Bell found that their response to his question about how many friends they had averaged 4.7 for women and 3.2 for men (p. 63). He writes: "The fact that men are trapped within themselves has come through in our interviews. Women overwhelmingly reveal many of their fears, anxieties and insecurities to their best friends, while men overwhelmingly do not" (p. 80). For further discussion of female friendships and male friendships, see chapters 3 and 4 of Bell's book.

page 193 "There are some things":
Ibid., pp. 81–82.

page 193 "I love my women friends":
Ibid., p. 63.

pages 193–194 the celebrated friendships of myth and folklore:
Ibid. Bell writes: "The great friendships recorded in history have been between men. In the past when friendships among men have been romanticized and eulogized, they have been friendships reflecting bravery, valor and physical sacrifice in coming to the aid of another. ... But rarely have the recollections been to celebrate interpersonal relationships of feeling, understanding and compassion of one male for another" (p. 75).

page 194 "men are for friendships":
Ibid., p. 104.

page 194 In one study:
Ibid. Both interviews appear on p. 111.

page 195 Lucy, a married woman:
The interview with Lucy appears on p. 38 of Judith Viorst's "Friends, Good Friends—and Such Good Friends," *Redbook*, October 1977, pp. 31–32, 38.

page 195 one of the following categories:
See Rangell's discussion of the three categories of friendship in "On Friendship," *Journal of the American Psychoanalytic Association*, Vol. 11, No. 1, pp. 30–31.

page 195 "not quite a 'friendship'":
Ibid., p. 40.

pages 195–196 both lovers and best friends:
In Bell's *Worlds of Friendship* he writes that in his research "about one-half of the women named their husbands as a very close friend. About 60 percent of the married men named their wives as a very close friend" (p. 125). He points out, however, that these figures also show, of course, that about half of all married people do *not* consider their spouses a close friend.

page 196 "a little bit of sex":
In Bell's *Worlds of Friendship* he cites a *Psychology Today* reader survey which found "that about three-fourths of the respondents felt that friendships with someone of the opposite sex were different from same-sex friendships. A major reason given for the difference was that sexual tensions complicated the relationship" (pp. 98–99).

page 196 Friendship, like civilization, is bought at the price:
In his paper "On Friendship," *Journal of the American Psychoanalytic Association*, Vol. 11, No. 1, Rangell writes: "True friendship is a

human trait which goes along with, and makes possible, civilization. Both are at the expense of instincts" (p. 49).

page 197 the following categories of friendship:
These categories and interviews are adapted from J. Viorst, "Friends, Good Friends—and Such Good Friends," *Redbook*, October 1977, pp. 31–32, 38.

page 199 "To be her friend":
Jane Howard, *Families*, p. 263.

page 199 "growth demands relatedness":
James McMahon, "Intimacy Among Friends and Lovers," *Intimacy*, Fisher and Stricker, eds., p. 297.

page 199 He quotes philosopher Martin Buber:
Ibid.

page 200 "Rosie is my friend":
J. Viorst, *Rosie and Michael*, unpaged.

page 201 "On Friendship":
Cicero, "On Friendship," *The Harvard Classics*, Vol. 9, *Letters of Marcus Tullius Cicero and Letters of Gaius Plinius Caecilius Secundus*, Charles Eliot, ed., p. 15 ("how can life . . ." and "a complete accord . . .") and p. 29 ("stainless" and "There must be complete harmony . . .").

page 202 "may be more likely":
Bell, *Worlds of Friendship*, p. 122. He is describing the ideas of sociologist Georg Simmel, who contrasted the friendship ideal of the past—"total psychological intimacy"—with our modern, partial, differentiated friendships.

pages 202–3 "If Rosie told me a secret":
J. Viorst, *Rosie and Michael*, unpaged.

page 203 "sacred and miraculous":
The lovely description of friendship as "sacred and miraculous" appears in Jane Howard's *Families*, p. 265.

CHAPTER THIRTEEN   LOVE AND HATE IN THE MARRIED STATE

page 204 "normal, crucial beginning":
Kernberg, "Adolescent Sexuality in the Light of Group Process," *The Psychoanalytic Quarterly*, Vol. 49, No. 1, p. 46.

page 205 "Last night, ah, yesternight":
This verse is from Ernest Dowson's poem "Non sum qualis eram

bonae sub regno Cynarae," *The Norton Anthology of Poetry*, Allison et al., eds., pp. 937–938.

page 205 In Freud's discussions of love:
See Hitschmann's paper on "Freud's Conception of Love," *The International Journal of Psycho-Analysis*, Vol. 33, Part 4, pp. 421–428. See also Freud's discussion of Being in Love and Hypnosis in *Standard Edition*, Vol. 18, "Group Psychology and the Analysis of the Ego."

page 205 "The silken texture":
Howells, *The Rise of Silas Lapham*, p. 43.

page 205 "One person, without any hostility":
The statement comes from University of Pennsylvania sociologist Otto Pollak and is quoted on p. 5 of Israel Charny's paper "Marital Love and Hate," *Family Process*, Vol. 8, No. 1, pp. 1–24.

page 206 Psychologist Israel Charny:
I. Charny, "Marital Love and Hate," *Family Process*, Vol. 8, No. 1. "The myth..." p. 3; "empirically it cannot..." p. 3; "a wise balancing..." pp. 2–3.

page 206 "So they were married":
Louis MacNeice, "Les Sylphides," *Modern Poetry*, Mack, Dean, Frost, eds., p. 296.

pages 206–7 a doctor's wife named Emma:
Gustave Flaubert, *Madame Bovary*. The "marvelous realm..." appears on p. 140. "Her too lofty..." and "the sole object" appear on p. 94. "That marvelous passion..." appears on p. 34.

page 207 "Marriage," writes anthropologist Bronislaw Malinowski:
The Malinowski quote appears in Nena O'Neill's book *The Marriage Premise*, p. 36.

page 208 "The true man or woman":
Kathrin Perutz, *Marriage Is Hell*, pp. 96–97. Both anecdotal and research material support this contention: See, for instance, Masters and Johnson's book *The Pleasure Bond*, where the sex therapists state, "Sex in a warm, emotionally committed relationship may change in character, and sexual response may become diffused after a while. It may not always reach the peaks of excitement that are sometimes experienced by a man and woman in their early, experimental encounters" (p. 99). And a married woman writing to me from Pennsylvania voices a frequently heard complaint: "Expectation: No matter what else happens in your lives, the sex part will always stay fresh and exciting. ... The truth is ... there is the sheer problem of boredom. I defy any couple married more than ten years or so to say this hasn't been the case."

pages 208–9 "I bring the children":
J. Viorst, *It's Hard to Be Hip Over Thirty and Other Tragedies of Married Life*, "Sex Is Not So Sexy Anymore," p. 63.

page 209 "multiple forms of transcendence":
O. Kernberg, "Boundaries and Structure in Love Relations," *Journal of the American Psychoanalytic Association*, Vol. 25, No. 1, p. 99. See his entire section on Sexual Passion and the Crossing of Boundaries in Love Relations, pp. 93–104.

page 209 "I have sought love":
B. Russell, *The Autobiography of Bertrand Russell, 1872–1914*, p. 3.

page 210 "haven in a heartless world":
The phrase is the title of Christopher Lasch's book *Haven in a Heartless World*.

page 210 "intimate enemies":
The phrase derives from Bach and Wyden's book on how to fight fair in love and marriage, *The Intimate Enemy*.

page 210 Listen to Millie:
J. Viorst, "Sometimes I Hate My Husband," *Redbook*, November 1976, pp. 73–74. The interview with Millie appears on p. 73.

page 212 "to distinguish between their conscious":
The Kubie quote appears on pp. 119–120 of Jessie Bernard's book *The Future of Marriage*.

page 213 "complementary marriages":
For a discussion of marital complementarity, see Bela Mittelmann's "Complementary Neurotic Reactions in Intimate Relationships," *The Psychoanalytic Quarterly*, Vol. 13, No. 4, pp. 479–491. He concludes: "Because of the continuous and intimate nature of marriage, every neurosis in a married person is strongly anchored in the marriage relationship. The presence of a complementary neurotic reaction in the marriage partner is an important aspect of the married patient's neurosis" (p. 491). See also Henry Dicks's classic work, *Marital Tensions*. Other references to complementarity can be found in Jessie Bernard's *The Future of Marriage*, where she refers to Robert Ryder's twenty-one different patterns of mating and Robert Winch's "fourfold classification of matings: an Ibsenite mating, in which the husband is dominant and nurturant, the wife the opposite; a Thurberian mating, in which the husband is submissive and nurturant rather than the wife; a Master-Servant Girl mating, in which the husband is dominant and the wife receptive; and a Mother-Son mating, in which the husband is submissive and receptive" (p. 119).

page 213 "couples in collusion":
The phrase, and (with some modifications) the preceding discussion

of shared assumptions in marriage, derive from Jurg Willi's book *Couples in Collusion*.

page 214 projective identification:
This definition and an excellent discussion of projective identification can be found in Thomas Ogden's book *Projective Identification and Psychotherapeutic Technique*. I am also indebted to therapist Anne Stephansky for a beautifully lucid explanation of this difficult concept.

page 214 "If a woman has been taught":
See "What Qualities Do Women Most Value in Husbands?" *Viewpoints*, Vol. 16, No. 5, pp. 77–90. Harriet Lerner's comments appear on p. 89.

page 215 A mid-thirties wife:
See Giovachinni's paper "Characterological Aspects of Marital Interaction" and the discussants' comments in *The Psychoanalytic Forum*, Vol. 2, No. 1, pp. 7–29. The quoted phrases appear on p. 9.

page 215 Ironically, the thrust of human development:
In Kernberg's "Boundaries and Structure in Love Relations," *Journal of the American Psychoanalytic Association*, Vol. 25, No. 1, pp. 81–114, he writes that in his analysis of love relations he was "forced to conclude that emotional maturity is no guarantee for a couple's non-conflictual stability. The very capacity for loving in depth and for realistically appreciating another person over the years . . . may both reconfirm and deepen the relationship or lead it to disillusionment and termination. The complication is that both individuals and couples change, and that developing maturity may open new degrees of freedom in the couple's re-examining realistically the basis of their life together" (p. 84).

page 216 "introduce[d] us to the human situation":
Dinnerstein, *The Mermaid and the Minotaur*, p. 234.

pages 216–17 "while much of our pleasure":
Ibid., pp. 5–6. While conceding that there are, of course, many exceptions to the rule, Dinnerstein mobilizes arguments to show "how female-dominated child care guarantees male insistence upon, and female compliance with, a double standard of sexual behavior"; how "it guarantees that women and men will regard each other, respectively, as silly overgrown children"; and how "it guarantees certain forms of antagonism—rampant in men, and largely shared by women as well—against women," including the conviction that women are defective, untrustworthy and malevolent (p. 36). Regarding this antagonism, Dinnerstein notes that there is no purpose in reproaching men "for a hatred they are bound to feel; when they claim—in many cases sincerely—not to feel it, there is no reason at all to believe them; when they recognize and deplore it in themselves, there is no sense at all in trusting them to keep it under control" (p. 90).

page 217 "So long as the first parent":
Ibid., pp. 111–112.

page 217 in the process of forming their gender identity:
See the discussion of gender-identity formation in this book, Chapter Eight, "Anatomy and Destiny."

page 218 "intimate strangers":
The phrase is the title of Dr. Rubin's book *Intimate Strangers*, which argues the nurture, not nature, theory of male-female psychological differences. Like Dorothy Dinnerstein in *The Mermaid and the Minotaur*, Dr. Rubin believes that men would have less trouble with intimacy, and girls would have less trouble with autonomy, if fathers were as involved as mothers with child-rearing.

page 218 "The whole goddam business":
Rubin, *Intimate Strangers*, p. 66.

page 220 "more wives than husbands report marital frustration":
Bernard, *The Future of Marriage*, pp. 26–27.

page 220 "conform more to husbands' expectations":
Ibid., p. 39.

page 220 "There are two marriages":
Ibid., p. 14.

page 220 "demonstrate this need":
Ibid., p. 53.

pages 220–21 "the demands men and women make":
Ibid., "the demands..." p. 289; "will continue..." p. 289; "intrinsically tragic..." pp. 265–266.

page 221 "cat and dog" marriages:
Dicks, in *Marital Tensions*, refers to cat and dog relationships on p. 52 and p. 69, and discusses those unions where there is "perpetual sunshine without a shadow" on p. 73. In Bowlby's *Loss*, pp. 209–210, there is reference to Cat and Dog marriages and Babes in the Wood marriages, the first characterized by perpetual conflict and the second by resolute denial of conflict.

page 222 Rachel's feelings:
J. Viorst, "Sometimes I Hate My Husband," *Redbook*, November 1976, pp. 73–74. The interview with Rachel appears on p. 74.

page 222 Connie, a gentle woman:
Ibid. The interview with Connie appears on p. 74.

page 222 Perhaps, says psychoanalyst Leon Altman:
In Altman's discussion of love in "Some Vicissitudes of Love," *Journal of the American Psychoanalytic Association*, Vol. 25, No. 1, pp. 35–52, he writes: "All the clinical evidence we have, including our

own personal experience, will testify to the presence of aggression and hate in the midst of what may seem the most perfect love affair. . . . The need to disown hate might even be the root cause of our need to place so much emphasis on love, to ask so much of it. . . . Perhaps man could love more if he could also hate cheerfully" (p. 43).

page 223 No aggression; no love:
See Lorenz's book *On Aggression,* particularly Chapter 11, "The Bond." Citing evidence from animal studies, he concludes that "aggression can certainly exist without its counterpart, love, but conversely there is no love without aggression" (p. 217).

page 223 "transforms a deep love relation":
See Kernberg's "Love, the Couple and the Group: A Psychoanalytic Frame," *The Psychoanalytic Quarterly,* Vol. 49, No. 1, pp. 78–108. The quote is on p. 83. Dicks, in *Marital Tensions,* is in agreement when he writes: "The opposite to love is not hate. These two always co-exist so long as there is a live relationship. The opposite to love is indifference" (p. 133).

page 223 "an attempt to arrive":
Erikson, *Childhood and Society,* p. 262.

page 223 "identity searching":
Ibid., p. 264.

page 224 open us to gratitude:
For a discussion of gratitude and other aspects of love, see Martin Bergmann's wide-ranging paper, "On the Intrapsychic Function of Falling in Love," *The Psychoanalytic Quarterly,* Vol. 49, No. 1, pp. 56–77.

page 224 "All human relationships must end":
O. Kernberg, *Object Relations Theory and Clinical Psychoanalysis,* p. 238.

page 225 "And down by the brimming river":
These verses are from Auden's poem "As I Walked Out One Evening," found in *Modern Poetry,* Mack, Dean, Frost, eds., pp. 184–185.

page 226 beloved enemies:
The phrase is from Altman's paper "Marriage—Dream and Reality," summarized in the "Bertram D. Lewin Memorial Symposium: Psychoanalytic Perspectives on Love and Marriage," *Journal of the Philadelphia Association for Psychoanalysis,* Vol. 2, 1975, pp. 191–201. "Even the most devoted mate, he states, can be one's beloved enemy and the marriage is the opportunity for a state of siege or battle in full array" (p. 193).

page 226 "love forever; hate never":
The phrase is from Benedek's paper "Ambivalence, Passion and Love,"

Journal of the American Psychoanalytic Association, Vol. 25, No. 1, pp. 53–79. "The ethos of marriage demands a great deal, probably the impossible," she writes, "love forever, hate never" (p. 77).

CHAPTER FOURTEEN   SAVING THE CHILDREN

page 228 "she felt this thing that she called life":
Virginia Woolf, *To the Lighthouse*, p. 92.

page 228 The World According to Garp:
In John Irving's novel, Garp and Helen warn their children, Duncan and Walt, about the undertow. One day, watching Walt at the water's edge peering uneasily into the waves, they ask what he's looking for. "I'm trying to see the Under Toad," he replies. And, "Long after the monster was clarified for Walt, ('Under*tow*, dummy, not Under Toad!' Duncan had howled), Garp and Helen evoked the beast as a way of referring to their own sense of danger" (p. 341).

page 229 One father says:
J. Viorst, "Letting Go: Why It's Hard to Let Children Grow Up," *Redbook*, May 1980, pp. 42, 44. This interview appears on p. 44.

page 229 "A man who cannot stand":
Louis Simpson, "The Goodnight," *Sound and Sense*, Laurence Perrine, ed., pp. 133–134.

page 230 "It only recently":
J. Viorst, "Letting Go: Why It's Hard to Let Children Grow Up," *Redbook*, May 1980, pp. 42, 44. This interview appears on p. 44.

page 230 Consider this mother:
Ibid., p. 42.

pages 230–31 Selena who, as a child:
Ibid. This interview appears on p. 42.

page 231 the "too-good" mother:
In a paper called "The Too-Good Mother," *The International Journal of Psycho-Analysis*, Vol. 45, Part 1, pp. 85–88, Robert Shields takes off from Winnicott's concept of the good-enough mother and discusses the mother who sees herself "only as the supplier of infinite satisfactions."

page 232 "had from early on":
H. Kohut, *The Restoration of the Self*, p. 146. See his discussion of "The Psychoanalyst's Child," pp. 146–151. Kohut calls such insights "distorted empathy," because while these parents' empathic grasp of certain details . . . was often quite accurate," they were "out of tune with their children's maturational needs" (p. 150).

page 232 I am told of a mother:
J. Viorst, "Letting Go: Why It's Hard to Let Children Grow Up," *Redbook*, May 1980, pp. 42, 44. This interview appears on p. 44.

page 232 "a mother might need to give up the fantasy":
T. Berry Brazelton and Catherine Buttenwieser, "Early Intervention in a Pediatric Multidisciplinary Clinic," *Infants and Parents*, Sally Provence, ed., p. 13.

page 234 "In erotic love":
E. Fromm, *The Art of Loving*, p. 51.

page 234 "goodness of fit":
A good discussion of mother-child "fit" can be found in "Infants, Mothers and Their Interaction: A Quantitative Clinical Approach to Developmental Assessment" by Stanley Greenspan and Alicia Lieberman, *The Course of Life*, Vol 1, pp. 271–312, Greenspan and Pollock, eds. A detailed assessment of "goodness of fit" based on four sets of samples of mother-child interactions begins on p. 289.

page 234 "The mother's love":
Winnicott, *Collected Papers*, "Psychoses and Child Care," p. 223.

page 234 stop being that all-accommodating mother:
Ibid. In Winnicott's *Collected Papers*, "Mind and Its Relation to the Psyche-Soma," p. 246, he calls this a "graduated failure of adaptation."

page 234 "primary maternal preoccupation":
Winnicott relates the special intensity of the mother-child bond to what he calls "primary maternal preoccupation," described as "a very special psychiatric condition of the mother" which "gradually develops and becomes a state of heightened sensitivity" toward the end of pregnancy and for a few weeks after birth. The mother's state of profound attachment to, and identification with, her baby allows her "to adapt delicately and sensitively to the infant's needs at the very beginning," and is, in Winnicott's view, a normal sickness from which mothers eventually recover (p. 302). See his *Collected Papers*, "Primary Maternal Preoccupation."

See Winnicott's *The Maturational Processes and the Facilitating Environment*, "The Theory of the Parent-Infant Relationship," for the statements beginning "to let go . . ." (p. 53) and "a difficult thing . . ." (p. 54).

page 235 "the emotional growth of the mother":
M. Mahler, *The Psychological Birth of the Human Infant*, p. 79. Mahler comments on the various reactions the mothers in her study had to their children's separation-individuation. One mother, for instance, could accept her little boy "only as a symbiotic part of herself and . . . actively interfered with his attempts to move away" (p. 67). Still other

mothers "liked the closeness of the symbiotic phase but once this phase was over they would have liked their children to be 'grown up' already" (p. 66). Other mothers, who had been very anxious in the early phases of mothering, were "greatly relieved when their children became less fragile and vulnerable and somewhat more independent" (p. 66).

page 235 The good-enough mother, Winnicott writes:
Winnicott, *Collected Papers*, "Paediatrics and Psychiatry," pp. 160–161, offers this list of "the following things about a mother [which] stand out as vitally important."

pages 235–36 "The loving mother teaches her child":
In *The Psychological Birth of the Human Infant*, Mahler credits E. J. Anthony with discovering this illustrative passage by Kierkegaard (pp. 72–73).

page 236 And we will renegotiate our relationship:
See the discussion of stages of parenthood in "The Experience of Separation-Individuation in Infancy and Its Reverberations Through the Course of Life: Maturity, Senescence and Sociological Implications," Irving Sternschein (reporter), *Journal of the American Psychoanalytic Association*, Vol. 21, No. 3, pp. 633–645.

page 236 "Each transition":
J. Kestenberg, "The Effect on Parents of the Child's Transition into and out of Latency," *Parenthood: Its Psychology and Psychopathology*, E. James Anthony and Therese Benedek, eds., p. 290.

page 237 "Not one of us":
Haim Ginott, *Between Parent and Child*, p. 92.

page 237 "I'd vowed to be rational":
This statement, from a mother of two girls now grown, appears in Shirley Radl's book *Mother's Day Is Over*, p. 128.

page 238 "tendency of adults to replay old fears and conflicts":
Group for the Advancement of Psychiatry, *The Joys and Sorrows of Parenthood*, p. 41. The book offers this example: "A physician's eldest daughter was sensitive, high-strung and emotional, like her grandfather. Her father had always hated and feared his father's volatility and temper tantrums, which he regarded as evil and self-centered. He had coped with his father's emotional demands by being a hard worker and helper and by a keen sensitivity to his moods. He could forestall his father's rage by anticipating his demands and being a model son. His attitude toward his daughter was suspicious and critical. Although he tried at times to appease her, he more often showed the resentment and anger that had been buried because of his fear" (p. 41).

page 238 "still there is only one image":
Jane Lazarre, from the preface of *The Mother Knot*, pp. vii–viii.

page 239 "The baby is an interference":
D. W. Winnicott, *Collected Papers*, "Hate in the Countertransference," p. 201.

page 239 "I am angry with my baby":
Jane Lazarre, *The Mother Knot*, p. 59.

page 240 the True Dilemma Theory of Parenthood:
See Group for the Advancement of Psychiatry, *The Joys and Sorrows of Parenthood*, pp. 43–44.

page 240 babies are born with specific temperaments:
See Chess and Alexander, "Temperament in the Normal Infant," *Individual Differences in Children*, Jack Westman, ed., for their discussion of temperamental individuality.

page 241 "the importance of innate (constitutional) factors":
In Freud's *Standard Edition*, Vol. 12, "The Dynamics of Transference," this footnote appears on p. 99: "I take this opportunity of defending myself against the mistaken charge of having denied the importance of innate (constitutional) factors because I have stressed that of infantile impressions. A charge such as this arises from the restricted nature of what men look for in the field of causation; in contrast to what ordinarily holds good in the real world, people prefer to be satisfied with a single causative factor. Psychoanalysis has talked a lot about the accidental factors in aetiology and little about the constitutional ones; but that is only because it was able to contribute something fresh to the former, while, to begin with, it knew no more than was commonly known about the latter. We refuse to posit any contrast in principle between two sets of aetiological factors; on the contrary, we assume that the two sets regularly act jointly in bringing about the observed result. [Endowment and Chance] determine a man's fate—rarely or never one of these powers alone."

page 241 And sometimes a bad fit:
For more on fit, see Daniel Stern's book *The First Relationship*, particularly Chapter 8, "Missteps in the Dance."

page 241 Psychoanalyst Stanley Greenspan:
Personal communication.

page 242 "we could get the baby through":
Ibid.

page 242 hypersensitive to sound:
See Greenspan's excellent book, *Psychopathology and Adaptation in Infancy and Early Childhood: Principles of Clinical Diagnosis and Preventive Intervention*, for his case history of Hilda, who—in her mother's presence—became rigid and cried most of the time. It was discovered that Hilda had a special sensitivity to sound that made her

mother's high-pitched voice a particular irritant. Her mother was taught to speak in a low-pitched, rhythmic voice, to soothe Hilda with rhythmic rocking motions, and to distract her from the upsetting sounds by presenting her with interesting visual stimuli. For further case histories of infant-parent interventions, see *Infants and Parents*, Sally Provence, ed.

page 245 Freud originally believed:
In Freud's *Standard Edition*, Vol. 20, "An Autobiographical Study," pp. 33–34, he discusses his abandonment of the seduction theory and his conclusion that "neurotic symptoms were not related directly to actual events but to wishful phantasies" (p. 34).

page 246 "soul-destroying" experiences:
See Shengold's eloquent paper "Child Abuse and Deprivation: Soul Murder," *Journal of the American Psychoanalytic Association*, Vol. 27, No. 3, pp. 533–559 for his discussion of soul-destroying experiences. The quotation appears on p. 550.

page 246 "Human beings are mysteriously resourceful":
Ibid., pp. 549–550.

page 246 "that as far as the neurosis was concerned":
Freud, *Standard Edition*, Vol. 20, "An Autobiographical Study," p. 34.

page 246 link between early experience and future emotional health is currently being challenged:
Spokesmen for this view include University of Chicago psychologist Bertram Cohler and Harvard's Jerome Kagan. See also Rudolph Schaffer's book *Mothering*, in which he challenges the persistent faith, among parents and professionals, in the permanent formative effects of early childhood experiences.

page 246 what happens in childhood matters enormously:
In Kliman and Rosenfeld's useful book *Responsible Parenthood*, they cite a number of studies (see pp. 243–244) supporting the view that what happens to a person in early childhood strongly affects his later emotional life. They concede that what they dub the Childhood-Doesn't-Matter Movement has some value in reminding us that there is no *necessary* connection between a disadvantaged childhood and a troubled adulthood—"inadequate parenting does not condemn a child to failure or unhappiness"; and that parents need not always take the blame when children, by whatever standard, "have turned out badly" (p. 240). They also concede that the movement has value in making the crucial point that childhood damage is surely not irreversible. "But such reversal," the authors note, "is achieved at great cost, and only with great effort. Prevention is so much better" (p. 244).
Dr. Sally Provence addresses the does-childhood-matter question

in her foreword to Stanley Greenspan's book *Psychopathology and Adaptation in Infancy and Early Childhood: Principles of Clinical Diagnosis and Preventive Intervention*: "It is true that in some instances infants with vulnerabilities and maladaptive behavior in the first year of life may improve in functioning without intervention, or, at least, without the sort of intervention that we can identify specifically. The fact that this occurs, that many infants are resilient and that many parents improve as nurturers, leads some to discount the importance of providing help early in the life of the child. And yet, other infants and parents fare far less well: Early dysfunctions may crystallize into maladaptive, psychopathological patterns that not only interfere with current development and parent-infant relationships, but exert long-lasting adverse effects as well" (p. xii). Dr. Provence agrees, however, that studies predicting future development and adaptive capacities have been frequently unreliable, in part because there is still much to be learned about those factors that promote *healthy* development and in part because earlier studies failed to reflect the fact that many factors—not one—determine human behavior.

page 247 "of ancient, fabulous forests":
V. Nabokov, *Speak, Memory*, p. 297.

page 247 "Who said that tenderness":
Louis Simpson, "The Goodnight," *Sound and Sense*, Laurence Perrine, ed., pp. 133–134.

CHAPTER FIFTEEN   FAMILY FEELINGS

page 249 family myths—unspoken or spoken themes:
Family themes (I am using the words "theme" and "myth" interchangeably) are discussed on pp. 17–19 of Robert Hess and Gerald Handel's "The Family as a Psychosocial Organization," *The Psychosocial Interior of the Family*, Gerald Handel, ed.

page 249 "corporate characteristic":
The concept of "corporate characteristics" is discussed in the introduction to *The Psychosocial Interior of the Family*, Gerald Handel, ed., p. 5.

page 249 But many family myths distort reality:
See Antonio Ferreira's "Family Myth and Homeostasis," *Archives of General Psychiatry*, Vol. 9, pp. 457–463. The quoted phrase appears on p. 462. See also Dennis Bagarozzi and Steven Anderson on "The Evolution of Family Mythological Systems: Considerations for Meaning, Clinical Assessment and Treatment," *The Journal of Psychoanalytic Anthropology*, 5:1, pp. 71–90. And see Lynn Wikler's "*Folie à Famille*: A Family Therapist's Perspective," *Family Process*, Vol. 19–

3, pp. 257–268, for her discussion of shared familial delusions. Wikler describes a hypothetical continuum of family beliefs ranging from *folie à famille* to family myths to incongruous shared concepts to shared idiosyncratic reality.

page 250 "We are all peaceful":
See "Pseudo-Mutuality in the Family Relations of Schizophrenics," by Lyman Wynne, Irving Ryckoff, Juliana Day and Stanley Hirsch, in *The Psychosocial Interior of the Family*, George Handel, ed., p. 451.

page 250 "pseudo-mutuality":
Ibid. The concept of pseudo-mutuality is defined on pp. 444–449.

page 250 "intense and enduring":
Ibid., p. 447.

page 251 even before we were actually born:
In his paper on "The Role of Family Life in Child Development," *The International Journal of Psycho-Analysis*, Vol. 57, Part 4, pp. 385–395, Horst-Eberhard Richter writes: "Frequently, even before the child is born, parents entertain fairly detailed fantasies concerning the position the child is to take in the family.... The more burdened the parents are by their own inner conflicts... the more rigidly and compulsively their educational behavior is governed by these fantasies. ...In this perspective the development of the child is seen as his lasting attempt to come to terms with the role that one or both parents have prescribed for him" (p. 387).

page 251 "like mother, dumb and stupid":
Ferreira, "Family Myth and Homeostasis," *General Archives of Psychiatry*, Vol. 9, p. 463.

page 251 There are all kinds of roles:
See Richter (two notes above), pp. 387–388, for a discussion of these four roles. For an interesting further look at the scapegoat role, see innovative family therapist Nathan Ackerman's chapter on "Rescuing the Scapegoat" in his book *Treating the Troubled Family.*

page 252 "It is often assumed":
Peter Lomas, "Family Role and Identity Formation," *The International Journal of Psycho-Analysis*, Vol. 42, Parts 4–5, p. 379.

page 252 Death of a Salesman:
Arthur Miller, *Death of a Salesman*, p. 54 ("can't take hold..."), p. 132 ("I am not..."), p. 133 ("Pop... happens").

page 252 The allotment of roles:
In "The Role of Family Life in Child Development," *The International Journal of Psycho-Analysis*, Vol. 57, Part 4, Richter writes: "Studies of families carried out over a number of years show that children

understand exactly the role which the parental unconscious seeks to allot to them, and that many of their reactions may be interpreted partly as identifications and partly as protests against the directives unconsciously imposed upon them" (p. 388).

page 253 *"Our subjective experience"*:
Roger Gould, "Transformational Tasks in Adulthood," *The Course of Life*, Vol. 3, Greenspan and Pollock, eds., p. 58.

page 255 *"Parents continue to monitor"*:
Ibid., p. 69.

page 255 *We begin to recognize our identifications*:
Gould (see above) writes: "During our twenties, our knowledge of these identifications had to be suppressed so we could believe in the illusion of our complete independence from parental influence. Now, in order to avoid blind repetition of their patterns and in order not to forfeit the piece of self underlying the parental identification, we must first acknowledge the presence of this mysterious, slightly foreign inner self."

But not all identifications are either an exact duplication or a complete repudiation of a parental quality. "The final solution to a successful processing of identifications comes when we find we have a *similarity* to a parent but are *not identical*. We may share the stem of a value but not the ramifications. We may share a temperament characteristic but use it for different purposes. Hostility might be spunk; niggardliness may be prudence. But only after the identification similarity is admitted can the necessary discriminations be made and the self attached to that characteristic allowed to live" (p. 73).

page 256 *Parenthood can be a constructive developmental phase*:
See Therese Benedek's "Parenthood as a Developmental Phase," *Journal of the American Psychoanalytic Association*, Vol. 7, pp. 389–417, where she argues that at each successive stage of a child's development his parents are afforded another chance to work through, or reinforce, solutions to conflicts arising at a comparable stage of their own childhood. She notes that each child "stirs up through his own phasic development the corresponding unconscious developmental conflict of the parent . . . [and] . . . the parent cannot help but deal with his own conflict unconsciously, while consciously he tries to help the child achieve his developmental goal" (pp. 404–405). "We assume that while parents thus deliberately manipulate the behavior of the child and their current relationship with him, unconsciously they also modify their own intrapsychic processes" (p. 408).

page 258 *"Grandparenthood," writes psychoanalyst Therese Benedek*:
T. Benedek. This material is an addendum to "Parenthood as a Developmental Phase" and appears on p. 406 of her *Psychoanalytic Investigations: Selected Papers*.

pages 259–60 "my friends are much more interested":
Featherstone, "Family Matters," *Harvard Educational Review*, Vol. 49, No. 1, pp. 29–30.

page 260 And we often discover secrets:
For a discussion of family secrets, see Theodore Jacobs's "Secrets, Alliances and Family Fictions: Some Psychoanalytic Observations," *Journal of the American Psychoanalytic Association*, Vol. 28, No. 1, pp. 21–42.

page 261 "I remember why skating":
Herbert Gold, *Fathers*, pp. 199–200.

page 261 "struck again and again":
Featherstone, "Family Matters," *Harvard Educational Review*, Vol. 49, No. 1, p. 51.

CHAPTER SIXTEEN   LOVE AND MOURNING

page 265 "a lifelong human condition":
Rochlin, "The Dread of Abandonment," *The Psychoanalytic Study of the Child*, Vol. 16, p. 452.

page 265 "In what, now":
Freud, *Standard Edition*, Vol. 14, "Mourning and Melancholia," p. 244.

page 266 phases of mourning:
The Institute of Medicine's exhaustive survey of bereavement research—*Bereavement: Reactions, Consequences, and Care*, Marian Osterweis, Frederic Solomon and Morris Green, eds.—notes that "most observers . . . speak of clusters of reactions or 'phases' of bereavement that change over time. Although observers divide the process into various numbers of phases and use different terminology to label them, there is general agreement about the nature of reactions over time. Clinicians also agree that there is substantial individual variation in terms of specific manifestations of grief and in the speed with which people move through the process" (p. 48).

page 266 "sorrow . . . turns out to be":
C. S. Lewis, *A Grief Observed*, p. 68.

page 266 "shock, numbness and a sense of disbelief":
Institute of Medicine, *Bereavement: Reactions, Consequences, and Care*, p. 49.

page 267 Mark Twain:
Clemens, *The Autobiography of Mark Twain*, p. 324 ("our wonder and our worship") and p. 323 ("It is one of the . . .").

page 267 "anticipatory mourning":
Many studies of bereavement take note of the phenomenon of "anticipatory mourning" or "mourning before the fact." In George Pollock's "Mourning and Adaptation," *The International Journal of Psycho-Analysis*, Vol. 42, Parts 4–5, pp. 341–361, he writes: "In instances where death is anticipated as a result of a long-standing debilitation, acute mourning reactions may occur prior to the actual death. In several patients, whose parents were dying of malignant conditions, the shock response came when the patients first heard of the hopeless malignant diagnosis, and only very slightly when the actual death occurred" (p. 346). Pollock notes, however, that after the death has in fact occurred, "mourning work is still required" (p. 349).

page 268 "An elderly woman":
This clinical illustration was presented by Channing Lipson in "Denial and Mourning," *The Interpretation of Death*, p. 269.

page 268 physical complaints:
According to the Institute of Medicine's *Bereavement: Reactions, Consequences, and Care*, "acute grief is associated with a variety of physical complaints, including pain, gastrointestinal disturbances and the very 'vegetative' symptoms that, at another time, might signal the presence of a depressive disorder (e.g., sleep disturbance, appetite disturbance, loss of energy)" (p. 51).

page 268 regression (to a needier, "Help me!" stage):
In *Death and the Family*, social worker Lily Pincus discusses (pp. 41–43) the importance of being allowed, as part of mourning, to regress. She cites "one widow who, after an initial period of sleeplessness, could happily go to sleep cuddling a bolster, just like a baby who needs a teddy bear to go to sleep without his mother. Why not acknowledge and satisfy without shame the baby needs stirred up by bereavement?" (pp. 114–115). Pincus later notes: "The three year old who starts wetting and soiling again after the birth of a rival sibling is asking for extra care and attention. Both the small child who wants to be a baby again and the adult in pain learn to use regression in their new situation to gain comfort and love. If the desired response is forthcoming, the toddler can move on and make a step toward growth. . . . Regression in grief must be seen and supported as a means toward adaptation and health" (pp. 122–123).

page 268 "how I hated the world":
Raphael, *The Anatomy of Bereavement*, p. 49.

page 269 "Your logic, my friend, is perfect":
These are verses nine and ten of James Russell Lowell's "After the Burial," *The Complete Poetical Works of James Russell Lowell*, pp. 308–309, written after his child's death.

page 269 anger—toward others, and also toward the dead:
Bowlby, in *Loss*, citing corroborating research, affirms the place of anger in normal mourning: "There can in fact be no doubt that in normal mourning anger expressed towards one target or another is the rule. . . . [N]either the occurrence nor the frequency of anger can be regarded any longer as an issue" (p. 29).

page 269 Guilty feelings too—:
In *The Anatomy of Bereavement*, psychiatrist Beverley Raphael, who has done extensive work with, and research on, bereaved people, notes that in mourning: "Guilt is frequent: it relates to the imperfection of human relationships. During the reviewing process of mourning, one may recall the love that was not given, the care that was not provided—the 'sins' of omission. Or, one may remember the hatred he felt for the dead person, the resentment, the violence that was fantasized—the 'sins' of commission. Where the relationship was basically loving, such guilt is transient; where ambivalence was high, it creates greater stress in the working through process. Relief may also be felt—relief that the illness is over, that the painful relationship is finished, that one did not die oneself—and this may be accepted or become a further cause of guilt" (p. 45).

page 270 "Missing him now":
These words by Frances Gunther appear in John Gunther's memoir of their son, *Death Be Not Proud*, p. 258, p. 259.

page 270 Canonizing—idealizing—the dead:
In Freud's *Standard Edition*, Vol. 14, "Thoughts for the Times on War and Death," he describes the way we idealize our dead: "We suspend criticism of him, overlook his possible misdeeds, declare that *de mortuis nil nisi bonum* [of the dead nothing but good], and think it justifiable to set out all that is most favourable to his memory in the funeral oration and upon the tombstone. Consideration for the dead, who, after all, no longer need it, is more important to us than the truth" (p. 290).

page 271 "the greatest little woman":
Raphael, *The Anatomy of Bereavement*, p. 207.

page 271 "He could say nothing negative":
Ibid.

page 271 "On the one hand":
Bowlby, *Loss*, p. 87. See searching discussion, pp. 87–90.

pages 271–72 ". . . I went to find you":
Anne Philipe, *No Longer Than a Sigh*, pp. 90–91.

page 272 A father dreams of his son:
This dream of Samuel Palmer was described by Bowlby in *Loss*, p. 112.

page 272 A mother dreams of her daughter:
This dream was described to me by a woman whose daughter died of cancer.

page 272 A woman dreams of her sister:
This dream was described by Geoffrey Gorer in *Death, Grief, and Mourning*, p. 53.

page 272 A daughter (Simone de Beauvoir) dreams of her mother:
This dream was described by de Beauvoir in *A Very Easy Death*, pp. 102–103.

page 272 A son dreams of his father:
This dream, from a man in his twenties who had a very *unpeaceful* relationship with his father, was described to me by his psychiatrist.

page 273 A son dreams of his mother:
These dreams were described to me by a man who had greatly idealized his mother after her death.

page 273 A daughter dreams of her father:
Gorer, *Death, Grief, and Mourning*, p. 55.

page 273 A widow dreams of her husband:
This dream was described to me by a woman whose husband, a manic-depressive, shot himself when he was fifty and she forty-six.

page 273 And the writer Edmund Wilson:
Wilson, *The Thirties*, pp. 367, 368, 369.

page 274 we can begin to come to the end of mourning:
In George Pollock's "Mourning and Adaptation," *The International Journal of Psycho-Analysis*, Vol. 42, parts 4–5, pp. 341–361, he writes: "The ego's ability to perceive the reality of the loss; to appreciate the temporal and spatial permanence of the loss; to acknowledge the significance of the loss; to be able to deal with the acute sudden disruption following the loss with attendant fears of weakness, helplessness, frustration, rage, pain and anger; to be able effectively to reinvest new objects or ideals with energy, and so re-establish different but satisfactory relationships, are the key factors in this process" (p. 355).

page 275 "one of the more universal forms":
Ibid., p. 345. See also Pollock's "The Mourning Process and Creative Organizational Change," *Journal of the American Psychoanalytic Association*, Vol. 25, No. 1, pp. 3–34.

pages 275–76 "... now I see what":
This is the final section of Linda Pastan's poem, "The Five Stages of Grief," from her book *The Five Stages of Grief*, p. 62.

page 276 "after the amputation":
Ibid., p. 61.

page 276 C. S. Lewis:
Both passages appear in Lewis's "A Grief Observed," p. 67.

page 276 "anniversary reactions":
See Pollock's "Anniversary Reactions, Trauma and Mourning," *The Psychoanalytic Quarterly*, Vol. 39, No. 3, pp. 347-371.

pages 276-77 this record of a daughter's grieving testifies:
These selections from Toby Talbot's *A Book About My Mother* appear on the following pages: 10, 16, 33, 75, 120, 121, 154, 166, 172, 178-179.

pages 277-78 "filled with her":
Ibid., p. 178.

page 278 It is by internalizing the dead:
Since some writers talk about *internalization* of the lost "object" and some talk about *identification* with it, let me distinguish between these two words. Internalization is most usefully defined as a general term for various processes (identification, incorporation, introjection, to name three) by which we transform our relationships and experiences with the outer world into inner relationships and experiences. Identification is the process of internalization by which we modify our self to become in some ways like this or that person out there.

In "Mourning and Melancholia" Freud argued that identification with the lost loved person only occurred when mourning was pathological, but he later (in "The Ego and the Id") took the position that identification is part of all mourning and is the means by which we are able to relinquish our relationship with the lost person.

page 278 The "loved object is not gone":
Abraham, *Selected Papers*, "A Short Study of the Development of the Libido, Viewed in the Light of Mental Disorders," p. 437.

page 278 One form of internalization:
See this book, Chapter Four, "The Private 'I,'" pp. 45-49.

page 278 Therapist Lily Pincus describes:
Pincus gives these examples in her book *Death and the Family*, noting further that the dull wife who became witty after her husband's death also "told me that she had always been amused by her husband's patient peeling of the top of his boiled egg, while she used to cut it off. 'Now,' she said, 'I just cannot bring myself to cut the top off, I have to peel it off patiently'" (p. 121).

page 278 identifications can be pathological:
Pincus (see above reference) describes a woman who had deplored her husband's bad table manners during his life, then acquired those same bad manners after his death. Pincus suggests that this was an attempt at restitution for her nagging (pp. 122-123). Pathological iden-

tifications include identifying with, and actually developing, the symptoms of the dead person's last, fatal illness. Pathological identifications may also occur when there has been great ambivalence in the relationship. The mourner has feelings of anger and reproach toward the person who died but directs them, instead, against himself. (See Freud's "Mourning and Melancholia.")

page 279 "There is continued crying":
Raphael, *The Anatomy of Mourning*, p. 60.

page 279 "it is as though":
Ibid., p. 60.

page 279 "Grief fills the room up":
Shakespeare, *King John*, Act 3, Scene 4.

page 279 "mummification":
Gorer discusses mummification in *Death, Grief, and Mourning*, pp. 85–87.

page 280 Bowlby says there are many different clues:
See Bowlby's discussion of absence of conscious grieving in *Loss*, pp. 152–156.

page 281 "Give sorrow words":
Shakespeare, *Macbeth*, Act 4, Scene 3.

page 281 harmful effects on the mental and physical health:
For a full discussion of the health consequences following a loss through death, see Chapter 2 of the Institute of Medicine's *Bereavement: Reactions, Consequences, and Care*. Among the conclusions reported on pp. 39–40 are:

"Following bereavement there is a statistically significant increase in mortality for men under the age of 75. . . . There is no higher mortality in women in the first year; whether there is an increase in the second year is unclear.

"There is an increase in suicide in the first year of bereavement, particularly by older widowers and by single men who lose their mothers. There may be a slight increase in suicide by widows.

"Among widowers, there is an increase in the relative risk of death from accidents, cardiovascular disease and some infectious diseases. In widows, the relative risk of death from cirrhosis rises.

"All studies document increases in alcohol consumption and smoking and greater use of tranquilizers or hypnotic medication (or both) among the bereaved. For the most part, these increases occur in people who already are using these substances; however, some of the increase is attributable to new users.

"Depressive symptoms are very common in the first months of bereavement. Between 10 and 20 per cent of men and women who lose a spouse are still depressed a year later."

See also Chapter 6 of that book, "To a Biology of Grieving," which explores the impact of grief on our biological systems.

page 281 "The father, Hermann Castorp":
The Institute of Medicine's study of bereavement (see reference above) begins its report with this apt selection from Thomas Mann's novel *The Magic Mountain*. It appears on p. 19.

pages 281–82 The statistics are these:
These figures come from the Institute of Medicine's bereavement study (see above reference, p. 4).

page 282 Here are some answers:
Ibid., pp. 35–41, and Chapter 5.

page 283 the losses of early childhood may continue:
See Chapter 5 of the Institute of Medicine's *Bereavement: Reactions, Consequences, and Care*, for a discussion of the immediate, intermediate and long-range reactions of children to loss.

page 283 The Danish writer Tove Ditlevsen:
Moffat's *In the Midst of Winter* introduced me to Ditlevsen's poem, translated from the Danish by Ann Freeman, and provided the biographical information about her on pp. 88–90. Ditlevsen's poems "Self-Portrait 1" and "Self-Portrait 2" can be found in *The Other Voice: Twentieth-Century Women's Poetry in Transition*, Bankier et al., eds., pp. 27–29.

page 284 no young child has the ego strength:
One of the more fatiguing debates among the experts is whether or not children are capable of mourning, with some (like Melanie Klein) claiming that even infants can mourn and others (like Martha Wolfenstein) claiming that mourning does not become possible until adolescence. Part of the confusion has to do with different definitions. But if complete mourning is defined not merely as the capacity to feel grief over the loss of someone you love but as the capacity to confront that loss and sustain that grief (and other emotions) and in time to internally detach yourself from the lost one, it seems likely that children find it harder than adults to mourn, and need more help from adults with the mourning process. In the Institute of Medicine's report (see earlier citation) it notes: "Generally it is agreed that prior to age 3 or 4 children are not able to achieve complete mourning and it is agreed that by adolescence youngsters can mourn but are still more vulnerable than adults because they are experiencing so many other losses and changes. The controversy centers on the years in between" (Chapter 5, pp. 2–3).

For more on this controversy, see Melanie Klein's "Mourning and Its Relation to Manic-Depressive States" in *The Interpretation of Death*, Hendrik Ruitenbeek, ed.; Martha Wolfenstein's "How is Mourning

Possible?", in *The Psychoanalytic Study of the Child*, Vol. 21; Edna Furman's *A Child's Parent Dies*; and John Bowlby's *Loss*.

page 284 Bowlby and others:
See Bowlby's *Loss* for his discussion of the conditions under which mourning in children leads to healthy and to unhealthy outcomes. In *The Anatomy of Bereavement*, pp. 114–119, Raphael discusses a variety of family contexts in which a child experiences loss and death.

pages 284–85 "Jessica was five":
Raphael, *The Anatomy of Bereavement*, p. 138.

page 286 grief for a dead grown child:
See pp. 121–126 of Gorer's *Death, Grief, and Mourning* for his discussion of parents' responses to the death of their children.

page 287 "They said it was nothing":
Raphael, *The Anatomy of Bereavement*, p. 236.

page 287 "then there was the empty room":
Ibid., pp. 251–252.

page 287 "may alter, forever":
Ibid., p. 281.

pages 287–88 "Although we know that after such a loss":
This is from Freud's letter to Ludwig Binswanger, *The Letters of Sigmund Freud*, Ernst Freud, ed., p. 386.

page 288 "Our society is set up":
Caine, *Widow*, p. 1.

page 289 "her own life had no meaning":
Raphael, *The Anatomy of Bereavement*, p. 207.

page 289 "I was just as crazy":
The Hayes statement appears in Lynn Caine's *Widow*, pp. 75–76.

page 289 "God has moved me up":
This poignant line appears in Etty Hillesum's *An Interrupted Life*, p. 182.

page 289 that other marital death called divorce:
For a fuller discussion of this subject, see Gerald Jacobson's *The Multiple Crises of Marital Separation and Divorce*.

page 290 "There was once a man":
de Beauvoir, "The Woman Destroyed," from her collection also entitled *The Woman Destroyed*, pp. 207–208.

page 290 "the 'bereaved' must mourn":
Raphael, *The Anatomy of Bereavement*, p. 228.

page 291 "The world breaks everyone":
Hemingway, *A Farewell to Arms*, p. 186.

pages 292–93 "When we found out what the disease would do":
This is all but the opening portion of Maxine Kumin's poem "The Man of Many L's," *Our Ground Time Here Will Be Brief*, pp. 30–31.

page 294 Jerome said Kaddish:
Many of the books mentioned in these notes discuss the great importance of such traditional rituals of mourning in facilitating the internal mourning process.

page 294 "You have grown wings of pain":
This is a portion of Linda Pastan's poem "Go Gentle," *PM/AM*, p. 41.

page 294 "I had grown very fond":
de Beauvoir, *A Very Easy Death*, p. 76.

page 295 "there is no loss":
Pincus, *Death and the Family*, p. 278.

page 295 "I am a more sensitive person":
Kushner, *When Bad Things Happen to Good People*, pp. 133–134.

CHAPTER SEVENTEEN   SHIFTING IMAGES

page 296 Confucius:
Daniel Levinson's book *The Seasons of a Man's Life* is the source for "the ages of man" according to Confucius (p. 326), Solon (p. 326) and the Talmud (p. 325). From Confucius:

The Master said, At 15 I set my heart upon learning.
At 30, I had planted my feet firm upon the ground.
At 40, I no longer suffered from perplexities.
At 50, I knew what were the biddings of heaven.
At 60, I heard them with a docile ear.
At 70, I could follow the dictates of my own heart; for what I desired no longer overstepped the boundaries of right.

page 296 Solon:

0– 7	A boy at first is the man; unripe; then he casts his teeth; milk-teeth befitting the child he sheds in his seventh year.
7–14	Then to his seven years God adding another seven, signs of approaching manhood show in the bud.
14–21	Still, in the third of the sevens his limbs are growing; his chin touched with a fleecy down, the bloom of the cheek gone.
21–28	Now, in the fourth of the sevens ripen to greatest completeness the powers of the man, and his worth becomes plain to see.

28–35   In the fifth he bethinks him that this is the season for courting, bethinks him that sons will preserve and continue his line.

35–42   Now in the sixth his mind, ever open to virtue, broadens, and never inspires him to profitless deeds.

42–56   Seven times seven, and eight; the tongue and the mind for fourteen years together are now at their best.

56–63   Still in the ninth is he able, but never so nimble in speech and in wit as he was in the days of his prime.

63–70   Who to the tenth has attained, and has lived to complete it, has come to the time to depart on the ebb-tide of Death.

page 296 The Talmud:

 5   years is the age for reading (Scripture);
10   for Mishnah (the laws);
13   for the Commandments (Bar Mitzvah, moral responsibility);
15   for Gemara (Talmudic discussions; abstract reasoning);
18   for Hupa (wedding canopy);
20   for seeking a livelihood (pursuing an occupation);
30   for attaining full strength ("Koah");
40   for understanding;
50   for giving counsel;
60   for becoming an elder (wisdom, old age);
70   for white hair;
80   for Gevurah (new, special strength of age);
90   for being bent under the weight of the years;
100   for being as if already dead and passed away from the world

page 296 Shakespeare:
From *As You Like It*, Act 2, Scene 7:

> All the world's a stage,
> And all the men and women merely players:
> They have their exits, and their entrances;
> And one man in his time plays many parts,—
> His acts being seven ages. At first, the infant,
> Mewling and puking in the nurse's arms:
> Then the whining schoolboy, with his satchel,
> And shining morning face, creeping like snail
> Unwillingly to school: and then the lover,
> Sighing like furnace, with a woeful ballad
> Made to his mistress' eyebrow: Then a soldier,
> Full of strange oaths, and bearded like a pard,
> Jealous in honour, sudden and quick in quarrel,
> Seeking the bubble Reputation
> Even in the cannon's mouth: and then the justice,
> In fair round belly, with good capon lin'd,
> With eyes severe, and beard of formal cut,
> Full of wise saws and modern instances,

And so he plays his part: The sixth age shifts
Into the lean and slipper'd pantaloon;
With spectacles on nose, and pouch on side
His youthful hose well sav'd, a world too wide
For his shrunk shank; and his big manly voice
Turning again toward childish treble, pipes
And whistles in his sound: Last scene of all,
That ends this strange eventful history,
Is second childishness, and mere oblivion;
Sans teeth, sans eyes, sans taste, sans—everything.

page 296 Erikson:

Erik Erikson's *Childhood and Society*, Chapter 7, describes "Eight Ages of Man," successive phases of the life cycle during which crucial turning-point decisions are made between:

> basic trust versus basic mistrust
> autonomy versus shame and doubt
> initiative versus guilt
> industry versus inferiority
> identity versus role confusion
> intimacy versus isolation
> generativity versus stagnation
> ego integrity versus despair.

page 296 Sheehy:

Gail Sheehy's *Passages* focuses on stages of adult development between what she calls "The Trying Twenties" and the "Deadline Decade" of mid-life.

page 296 Jaques:

Elliott Jaques's "The Midlife Crisis," *The Course of Life*, Vol. 3, Greenspan and Pollock, eds., describes the following developmental stages: "*infancy*: the critical first year of life terminated by what might be termed the *depressive crisis* ...; *early childhood*: the period of emergence of organized conscious ego functioning and language, separated by the *oedipal crisis* from the *latency stage* of development which in turn is ended by the *crisis of puberty and adolescence*. There then emerges the state of *early childhood*, from roughly the late teens to the middle thirties; in the middle and late thirties occur the *midlife crisis* and the transition to *mature adulthood* which runs from around forty to the middle or late fifties. There then occurs what I would term the *late adult crisis*, leading into *late adulthood*, the period of the sixties and seventies. There is some evidence ... that there is a further maturational step at around the age of eighty if senility does not step in, but we leave this possibility as an open question" (p. 2).

page 296 Gould:

Roger Gould's *Transformations* presents a series of false assumptions

which, in sequential stages between adolescence and mid-life, must be challenged. These will be discussed later in this chapter.

page 296 Levinson:
Daniel Levinson's *The Seasons of a Man's Life* is based on his intensive study of the lives of forty men representing four different occupations—industrial workers, business executives, university biologists and novelists—between the ages of thirty-five and forty-five. Generalizing from in-depth biographical interviews, Levinson and his colleagues have formulated a developmental theory of men in the years between their entry into adulthood and mid-life. The life cycle is viewed as a sequence of partially overlapping eras:

0–22   childhood and adolescence;
17–45 early adulthood;
40–65 middle adulthood;
60–?   late adulthood.

The transition from one era to the next takes place over several years; the zone of overlap between eras is the transition period. Thus the Early Adult Transition extends from seventeen to twenty-two; the Mid-Life Transition extends from forty to forty-five; the Late Adult Transition extends from sixty to sixty-five. The eras, according to Levinson, are further subdivided into developmental periods (to be discussed in the text of this chapter).

page 296 normal predictable stages of adult development:
Freud's work emphasized the developmental stages of childhood. In recent years, however, much attention has been paid to adult stages of development. The father of these adult developmental studies, in the view of Levinson and others, is Freud's disciple Carl Jung, who later split with Freud and founded his own school of "analytical psychology." Jung wrote forcefully of change and development in the second half of life, the "afternoon of life." See, for instance, his "The Stages of Life" in *The Portable Jung*, Joseph Campbell, ed.

page 297 "is an ending":
Levinson, *The Seasons of a Man's Life*, p. 50, p. 51.

page 297 "In the course of these changes":
This paragraph is based on Levinson's divisions of the developmental periods between early adulthood and mid-life: Early Adult Transition; Entering the Adult World; Age Thirty Transition; Settling Down and Becoming One's Own Man; Mid-Life Transition and Entering Middle Adulthood (p. 68). Although his research is on men only, the general time frames seem applicable—to some extent—to both sexes.

page 298 "What am I doing with a mid-life crisis":
J. Viorst, *How Did I Get to Be Forty and Other Atrocities*, "Mid-Life Crisis," p. 17.

page 299 "When I was young and miserable and pretty":
These lines are from Randall Jarrell's poem, "Next Day," quoted by
Charles Simmons in "The Age of Maturity," *The New York Times
Magazine*, Dec. 11, 1983, p. 114.

page 299 Quoting that poem in a wistful essay:
Charles Simmons, "The Age of Maturity," *The New York Times Magazine*, Dec. 11, 1983, p. 114.

page 300 "Being physically attractive":
Susan Sontag, "The Double Standard of Aging," *Saturday Review*,
Oct. 1972, pp. 29–38. The statements quoted appear on p. 31.

page 300 "Most men experience getting older":
Ibid., p. 34.

page 302 empty nests have advantages:
Many women will attest to the pleasures of the empty nest: the new
neatness and quiet of the house, the freedom to eat, sleep and make
love on their own schedule, the freedom from anxiety which comes
from not knowing, on any given blizzardy night, whether or not their
children are out in a car. Indeed, Lillian Rubin's book, *Women of a
Certain Age*, challenges the concept of an empty-nest syndrome of
sadness, loneliness and depression. "Almost all the women I spoke
with," she writes, "respond to the departure of their children, whether
actual or impending, with a decided sense of relief" (p. 15). Almost
all of the women *I* spoke with, however, felt both the relief and a
sense of sadness, particularly in the period just following departure.
And with the departure of the last child, they note, all the friends of
that child also vanish from the household. The loss, then, is not only
of their own children—but of children's presence in their daily life.

page 303 "renunciation of what has been inexorably outlived":
Dinnerstein, *The Mermaid and the Minotaur*, p. 140.

page 304 "the one major institution in our society":
Gutmann, "Psychoanalysis and Aging: A Developmental View," *The
Course of Life*, Vol. 3, Greenspan and Pollock, eds., p. 513.

page 305 "I've finished six pillows":
Judith Viorst, *How Did I Get to Be Forty and Other Atrocities*, "Self-Improvement Program," p. 45.

page 306 "our ground time here":
Our Ground Time Here Will Be Brief is the title and title poem of a
book of poetry by Maxine Kumin.

page 306 "a dark wood":
Many of those who have written about the mid-life crisis find it most
movingly rendered in the opening lines of Dante's *The Divine Comedy*:
"Midway in the journey of our life I found myself in a dark wood, for

the straight way was lost. Ah, how hard it is to tell what that wood was, wild, rugged, harsh; the very thought of it renews the fear! It is so bitter that death is hardly more so" (p. 3).

page 307 "God ordains":
Jaques quotes Shaw in "The Midlife Crisis," *The Course of Life*, Vol. 3, Greenspan and Pollock, eds., p. 4.

page 310 "The old conspiracies":
Gould, *Transformations*, p. 291.

page 311 "I might as well have a roommate":
Mary Bralove, "Husband's Hazard," *The Wall Street Journal*, Nov. 9, 1981. See p. 1 for headline and quote about roommate.

page 311 "out of phase":
Ibid., p. 24.

page 311 what psychologist Gilligan calls both "voices":
See Carol Gilligan's book *In a Different Voice*.

page 312 masculine autonomy is far more valued:
Gilligan takes issue in Chapter 6 of *In a Different Voice* with studies of adult development (like Levinson's and George Vaillant's) "that convey a view of adulthood where relationships are subordinated to the ongoing process of individuation and achievement" (p. 154).

page 312 "the chronic emergency of parenthood":
Gutmann, "Psychoanalysis and Aging: A Developmental View," *The Course of Life*, Vol. 3, Greenspan and Pollock, eds., p. 499.

page 312 "During the active and critical period":
Ibid., p. 500.

page 313 "Thus, men begin to live out directly":
Ibid., p. 502.

page 313 creativeness/destructiveness duality:
This duality is one of four sets of polarities discussed by Levinson in *The Seasons of a Man's Life* (pp. 197–198, pp. 209–244). According to Levinson, the four polarities, "whose resolution is the principal task of mid-life individuation, are: (1) Young/ Old, (2) Destruction/ Creation, (3) Masculine/Feminine and (4) Attachment/Separateness" (p. 197).

page 313 "childhood consciousness":
Gould, *Transformations*, see Section I, "Childhood Consciousness vs. Adult Consciousness."

page 313 four assumptions:
These four false assumptions are described in Gould's "Transformational Tasks in Adulthood," *The Course of Life*, Vol. 3, Greenspan and Pollock, eds., p. 66.

page 314 "our darker, mysterious center":
Gould, *Transformations*, p. 294.

page 315 "the madness of unbridled rationality":
Loewald, *Psychoanalysis and the History of the Individual*, p. 56.

page 315 connecting "with the insane in us":
Gould, *Transformations*, p. 305.

page 315 Analyst Elliott Jaques:
See Jaques, "The Midlife Crisis," *The Course of Life*, Vol. 3, Greenspan and Pollock, eds. The quoted material appears on p. 6, p. 8, p. 9 and p. 9 again.

page 316 "The Mid-Life Transition":
Levinson, *The Seasons of a Man's Life*, p. 197.

CHAPTER EIGHTEEN   I GROW OLD... I GROW OLD

The Boston Society for Gerontologic Psychiatry produced three books which I found invaluable background reading for this chapter: *Normal Psychology of the Aging Process*, Zinberg and Kaufman, eds.; *Geriatric Psychiatry: Grief, Loss and Emotional Disorders in the Aging Process*, Berezin and Cath, eds.; and *Psychodynamic Studies on Aging: Creativity, Reminiscing and Dying*, Levin and Kahana, eds.

page 318 "creative freedoms":
George Pollock, "Aging or Aged: Development or Pathology," *The Course of Life*, Vol. 3., Greenspan and Pollock, eds., p. 573.

page 319 "How hard and painful":
de Beauvoir, *The Coming of Age*, p. 92.

page 319 From Ovid:
Ibid., p. 121

page 319 From Montaigne:
Ibid., p. 159.

page 319 From Chateaubriand:
Ibid., p. 299.

page 319 From Gide:
Ibid., p. 460.

page 319 "Old age," says de Beauvoir:
Ibid., p. 539.

pages 320–21 "Eighty years old! No eyes left":
Ibid., p. 303. Although de Beauvoir's book emphasizes the miseries of age, she does—from time to time—present some spokesmen for a more positive view of aging.

page 321 "body preoccupation" and "body transcendence":
See Robert Peck, "Psychological Development in the Second Half of Life," *Middle Age and Aging*, Bernice Neugarten, ed., pp. 90–91, for a discussion of body transcendence vs. body preoccupation.

page 321 (a health pessimist):
See Ethel Shanas, et al., "The Psychology of Health," *Middle Age and Aging*, Bernice Neugarten, ed., for a discussion of health optimists, pessimists and realists.

page 321 "all the boring physical symptoms":
Fisher, *Sister Age*, p. 237.

page 321 "We who are old":
Florida Scott-Maxwell, *The Measure of My Days*, p. 5, p. 36.

page 322 Although aging is not an illness:
A helpful discussion of mental and physical changes with normal aging can be found in Chapters 6 through 12 of *Aging*, Woodruff and Birren, eds.

page 322 Malcolm Cowley writes:
Cowley, *The View from 80*, pp. 3–4.

page 322 "Put cotton in your ears":
Ibid., p. 5.

page 323 For although in today's America:
These statistics, obtained from the National Institute on Aging, were the latest available as of August 1984.

page 323 "Old age in America is often a tragedy":
Butler, *Why Survive?*, p. xi.

page 323 "We start by growing old":
Cowley, *The View from 80*, p. 5.

page 324 "should an old person":
Blythe, *The View in Winter*, p. 80. See also de Beauvoir's discussion of sex and the elderly in *The Coming of Age*, pp. 317–351.

page 324 "I was depressed":
Ibid., p. 220.

page 325 "while we unburden'd":
Shakespeare, *King Lear*, Act 1, Scene 1.

page 325 "of rule, interest of territory":
Ibid., Act 1, Scene 1.

page 326 "I'll resume the shape":
Ibid., Act 1, Scene 5.

page 326 a "mounting distaste":
Blythe, *The View in Winter*, p. 22, p. 73.

page 326 "profound, underlying problem":
Ibid., p. 13. Blythe is quoting geriatrician Paul Tournier.

page 326 For we live in a society:
In Butler's *Why Survive?* he passionately documents our present society's responsibilities for much of the suffering of the elderly, arguing that America "is extremely harsh to live in when one is old" (p. 2). He urges humane reforms that would assure the elderly adequate incomes, decent housing, appropriate medical care, community support systems, useful roles, workable transportation, available recreation, diverse companionship and physical safety.

For a discussion of different societies' treatment of the elderly, see de Beauvoir's *The Coming of Age*. See also Gutmann's discussion of the psychosocial function of the elderly in his fine paper "Psychoanalysis and Aging: A Developmental View," *The Course of Life*, Vol. 3, Greenspan and Pollock, eds., pp. 489–517.

page 327 "this absurdity . . . this caricature":
Yeats, *The Collected Poems of W. B. Yeats*, from "The Tower," pp. 192–197. These lines appear on p. 192.

page 327 My friend Irene:
J. Viorst, "In Praise of Older Women," *Redbook*, September 1980, pp. 42, 44. A longer version of the interview with Irene appears on p. 42.

page 328 the English professor:
Personal communication.

page 328 "nothing is too late":
Longfellow, "Morituri Salutamus," *The Complete Poetical Works of Henry Wadsworth Longfellow*. The full poem appears on pp. 310–314, these lines on p. 313.

page 329 Hear the miner's mother:
Blythe, *The View in Winter*, p. 167.

page 329 Hear the artist Goya:
Cowley, *The View from 80*, pp. 16–17.

page 329 Hear the Montessori teacher:
Blythe, *The View in Winter*, p. 200.

page 329 Hear the student:
This man, who had left the business world at the age of sixty-five, also told me, "I didn't retire. I turned the page."

page 329 And hear Lady Thelma:
Blythe, *The View in Winter*, p. 232.

page 329 I must mention one more woman:
J. Viorst, "In Praise of Older Women," *Redbook*, September 1980, pp. 42, 44. This material appears on p. 44.

page 331 People age well in many different modes:
Two opposing theories of aging have related "optimal aging" to (1) high activity levels and (2) disengagement from activity. However, in Bernice Neugarten, Robert Havighurst, and Sheldon Tobin's "Personality and Patterns of Aging," *Middle Age and Aging*, Bernice Neugarten, ed., the authors argue that neither the activity nor the disengagement theory is adequate and that different patterns of optimal aging characterize different personality types. They describe a study in which they measured life satisfaction against different patterns of aging in a group of seventy-year-olds.

Among the so-called "integrated" personalities in this group, there were three different types, distinguished by their different approaches to aging: the high-activity reorganizers, the medium-activity focused and the low-activity disengaged. All three types measured high in life satisfaction.

The study also reported on the aging patterns of the "armored" or "defended" personalities in this group, for whom there was a need for tight controls and strong defenses against the anxiety evoked by the threat of aging. Two patterns were perceived: a high-activity "holding on" to former ways of doing things and a low-activity "constricted" retreat from any new experiences. Both types of these "defended" personalities measured high to medium in life satisfaction.

A third category—"passive dependent" personalities—had strong needs for someone on whom they could lean. Those who were "succorance-seeking" had a medium activity level, looked for someone to meet their emotional needs, and if successful, measured medium in life satisfaction. Those who were "apathetic" had a low activity level, were immobilized by their passivity and measured low in life satisfaction.

In a fourth category were the "unintegrated" personalities, who displayed severe defects in psychological functions, loss of emotional control and deterioration in thought process. They were low both in activity and in life satisfaction.

page 331 "for social initiative":
Butler, *Why Survive?*, p. 341. The Gray Panthers, started by Maggie Kuhn at age sixty-seven, is an organization of retired older persons committed to social change.

page 332 "When I am an old woman I shall wear purple":
This is the first verse of Jenny Joseph's poem "Warning" in *The Oxford Book of Twentieth Century English Verse*, Philip Larkin, ed., pp. 609–610.

page 332 "ego transcendence":
See Robert Peck, "Psychological Developments in the Second Half of Life," *Middle Age and Aging*, Bernice Neugarten, ed., pp. 91–92, for a discussion of ego transcendence vs. ego preoccupation. See also Gutmann, "Psychoanalysis and Aging: A Developmental View," *The Course of Life*, Vol. 3, Greenspan and Pollock, eds., where he is surely describing ego transcendence in his reference to a capacity for the "cathexis of otherness"—the "capacity to cathect [invest intensely in] and to make real those agencies which do not in any direct way bear on the security and priorities of the self" (p. 492).

page 333 "a sense of presentness":
Butler, *Why Survive?*, p. 410.

page 333 "when the sound of a child's laugh":
Fisher, *Sister Age*, p. 237.

page 333 "vanished geography":
Blythe, *The View in Winter*, p. 82, p. 87.

page 333 "the life review":
See Butler's "The Life Review: An Interpretation of Reminiscence in the Aged," *Psychiatry*, Vol. 26, No. 1, pp. 65–76, in which he postulates "the universal occurrence in older people of an inner experience or mental process of reviewing one's life," sometimes leading to depression and sometimes leading to "candor, serenity and wisdom" (p. 65).

page 333 "one and only life cycle":
Erikson, *Identity: Youth and Crisis*, p. 139.

page 333 "the fact that one's life":
Ibid., p. 139.

page 334 "How can you expect us":
Blythe, *The View in Winter*, p. 23.

page 334 "denigrates their humanness":
Butler, *Why Survive?*, p. 414.

page 334 "have made and—continue to make":
Ibid., p. 414.

page 334 "bright souls":
Fisher, *Sister Age*, pp. 234–235.

page 335 "a wide range of social and biological changes":
Neugarten, Havighurst, Tobin, "Personality and Patterns of Aging," *Middle Age and Aging*, Bernice Neugarten, ed., pp. 176–177.

page 335 new opportunities for change:
See Colarusso and Nemiroff, *Adult Development*, Chapters 4 and 12, for a useful discussion of development and change in adult life.

page 335 "All is uncharted and uncertain":
Scott-Maxwell, *The Measure of My Days*, pp. 139–140.

page 335 Benjamin Spock:
This discussion is based on several interviews with Dr. Spock in person, by phone and through the mails during 1983.

page 339 But age itself may also call forth new strengths:
In Scott-Maxwell's *The Measure of My Days*, she writes: "Age can seem a debacle, a rout of all one most needs, but that is not the whole truth. What of the part of us, the nameless, boundless part who experienced the rout, the witness who saw so much go, who remains undaunted and knows with clear conviction that there is more to us than age? Part of that which is outside age has been created by age, so there is gain as well as loss. If we have suffered defeat we are somewhere, somehow beyond the battle" (pp. 140–141).

page 340 though Sigmund Freud said otherwise:
Freud and others have argued that treatment of older people is contraindicated because they become more rigid and inflexible with age. Analysts working with older patients, however, have found that they can be as flexible and as well-motivated for change as younger patients.

page 340 the emotional problems that the coming of age may initiate:
Among the elderly, depression is the most prevalent of the mental health disorders. In addition, depression—as well as the risk of suicide—is more prevalent among the elderly than it is in any other age group. See *Physicians' Guide to the Diagnosis and Treatment of Depression in the Elderly*, Crook and Cohen, eds.

page 340 "The basic insight is that parts of self":
Pollock, "Aging or Aged: Development or Pathology," *The Course of Life*, Vol. 3, Greenspan and Pollock, eds., p. 579.

page 340 Psychoanalysts report that psychoanalysis with the elderly:
Panel Report: "The Psychoanalysis of the Older Patient," reported by Nancy Miller. For *Journal of the American Psychoanalytic Association* (in press).

page 341 Why, a seventy-six-year-old woman was asked:
This vignette is described by analyst Martin Berezin in "Psychotherapy of the Elderly," *Aspects of Aging*, No. 4, unpaged.

page 341 "Though he has watched a decent age pass by":
Sophocles, "Oedipus at Colonus," *Sophocles I*, Grene and Lattimore, eds., p. 134.

CHAPTER NINETEEN   THE ABC OF DYING

page 343 "Death is the mother of beauty":
This line is from Stevens's poem "Sunday Morning," *The Norton Anthology of Poetry*, Allison et al., eds., pp. 968–970. The line appears on p. 970.

page 343 "Life without death is meaningless":
See Lisl Marburg Goodman's *Death and the Creative Life*, where she interviews eminent artists and scientists on death. The interview with Wheeler appears on pp. 76–83; the quoted line appears on p. 78.

page 343 "And if one is not able to die":
See Tillich's "The Eternal Now" in *The Meaning of Death*, Herman Feifel, ed., p. 32.

page 344 "If I had my life over again":
Spark, *Memento Mori*, p. 149.

page 345 Why were we born:
In *The Broken Connection*, Robert Jay Lifton quotes Ionesco's poignant line: "Why was I born if it wasn't forever?" (p. 70).

page 345 "to every thing there is a season":
Holy Bible, Ecclesiastes 3:1, 2.

page 345 arrange with cryonics companies to be deep-frozen:
The theory of cryonics is that if a dead body is frozen and preserved, it then can be thawed and revived sometime in the future, when a cure has been found for whatever has been the cause of the death. Several cryonics companies now are freezing the dead bodies of people who have made prior arrangements for such preservation.

page 345 perhaps to eternity:
In his foreword to John A. Mann's *Secrets of Life Extension*, Saul Kent notes that "pioneering 'longevists' . . . have embarked upon a fantastic journey that could, eventually, lead to the achievement of physical immortality" (p. xi). And in Salholz and Smith's article in *Newsweek*, March 26, 1984, on life-extension practitioners Durk Pearson and Sandy Shaw, they are described as believing "that ultimately the only causes of death will be suicide, murder or accident" (p. 81).

page 346 a dread of abandonment:
See Gregory Rochlin's "The Dread of Abandonment: A Contribution to the Etiology of the Loss Complex and to Depression," *The Psychoanalytic Study of the Child*, Vol. 16, where he discusses the "two great inseparable fears of man . . . the fear of not surviving or death, and . . . the dread of abandonment" (p. 460). He further argues that what he calls the "paradise myth" (p. 467) is an effort to transform

the meaning of death and abandonment from separation to reunion—
a joining with others.

pages 346–47 "The Death of Ivan Ilych":
These lines and passages from Tolstoy's "The Death of Ivan Ilych"
are found in *Great Short Works of Leo Tolstoy* on the following pages:
"something terrible, new . . ." p. 274; "My God . . ." p. 278; "It is impossible . . ." p. 279; "the syllogism . . ." p. 280; "It cannot be . . ." p.
280; "stand before him . . ." p. 281; "alone with It . . ." p. 282; "Why,
and for what . . ." p. 296; "Agony, death . . ." p. 298.

page 347 "This deception tortured him":
Ibid., p. 285.

pages 347–48 On Death and Dying:
Kübler-Ross's book *On Death and Dying* arose out of a seminar on
death, which she originated and conducted at the University of Chicago. In this seminar, students of medicine, sociology, psychology and
theology listened to the terminally ill discussing their wants and fears.
Kübler-Ross maintains that all terminally ill patients are "aware of
the seriousness of their illness whether they are told or not" (p. 233).
She says that although they may be initially glad that their doctors
and relatives (because of their own anxieties) don't want to discuss
it, there comes a time when the dying have a need for an understanding
person with whom to share some of their feelings and concerns, with
whom "to lift the mask, to face reality" and with whom to talk about
their impending death (p. 234). Kübler-Ross notes, however, that even
very realistic patients will leave "the possibility open for some cure"
and that it is important—without telling lies—to "share with them
the hope that something unforeseen may happen" (p. 123).

Although Kübler-Ross believes that doctors and family should make
themselves available to talk frankly about death, she also makes the
important point "that we do not always state explicitly that the patient
is actually terminally ill. We attempt to elicit the patients' needs first
. . . and look for overt or hidden communications to determine how
much a patient wants to face reality at a given moment" (p. 41).

Some doctors say that there will always be certain patients who
don't want to know, and should never be told, that they are dying.
Eissler discusses such a patient (case three) in his book *The Psychiatrist and the Dying Patient*. For more on the subject of telling patients
about their fatal illnesses, see Payne's "The Physician and His Patient
Who Is Dying," *Psychodynamic Studies of the Aging: Creativity, Reminiscing, Dying*, Levin and Kahana, eds., pp. 135–139.

page 348 Denial:
In Kübler-Ross's *On Death and Dying* she notes that after an initial
state of shock, patients respond to news that they are terminally ill
with denial. She says that complete denial is rarely maintained until

the end although partial denial is used by almost all patients from time to time. Patients, she says, "may briefly talk about the reality of their situation, and suddenly indicate their inability to look at it realistically any longer" (pp. 36–37). Later, she says, they may use the defense of isolation rather than denial, and thus talk about health and illness, mortality and immortality, death and hope, as if there were no inherent contradictions.

There is also a good discussion of denial in Payne's "The Physician and His Patient Who Is Dying," see note above, pp. 131–135.

page 348 Anger:

Kübler-Ross notes that the anger and resentment of the dying about having to die may be redirected—displaced onto—family and friends and hospital staff and procedures. She also notes that this anger may be quite rational (having to do, say, with insensitive and incompetent treatment) as well as irrational ("Why couldn't it have been, instead of me, that old and useless fellow down the street?").

page 348 Bargaining:

Kübler-Ross is describing (*On Death and Dying*, p. 73) the bargaining strategy of one of her patients. She notes that such bargaining includes the implicit promise (to the doctor, to God) that if this postponement is granted the patient will not ask for further postponements. She says that none of the patients that she has worked with have kept this promise.

page 348 Depression:

Kübler-Ross distinguishes between two kinds of depression—reactive and preparatory. She says that depression over past losses (reactive depression) may involve sorrows a listener can help to alleviate, whether it is reassurance of a mastectomy patient's continuing femininity or offers of assistance with the management of a household when a patient can no longer manage it him- or herself. However, she says, depression over one's death (preparatory depression) does not call for encouragements and reassurances. She writes: "The patient is in the process of losing everything and everybody he loves. If he is allowed to express his sorrow he will find a final acceptance much easier, and he will be grateful to those who can sit with him during this stage of depression without constantly telling him not to be sad" (*On Death and Dying*, p. 77).

page 348 Acceptance:

Ibid., p. 99, p. 100.

page 349 "against the dying of the light":

In Thomas's "Do Not Go Gentle into That Good Night," *Sound and Sense*, Laurence Perrine, ed., pp. 345–346, his first stanza tells us:

Do not go gentle into that good night,

Old age should burn and rave at close of day;
Rage, rage against the dying of the light.

page 349 And some critics fear:
Another criticism of Kübler-Ross, though it has no bearing on the
validity of *On Death and Dying*, has been her subsequent interest in
supernatural post-death communication.

page 349 Dr. Edwin Shneidman:
Shneidman, *Voices of Death*, "my own..." p. 108; "...I reject..."
p. 108, p. 109; "natural law..." p. 109.

page 349 allowed to be a baby again:
See Payne's "The Physician and His Patient Who Is Dying," *Psychodynamic Studies of the Aging: Creativity, Reminiscing, Dying*, Levin
and Kahana, eds., pp. 141–143, for his discussion of regression. In
The Interpretation of Death, Ruitenbeek, ed., Ruitenbeek quotes from
a tender letter written by a therapist to a girl dying of cancer: "Above
all do not be ashamed of being a baby. We all regress into childhood
when we are in deep discomfort and physical pain" (pp. 3–4). And in
Tolstoy's "The Death of Ivan Ilych" the dying man speaks of his
longing to regress: "At certain moments after prolonged suffering he
wished most of all (though he would have been ashamed to confess
it) for someone to pity him as a sick child is pitied. He longed to be
petted and comforted. He knew that he was an important functionary,
that he had a beard turning gray and that therefore what he longed
for was impossible, but still he longed for it" (p. 286).

page 350 they will teach us:
In addition to Payne (see previous note), several other writings offer
valuable discussions of work with the dying: Eissler, *The Psychiatrist
and the Dying Patient*; Feifel, "Attitudes toward Death in Some Normal and Mentally Ill Populations," *The Meaning of Death*, Feifel, ed.;
Tor-Bjorn Hagglund's *Dying*; and in *The Interpretation of Death*, Ruitenbeek, ed., Janice Norton's "Treatment of a Dying Patient," Hattie
Rosenthal's "Psychotherapy for the Dying" and Lawrence and Eda
LeShan's "Psychotherapy and the Patient with a Limited Life-Span."

page 352 In videotapes about a thirty-nine-year-old doctor:
This material about Dr. Gary Leinbach appears in "A Fatally Ill Doctor's Reaction to Dying," by Lawrence Altman, *The New York Times*,
July 22, 1974, p. 1, p. 26. The story notes that "there are many other
dying patients who, like Dr. Leinbach, put up a fight to the very last."
According to the story the therapy called hyperalimentation (feeding
a patient, through a vein in the neck, a sugar and protein-rich solution)
is usually a temporary post-operative procedure. But when the doctors
hesitated about continuing the hyperalimentation, Dr. Leinbach pressed
them to keep it going, asking them, "How can I live without it?" (p.
26).

page 353 "the condemned cheats the executioner":
Eissler, *The Psychiatrist and the Dying Patient*, p. 66.

page 353 In 1982, for instance:
These are the latest available statistics from the National Center for Health Statistics. The actual suicide rate may be considerably higher; many probable suicides—from overdoses, for instance—may be officially listed as "natural causes."

page 353 Thus Cecil and Julia Saunders:
The story of the Saunderses and of other elderly and terminally ill suicides appears in "Some Elderly Choose Suicide Over Lonely, Dependent Life," by Andrew Malcolm, *The New York Times*, September 24, 1984, p. 1, p. B6. The Saunderses' letter appears on p. B6.

page 354 to reach out a rescuing hand:
In Eissler's *The Psychiatrist and the Dying Patient* he discusses his efforts to dissuade a dying patient from suicide, pp. 186–194.

page 354 "Who knows how he may be tempted":
This quote from Robert Burton's *Anatomy of Melancholy*, a study of suicide published in 1621, is cited in A. Alvarez's *The Savage God*, p. 167. In addition to Alvarez, I found useful discussions of suicide in *Suicide in America*, by Herbert Hendin; and Lifton's *The Broken Connection*, pp. 239–280.

page 354 "care, grief [and] perplexity":
Clemens, *The Autobiography of Mark Twain*, p. 249.

page 355 "Men must endure":
Shakespeare, *King Lear*, Act 5, Scene 2.

page 355 "When I catch myself resenting":
Arnold J. Toynbee, "Why and How I Work," *Saturday Review*, p. 15, April 5, 1969.

page 355 "Without regret for father":
Philippe Ariès quotes these lines from Marguerite de Navarre in his book *The Hour of Our Death*, p. 309.

page 355 "Thou shalt lie down":
William Cullen Bryant, "Thanatopsis," *A Treasury of the World's Best Loved Poems*, pp. 161–163. The lines quoted appear on p. 162.

page 356 "And does it not seem hard to you":
Robert Louis Stevenson, *A Child's Garden of Verses*, "Bed in Summer," p. 9.

page 356 "makes all the difference":
Kaufmann, "Existentialism and Death," *The Meaning of Death*, Herman Feifel, ed., p. 62.

pages 356–57 "A single summer grant me":
This translation, by Kaufmann, of Holderlin's poem appears in Kaufmann's "Existentialism and Death" (see above reference), p. 59.

page 357 "in the face of death":
Ibid., p. 59.

page 357 it "is the person who is convinced":
Rosenthal, "Psychotherapy for the Dying," *The Interpretation of Death*,
Ruitenbeek, ed., p. 94.

page 357 die the way we live:
"They died as they lived," writes Daniel Cappon of some twenty
patients dying in a general hospital in "The Psychology of Dying,"
The Interpretation of Death, Ruitenbeek, ed. "The hostile became
more hostile, the fearful more fearful, the weak weaker" (pp. 62–63).
Shneidman, in his *Voices of Death*, agrees, arguing that "each individual tends to die as he or she has lived, especially as he or she has
previously reacted in periods of threat, stress, failure, challenge, shock
and loss" (p. 110).

pages 357–58 "the knowledge or the vague feeling":
Eissler, *The Psychiatrist and the Dying Patient*, p. 53.

page 358 "a last step forward":
Ibid., p. 54.

page 358 the "perfect death" that is described by Lily Pincus:
Pincus, *Death and the Family*, pp. 6–8.

pages 358–59 "The full awareness of each step":
Eissler, *The Psychiatrist and the Dying Patient*, p. 57.

page 359 rather not be there when it happens:
This is a play on Woody Allen's famous crack: "I'm not afraid to die.
I just don't want to be there when it happens."

page 359 "corresponds exactly":
Ariès, *The Hour of Our Death*, p. 587.

page 359 hospice movement:
See the Institute of Medicine's *Cancer Today: Origins, Prevention and
Treatment*, "Alternative Care for the Dying: American Hospices," pp.
103–116. On a personal note, I was tremendously impressed with the
kindness and competence of the hospice people in their home treatment of my sister during her last days.

page 360 "avoid looking it":
La Rochefoucauld, *The Maxims of the Duc de la Rochefoucauld*, p.
128.

page 360 modes of immortality:
See Lifton's *The Broken Connection*, pp. 13–35, where he discusses the five general modes in which a sense of immortality may be expressed.

page 360 "derived from a more-than-natural source":
Ibid., p. 21.

page 360 "death-transcending truths":
Ibid., p. 20.

page 360 "exorcise the terrors":
Freud, *Standard Edition*, Vol. 21, "The Future of an Illusion," p. 18. In arguing that men can do without "the consolation of the religious illusion," he states that "surely infantilism is destined to be surmounted. Men cannot remain children for ever" (p. 49).

page 361 We can agree with Robert Lifton:
Lifton, *The Broken Connection*, p. 18. Lifton is talking about symbolic—not literal—immortality.

page 361 ". . . Earth, that nourished thee, shall claim":
William Cullen Bryant, "Thanatopsis," *A Treasury of the World's Best Loved Poems*, pp. 161–163. The quoted lines appear on p. 162.

pages 361–62 "Life is atrocious":
Yourcenar, *Memoirs of Hadrian*, p. 293.

page 362 a broader—"biosocial"—image of living on:
Lifton notes in *The Broken Connection* that "the biosocial mode of immortality can be extended outward from family to tribe, organization, subculture, people, nation, or even species. . . . An encompassing vision of biosocial immortality . . . would provide each individual anticipating death with the image: 'I live on in humankind'" (pp. 19–20).

page 362 "an indissoluble bond":
Freud, *Standard Edition*, Vol. 21, "Civilization and Its Discontents," p. 65. Freud is paraphrasing a letter from Romain Rolland, who wrote about his "oceanic" feelings.

page 362 "I cannot discover":
Ibid., p. 65. Freud argues that Rolland's feelings of oneness with the universe can be traced back to babyhood's blurred-boundaries stage. Lifton, however, says that these oneness experiences should not be viewed as merely regressive, for the rediscovery of the harmony, the inner unity, of early childhood is occurring now within an adult framework. See his chapter "The Experience of Transcendence" in *The Broken Connection*, pp. 24–35.

pages 362–63 "Whether you think of it":
de Beauvoir, *A Very Easy Death*, p. 92.

page 363 "I don't want to gain immortality":
Mr. Allen confirms having made this statement, but neither I nor his office have been able to establish where it originally appeared.

page 363 "Not unless I be aware":
In Karen Snow's novel *Willo*, p. 98, her heroine recalls this exchange between the dying Flavian and his friend Marius in the novel *Marius the Epicurean*.

page 363 "a corollary of the knowledge of death":
Lifton, *The Broken Connection*, p. 17.

page 364 "The sunlight on the garden":
MacNeice, "The Sunlight on the Garden," *The Norton Anthology of Poetry*, Allison et al., eds., p. 1127.

Bibliography

Abraham, Karl. 1927. *Selected Papers of Karl Abraham*. New York: Basic Books, Inc.

Ackerman, Nathan. 1966. *Treating the Troubled Family*. New York: Basic Books, Inc.

Adler, Alfred. 1929. *Problems of Neurosis*. London: Kegan Paul, Trench, Trubner & Co., Ltd.

Albee, Edward. 1978. *Who's Afraid of Virginia Woolf?*. New York: Atheneum. (paperback)

Allison, Alexander; Barrows, Herbert; Blake, Caesar; Carr, Arthur; Eastman, Arthur; English, Hubert. 1970, 1975. *The Norton Anthology of Poetry*. New York: W. W. Norton & Co., Inc. (paperback)

Altman, Lawrence. July 22, 1974. "A Fatally Ill Doctor's Reactions to Dying." *The New York Times*, p. 1, p. 26.

Altman, Leon. 1969. *The Dream in Psychoanalysis*. New York: International Universities Press, Inc.

_____. 1977. "Some Vicissitudes of Love." *Journal of the American Psychoanalytic Association*, Vol. 25, No. 1, pp. 35–52.

Alvarez, A. 1970, 1971, 1972. *The Savage God*. New York: Random House.

American Psychiatric Association. 1980. *Diagnostic and Statistical Manual of Mental Disorders*, Third Edition. Washington, D.C.: American Psychiatric Association.

Applegarth, Adrienne. 1976. "Some Observations on Work Inhibitions in Women." *Journal of the American Psychoanalytic Association*, Vol. 24, No. 5, pp. 251–268.

Ariès, Philippe. 1962. *Centuries of Childhood*. New York: Alfred A. Knopf.

_____. 1981. *The Hour of Our Death*. New York: Alfred A. Knopf.

Arnstein, Helene. 1979. *Brothers and Sisters/Sisters and Brothers*. New York: E. P. Dutton.

Auden, W. H. 1950. "As I Walked Out One Evening." *Modern Poetry*, Mack, Dean, Frost, eds. New York: Prentice-Hall, Inc.

_____. 1979. "September 1, 1939." *Selected Poems*, Edward Mendelson, ed. New York: Vintage Books. (paperback)

Bach, George, and Wyden, Peter. 1969. *The Intimate Enemy*. New York: William Morrow and Company, Inc.

Bagarozzi, Dennis, and Anderson, Steven. Winter 1982. "The Evo-

lution of Family Mythological Systems: Considerations for Meaning, Clinical Assessment and Treatment." *The Journal of Psychoanalytic Anthropology*, 5:1, pp. 71–90.

Bak, Robert. 1973. "Being in Love and Object Loss." *The International Journal of Psycho-Analysis*, Vol. 54, Part 1, pp. 1–7.

Balint, Alice. 1949. "Love for the Mother and Mother-Love." *The International Journal of Psycho-Analysis*, Vol. 30, pp. 251–259.

Balint, Michael. 1968. *The Basic Fault*. London: Tavistock Publications.

Bank, Stephen, and Kahn, Michael. 1982. *The Sibling Bond*. New York: Basic Books, Inc.

Bankier, Joanna; Cosman, Carol; Earnshaw, Doris; Keefe, Joan; Lashgari, Deirdre; Weaver, Kathleen. 1976. *The Other Voice: Twentieth-Century Women's Poetry in Transition*. New York: W. W. Norton & Co., Inc.

Becker, Ernest. 1973. *The Denial of Death*. New York: The Free Press. (paperback)

Bell, Robert. 1981. *Worlds of Friendship*. Beverly Hills: Sage Publications.

Benedek, Therese, 1959. "Parenthood as a Developmental Phase." *Journal of the American Psychoanalytic Association*, Vol. 7, pp. 389–417.

———. 1973. *Psychoanalytic Investigations: Selected Papers*. New York: Quadrangle/New York Times.

———. 1977. "Ambivalence, Passion and Love." *Journal of the American Psychoanalytic Association*, Vol. 25, No. 1, pp. 53–79.

Berezin, Martin, 1984. "Psychotherapy of the Elderly." *Aspects of Aging*, No. 4. Philadelphia: SmithKline Beckman Corporation. (unpaged)

Berezin, Martin, and Cath, Stanley, eds. 1965. *Geriatric Psychiatry: Grief, Loss and Emotional Disorders in the Aging Process*. New York: International Universities Press, Inc.

Bergmann, Martin. 1980. "On the Intrapsychic Function of Falling in Love." *The Psychoanalytic Quarterly*, Vol. 49, No. 1, pp. 56–77.

Bernard, Jessie. 1982. *The Future of Marriage*. New Haven and London: Yale University Press. (paperback)

Bettelheim, Bruno. 1954. *Symbolic Wounds*. Glencoe, Illinois: The Free Press.

———. 1983. *Freud and Man's Soul*. New York: Alfred A. Knopf.

Blos, Peter. 1962. *On Adolescence*. New York: The Free Press.

Blume, Judy. 1970. *Are You There, God? It's Me, Margaret*. New York: Dell Publishing Co., Inc. (paperback)

Blythe, Ronald. 1979. *The View in Winter*. New York and London:

Harcourt Brace Jovanovich.

Boehm, Felix. October 1930. "The Femininity-Complex in Men." *The International Journal of Psycho-Analysis*, Vol. 11, Part 4, pp. 444–469.

Bowlby, John. 1969. *Attachment*. New York: Basic Books, Inc.

———. 1973. *Separation*. New York: Basic Books, Inc.

———. 1980. *Loss*. New York: Basic Books, Inc.

Brain, Robert. 1976. *Friends and Lovers*. New York: Basic Books, Inc.

Bralove, Mary. Nov. 9, 1981. "Husband's Hazard." *The Wall Street Journal*, pp. 1, 24.

Breger, Louis. 1974. *From Instinct to Identity*. Englewood Cliffs, New Jersey: Prentice-Hall, Inc.

Brenner, Charles. 1974. *An Elementary Textbook of Psychoanalysis*. New York: Anchor Books. (paperback)

Bruch, Hilde. 1980. "The Sleeping Beauty: Escape from Change." *The Course of Life*, Vol. 2, Greenspan and Pollock, eds.

Bryant, William Cullen. 1961. "Thanatopsis." *A Treasury of the World's Best Loved Poetry*. New York: Avenel Books.

Buber, Martin. May 1957. "Guilt and Guilt Feelings." *Psychiatry*, Vol. 20, No. 2, pp. 114–129.

Busse, Ewald, and Feiffer, Eric. 1969. *Behavior and Adaptation in Late Life*. Boston: Little, Brown and Company.

Butler, Robert. February 1963. "The Life Review: An Interpretation of Reminiscence in the Aged." *Psychiatry*, Vol. 26, No. 1, pp. 65–76.

———. 1975. *Why Survive?* New York: Harper & Row.

Caine, Lynn. 1974. *Widow*. New York: Bantam Books. (paperback)

Cappon, Daniel. 1969, 1973. "The Psychology of Dying." *The Interpretation of Death*, Hendrik Ruitenbeek, ed. New York: Jason Aronson.

Cath, Stanley, Gurwitt, Alan, and Ross, John Munder. 1982. *Father and Child*. Boston: Little, Brown and Company.

Charny, Israel. March 1969. "Marital Love and Hate." *Family Process*, Vol. 8, No. 1, pp. 1–24.

Chasseguet-Smirgel, Janine. 1976. "Freud and Female Sexuality: The Consideration of Some Blind Spots in the Exploration of the 'Dark Continent.'" *The International Journal of Psycho-Analysis*, Vol. 57, Part 3, pp. 275–286.

Chess, Stella, and Thomas, Alexander. 1973. "Temperament in the Normal Infant." *Individual Differences in Children*, Jack Westman, ed. New York: John Wiley & Sons.

Cicero, Marcus Tullius. 1909. "On Friendship." *The Harvard Classics*, Vol. 9, *Letters of Marcus Tullius Cicero and Letters of Gaius Plinius Caecilius Secundus*, Charles Eliot, ed. New York: P. F. Collier & Son.

Cicirelli, Victor. 1982. "Sibling Influence Throughout the Lifespan." *Sibling Relationships: Their Nature and Significance Across the Lifespan*, Michael Lamb and Brian Sutton-Smith, eds. Hillsdale, New Jersey: Lawrence Erlbaum Associates.

Cleckley, Hervey. 1964. *The Mask of Sanity*. Saint Louis: The C. V. Mosby Company.

Clemens, Samuel. 1959. *The Autobiography of Mark Twain*, arranged and edited by Charles Neider. New York: Harper.

Colarusso, Calvin, and Nemiroff, Robert. 1981. *Adult Development*. New York and London: Plenum Press.

Conrad, Joseph. 1902. *Heart of Darkness*. Great Britain: Penguin Books. (paperback)

Cowley, Malcolm. 1980. *The View from 80*. New York: The Viking Press.

Crook, Thomas, and Cohen, Gene. 1983. *Physicians' Guide to the Diagnosis and Treatment of Depression in the Elderly*. New Canaan: Mark Powley Associates, Inc.

Dante Alighieri. 1980. *The Divine Comedy*, Charles Singleton, translator. Princeton: Princeton University Press. (paperback)

de Beauvoir, Simone. 1966. *A Very Easy Death* (originally published in 1964). New York: G. P. Putnam's Sons.

———. 1971. *The Woman Destroyed*. Great Britain: Fontana/Collins. (paperback)

———. 1972. *The Coming of Age*. New York: G. P. Putnam's Sons.

Deutsch, Helene. 1965. *Neuroses and Character Types*. New York: International Universities Press, Inc.

Dew, Robb Forman. 1979, 1981. *Dale Loves Sophie to Death*. New York: Penguin Books. (paperback)

Dicks, Henry. 1967. *Marital Tensions*. New York: Basic Books.

Dillard, Annie. 1974. *Pilgrim at Tinker Creek*. New York: Harper's Magazine Press.

———. 1982. *Teaching a Stone to Talk*. New York: Harper & Row.

Dinnerstein, Dorothy. 1977. *The Mermaid and the Minotaur*. New York: Harper & Row. (paperback)

Dowling, Colette. 1982. *The Cinderella Complex*. New York: Pocket Books. (paperback)

Dowson, Ernest. 1970, 1975. "Non sum qualis eram bonae subregno Cynarae." *The Norton Anthology of Poetry*, Allison et al., eds. (paperback)

Edel, Leon. 1972. *Henry James, The Master: 1901–1916*. Vol. 5. New York: Avon Books. (paperback)

———. 1982. *Stuff of Sleep and Dreams*. New York: Avon Books. (paperback)

Eissler, K. R. 1955. *The Psychiatrist and the Dying Patient*. New York: International Universities Press, Inc. (paperback)

———. 1977. "Comments on Penis Envy and Orgasm in Women." *The Psychoanalytic Study of the Child*, Vol. 32. New York:

International Universities Press, Inc.

Ephron, Delia. 1981. *Teenage Romance*. New York: Ballantine Books. (paperback)

Erikson, Erik. 1950, 1963. *Childhood and Society*. New York: W. W. Norton & Co., Inc. (paperback)

———. January 1954. "The Dream Specimen of Psychoanalysis." *Journal of the American Psychoanalytic Association*, Vol. 2, No. 1, pp. 5–56.

———. 1968. *Identity: Youth and Crisis*. New York: W. W. Norton & Co., Inc.

Esman, Aaron. 1980. "Mid-Adolescence—Foundations for Later Psychopathology." *The Course of Life*, Vol. 2, Greenspan and Pollock, eds.

Fairbairn, W. R. D. 1952. *Psychoanalytic Studies of the Personality*. London: Tavistock Publications Limited.

———. 1954. *An Object-Relations Theory of the Personality*. New York: Basic Books, Inc.

Farber, Leslie. October 1973. "On Jealousy." *Commentary*, pp. 50–58.

Featherstone, Joseph. February 1979. "Family Matters." *Harvard Educational Review*, Vol. 49, No. 1, pp. 20–52.

Feifel, Herman. 1959. "Attitudes Toward Death in Some Normal and Mentally Ill Populations." *The Meaning of Death*, Herman Feifel, ed. New York: McGraw-Hill Book Company, Inc.

———, ed. 1959. *The Meaning of Death*. New York: McGraw-Hill Book Company, Inc.

Feldman, Sandor. September 1969. "On Romance." *Bulletin of the Philadelphia Association for Psychoanalysis*, Vol. 19, No. 3, pp. 153–157.

Fenichel, Otto. 1953. *The Collected Papers of Otto Fenichel*. New York: W. W. Norton & Co., Inc.

Ferenczi, Sandor. 1950. *Sex in Psychoanalysis*. New York: Basic Books, Inc.

Ferreira, Antonio. November 1963. "Family Myth and Homeostasis." *Archives of General Psychiatry*, Vol. 9, pp. 457–463.

Fields, Suzanne. 1983. *Like Father, Like Daughter*. Boston: Little, Brown and Company.

Fishel, Elizabeth. 1979. *Sisters*. New York: William Morrow and Co., Inc.

Fisher, M. F. K. 1983. *Sister Age*. New York: Alfred A. Knopf.

Fitzgerald, F. Scott. 1933. *Tender Is the Night*. New York: Charles Scribner's Sons. (paperback)

Flaubert, Gustave. 1981. *Madame Bovary* (originally published in 1857). New York, Toronto, London: Bantam Books. (paperback)

Fontaine, Joan. 1978. *No Bed of Roses*. New York: William Morrow & Company, Inc.

Forster, E. M. 1921. *Howards End*. New York: Vintage Books.

The Foster Care Monitoring Committee. 1984. *Foster Care 1984: A Report on the Implementation of the Recommendations of the Mayor's Task Force on Foster Care*.

Fraiberg, Selma. 1959. *The Magic Years*. New York: Charles Scribner's Sons.

—————. 1969. "Libidinal Object Constancy and Mental Representation." *The Psychoanalytic Study of the Child*, Vol. 24. New York: International Universities Press, Inc.

—————. 1977. *Every Child's Birthright*. New York: Basic Books, Inc.

Francke, Linda Bird. May 22, 1983. "The Sons of Divorce." *The New York Times Magazine*, pp. 40–41, 54–57.

Freud, Anna. 1952. "A Connection Between the States of Negativism and of Emotional Surrender." *The International Journal of Psycho-Analysis*, Vol. 33, Part 3, p. 265.

—————. 1958. "Adolescence." *The Psychoanalytic Study of the Child*, Vol. 13. New York: International Universities Press, Inc.

—————. 1965. *Normality and Pathology in Childhood*. New York: International Universities Press, Inc.

—————. 1966. *The Ego and the Mechanisms of Defense*. New York: International Universities Press, Inc. (paperback)

Freud, Anna, and Burlingham, Dorothy. 1943. *War and Children*. New York: International Universities Press, Inc.

Freud, Anna, and Burlingham, Dorothy. 1944. *Infants Without Families*. New York: International Universities Press, Inc.

Freud, Ernst, ed. 1960, 1975. *The Letters of Sigmund Freud*. New York: Basic Books, Inc. (paperback)

Freud, Sigmund. 1953. "The Interpretation of Dreams" (originally published in 1900). *Standard Edition*, Vols. 4 and 5, James Strachey, ed. London: The Hogarth Press.

—————. 1953. "Some Reflections on Schoolboy Psychology" (originally published in 1914). *Standard Edition*, Vol. 13, James Strachey, ed. London: The Hogarth Press.

—————. 1953. "Three Essays on the Theory of Sexuality" (originally published in 1905). *Standard Edition*, Vol. 7, James Strachey, ed. London: The Hogarth Press.

—————. 1953. "Totem and Taboo" (originally published in 1913 [1912–1913]). *Standard Edition*, Vol. 13, James Strachey, ed. London: The Hogarth Press.

—————. 1955. "Beyond the Pleasure Principle" (originally published in 1920). *Standard Edition*, Vol. 18, James Strachey, ed. London: The Hogarth Press.

—————. 1955. "Group Psychology and the Analysis of the Ego" (originally published in 1921). *Standard Edition*, Vol. 18, James Strachey, ed. London: The Hogarth Press.

—————. 1957. "A Metapsychological Supplement to the Theory of Dreams" (originally published in 1917 [1915]). *Standard Edi-*

tion, Vol. 14, James Strachey, ed. London: The Hogarth Press.

_____. 1957. "Mourning and Melancholia" (originally published in 1917 [1915]). *Standard Edition*, Vol. 14, James Strachey, ed. London: The Hogarth Press.

_____. 1957. "On Narcissism: An Introduction" (originally published in 1914). *Standard Edition*, Vol. 14, James Strachey, ed. London: The Hogarth Press.

_____. 1957. "Some Character-Types Met With in Psycho-Analytic Work" (originally published in 1916). *Standard Edition*, Vol. 14, James Strachey, ed. London: The Hogarth Press.

_____. 1957. "A Special Type of Choice of Object Made by Men" (originally published in 1910). *Standard Edition*, Vol. 11, James Strachey, ed. London: The Hogarth Press.

_____. 1957. "Thoughts for the Times on War and Death" (originally published in 1915). *Standard Edition*, Vol. 14, James Strachey, ed. London: The Hogarth Press.

_____. 1958. "The Dynamics of Transference" (originally published in 1912). *Standard Edition*, Vol. 12, James Strachey, ed. London: The Hogarth Press.

_____. 1958. "Observations on Transference-Love" (originally published in 1915 [1914]). *Standard Edition*, Vol. 12, James Strachey, ed. London: The Hogarth Press.

_____. 1958. "Remembering, Repeating and Working-Through" (originally published in 1914). *Standard Edition*, Vol. 12, James Strachey, ed. London: The Hogarth Press.

_____. 1959. "An Autobiographical Study" (originally published in 1925 [1924]). *Standard Edition*, Vol. 20, James Strachey, ed. London: The Hogarth Press.

_____. 1959. "Inhibitions, Symptoms and Anxiety" (originally published in 1926 [1925]). *Standard Edition*, Vol. 20, James Strachey, ed. London: The Hogarth Press.

_____. 1961. "Civilization and Its Discontents" (originally published in 1930 [1929]). *Standard Edition*, Vol. 21, James Strachey, ed. London: The Hogarth Press.

_____. 1961. "The Dissolution of the Oedipus Complex" (originally published in 1924). *Standard Edition*, Vol. 19, James Strachey, ed. London: The Hogarth Press.

_____. 1961. "The Economic Problem of Masochism" (originally published in 1924). *Standard Edition*, Vol. 19, James Strachey, ed. London: The Hogarth Press.

_____. 1961. "The Ego and the Id" (originally published in 1923). *Standard Edition*, Vol. 19, James Strachey, ed. London: The Hogarth Press.

_____. 1961. "Female Sexuality" (originally published in 1931). *Standard Edition*, Vol. 21, James Strachey, ed. London: The Hogarth Press.

————. 1961. "The Future of an Illusion" (originally published in 1927). *Standard Edition*, Vol. 21, James Strachey, ed. London: The Hogarth Press.

————. 1961. "Introductory Lectures on Psycho-Analysis, Parts I and II" (originally published in 1916–1917 [1915–1917]). *Standard Edition*, Vol. 15, James Strachey, ed. London: The Hogarth Press.

————. 1961. "Some Psychical Consequences of the Anatomical Distinction Between the Sexes" (originally published in 1925). *Standard Edition*, Vol. 19, James Strachey, ed. London: The Hogarth Press.

————. 1963. "Introductory Lectures on Psycho-Analysis, Part III" (originally published in 1916–1917 [1915–1917]). *Standard Edition*, Vol. 16, James Strachey, ed. London: The Hogarth Press.

————. 1964. "New Introductory Lectures on Psycho-Analysis" (originally published in 1933 [1932]). *Standard Edition*, Vol. 22, James Strachey, ed. London: The Hogarth Press.

————. 1964. "An Outline of Psycho-Analysis" (originally published in 1940 [1938]). *Standard Edition*, Vol. 23, James Strachey, ed. London: The Hogarth Press.

Frisch, Max. 1958. *I'm Not Stiller*. New York: Vintage Books. (paperback)

Fromm, Erich. 1956. *The Art of Loving*. New York: Harper & Brothers.

Furman, Edna. 1974. *A Child's Parent Dies*. New Haven and London: Yale University Press.

Gilligan, Carol. 1982. *In a Different Voice*. Cambridge, Mass: Harvard University Press. (paperback)

Ginott, Haim. 1965. *Between Parent and Child*. New York: The Macmillan Company.

Giovacchini, Peter. Spring 1967. "Characterological Aspects of Marital Interaction." *The Psychoanalytic Forum*, Vol. 2, No. 1, pp. 7–29.

Gold, Herbert. 1968. *Fathers*. Greenwich, Conn.: Fawcett Publications, Inc. (paperback)

Goldstein, Joseph; Freud, Anna; Solnit, Albert J. 1973, 1979. *Beyond the Best Interests of the Child*. New York: The Free Press. (paperback)

Goodman, Lisl. 1981, 1983. *Death and the Creative Life*. New York: Penguin Books. (paperback)

Gorer, Geoffrey. 1965. *Death, Grief, and Mourning*. New York: Doubleday & Company, Inc.

Gornick, Vivian. May 31, 1973. "Toward a Definition of a Female Sensibility." *The Village Voice*.

Gould, Roger. 1978. *Transformations*. New York: Simon and Schuster. (paperback)

_____. 1981. "Transformational Tasks in Adulthood." *The Course of Life*, Vol. 3, Greenspan and Pollock, eds., pp. 55–89.

Greenacre, Phyllis. 1971. *Emotional Growth*, Vol. 2. New York: International Universities Press, Inc.

Greene, Bob. 1985. *Good Morning, Merry Sunshine*. New York: Penguin Books. (paperback)

Greenspan, Stanley. 1981. *Psychopathology and Adaptation in Infancy and Early Childhood*. New York: International Universities Press, Inc.

_____. 1982. "'The Second Other'—The Role of the Father in Early Personality Formation and in the Dyadic-Phallic Phase of Development." *Anthology on Fatherhood*, S. Cath, A. Gurwitt, J. Ross, eds. Boston: Little, Brown and Company.

Greenspan, Stanley, and Lieberman, Alicia. 1980. "Infants, Mothers and Their Interaction: A Quantitative Clinical Approach to Development Assessment." *The Course of Life*, Vol. 1, Greenspan and Pollock, eds.

Greenspan, Stanley, and Pollock, George, eds. 1980. *The Course of Life*, Vol. 1: *Infancy and Early Childhood*. Washington, D.C.: Government Printing Office. DHHS Pub. No. (ADM) 80–786.

_____. 1980. *The Course of Life*, Vol. 2: *Latency, Adolescence and Youth*. Washington, D.C.: Government Printing Office. DHHS Pub. No. (ADM) 80–999.

_____. 1981. *The Course of Life*, Vol. 3: *Adulthood and the Aging Process*. Washington, D.C.: Government Printing Office. DHHS Pub. No. (ADM) 81–1000.

Grene, David, and Lattimore, Richmond, eds. 1954. *Sophocles I*. Chicago and London: The University of Chicago Press. (paperback)

Grossman, William, and Stewart, Walter. 1976. "Penis Envy: From Childhood Wish to Development Metaphor." *Journal of the American Psychoanalytic Association*, Vol. 24, No. 5, pp. 193–212.

Group for the Advancement of Psychiatry. 1973. *The Joys and Sorrows of Parenthood*. New York: Charles Scribner's Sons.

_____. 1983. *Friends and Lovers in the College Years*. New York: Mental Health Materials Center. (paperback)

Gunther, John. 1949. *Death Be Not Proud*. New York: Harper & Brothers.

Gutmann, David. 1981. "Psychoanalysis and Aging: A Development View." *The Course of Life*, Vol. 3, Greenspan and Pollock, eds.

Hagglund, Tor-Bjorn. 1978. *Dying*. New York: International Universities Press, Inc.

Handel, Gerald, ed. 1967. *The Psychosocial Interior of the Family*. Chicago: Aldine Atherton.

Hartmann, Heinz, and Loewenstein, R. M. 1962. "Notes on the Su-

perego." *The Psychoanalytic Study of the Child*, Vol. 17. New York: International Universities Press, Inc.

Hayward, Brooke. 1978. *Haywire*. New York: Bantam Books. (paperback)

Heinicke, Christoph, and Westheimer, Ilse. 1965. *Brief Separations*. New York: International Universities Press, Inc.

Hemingway, Ernest. 1929. *A Farewell to Arms*. New York: Bantam Books. (paperback)

Hendin, Herbert. 1982. *Suicide in America*. New York: W. W. Norton & Co.

Hess, Robert, and Handel, Gerald. 1967. "The Family as a Psychosocial Organization." *The Psychosocial Interior of the Family*, Gerald Handel, ed.

Hilgard, Josephine. 1951. "Sibling Rivalry and Social Heredity." *Psychiatry*, Vol. 14, No. 4, pp. 375–385.

Hillesum, Etty. 1981, 1983. *An Interrupted Life*. New York: Pantheon Books.

Hite, Shere. 1976. *The Hite Report*. New York: Macmillan Publishing Co., Inc.

Hitschmann, Edward. 1952. "Freud's Conception of Love." *The International Journal of Psycho-Analysis*, Vol. 33, Part 4, pp. 421–428.

Holy Bible

Howard, Jane. 1978. *Families*. New York: Simon and Schuster.

Howells, William Dean. 1951 (originally published in 1885). *The Rise of Silas Lapham*. New York: Random House, Inc.

Institute of Medicine, Marian Osterweis, Fredric Solomon and Morris Green, eds. 1984. *Bereavement: Reactions, Consequences, and Care*. Washington, D.C.: National Academy Press.

Institute of Medicine. 1984. *Cancer Today: Origins, Prevention and Treatment*. Washington, D.C.: National Academy Press. (paperback)

Irving, John. 1976, 1977, 1978. *The World According to Garp*. New York: E. P. Dutton.

Jacobs, Theodore. 1980. "Secrets, Alliances and Family Fictions: Some Psychoanalytic Observations." *Journal of the American Psychoanalytic Association*, Vol. 28, No. 1, pp. 21–42.

Jacobson, Edith. 1964. *The Self and the Object World*. New York: International Universities Press, Inc.

Jacobson, Gerald. 1983. *The Multiple Crises of Marital Separation and Divorce*. New York: Grune & Stratton.

Jaffe, Daniel. 1968. "The Masculine Envy of Woman's Procreative Function." *Journal of the American Psychoanalytic Association*, Vol. 16, No. 3, pp. 521–548.

James, William. 1950. *The Principles of Psychology* (originally published in 1890). New York: Dover Publications, Inc.

_____. 1961. *The Varieties of Religious Experience*. New York: Collier Books. (paperback)

Jaques, Elliott. 1981. "The Midlife Crisis." *The Course of Life*, Vol. 3, Greenspan and Pollock, eds.

Johnson, Ann Braden. 1977. "A Temple of Last Resorts: Youth and Shared Narcissisms." *The Narcissistic Condition*, Marie Coleman Nelson, ed. New York: Human Science Press.

Jones, Ernest. 1955. *Hamlet and Oedipus*. New York: Doubleday Anchor Books. (paperback)

Joseph, Jenny. 1973. "Warning." *The Oxford Book of Twentieth Century English Verse*, Philip Larkin, ed. London: Oxford University Press.

Jung, Carl. 1971. *The Portable Jung*, Joseph Campbell, ed. New York: The Viking Press. (paperback)

Kagan, Jerome; Kearsley, Richard B., and Zelazo, Philip R. 1978. *Infancy*. Cambridge, Massachusetts, and London: Harvard University Press.

Kaplan, Louis. 1970. "Some Thoughts on the Nature of Women." *Bulletin of the Philadelphia Association of Psychoanalysis*, Vol. 20, pp. 319–328.

Kaufmann, Walter. 1959. "Existentialism and Death." *The Meaning of Death*, Herman Feifel, ed. New York: McGraw-Hill Book Company, Inc.

Kernberg, Otto. 1975. *Borderline Conditions and Pathological Narcissism*. New York: Jason Aronson, Inc.

_____. 1976. *Object-Relations Theory and Clinical Psychoanalysis*. New York: Jason Aronson, Inc.

_____. 1977. "Boundaries and Structure in Love Relations." *Journal of the American Psychoanalytic Association*, Vol. 25, No. 1, pp. 81–114.

_____. 1980. "Adolescent Sexuality in the Light of Group Process." *The Psychoanalytic Quarterly*, Vol. 49, No. 1, pp. 26–47.

_____. 1980. "Love, the Couple and the Group: A Psychoanalytic Frame." *The Psychoanalytic Quarterly*, Vol. 49, No. 1, pp. 78–108.

Kestenberg, Judith. 1970. "The Effect on Parents of the Child's Transition Into and Out of Latency." *Parenthood: Its Psychology and Psychopathology*. E. James Anthony and Therese Benedek, eds. Boston: Little, Brown and Company.

_____. 1980. "Eleven, Twelve, Thirteen: Years of Transition From the Barrenness of Childhood to the Fertility of Adolescence." *The Course of Life*, Vol. 2, Greenspan and Pollock, eds.

Kleeman, James. 1976. "Freud's Views on Early Female Sexuality in the Light of Direct Child Observation." *Journal of the American Psychoanalytic Association*, Vol. 24, No. 5, pp. 3–27.

Klein, Melanie. 1969, 1973. "Mourning and Its Relation to Manic-

Depressive States." *The Interpretation of Death*, Hendrik Ruitenbeek, ed. New York: Jason Aronson, Inc.

Kliman, Gilbert, and Rosenfeld, Albert. 1980. *Responsible Parenthood*. New York: Holt, Rinehart and Winston.

Kohlberg, Lawrence, and Gilligan, Carol. 1971. "The Adolescent as a Philosopher: The Discovery of the Self in a Postconventional World." *Daedalus* 100, pp. 1051–1086.

Kohlberg, L., and Kramer, R. 1969. "Continuities and Discontinuities in Child and Adult Moral Development." *Human Development* 12, pp. 93–120.

Kohut, Heinz. 1971. *The Analysis of the Self*. New York: International Universities Press, Inc.

———. 1977. *The Restoration of the Self*. New York: International Universities Press, Inc.

Krent, Justin. 1978. "Some Thoughts on Aggression." *Journal of the American Psychoanalytic Association*, Vol. 26, No. 1, pp. 185–232.

Kris, Ernst. 1975. *Selected Papers of Ernst Kris*. New Haven and London: Yale University Press.

Kubie, Lawrence. 1939. "A Critical Analysis of the Concept of a Repetition Compulsion." *The International Journal of Psycho-Analysis*, Vol. 20, Parts 3 and 4, pp. 390–402.

———. 1974. "The Drive to Become Both Sexes." *The Psychoanalytic Quarterly*, Vol. 43, No. 3, pp. 349–426.

Kübler-Ross, Elizabeth. 1969. *On Death and Dying*. London: Collier-Macmillan Ltd.

Kumin, Maxine. 1982. *Our Ground Time Here Will Be Brief*. New York: Penguin Books. (paperback)

Kushner, Harold. 1981. *When Bad Things Happen to Good People*. New York: Schocken Books.

Lamb, Michael, ed. 1976. *The Role of the Father in Child Development*. New York: John Wiley and Sons.

Lamb, Michael E., and Sutton-Smith, Brian, eds. 1982. *Sibling Relationships: Their Nature and Significance Across the Lifespan*. Hillsdale, New Jersey: Lawrence Erlbaum Associates.

Lampl-De Groot, J. 1928. "The Evolution of the Oedipus Complex in Women." *The International Journal of Psycho-Analysis*, Vol. 9, pp. 332–345.

Larkin, Philip, ed. 1973. *The Oxford Book of Twentieth Century English Verse*. London: Oxford University Press.

La Rochefoucauld, François, Duc de. 1957. *The Maxims of the Duc de la Rochefoucauld*. London: Allan Wingate.

Lasch, Christopher. 1977. *Haven in a Heartless World*. New York: Basic Books, Inc.

———. 1978. *The Culture of Narcissism*. New York: W. W. Norton & Co., Inc.

Lawrence, D. H. 1957. *Lady Chatterley's Lover*. New York: Grove Press, Inc.

Lazarre, Jane. 1976. *The Mother Knot*. New York: McGraw-Hill.

LeShan, Lawrence, and LeShan, Eda. 1969, 1973. "Psychotherapy and the Patient with a Limited Lifespan." *The Interpretation of Death*, Hendrik Ruitenbeek, ed. New York: Jason Aronson, Inc., Publishers.

Levin, Sidney, and Kahana, Ralph, eds. 1967. *Psychodynamic Studies on Aging: Creativity, Reminiscing and Dying*. New York: International Universities Press, Inc.

Levinson, Daniel. 1978. *The Seasons of a Man's Life*. New York: Ballantine Books. (paperback)

Levy, David. 1937. *Studies in Sibling Rivalry*. American Orthopsychiatric Association.

Lewis, C. S. 1963. *A Grief Observed*. New York: Bantam Books. (paperback)

Lichtenstein, Heinz. 1963. "The Dilemma of Human Identity: Notes on Self-Transformation, Self-Objectivation and Metamorphosis." *Journal of the American Psychoanalytic Association*, Vol. 11, No. 1, pp. 173–223.

Lidz, Theodore. 1975. *Hamlet's Enemy*. New York: Basic Books, Inc.

Lifton, Robert Jay. 1979. *The Broken Connection*. New York: Simon and Schuster.

Lipson, Channing. 1969, 1973. "Denial and Mourning." *The Interpretation of Death*, Hendrik Ruitenbeek, ed. New York: Jason Aronson, Inc.

Loewald, Hans. 1960. "On the Therapeutic Action of Psychoanalysis." *The International Journal of Psycho-Analysis*, Vol. 41, Part 1, pp. 16–33.

———. 1978. "Instinct Theory, Object Relations and Psychic-Structure Formation." *Journal of the American Psychoanalytic Association*, Vol. 26, No. 3, pp. 493–506.

———. 1978. *Psychoanalysis and the History of the Individual*. New Haven and London: Yale University Press.

———. 1979. "The Waning of the Oedipus Complex." *Journal of the American Psychoanalytic Association*, Vol. 27, No. 4, pp. 751–775.

Lomas, Peter. 1961. "Family Role and Identity Formation." *The International Journal of Psycho-Analysis*, Vol. 42, Parts 4–5, pp. 371–380.

Longfellow, Henry Wadsworth. 1893. "Morituri Salutamus." *The Complete Poetical Works of Henry Wadsworth Longfellow*. Boston: Houghton Mifflin Company.

Lorenz, Konrad. 1974. *On Aggression*. New York and London: Harcourt Brace Jovanovich, Publishers. (paperback)

Lowell, James Russell. 1925. *The Complete Poetical Works of James*

Russell Lowell. Cambridge: The Riverside Press.

Maccoby, Eleanor, and Jacklin, Carol. 1974. *The Psychology of Sex Differences*. Stanford, California: Stanford University Press.

Macdonald, Cynthia. 1979. "Accomplishments." *A Geography of Poets*, Edward Field, ed. New York: Bantam Books.

Mack, Maynard; Dean, Leonard; Frost, William, eds. 1950. *Modern Poetry*. New York: Prentice-Hall, Inc.

MacLeish, Archibald. 1956. *J.B.* Cambridge, Mass.: The Riverside Press.

MacNeice, Louis. 1950. "Les Sylphides." *Modern Poetry*, Mack, Dean, Frost, eds. New York: Prentice-Hall, Inc.

————. 1970, 1975. "The Sunlight on the Garden." *The Norton Anthology of Poetry*, Allison et al., eds. New York: W. W. Norton & Company. (paperback)

Mahler, Margaret. 1968. *On Human Symbiosis and the Vicissitudes of Individuation*, Vol. I. New York: International Universities Press, Inc.

Mahler, Margaret, and McDevitt, John. 1980. "The Separation-Individuation Process and Identity Formation." *The Course of Life*, Vol. 1, Greenspan and Pollock, eds.

Mahler, Margaret; Pine, Fred; and Bergman, Anni. 1975. *The Psychological Birth of the Human Infant*. New York: Basic Books, Inc.

Malcolm, Andrew. September 24, 1984. "Some Elderly Choose Suicide Over Lonely, Dependent Life." *The New York Times*, pp. 1, B6.

Mann, John. 1980, 1982. *Secrets of Life Extension*. New York: Bantam Books. (paperback)

Mann, Thomas. 1969. *The Magic Mountain* (originally published in German, 1924, and in English, 1927). New York: Random House. (Vintage Books paperback)

Marquis, Don. 1927. *archy and mehitabel*. New York: Doubleday & Co., Inc.

Masters, William, and Johnson, Virginia, in association with Robert Levin. 1976. *The Pleasure Bond*. Toronto/New York/London: Bantam Books. (paperback)

May, Rollo. 1969. *Love and Will*. New York: Dell Publishing Co., Inc.

McDevitt, John. 1979. "The Role of Internalization in the Development of Object Relations During the Separation-Individuation Phase." *Journal of the American Psychoanalytic Association*, Vol. 27, No. 2, pp. 327–343.

McDevitt, John, and Mahler, Margaret. 1980. "Object Constancy, Individuality and Internalization." *The Course of Life*, Vol. 1, Greenspan and Pollock, eds.

McGlashan, Thomas, and Miller, Glenn. April 1982. "The Goals of Psychoanalysis and Psychoanalytic Psychotherapy." *Archives of General Psychiatry*, Vol. 39.

McMahon, James. 1982. "Intimacy Among Friends and Lovers." *Intimacy*, Martin Fisher and George Stricker, eds. New York: Plenum Press.

Mead, Margaret. 1972. *Blackberry Winter*. New York: William Morrow & Co., Inc.

———. 1975. *Male and Female* (originally published in 1949). New York: William Morrow & Co., Inc. (paperback)

Menninger, Karl. 1942. *Love Against Hate*. New York: Harcourt, Brace and Co.

Michaels, Leonard. 1978. *The Men's Club*. New York: Farrar, Straus and Giroux.

Milgram, Stanley. 1974. *Obedience to Authority*. New York: Harper & Row.

Miller, Alice. *Prisoners of Childhood*. 1981. New York: Basic Books, Inc.

Miller, Arthur. 1958. *Death of a Salesman*. New York: The Viking Press. (paperback)

Mittelmann, Bela. 1944. "Complementary Neurotic Reactions in Intimate Relationships." *The Psychoanalytic Quarterly*, Vol. 13, No. 4, pp. 479–491.

Modell, Arnold. 1965. "On Having the Right to a Life: An Aspect of the Superego's Development." *The International Journal of Psycho-Analysis*, Vol. 46, Part 3, pp. 323–331.

———. 1975. "The Ego and the Id: Fifty Years Later." *The International Journal of Psycho-Analysis*, Vol. 56, Part 1, pp. 57–68.

Moffat, Mary Jane, ed. 1982. *In the Midst of Winter: Selections from the Literature of Mourning*. New York: Random House.

Moore, Burness. 1976. "Freud and Female Sexuality: A Current View." *The International Journal of Psycho-Analysis*, Vol. 57, Part 3, pp. 287–300.

Morrison, Toni. 1972. *The Bluest Eye*. New York: Pocket Books. (paperback)

Nabokov, Vladimir. 1966. *Speak, Memory*. New York: G. P. Putnam's Sons.

Nacht, Sacha, and Viderman, S. 1960. "The Pre-Object Universe in the Transference Situation." *The International Journal of Psycho-Analysis*, Vol. 41, Parts 4–5, pp. 385–388.

Natterson, Joseph, ed. 1980. *The Dream in Clinical Practice*. New York: Jason Aronson.

Nelson, Bryce. February 15, 1983. "Self-Sabotage in Careers—A Common Trap." *The New York Times*.

Nelson, John, and Cargill, Oscar, eds. 1949. *Contemporary Trends*. New York: The Macmillan Company.

Neubauer, Peter. 1960. "The One-Parent Child and His Oedipal Development." *The Psychoanalytic Study of the Child*, Vol. 15. New York: International Universities Press, Inc.

Neugarten, Bernice; Havighurst, Robert; and Tobin, Sheldon. 1968. "Personality and Patterns of Aging." *Middle Age and Aging*, Bernice Neugarten, ed. Chicago and London: The University of Chicago Press.

Neugarten, Bernice, ed. 1968. *Middle Age and Aging*. Chicago and London: The University of Chicago Press.

Norton, Janice. 1969, 1973. "Treatment of a Dying Patient." *The Interpretation of Death*, Hendrik Ruitenbeek, ed. New York: Jason Aronson.

Noshpitz, Joseph. 1980. "Disturbances in Early Adolescent Development." *The Course of Life*, Vol. 2, Greenspan and Pollock, eds.

Offer, Daniel. 1980. "Adolescent Development: A Normative Perspective." *The Course of Life*, Vol. 2, Greenspan and Pollock, eds.

Ogden, Thomas. 1982. *Projective Identification and Psychotherapeutic Technique*. New York and London: Jason Aronson.

O'Neill, Eugene. 1955. *Long Day's Journey Into Night*. New Haven and London: Yale University Press. (paperback)

O'Neill, Nena. 1978. *The Marriage Premise*. New York: Bantam Books. (paperback)

Panel, David Rubinfine, reporter 1958. "Problems of Identity." *Journal of the American Psychoanalytic Association*, Vol. 6, No. 1, pp. 131–142.

Panel, Irving Sternschein, reporter. 1973. "The Experience of Separation-Individuation in Infancy and Its Reverberations Through the Course of Life: Maturity, Senescence, and Sociological Implications." *Journal of the American Psychoanalytic Association*, Vol. 21, No. 3, pp. 633–645.

Panel. 1975. "Bertram D. Lewin Memorial Symposium: Psychoanalytic Perspectives on Love and Marriage." *Journal of the Philadelphia Association for Psychoanalysis*, Vol. 2, pp. 191–201.

Panel, Robert C. Prall, reporter. 1978. "The Role of the Father in the Preoedipal Years." *Journal of the American Psychoanalytic Association*, Vol. 26, No. 1, pp. 143–161.

Panel. May 1982. "What Qualities Do Women Most Value in Husbands?" *Viewpoints*, Vol. 16, No. 5, pp. 77–90.

Panel, Nancy Miller, reporter (in press). "The Psychoanalysis of the Older Patient." For *Journal of the American Psychoanalytic Association*.

Pastan, Linda. 1978. *The Five Stages of Grief*. New York: W. W. Norton. (paperback)

————. 1982. *PM/AM*. New York: W. W. Norton. (paperback)

Payne, Edmund. "The Physician and His Patient Who Is Dying." *Psychodynamic Studies of Aging: Creativity, Reminiscing and Dying*, Sidney Levin and Ralph Kahana, eds. New York: International Universities Press, Inc.

Pearson, Gerald. 1952. "A Survey of Learning Difficulties in Children." *The Psychoanalytic Study of the Child*, Vol. 7. New York: International Universities Press, Inc.

Peck, Robert. 1968. "Psychological Developments in the Second Half of Life." *Middle Age and Aging*, Bernice Neugarten, ed. Chicago and London: The University of Chicago Press.

Perrine, Laurence, ed. 1956, 1963, 1969, 1973, 1977. *Sound and Sense*. New York: Harcourt Brace Jovanovich, Inc. (paperback)

Perutz, Kathrin. 1972. *Marriage Is Hell*. New York: William Morrow & Company, Inc.

Philipe, Anne. 1964. *No Longer Than a Sigh*. New York: Atheneum.

Piaget, Jean. 1969. "The Intellectual Development of the Adolescent." *Adolescence: Psychosocial Perspectives*, Caplan and Lebovici, eds. New York: Basic Books.

Piercy, Marge. 1982. *Circles on the Water*. "Doing It Differently." New York: Alfred A Knopf. (paperback)

Pincus, Lily. 1974. *Death and the Family*. New York: Random House. (Vintage Books paperback)

Pollock, George. July–October 1961. "Mourning and Adaptation." *The International Journal of Psycho-Analysis*, Vol. 42, Parts 4–5, pp. 341–361.

_____. 1964. "On Symbiosis and Symbiotic Neurosis." *The International Journal of Psycho-Analysis*, Vol. 45, Part 1, pp. 1–30.

_____. 1970. "Anniversary Reactions, Trauma, and Mourning." *The Psychoanalytic Quarterly*, Vol. 39, No. 3, pp. 347–371.

_____. 1977. "The Mourning Process and Creative Organizational Change." *Journal of the American Psychoanalytic Association*, Vol. 25, No. 1, pp. 3–34.

_____. 1981. "Aging or Aged: Development or Pathology." *The Course of Life*, Vol. 3, Greenspan and Pollock, eds.

Provence, Sally, ed. 1983. *Infants and Parents*. New York: International Universities Press, Inc.

Racine, Jean. 1961. *Three Plays of Racine* (originally presented in 1667). George Dillon, translator. Chicago: The University of Chicago Press.

Radl, Shirley. 1973. *Mother's Day Is Over*. New York: Charterhouse.

Rangell, Leo. 1963. "On Friendship." *Journal of the American Psychoanalytic Association*, Vol. 11, No. 1, pp. 3–54.

Rank, Otto. 1952. *The Trauma of Birth*. New York: Robert Brunner.

Raphael, Beverley. 1983. *The Anatomy of Bereavement*. New York: Basic Books, Inc.

Richter, Horst-Eberhard. 1976. "The Role of Family Life in Child Development." *The International Journal of Psycho-Analysis*, Vol. 57, Part 4, pp. 385–395.

Robinson, Edwin Arlington. 1949. "Richard Cory" (originally published in 1897). *Contemporary Trends*, John Nelson and Oscar

Cargill, eds. New York: The Macmillan Co.

Robinson, Marilynne. 1982. *Housekeeping*. New York: Bantam Books. (paperback)

Rochlin, Gregory. 1961. "The Dread of Abandonment: A Contribution to the Etiology of the Loss Complex and to Depression." *The Psychoanalytic Study of the Child*, Vol. 16. New York: International Universities Press, Inc.

Rosenthal, Hattie. 1969, 1973. "Psychotherapy for the Dying." *The Interpretation of Death*, Hendrik Ruitenbeek, ed. New York: Jason Aronson.

Ross, Helgola, and Milgram, Joel. 1982. "Important Variables in Adult Sibling Relationships: A Qualitative Study." *Sibling Relationships: Their Nature and Significance Across the Life-Span*, Lamb and Sutton-Smith, eds.

Ross, John Munder. 1979. "Fathering: A Review of Some Psychoanalytic Contributions on Paternity." *The International Journal of Psycho-Analysis*, Vol. 60, Part 3, pp. 317–327.

Rossi, Alice. Spring 1977. "A Biosocial Perspective on Parenting." *Daedalus*, pp. 1–31.

Roth, Philip. 1967, 1968, 1969. *Portnoy's Complaint*. New York: Random House.

Rubin, Lillian. 1979. *Women of a Certain Age*. New York: Harper & Row. (paperback)

———. 1983. *Intimate Strangers*. New York: Harper & Row.

Ruitenbeek, Hendrik, ed. 1969, 1973. *The Interpretation of Death*. New York: Jason Aronson.

Russell, Bertrand. 1967. *The Autobiography of Bertrand Russell, 1872–1914*. London: Allen & Unwin.

Rycroft, Charles. 1979. *The Innocence of Dreams*. New York: Pantheon.

Salholz, Eloise, with Jennifer Smith. March 26, 1984. "How to Live Forever." *Newsweek*, p. 81.

Salinger, J. D. 1945, 1946, 1951. *The Catcher in the Rye*. New York: Bantam Books. (paperback)

Sandler, Joseph. 1960. "On the Concept of Superego." *The Psychoanalytic Study of the Child*, Vol. 15. New York: International Universities Press, Inc., pp. 128–162.

Sass, Louis. August 22, 1982. "The Borderline Personality." *The New York Times Magazine*, pp. 12–15, 66–67.

Scarf, Maggie. 1980. *Unfinished Business*. New York: Doubleday & Co.

Schachter, Frances Fuchs. 1982. "Sibling Deidentification and Split-Parent Identification: A Family Tetrad." *Sibling Relationships: Their Nature and Significance Across the Lifespan*. Michael Lamb and Brian Sutton-Smith, eds. Hillsdale, New Jersey: Lawrence Erlbaum Associates.

Schafer, Roy. 1960. "The Loving and Beloved Superego in Freud's Structural Theory." *The Psychoanalytic Study of the Child*, Vol. 15. New York: International Universities Press, Inc.

_____. 1968. *Aspects of Internalization*. New York: International Universities Press, Inc.

Schaffer, Rudolph. 1977. *Mothering*. Cambridge, Mass.: Harvard University Press.

Scott-Maxwell, Florida. 1979. *The Measures of My Days*. New York: Penguin Books. (paperback)

Searles, Harold. 1979. *Countertransference*. New York: International Universities Press, Inc.

Segal, Hanna. 1964, 1973. *Introduction to the Works of Melanie Klein*. New York: Basic Books, Inc.

Sendak, Maurice. 1963. *Where the Wild Things Are*. New York: Harper & Row.

_____. 1970. *In the Night Kitchen*. New York: Harper & Row.

Shakespeare, William. *As You Like it*.

_____. *King John*.

_____. *King Lear*.

_____. *Macbeth*.

_____. *Romeo and Juliet*.

Shanas, Ethel; Townsend, Peter; Wedderburn, Dorothy; Friis, Hennig; Milhoj, Poul; and Stehouwer, Jan. 1968. "The Psychology of Health." *Middle Age and Aging*, Bernice Neugarten, ed. Chicago and London: The University of Chicago Press.

Shapiro, Theodore, and Perry, Richard. 1976. "Latency Revisited." *The Psychoanalytic Study of the Child*, Vol. 31, pp. 79–105.

Sheehy, Gail. 1974, 1976. *Passages*. New York: E. P. Dutton & Co., Inc.

Shengold, Leonard. 1979. "Child Abuse and Deprivation: Soul Murder." *Journal of the American Psychoanalytic Association*, Vol. 27, No. 3, pp. 533–559.

Shields, Robert. 1964. "The Too-Good Mother." *The International Journal of Psycho-Analysis*, Vol. 45, Part 1, pp. 85–88.

Shneidman, Edwin. 1980, 1982. *Voices of Death*. New York: Bantam Books. (paperback)

Silverman, Lloyd; Lachmann, Frank; Milich, Robert. 1982. *The Search for Oneness*. New York: International Universities Press, Inc.

Simmons, Charles. Dec. 11, 1984. "The Age of Maturity." *The New York Times Magazine*, p. 114.

Simpson, Louis. 1956, 1963, 1969, 1973, 1977. "The Goodnight." *Sound and Sense*, Laurence Perrine, ed. New York: Harcourt Brace Jovanovich. (paperback)

Sklansky, Morris. 1980. "The Pubescent Years: Eleven to Fourteen." *The Course of Life*, Vol. 2, Greenspan and Pollock, eds.

Smith, Sydney. 1977. "The Golden Fantasy: A Regressive Reaction

to Separation Anxiety." *The International Journal of Psycho-Analysis*, Vol. 58, Part 3, pp. 311–324.

Snow, Karen. 1976. *Willo*. Ann Arbor: Street Fiction Press, Inc.

Solnit, Albert. 1980. "Psychoanalytic Perspectives on Children One–Three Years of Age." *The Course of Life*, Vol. 1, Greenspan and Pollock, eds.

Sontag, Susan. October 1972. "The Double Standard of Aging." *Saturday Review*, pp. 29–38.

Sophocles. 1954. "Oedipus at Colonus." *Sophocles I*, Grene and Lattimore, eds. Chicago and London: The University of Chicago Press. (paperback)

——. 1954. "Oedipus the King." *Sophocles I*, Grene and Lattimore, eds. Chicago and London: The University of Chicago Press. (paperback)

Spark, Muriel. 1966. *Memento Mori*. New York: The Modern Library.

Spitz, René. 1945. "Hospitalism." *The Psychoanalytic Study of the Child*, Vol. 1. New York: International Universities Press, Inc.

——. 1965. *The First Year of Life*. New York: International Universities Press, Inc.

Stern, Daniel. 1977. *The First Relationship*. Cambridge, Mass.: Harvard University Press.

Stevens, Wallace. 1970, 1975. "Sunday Morning." *The Norton Anthology of Poetry*, Allison et al., eds. New York: W. W. Norton & Company. (paperback)

Stevenson, Robert Louis. 1885. *A Child's Garden of Verses*. "Bed in Summer." London: George C. Harrap and Company Ltd.

Stoller, Robert. 1976. "Primary Femininity." *Journal of the American Psychoanalytic Association*, Vol. 24, No. 5, pp. 59–78.

——. 1980. "A Different View of Oedipal Conflict." *The Course of Life*, Vol. 1, Greenspan and Pollock, eds.

Stoller, Robert, and Herdt, Gilbert. 1982. "The Development of Masculinity: A Cross-Cultural Contribution." *Journal of the American Psychoanalytic Association*, Vol. 30, No. 1, pp. 29–59.

Sutherland, John D. 1980. "The British Object Relations Theorists: Balint, Winnicott, Fairbairn, Guntrip." *Journal of the American Psychoanalytic Association*, Vol. 28, No. 4, pp. 829–860.

Suttie, Ian. 1935. *The Origins of Love and Hate*. London: Kegan Paul, Trench, Trubner & Co., Ltd.

Sweet, Ellen. May 1984. "The Electra Complex: How Can I Be Jealous of My Four-Year-Old Daughter?" *Ms.*, pp. 148–149.

Talbot, Toby. 1980. *A Book About My Mother*. New York: Farrar, Straus and Giroux.

Tavris, Carol, with Dr. Alice Baumgartner. February 1983. "How Would Your Life Be Different If You'd Been Born a Boy?" *Redbook*, pp. 92–95.

Teicholz, Judith Guss. 1978. "A Selective Review of the Psychoanalytic Literature on Theoretical Conceptualizations of Narcissism." *Journal of the American Psychoanalytic Association*, Vol. 26, No. 4, pp. 831–861.

Tennyson, Alfred, Lord. 1970, 1975. "Ulysses" (originally published 1833, 1842). *The Norton Anthology of Poetry*, Allison et al., eds. New York: W. W. Norton. (paperback)

Thomas, Dylan. 1970, 1975. "Fern Hill." *The Norton Anthology of Poetry*, Allison et al., eds. New York: W. W. Norton. (paperback)

_____. 1977. "Do Not Go Gentle into That Good Night." *Sound and Sense*, Laurence Perrine, ed. New York: Harcourt Brace Jovanovich, Inc. (paperback)

Tillich, Paul. 1959. "The Eternal Now." *The Meaning of Death*, Herman Feifel, ed. New York: McGraw-Hill.

Tolstoy, Leo. 1967. *Great Short Works of Leo Tolstoy*. "The Death of Ivan Ilych." New York: Harper & Row. (paperback)

Toynbee, Arnold J. April 5, 1969. "Why and How I Work." *Saturday Review*, pp. 22–27, 62.

Tyson, Phyllis. 1982. "A Developmental Line of Gender Identity, Gender Role and Choice of Love Object." *Journal of the American Psychoanalytic Association*, Vol. 30, No. 1, pp. 61–86.

Ulanov, Ann and Barry. 1975. *Religion and the Unconscious*. Philadelphia: The Westminster Press.

Ullmann, Liv. 1977. *Changing*. New York: Alfred A Knopf.

Viorst, Judith. 1968. *It's Hard to Be Hip Over Thirty and Other Tragedies of Married Life*. New York and Cleveland: World Publishing Company.

_____. 1973, 1974, 1976. *How Did I Get To Be Forty and Other Atrocities*. New York: Simon and Schuster.

_____. 1974. *Rosie and Michael*. New York: Atheneum.

_____. November 1976. "Sometimes I Hate My Husband." *Redbook*, pp. 73–74.

_____. February 1977. "The Hospital That Has Patience for Its Patients: A Look at Children's Hospital, in Washington, D.C." *Redbook*, pp. 48–54.

_____. October 1977. "Friends, Good Friends—and Such Good Friends." *Redbook*, pp. 31–32, 38.

_____. November 1978. "Are Men and Women Different?" *Redbook*, pp. 46–50.

_____. May 1980. "Letting Go: Why It's Hard to Let Children Grow Up." *Redbook*, pp. 42, 44.

_____. September 1980. "In Praise of Older Women." *Redbook*, pp. 42, 44.

_____. 1981. *If I Were In Charge of the World and Other Worries*. New York: Atheneum.

Wagenvoord, James, and Bailey, Peyton. 1978. *Men: A Book for Women*. New York: Avon. (paperback)

White, E. B. *Poems and Sketches of E. B. White*. 1981. New York: Harper & Row.

Wikler, Lynn. 1980. "Folie à Famille: A Family Therapist's Perspective." *Family Process*, Vol. 19:3, pp. 257–268.

Wilbur, Richard. 1970, 1975. "Seed Leaves" (originally published in 1969). *The Norton Anthology of Poetry*, Allison et al., eds. New York: W. W. Norton. (paperback)

Willi, Jurg. 1982. *Couples in Collusion*. New York and London: Jason Aronson.

Wilson, Edmund. 1980. *The Thirties*. New York: Farrar, Straus and Giroux.

Winnicott, D. W. 1958. *Collected Papers*. New York: Basic Books, Inc.

———. 1965. *The Maturational Processes and the Facilitating Environment*. New York: International Universities Press, Inc.

Wisdom, J. O. 1976. "The Role of the Father in the Mind of Parents, in Psychoanalytic Theory and in the Life of the Infant." *The International Review of Psychoanalysis*, Vol. 3, Part 2, pp. 231–239.

Wolfenstein, Martha. 1966. "How Is Mourning Possible?" *The Psychoanalytic Study of the Child*, Vol. 21. New York: International Universities Press, Inc.

Woodruff, Diana, and Birren, James. 1975. *Aging*. New York: D. Van Nostrand Company.

Woolf, Virginia. 1927. *To the Lighthouse*. New York: Harcourt, Brace and World, Inc. (paperback)

———. 1928, 1956. *Orlando*. New York and London: Harcourt Brace Jovanovich. (paperback)

Wynne, Lyman; Ryckoff, Irving; Day, Juliana; and Hirsch, Stanley. 1967. "Pseudo-Mutuality in the Family Relations of Schizophrenics." *The Psychosocial Interior of the Family*, Gerald Handel, ed. Chicago: Aldine.

Yeats, W. B. 1956. *The Collected Poems of W. B. Yeats*. New York: Macmillan Publishing Co., Inc.

Yogman, Michael. 1982. "Development of the Father-Infant Relationship." Fitzgerald, Lester, Yogman, eds. *Theory and Research in Behavioral Pediatrics*, Vol. 1. New York: Plenum Publishing Corporation.

Yourcenar, Marguerite. 1954. *Memoirs of Hadrian*. New York: Farrar, Straus and Giroux. (paperback)

Zinberg, Norman, and Kaufman, Irving, eds. 1963. *Normal Psychology of the Aging Process*. New York: International Universities Press, Inc.

Index

About the Author

JUDITH VIORST, author of numerous books of poetry and prose and a contributing editor to *Redbook* magazine, graduated from the Washington Psychoanalytic Institute in 1981 after six years of study. Mrs. Viorst lives in Washington, D.C., with her husband, Milton Viorst, the political writer. They have three sons—Anthony, Nicholas, and Alexander.

Cedar River Daydreams

The Suspect

The Kelowna Alliance Church

Published by Bethany House Publishers
A Ministry of Bethany Fellowship, Inc.
11300 Hampshire Avenue South
Minneapolis, Minnesota 55438

Printed in the United States of America.

Library of Congress Cataloging-in-Publication Data

Baer, Judy.
    The suspect / Judy Baer.
        p.   cm. — (Cedar River daydreams ; #24)
    Summary: To complete an assignment for their
marketing class, Binky and her brother Egg become
student managers of the school store.

    [1. Stores, Retail—Fiction.   2. High schools—
Fiction.   3. Schools—Fiction.   4. Christian life—
Fiction.]   I. Title.   II. Series: Baer, Judy. Cedar River
daydreams ; 24.
PZ7.B1395Su   1996
[Fic]—dc20   96–9942
ISBN 1–55661–834–4   CIP
                                                       AC

For Tressa Vesterso—
Congratulations on your graduation!

Chapter One

"Have you heard the news?" Egg McNaughton's thin face glowed with excitement as he raced into the Hamburger Shack and skidded to a stop at a large table near the back of Cedar River's most popular high-school hangout.

Egg's sister, Binky, was close behind him. Her reddish brown hair practically stood on end and her eyes gleamed beneath pale lashes. "You'll never believe it! Never!"

Something momentous had obviously occurred.

Binky danced back and forth on her tiptoes like a spindly legged bird until Todd Winston reached out and grabbed her hand.

"Settle down and tell us what's up. We aren't mind readers."

"You're assuming they have *minds*. It's my guess that the McNaughtons have lost theirs entirely." Jennifer Golden tossed her blond hair away from her face and took a deep swig from the root beer mug in front of her. Egg and Binky were always excited about something. It was hard to take them seriously. Lexi Leighton and Peggy Madison burst out laughing.

Even the group at a neighboring table was

drawn into Egg and Binky's exuberance. Minda Hannaford, Tressa and Gina Williams, Mary Beth Adamson, and Rita Leonard, all members of a clique of girls who called themselves the High Fives, were watching with growing interest.

Only Matt Windsor appeared to be actually listening to the agitated pair. "Quiet," he muttered. "Let them talk."

Matt, a dark, brooding boy who rarely smiled, actually grinned at Egg and Binky. "Ignore them," he advised.

"I'm glad *somebody* is taking us seriously," Egg said pompously. "And when you hear our news, you'll be sorry you didn't too." He glared at Jennifer accusingly.

"All right, what is it?" Jennifer rolled her eyes, sure that their news wasn't worth all this fuss.

"As you all know," Egg began importantly, "Binky and I are in marketing class this quarter."

"So? I'm in physics and I'm not bragging about it."

"That's because you're probably flunking it, Golden," Minda Hannaford sneered. A pouty blue-eyed blonde who always had a tart remark, Minda was not Jennifer's favorite person.

"Am not."

"Are too."

"Not."

"Too."

"Break it up," Egg ordered. "You're not paying attention."

Minda and Jennifer glared at each other but turned toward Egg.

He cleared his throat. "Binky and I have been

named class managers of the *School Store!*"

There was a moment of startled silence at both tables. The School Store was a small retail operation run by the marketing class as a hands-on learning opportunity. The store sold school supplies, sweat shirts, running suits, even jackets with the Cedar River logo emblazoned on them. At Christmastime the store usually did a brisk gift business selling stuffed animals and affordable trinkets to impoverished high-school students. It was also a popular hangout between classes because two years earlier the enterprising marketing class had installed an iced cappucino maker and gained permission from the school administration to sell it during the lunch hour. Being selected to be manager of the School Store was the equivalent of being chosen class president or Student Council member. Those spots usually went to the brightest and most organized students.

"You two? Get outta here!" Minda was the first to express the doubt and amazement that everyone felt. "I thought they had accounting brains do that."

"Are you saying I'm *not* an accounting brain?" Egg asked huffily.

"You're more of a *bird* brain, McNaughton," Tressa said.

The High Fives cackled at her humor. They were a tight-knit group, bound by loyalty to one another. Even if Tressa's statement *hadn't* contained the least bit of humor, they all would have laughed. Becoming a member of the elite club of girls wasn't easy. Lexi had learned that hard lesson when she first moved to Cedar River. When she had rejected their rite of initiation, she had made more enemies than friends in the group.

Egg was blustering a retort to Tressa when Matt spoke. "I don't think I've ever set foot in the School Store."

Everyone stared at him in amazement. "Where have *you* been?"

Matt shrugged. "Around. But I'm not crazy about school. Why would I want to *shop* there?"

"Matt's right," Rita said. "Who wants a bunch of goofy clothes with 'Cedar River High' written all over them?"

"I do!" Binky said. "There are great things in the store. Cheap too."

"It *is* a school tradition," Lexi pointed out. "When I moved to Cedar River I asked someone about the store. I was told that it's been a part of the school for nearly twenty years, ever since they started the marketing program. It's where the marketing students get to practice what they learn in the classroom."

"Exactly!" Egg agreed. "We're involved in every aspect of running the store. We make the displays, keep the books and deposit the money, handle the customers—"

"And we get to go on a buying trip!" Binky interjected enthusiastically.

"What do you need to buy if you already work at the store?" Rita asked.

"The stuff we'll sell, of course. Our class has already decided to put in a line of cards and stationery. We get to pick them out."

"Get something funny," Todd advised. "And something for parents. I almost forgot my mom's birthday this year. It would have been great if I could have found a card at the School Store."

"Good idea." Egg whipped a tiny notebook out of his pocket and scribbled a note. "We want our customers to be happy."

"I can guess what we'll be hearing about for the rest of the month," Jennifer groaned.

Egg ignored her. "We have almost five hundred dollars to spend on our buying trip, so suggestions for things you'd like to see in the store are welcome."

"Five hundred dollars?" Mary Beth Adamson had been the quietest of the High Fives until now. Her eyes grew round with surprise. "That's a lot of money!"

"I told you that you'd be impressed!" Egg said, his expression one of smug satisfaction.

"Who works for you? In the store, I mean." Mary Beth was paying close attention now.

"Students. The people we hire. The marketing students do the big stuff, but regular students can come in for an interview and be hired to work during their free hour. We're going to be open longer hours this year. We'll open before school starts and close half an hour after the last bell. Marketing students work there once or twice a month during marketing class as well. We'll train our employees and oversee their work."

"Cool," Mary Beth said.

"You should come and apply," Egg suggested importantly. "After all, you know the manager."

"I'm a manager too," Binky pointed out, tired of having Egg take all the glory for their new venture.

Egg scowled at her, annoyed that she'd try to take the wind from his sails.

"Well, I *am*!"

Hoping to diffuse the inevitable fight the Mc-Naughtons would have if this conversation was allowed to continue, Lexi hurried to ask, "How were you two chosen to be managers?"

"Because they're the best for the job, of course!" Angela Hardy beamed at Egg and Binky as if they'd just successfully completed a moon landing or delicate brain surgery. Egg's response was a goofy, smitten grin. Angela was a slender, dark-haired girl with smooth, clear skin. She was quite beautiful when she smiled.

Egg and Angela had been dating since Angela came to Cedar River. She'd had a bumpy beginning here, first being homeless, then living with her mother at the city mission. Egg's initial curiosity about Angela and her homelessness had caused him to spend a night on the streets trying to comprehend what it might be like. Somehow, that strange and not-too-wise decision had created a bond between them that had grown even stronger over time.

Things had steadily improved for the Hardys since then. Now they had their own apartment, and Angela's mother had a job she could support them with. Egg had been Angela's enthusiastic champion through those dark days, and Angela had never forgotten his kindness. What's more, the gang agreed that they made a perfect—if unlikely—couple.

Angela scrambled out of her seat to fling her arms around Binky and Egg. Her arms lingered around his waist, and he seemed unwilling to drop his hand from her shoulder. It wasn't until Tressa and the rest of the eavesdropping High Fives started to make kissy noises on the backs of their hands that Angela stepped out of his embrace.

Uncharacteristically, Egg was not embarrassed by the teasing. The appointment as School Store manager had already given him newfound confidence.

"I think we should congratulate our friends," Todd suggested, "and buy them a burger to celebrate."

"I'm not *that* happy," Minda huffed and turned back to her own table. Tressa, Gina, Rita, and Mary Beth followed.

"Ignore them," Peggy Madison advised. *"We'll buy."*

Egg and Binky maneuvered two more chairs around the table. As Egg sat down, Binky threw her arms around him and gave him a noisy smack on the cheek.

"What was that about?" Jennifer wondered. "You *kissed* your brother! Yuk."

"I couldn't help it. I'm just so excited about the store. Isn't it the greatest news you've ever heard?"

"I didn't know you and Egg were so interested in retail merchandising," Peggy said.

"We're not. Or, at least, we weren't—until now. When you get picked for something special you can't help being excited." Binky glowed like a little lantern.

Egg and Binky, while two of the sweetest, funniest students in the school, were not necessarily the most popular. Their quirkiness and Egg's gangly bean-pole appearance had always set them apart. This was a notable moment for the Mc-Naughtons.

As might be expected, their friends were still a little doubtful about this honor.

"How many people were considered for management?" Jennifer inquired.

Lexi shot her a warning glance.

Jennifer was trying to discover if Egg and Binky had had competition or if they'd become managers by default. She shrugged when she caught Lexi's stern look. *Can I help it if I'm curious?* her expression said.

Fortunately Egg and Binky didn't catch on. "Several people," Binky said. "Our teacher and advisor Mr. Kahler said . . . Look! There he is now!"

Mr. Walter Kahler had entered the Hamburger Shack and was winding his way through the crowded tables to the back of the room like a man with a purpose. He stopped when he reached their table.

"Edward, Bonita, I'd like to talk with you for a moment."

Todd blinked. Lexi and Peggy shifted in their chairs. Jennifer covered her mouth to hide a smile. None of them were used to hearing Egg and Binky called by their real names.

"I have some catalogs in my car I'd like you to take a look at. I want you to be familiar with the kinds of items you'll be seeing at the market when we go on our buying trip for the store. I meant to give them to you at school today, but I was called to the office last hour and missed you. Can you take them home and scan them tonight?"

"Sure." Egg jumped to his feet and Binky followed. "We'll get them out of your car."

"Hi, Mr. Kahler," Minda said. She and her

friends had watched this exchange with rapt interest.

"Hello, Minda. We've missed you in accounting class this quarter."

"I don't want you to be offended, Mr. Kahler," Minda began, "but are you sure you've made the right choice for store managers?"

Lexi swung around in her seat and stared at Minda. How *dare* she. . . .

But Mr. Kahler did not interpret the question as an insult at all.

"Positive. Mr. and Miss McNaughton will be excellent. They have the drive, the determination, the energy. . . ."

"They do have that, all right," Todd agreed. "Egg and Binky have more energy than any other people I know."

"Exactly. And their enthusiasm is contagious. I think they'll be the right combination to make the store work. We've got a lot of changes planned for the future, and I believe Edward and Bonita are the ones to implement them. I'm looking forward to a good experience."

After Mr. Kahler left, the kids stared at one another in amazement.

"Was he talking about the same people we know?" Jennifer asked in surprise. "Maybe there's another Edward and Bonita that we haven't met."

"Very funny," Angela huffed. "They'll be great. Why don't you believe in them?"

"We do believe in them. It's just that we didn't know anyone else did!" Jennifer skewered Angela with a gaze. "They are a little quirky, you know."

Angela laughed. "I know. But I also know they

can make this work. I'm happy for them."

"Me too," said someone from the adjoining booth. Amazingly, the statement had come out the mouth of Minda Hannaford.

Minda was usually Egg's worst tormentor. She never missed an opportunity to tease him relentlessly. What made it so much worse was that for a long time Egg had had a hopeless crush on Minda.

When Angela had appeared on the scene and Egg had transferred his love interest to her, Minda had been strangely upset. She didn't want Egg herself, but she wasn't accustomed to being rejected by him either.

"*You're* glad? Why?" Jennifer was painfully blunt.

"Maybe Egg and Binky will need a fashion buyer. After all, they don't have any sense of style. I'd hate to see them spend money on stupid sweat shirts. They need something in the store with *style*. And since I am the fashion columnist for the *Cedar River Review*, maybe I can help." Minda referred to the school newspaper which several of them worked on.

"I've got some great ideas for awesome new sweats and jackets."

"What makes you think Egg would ask for your help?"

Minda ignored Jennifer. "I wish everything in the School Store didn't have to have that stupid logo on it."

"Merchandise has to carry the school logo. It's a store rule. We're not supposed to compete with local businesses."

"I'd never wear a bathing suit with that logo on

it," Minda said derisively. "Egg and Binky had better be careful what they order, that's all I can say." She stood, and the rest of the High Fives rose with her. "Let's get out of here."

Obediently, the other girls followed.

"She sure leads them around," Peggy commented after they'd disappeared through the door of the Shack.

"And they let her. It's surprising. The only one I'd expect that of is Mary Beth Adamson," Angela commented. "She's very quiet and seems different from the others. The rest should be able to hold their own with Minda."

"We've talked enough about them," Todd said. "What do you think about Egg and Binky's news?"

"It's great, but . . ."

"We all know what you mean, Angela," Lexi assured her. "Egg and Binky are the best, but sometimes things do turn out . . . oddly . . . for them."

"I hope they know what they're doing," Peggy said quietly. "After all, the School Store has a pretty big budget. I hope they don't break the bank."

The Kelowna Alliance Church

Chapter Two

"It's starting already," Jennifer groaned to Lexi the next morning as they were getting books from their lockers for the first-hour class.

"We still have fifteen minutes before class."

"Not that. *Them*." Jennifer tipped her head to the left.

Lexi turned and saw Binky and Egg making their way toward the bank of lockers. Binky looked smug as a cat with a pocketful of mice. Egg wore a wide, complacent grin as he strutted down the hallway, thrusting his thin, unsubstantial chest into the faces of those he met.

"Now what?" Lexi asked. "Egg's acting weird even for Egg."

"I think we'll find out as soon as we can read those buttons they're wearing." Todd joined the girls to watch the McNaughtons' progress.

"Buttons? Those look like dinner plates!" Jennifer scowled as she attempted to read the words. "Tell me what they say. I don't think I want to strain my brain on this one." Jennifer was dyslexic, and the homemade, handwritten buttons Egg and Binky wore were a special challenge.

" 'Shop At The School Store,' " Todd read. " 'Bargains Galore!' "

"That rhymes," Lexi observed. "Do you think they meant for that to happen?"

"Do the McNaughtons actually *think*?" Minda sneered as she and Mary Beth came by. Her contempt for Egg and Binky was apparent.

Mary Beth tugged on Minda's sleeve. "Let's go." Minda allowed herself to be pulled away.

"I'm glad Egg and Binky didn't hear Minda," Lexi said. "I'd hate to have her rain on their parade."

"Who's having a parade?" Binky overheard the last of Lexi's comment.

Before Lexi could explain, Todd took over. "Are you going on a trip, Egg?"

"No." Egg looked puzzled.

"Then why are you carrying a suitcase?"

"This isn't a suitcase. It's my *briefcase*!"

"When did you start carrying a briefcase?"

"When I became a businessman," Egg said importantly. "I have a lot of papers to keep track of now."

"Your teachers will be very excited," Todd said with gentle sarcasm. "What have you done with *their* papers?"

"Oh, those are still in his backpack," Binky said. "The briefcase is for *business* papers."

"What's in there now?" Todd persisted.

"Just a few catalogs so far, but I'm sure there will be more later."

"What kind of catalogs?" Todd eyed the latches on the leather case.

"Sports clothing, mugs, pencils . . . what are you doing?"

Without a word, Todd undid the gold latches on the case. Several sandwiches, three candy bars, a bag of marshmallows, and two slim catalogs fell to the floor.

"Important stuff, huh? Like snacks?"

Egg blushed. "I never know when I'm going to get hungry."

"He won't have room for food for long. We'll be getting order forms and evaluations to fill out soon." Binky picked up the food and stuffed it back into the case but kept one candy bar for herself. "Just wait and see. Egg and I are going to do great things with the store. We're meeting with Mr. Kahler second hour to discuss our future."

"That should be interesting," Jennifer muttered after the McNaughtons were gone. "Poor Mr. Kahler. He probably doesn't realize what he's gotten himself into!"

———

Angela Hardy and Peggy Madison had saved the gang a table in the cafeteria. Egg was still clinging to his briefcase. Now that everyone knew there was food in it, he protected it more than ever.

"Why are you carrying that briefcase in here?" Todd eyed Egg's lunch tray. "Don't you think you have enough food already?"

Egg's tray was loaded until it threatened to spill onto the floor. Two burgers, fries covered with mustard and jelly, pudding, cookies, slices of bread, soda crackers, soup, and three cartons of milk teetered precariously as he headed for the table.

"If you eat all that you'll be sick." Jennifer looked as though Egg would not be the only one.

"Have I ever gotten sick?" Egg retorted as he settled his tray on the table.

"There was that time when you stuffed yourself with those cream-filled Easter eggs," Binky offered helpfully.

"I mean at school. Besides, that wasn't my fault. Mom shouldn't have hid so many. That was practically like asking me to be sick!"

"You ate all mine too, if I remember."

"You're driving me crazy!" Jennifer yelped. "Can't you talk about something important for a change?"

"Important!" Egg nearly tumbled off the bench. He flailed his arms. Napkins and paper-wrapped straws fluttered across the table. "You're right! We almost forgot! Mr. Kahler had some great news for us."

"You've been chosen for the next space shuttle shot, right?" Jennifer was growing impatient. "You'll be busy training and won't have time to pester us. Say it's true, please."

The McNaughtons ignored her. "The School Store is moving!" Binky crowed.

"You've already driven it out of the school? You've only been managers a couple of days!"

"It's moving into a bigger space. The current store was a janitor's store room until the School Store was created."

"So that's why it's tucked into a corner," Angela observed. "I didn't even know it was there for two months after I started school here."

"Where's it going?" Peggy asked.

"That's the big news! The administration has decided it should be moved to rooms near the main office. It will be the first thing you see when you walk in the front door of the school. Isn't that cool?"

"But why?" Jennifer was still skeptical. "It can't do that much business."

"Until now it's been in a poor location. Egg and I will be the first managers to see what we can do with a new look, a new location, and a brand-new store!

"The teacher's workroom is going to be moved to bigger quarters. Their old room will be remodeled so that it has big plate-glass windows. We've seen the blueprints. You guys will be so impressed."

"Sounds expensive to me," Angela commented. She was always very conscious of money. It was usually in short supply for her because Mrs. Hardy's job pay seldom stretched further than the necessities.

"Mr. Kahler hopes we'll pick up sales not only from students but also from visitors and guests. We might even get an advertising budget if things work out."

"This actually *is* a big deal?" Jennifer mused. "You aren't just exaggerating to impress us?"

"Big deal? Of course it is! We're responsible for decisions concerning the renovations, purchasing for the new store, the move itself, sales, staff. . . ." Binky took a deep breath. "It's going to be great."

Egg and Binky acted as though they'd gotten in on the ground floor of a huge new business operation.

"Mr. Kahler says we should act as if we're spending our own money on the store," Egg said. "That way we will make smart decisions and not waste any money."

"Uh-oh." Matt had been silent until now. "Mr. Kahler doesn't know Egg and Binky very well." The McNaughtons were magnets for financial disasters just as frequently as they attracted other minor catastrophes.

"We've already decided what look we want for the store. Shall we tell them, Egg?"

"The 'look'?"

"Colors, design, theme. We want something flashy, unusual—a big graphic design on the wall behind the cash register in colors that make a statement. I like lavender and purple, but Egg is leaning toward black and orange."

"What kind of statement do you want to make? Seems to me both of those choices make the statement that you're nuts." Jennifer was blunt.

Binky continued as if Jennifer had never spoken. "We haven't told Mr. Kahler our ideas yet, but we have some great ones for displaying merchandise—bright colors, music, graphics. . . ."

"And I want to have mannequins," Egg added. "Wearing the school colors. We can pose them in weird positions to attract attention."

"Oh, I don't think you'll have any problem attracting attention," Lexi said softly. "In fact, you might have to worry about just the opposite."

Chapter Three

"What's up?" Todd's voice was warm and low on the other end of the line when Lexi answered the telephone.

"Not much. Mom is working on an illustration for her book and Dad's reading the paper." Lexi's mother, an artist, was writing and illustrating a book for children on the topic of multiple sclerosis. She'd recently been diagnosed with the disease and was determined to turn the experience into something positive.

"Where's Ben?" Todd had a special place in his heart for Lexi's younger brother who had Down's syndrome.

"Driving Wiggles crazy. He's trying to teach the dog to roll over and play dead. Wiggles is more interested in tearing the curtains off the walls. I wish they'd quit making so much noise. I'm reading. Another exciting Friday night. What's up with you?"

"I was wondering if you wanted to do something."

"Sounds great. What do you have in mind?"

"Egg just called. He and Angela want to get together."

"Good. I haven't had a chance to spend time with Angela in ages."

"Who says you'll get to spend time with her tonight?" Todd asked with a laugh. "You know how Egg dominates Angela when they're together."

"He's crazy about her, that's all."

"That's for sure," Todd agreed.

"What are we going to do?" Lexi asked.

"It's a surprise. Egg planned it."

"Uh-oh."

"Don't worry. It's harmless enough. Pick you up in half an hour?"

"I'll be ready."

———

Egg and Angela were already in Todd's car when he pulled up in front of Lexi's house. Egg was hanging out the passenger-side window with his mouth open.

"What are you doing?" Lexi demanded when she reached the car. "I saw you all the way down the street with your cheeks flapping in the breeze."

"Were they? Great. I saw a documentary on the stuff pilots and astronauts go through," he explained. "There's one machine that sends you through the air so fast that if you open your mouth it stretches out your cheeks . . ." he grabbed a chunk of his face in each hand, "like this."

"And you wondered if it would happen if you stuck your head out of a car."

"I tried to get Todd to go faster, but he's some kind of a rule freak and wouldn't go over the speed limit."

"How do you do it, Angela?" Lexi asked as she

got into the front seat after Egg and Angela had scrambled into the back. "Put up with that, I mean."

Angela smiled serenely. "What? Who? Is there someone besides us in the car?"

"You mean you ignore him?"

"Exactly. Works great."

"You won't ignore me when you see what I brought." Egg dived toward the floor of the car and came up holding a grocery bag. "Chips, dip, sodas, cookies. . . ."

"Where *are* we going?" Lexi dared to ask. "On a camping trip?"

"Close," Todd said. "We're going to Snyder's Lake. We thought it would be fun to build a fire and watch the moon on the water."

At the mention of the word "moon," Egg began to yowl like a coyote baying. Then he slipped directly into a verse of a song talking about someone named Katie and seeing the moon over a cowshed. The ride to the lake flew by.

———

"It's beautiful out here tonight." Lexi and Angela were perched on a log near the water while Todd and Egg unloaded the food and started a small fire in the submerged grills provided for that purpose. "I'm glad Egg thought of it."

"He's so sweet," Angela said with a soft smile.

"I'm surprised you can say that after listening to Egg sing for the entire ride."

Angela looked surprised. "I *like* Egg's voice."

"You must be in love," Lexi said. "He was only

in tune about half the time, and I don't think he meant to be then."

"I know he can sing better than he did tonight. Egg's just . . ." Angela searched for a word, ". . . unique."

Lexi agreed with that assessment wholeheartedly. There was no one more unique than Egg.

"Fire's ready. Let's roast marshmallows," Todd called.

The girls meandered lazily back to the campsite where the guys had spread the food on a picnic table. A large collection of beach toys lay on the ground nearby.

"Looks like you're going to make us work," Angela commented.

"Yes, but first we eat. Want a marshmallow?"

Lexi glanced around. "How are we going to cook it?"

"That's what we forgot! Roasting sticks."

"No problem," Egg said, looking up at the overhead tree. "I know where sticks come from."

Before anyone could respond, he swung monkeylike into the tree and scrambled upward.

"Egg, there are sticks down here!" Angela yelled.

"Not as good as the ones up here. I see a nice straight one just above my head."

"Come down from there," Lexi ordered, half laughing as she watched the top half of Egg's body disappear into the leaves.

"I can just about reach it," Egg was muttering. "If I get a good foothold with my right foot, I can stretch a little and . . ." A sound came out of the tree that was part grunt, part groan, and all panic. The next thing that came out of the tree was Egg, like a rock dropping out of the sky.

He landed on his back at Lexi's and Angela's feet. Egg's head bounced slightly as he hit the ground, and his arms flew backward until his hands, palms up, landed near his ears. His long, scrawny legs were a tangle of denim. Alarming as all this was, it was nothing like the strange whistling scream that emanated from Egg's mouth.

"E . . . wh . . . eee . . ." he gasped as he tried to catch his breath. The thin barrel of his chest swelled and sank, and a rough gasping sound came from somewhere deep inside him.

"Egg! Oh, Egg!" Tears streamed down Angela's face as she knelt beside him. "Don't try to move. We'll get a doctor, call 911." She turned a tear-streaked face to Lexi. "Do you think he's dying?"

"Hardly." Todd leaned forward and peered into Egg's red, mottled face. "Got the wind knocked out of you, huh, old man?"

Egg nodded his head slightly and gave another hideous gasp.

"He could be *dying*!" Angela exclaimed frantically.

Egg was beginning to pant as air began to refill his lungs. He was sounding more like a dog after a long run and less like a crazed escapee from a zoo.

"Air. Air. Air."

"He can talk!" Angela stroked Egg's hair away from his face. Egg wheezed.

After an agonizing few moments, Egg's breathing became more regular and he struggled to sit up.

"You shouldn't move," Angela advised. "What if you broke something?"

"Just my pride," Egg gasped.

"Are you sure?"

"Haven't you ever had the wind knocked out of you, Angela?" Todd asked. "Don't you know what it feels like?"

"I fell off of a swing once," Lexi said. "I landed on my back and I could feel the air puffing out of my lungs. It's a terrible feeling."

"And you deserve it," Todd noted harshly to his friend.

"Huh?" Egg looked hurt and puzzled.

"It was a dumb thing to do, climbing into that tree. There were plenty of sticks down here."

"Todd's right," Angela agreed. "You could have been seriously hurt."

"But . . ."

"You were showing off, Egg, admit it."

Egg didn't even try to defend himself. But, because he looked so pitiful sitting there on the ground with dirt on his clothing and leaves in his hair, still panting like a winded puppy, even Todd relented.

"Just don't do it again," Todd ordered.

Lexi touched Egg's cheek with the tip of her finger. "You're too important to us to let you do crazy tricks like that. We'd all be crushed if something happened to you."

"I couldn't bear it if you got hurt." Angela's lower lip wobbled precariously and the tears threatened to return.

"Aw, quit it, will you?" Egg's face was red with embarrassment. "Don't yell at me. I feel stupid enough already." He kicked at a rock with the heel of his shoe. "I can't do anything right."

His thin shoulders slumped forward, and his chin disappeared down the front of his shirt until he looked like an abandoned stork.

"Come off it, Egg. You just fell out of a tree. You didn't push the button on the atomic bomb!"

"You guys just don't get it because you never make fools of yourselves!" Egg protested. The expression on his face changed from embarrassment to something deeper and more painful. "I know I'm a klutz. I try, I really do, but things just never seem to work out.

"When I was a little kid, my classmates used to laugh at me." His voice grew soft and distant, as if he were speaking more to himself than to the others. "I hated that. And I never knew how to make them stop. Here I am, *still* doing klutzy things. Will I ever outgrow it?"

"Don't you dare!"

"Huh?"

Angela took his hands and peered earnestly into his face. "That's the best part of you!"

"Being klutzy?"

"No. Being real. Being funny. Being you. Egg, do you have any enemies?"

He looked surprised at the question. "No, not really. Minda Hannaford and the High Fives aren't crazy about me, but . . ."

"Do they actually like *anybody*?"

"Well, no."

"That's what I mean. Everybody likes you. You aren't intimidating or stuck on yourself. You're easy to be around. Comfortable."

"Like old slippers or my dad's recliner? Great. Just what a guy likes to hear."

"No, silly! You are a *friend* to everyone. Why do you think *I* like you?" Angela asked sternly. "It's not because you act tough or macho, that's for sure. It's because you are genuinely *nice*. So get over your pity party. You've got it all wrong!"

Egg stared at Angela in genuine amazement. "You mean that?"

"Of course. I wouldn't have said it if I didn't."

He looked to Todd and Lexi. "Do you think she's right?"

"She's on target, Egg-o," Todd said. "Hard as it might be for you to accept, people do like you. Even when you fall out of trees."

Egg turned to Angela with shining eyes. "Thank you."

"No, Egg. Thank *you*."

———

Egg and Angela were still gazing dreamily at each other when Todd and Lexi dropped them off at Egg's house three hours later. The tree incident had provoked more laughter and more conversation than anyone could have imagined.

"That was fun," Lexi commented as they pulled into the Leighton driveway. "Especially once we realized Egg didn't kill himself falling out of that tree."

"Pretty interesting," Todd agreed. "Egg realized tonight how Angela feels about him."

"She's so good for Egg."

"And he's good for her. They really care what happens to each other."

"She's a neat girl," Lexi concluded. "It's amazing, really, when you consider what a difficult life

she's had. She's lived through poverty, homelessness, shame, ridicule—and still turned out to be a
great person."

Todd nodded thoughtfully. "You'd think,
wouldn't you, that a life like she's had would have
had more of an effect on her. Who knows? Maybe
something dark and secret *is* lurking somewhere
inside her and just hasn't come out yet."

"Oh, Todd, don't be so negative! You saw what
she did for Egg tonight. Angela is a super person."

"You're right," Todd said as he leaned over to
give Lexi a good-night kiss. "That was my imagination talking. I'm glad Egg has Angela. And," he
smiled into her eyes, "I'm glad I have you."

Chapter Four

"Got a minute?" Peggy Madison caught up with Lexi as she left the music room after rehearsal for the Emerald Tones. Cedar River High's swing choir was an elite group of musicians who performed often at events at school and around the community.

"Mrs. Waverly can really get carried away," Lexi said, referring to the much-loved Emerald Tones advisor. "I thought my voice was going to give out before she dismissed us."

As the girls walked down the hall, a clatter erupted in the area that was to become the new store. Curious, Lexi and Peggy peeked through the half-open door. Inside, amid stacks of boxes and a slightly gory pile of arms and legs from dismembered mannequins, were Egg and Binky.

Egg was wrestling with a one-armed torso of one of the mannequins. He appeared to be losing.

"Help me get this thing into the window, Binky. I'll dress it up there. I want to use the new sweat shirt and pants we ordered."

"It doesn't have any legs," Binky observed. "What are you going to use for legs?"

"I'll find some. For now, help me lift this. . . ." Egg turned around and the torso's single good arm thwacked Binky in the back of the head.

"Ouch! Watch where you move that thing." Binky picked up a disembodied leg and parried at him as though they were sword fighting.

Startled, Egg took a step backward, stumbled over a pile of boxes, and sent them crashing to the floor. At that moment, Angela Hardy and Mary Beth Adamson, two of Egg's new employees, popped out from behind another set of boxes.

"We just got those sorted out!" Angela yelped. "Now you've messed them up again."

"It's okay," Mary Beth murmured. "They didn't spill the contents all over the floor *this time*."

Egg looked as though he were about to skewer Binky with a coat hanger when Lexi cleared her throat to announce their presence.

Distracted, Egg looked up from the mayhem he was about to commit. "Hi, did you come to see our store?"

"What's left of it." Peggy's eyes were wide with wonder at the magnitude of the mess around them.

They were up to their ears in clutter. Boxes teetered higher than Binky's head. Mary Beth bent to pick up a rat's nest of hangers. Angela stumbled on a paint can and caught it just as it was about to spill.

Mary Beth was a rather nondescript girl compared to the other High Fives. Her clothes weren't as fashionable, her haircut not quite as professional. Today she looked especially ordinary in faded jeans and a T-shirt. Her money obviously didn't go for designer brand jeans and hand-knit sweaters like the other High Fives. She blew her bangs out of her eyes and swiped a hand across her forehead in frustration.

"We haven't got our system perfected yet," Egg understated subtly.

"Obviously. It looks like you had an explosion in here."

"Help me put this clothing rack together," Egg ordered, recruiting both Lexi and Peggy. "Then we can empty some of these boxes and make more room."

"What do you think?" Peggy asked. "Do you have time?"

"It looks as though we're needed here," Lexi responded. "Badly."

Just then a pole came swinging dangerously near her head. Lexi grabbed it, more to protect herself than to help Egg, who was holding the other end. Following Egg's barked orders, they got the clothing rack assembled in record time.

"Now what?" Peggy looked up from the tangle of clothes hangers she was unsnarling.

"We've got to empty these boxes. I found them in the store room. It's old unsold merchandise. For now, this can be the sale rack."

Lexi stuck her hand into one of the boxes and pulled out a bright yellow and lime green nightgown. "This is incredibly ugly!"

"That thing would keep you awake at night," Angela said. "When did the School Store sell those?"

"About the same time they sold this." Mary Beth was giggling. She held up a dish towel.

"Mr. Kahler said there were some 'poor merchandise selections' over the years. I see now what he meant. I guess the managers thought that as long as they put the high school logo on something, it should sell."

"Like bedroom slippers?" Peggy dug deeper into the box. "And baby clothes?"

"Actually, that's kind of cute." Lexi eyed a baby bib with the school logo on the front.

"I'm glad you think so." Binky had been tipped headfirst into another box. When she stood up, her hair frizzed around her head like an electric halo. The smudge of dirt on her nose matched one on Egg's cheek. They were without a doubt the most pitiful-looking pair of store managers Lexi had ever seen.

"Angela, you and Mary Beth can finish that," Binky directed. "I'd like Lexi and Peggy to give me their opinions on the carpet."

"*You* are going to pick out the carpet for the store?" Peggy gasped.

"Don't sound so surprised," Egg retorted. "Don't you think we can do it?"

"I didn't mean that, exactly." Peggy visibly bit her lip to keep from saying more.

"This is what I wanted," Binky said proudly. She held up a hot pink carpet sample. "Neon. Wouldn't that be great? Green, blue, yellow, and this pink. I thought we could set a neon sign for the window too, but Mr. Kahler said we didn't have that kind of money."

"Fortunately!" Peggy whispered to Lexi.

"And I like this." Egg's choice was an electric blue carpet and wallpaper that looked as though it were raining bolts of lightning in red and orange. "Eye-catching, isn't it?"

"You've got that right," Peggy said.

"So what did you finally choose?" Lexi hesitated, almost afraid of the answer.

"This." Egg and Binky both sounded disappointed. The carpet was a deep blue color. "Mr. Kahler says it won't show dirt. He also says we can paint the walls a soft yellow and bring color in with art posters. Sounds pretty boring to me, but the rest of the class voted for it."

"Mr. Kahler's smarter than we thought," Peggy muttered to herself.

"I like the choice," Lexi said. "It's classy."

"I guess—if you like classy." Binky obviously didn't. "We'll still be going over the carpet allowance the school budgeted for us. That means we'll have to make up the difference somewhere else."

"It's weird to hear you two worrying about budgets and carpets," Peggy said.

"And that's not the worst!" Binky complained. "The men who've been doing the remodeling have been smoking in here. Can you smell it?"

"Can't miss that."

"It's going to stink up our new merchandise. I've been putting up 'No Smoking' signs but they don't pay any attention. If they do it again today, I'm going to have to get tough with them." Binky balled her hands on her hips and thrust her jaw forward. Even in that pose she looked as tough as a hummingbird.

Egg sighed. His attention was not on Binky or even on the mess surrounding them. He stared forlornly out the window into the hallway.

"What's wrong, Egg?"

"Pressure. Too much pressure. Mr. Kahler says

we should get the store open as soon as possible. We lose money every day it's closed. The workmen, on the other hand, seem to think that this is their least important job and they come and go as they please. The carpet's shipping date has changed twice already, and we're not sure when it will be in now. I never realized how difficult it would be to run a business!"

"Me either." Binky gave a moan as she sank down on a stool. "There's still a bunch of stuff to be packed and moved from the other location. The merchandising class is small this quarter and there's not enough help. Now Egg tells me we'll have to work nights to pull this all together."

Lexi and Peggy exchanged a glance. Peggy's expression held a note of warning, but Lexi plunged forward anyway. "Would you like Peggy and me to help you? Maybe Todd, Matt, or Jennifer could."

"Would you? Help us? Oh, that would be the best!" Binky jumped up and threw her arms around Lexi. "Thank you, thank you, thank you!"

"It really would help. Angela and Tim Anders said they'd help and Mary Beth has been great, but with play rehearsal going on and an orchestra concert coming up, most everyone else has other things to do at night." Egg looked pitifully grateful for the offer.

There was no way out now. The gang was committed to another night of chaos with the Mc-Naughtons.

Chapter Five

"Don't step on him."

"Why not? If you act like a rug, you should expect to be treated like one."

"Get off the floor, Egg. You're in the way."

Egg, lying flat on his back in the middle of the Winstons' living room, appeared not to hear any of the conversation going on around him. His eyes were closed and his body limp. His feet splayed outward, the toes of each foot pointing in opposite directions. He lay there with his elbows bent and palms upward. His breathing was deep and rhythmic.

"Do you know what he reminds me of?" Peggy asked as she put a puzzle piece into place.

"Road kill?" Jennifer responded sweetly. "That's what he looks like to me. Flattened out. Smooshed. A grease spot on pavement."

Peggy considered the response. "Sort of. Actually, he looks more like a flattened scarecrow to me. You know, Scarecrow in the Wizard of Oz meets semi-truck."

"Scarecrow road kill, then." Jennifer pressed another piece of the puzzle into place.

"Shhhh. He might hear you."

"That's what we're hoping for, Lexi. If he responds, we'll know he's got a brain instead of straw under that mop of uncombed hair."

"Are you picking on my brother?" Binky and Angela stood over the prone body on the floor and stared down into Egg's face.

"Not any more than usual. Why doesn't he get up?"

"He's been that way ever since he got here," Todd said. He and Matt were intently watching a ball game on television and neither bothered to turn his head toward the girls.

"He said he was 'exhausted,'" Matt added. "Then he fell into that puddle and hasn't moved since."

"I think you're being a little overdramatic, Egg. I'm tired too, but do you see *me* lying around feeling sorry for myself? No, sir! Not me!"

"Be quiet, Binky. You're making my head hurt."

"It lives!" Jennifer crowed. "Get up and help us with this puzzle, Egg. We've got all the straight outside pieces. Now we need someone to help us with this stuff in the center. It looks all the same to me. Whose idea was it to buy a puzzle with all blue pieces, anyway?"

"I can't move," Egg whined. "My head hurts. My legs hurt. My back hurts."

"Anything else?" Matt asked absently.

"Yes, actually. My jaw." Egg lifted a hand to rub his face. "My teeth are killing me."

"You've moved a lot of boxes and lifted heavy things, but you didn't use your teeth, did you?" They'd all helped Egg and Binky move the last of the merchandise from the old store to the new one that evening. Not once had any of them seen Egg use his teeth for anything but candy bars.

"It's not surprising his teeth hurt," Binky snorted. "He's been keeping me awake at night with them."

That statement got everyone's attention. Even Todd and Matt turned away from the television set.

"What's that supposed to mean?"

"Ever since we got the management positions, Egg's been griping and worrying. When he gets upset, he grinds his teeth in his sleep. Some nights lately it sounds like he's filing iron in his room." Binky demonstrated a dreadful grinding noise with her own teeth, which caused Lexi and Jennifer to put their hands over their ears.

"Mom sleeps with earplugs and Dad snores, so I'm the one who really has to suffer." Binky peered grumpily at her brother. "I figure he'll have them worn down to little flat pegs pretty soon, and then it will get quiet again."

"Go to the dentist!" Lexi said.

"I don't like the dentist."

"He'll fit you for a night guard that will keep your teeth apart while you sleep. I had one for a little while. It's easy. No big deal," Peggy said.

"Can't. No time. We've got to get moved into the new store."

"You'll drive away business if you greet customers with a toothless smile."

"Lexi's right. You're scary enough *with* teeth. Without them, well, it's too bad to think about!" Jennifer remarked.

"If you can't find time to take care of yourself, I think you should quit the job."

That statement brought Egg to a sitting position. "Quit? Are you crazy?"

"Peggy's right," Lexi added. "What's more important? Your teeth or the job?"

"You're turning into a crazed type-A workaholic, and it's not pretty," Jennifer stated accusingly.

Egg sat in the center of the floor shaking his head morosely.

"What *is* so important that you'd let it hurt you?" Todd volunteered. "Your friends are even beginning to feel the pressure. Maybe it's too much."

"The store is beginning to shape up," Egg said stubbornly. "I'm not quitting now."

"Ease up, anyway. Don't let it get to you."

"I agree with Todd," Peggy said. "I certainly wouldn't keep any job that didn't allow me time to take care of myself. You're too young for false teeth, Egg."

"Dumb, dumber, dumbest," Jennifer chanted, "that's you. What's so important about this anyway? The School Store has been in operation for years. You aren't going to ruin the program if you take time out to go see a dentist and get a few good nights' sleep."

Egg pondered the question for a long time. Deep furrows channeled across his forehead. "I know the store will do fine even if I don't spend much time there. We sell paper, pencils, souvenir stuff, things people need or want. About the same number of dollars is earned every year, give or take a couple hundred. It's just that I want to make this semester *special*.

"Nobody's ever given me a chance to prove myself. I'm always 'goofy old Egg'! I'm a 'nice' guy but nobody outstanding. I wanted to play basketball but how did I end up? As student manager of the team. That's fine, but we all know that student managers are the guys everyone likes but that everyone knows can't play ball. I'm not a total loser, but I'm close."

Several started to protest, but Egg held up his hand. "Don't try to tell me it's not true. I know who and what I am. And for once, I want to prove that goofy Egg can be a success at something."

Everyone was quiet. It was obvious that no one, except perhaps Binky or Angela, had had any idea how much this manager position meant to Egg.

"You can do it," Todd finally said. "How can we help?" There was a sense of warmth and unity throughout the room. Egg's friends were there for him, totally and without reserve.

"You have already. You moved boxes. And you've listened to me."

"So what are you worried about now?" Lexi asked. "Anything we can talk about?"

"We have to purchase the new merchandise," he said off-handedly. "Lot's of it. We want to upgrade the quality because we think that the students are discriminating shoppers. Though higher prices might scare a few away, most like the idea of good quality stuff."

"Seems smart," Angela mused.

"Why don't you sell basketball and football jerseys, the good ones, not the cheap ones?" Todd suggested.

"Do you know how expensive they are?" Egg retorted.

"Sure, but they last," Todd pointed out.

"I wish you'd sell umbrellas," Jennifer commented. "It always rains on my good hair days."

"I'd like to be able to buy hand lotion," Lexi said.

"And hair spray!" Angela added.

Egg grabbed for a piece of paper and pencil and began scribbling. His head bobbed as he wrote down all the ideas.

"Keep going," he encouraged. "We're going to talk about this in class on Monday. Binky and I need all the suggestions we can get!"

"I want to sell hair accessories and socks with the school logo," Binky said. "What do you think?"

"How many of these decisions do you actually have to make?" Lexi asked.

"Even though the class votes, the final decisions always rest with the managers. In fact, part of our grade depends on what Mr. Kahler calls our 'wisdom.' " Egg looked anguished. "It makes my stomach hurt."

"It can't be *that* bad!" Matt interjected.

"Oh no? We have boxes of 'boo-boos' from other years that we'll never be able to get rid of—unless you can find a use for sixty T-shirts sized extra small, a dozen doggy jackets for pampered pets that might want to wear the school logo, and an entire carton of fuzzy-haired trolls."

Matt whistled. "I see your problem."

"Maybe you could have a rummage sale," Todd suggested. "My mom has one when she wants to get rid of her extra junk."

"I think Todd might have a good idea," Lexi said. "The School Store doesn't have to have a *rummage* sale, exactly, but it could have 'Crazy Days' or 'Midnight Madness' like the stores at the mall. People always like to find a bargain. Sell everything at rock-bottom prices. Even if you lose money, it's better than having boxes of junk sitting around. Then you can use the cash to buy new merchandise."

"You know, it just might work." Egg brightened as he spoke. "It could be fun and good promotion for the store too."

"It would help to have some extra cash for purchases," Binky admitted. "Having a nice operation takes a lot of money."

"I hope you aren't going to make it so nice that people like me won't be able to afford to shop there," Angela said quietly.

"That's a good point," Lexi said tactfully. "Not everyone wants to spend all their money at the School Store. There are people who want—and like—less expensive things."

"But we don't want the store to be junky!" Binky protested.

"It doesn't have to be junky to offer variety. That's where creative displays can help."

"Who's going to work in the store besides the class members?" Matt asked.

"Whoever we hire. In fact, we might already have our full staff."

"So soon?"

"Our first three applicants outside the class were acceptable to Mr. Kahler and the others. So far we've hired Angela, Tim Anders, and Mary Beth Adamson."

"Good going, Angela," Peggy congratulated her friend.

"Mary Beth Adamson?" Jennifer gasped. "You hired a High Five to work for you?"

"She's a pretty nice girl," Egg said defensively. "It's not like I hired Minda or anything."

The High Fives tended to be snobbish, exclusive, and a real pain in the neck to those who did not meet their "in crowd" requirements.

Minda Hannaford, their leader, had given Egg, Binky, and Lexi plenty of headaches over just about everything. Minda did not have a happy homelife, and as a consequence her frustration and unhappiness often translated itself into snobby behavior.

"We're planning a training session for the new employees," Binky explained. "Mr. Kahler says Egg and I have to run it."

"That should be interesting." Matt was always the master of understatement.

"It's going to be great," Egg said confidently. "We've been role-playing in class, taking turns doing the training. I've learned a lot."

"What do you have to teach? How hard can it be to sell T-shirts and junk?"

Egg gave Jennifer a withering stare. "That shows how little you know! Everyone has to learn about creating displays, running the cash register, making out receipts, taking inventory, ordering and reordering. . . ."

When Egg paused to draw a breath before continuing, Jennifer threw her hands in the air. "All right, I get it. This is very important. Once your staff learns this they can go to work at the mall."

"That's the idea."

Jennifer looked surprised. She was obviously being sarcastic. "Really? You could?"

"Sure. It's great work experience. Mr. Kahler says the people at the mall love to hire students who've worked at the School Store."

"Wow. Maybe I should apply." Now Jennifer was thoughtful. "This whole deal is bigger than I thought!"

Chapter Six

Todd caught Lexi's elbow in the hallway. "What's your hurry?" he asked with a lopsided grin. His wheat blond hair fell appealingly over one eye and his hand was warm and firm on her arm.

"I'm escaping from Minda. She's on a rampage about the layout for the *Cedar River Review*. Her fashion column got pushed to what she considers a 'demeaning' spot because of all the sports news this issue."

"Right. A fashion report is much more news-worthy than a winning team," Todd said sarcastically.

"Where are you going?"

"To the School Store. I need a new notebook and pen. I thought I'd give Egg and Binky the business."

"I'll walk with you. I haven't been in the store since they had their official 'grand reopening' and Egg and Binky took over as managers."

The School Store had evolved into a surprisingly attractive business. The walls were light yellow. A contemporary-looking arrow in blue meandered its way around the walls near the top of the store, finally ending with the point of the arrow targeted at the cash register. The lighting highlighted well-done displays, mannequins wearing logo-emblazoned sweats, jackets, and other sportswear.

"Impressive," Lexi murmured. "Very impressive."

"Didn't think Egg and Binky could do it?" Todd paused before adding, "Me either."

The shelves held just about everything a student could need—pens, paper, rulers, blank tapes, erasers, file cards, and dozens of other items. A glass case near the cash register contained more expensive items like calculators and small cameras.

Several students were shopping in the store. Angela Hardy and Mary Beth Adamson were busy ringing up sales at the register.

"How'd you get so lucky, Mary Beth?" Anna Marie Arnold asked as she paid for a spiral-bound notebook and two pencils. "It must be fun to handle all that money."

Mary Beth looked up sharply. "What do you mean?"

"N-nothing," Anna Marie stammered. "Just making conversation, that's all."

"Everybody's a little nervous," Lexi commented. "And touchy."

From the back room came the sound of angry but familiar voices. Binky and Egg were arguing.

"You can't put that on a mannequin!" Binky screeched. "It's bizarre. You're crazy if you think you can do that to the display."

"Eye catching, that's what it is. We have to have exciting displays or no one will buy anything," Egg retorted.

"No one will buy *that*."

"I like it."

Todd and Lexi exchanged a weary glance as they headed for the back room.

There, Egg and Binky were glaring at each other, each clutching a body part of a half-dressed mannequin. Egg was holding its feet, Binky, an arm and a wig. The mannequin was dressed in orange and yellow leggings, decorated in licking flames; a pair of red and black polka-dotted boxer shorts dangled off one leg. Fishline sprung from the head Binky held as well as the wrist of the arm. All in all, it was a very strange-looking sight.

"What are you two trying to do? Pull her apart at the seams?" Todd inquired.

"Talk some sense into this fruitcake. Tell my brother that red, black, orange, and yellow don't go together—especially with *that*." Binky nodded toward a green and purple jacket that was apparently going to finish the ensemble.

"It's . . . colorful," Todd remarked.

"See? I told you so! That's what we need in here—color. We went with muted yellows so we could make our displays stand out. This will be perfect."

"Who'd buy this outfit, Egg? A color-blind clown? I don't think so."

"We want it to be noticed."

"That's the other thing," Binky wailed in explanation to Todd and Lexi. "He wants to hang it from the ceiling!" She waved the mannequin's arm and the fishline danced. "It's too heavy."

"It will be great. We'll put her in a surreal pose. Everybody will notice her."

"And what if she drops on a customer's head? Mr. Kahler will be furious if we have to put a claim in on our insurance. No School Store manager has ever had to do that before. It's a crazy idea, Egg. Sooner or later you'll have to admit it."

In the store, Angela was busy pricing candy bars and trying not to smile. Mary Beth didn't seem to be paying any attention to the McNaughton family argument. She wore a somber expression as she unpacked pens and loaded them into a small display.

"Oh, all right. Have it your way." A clatter erupted as the mannequin fell to the floor. Egg stomped to the other side of the room and flopped into a chair. Binky looked dumbfounded. Egg rarely gave in so easily.

"Now what was that all about?" Todd was startled by his friend's behavior.

"Nothing. It's just not worth fighting about. Binky can have her way."

"Egg, are you all right?" Binky asked, concern creasing her pixielike face. "You *never* let me win an argument if you can help it."

"I wish everyone would leave me alone. Quit bugging me, would you? Nag, nag, nag, that's all I hear. Why do people keep telling me what I have to do?" Egg crossed his arms over his skinny chest and dropped his chin until he looked like a pouting toddler. His lower lip even wobbled.

Lexi put out a hand and felt his forehead. "No temperature, but he sure *acts* sick."

"You better tell us what's wrong, Egg-O," Todd said gently. "I've never seen you like this before."

"I'm okay. Just stressed." Egg gave his sister an odd glance, as if to warn her against saying more.

"Oh, tell them, Egg," she said, ignoring the look

he'd given her. "They'll find out sooner or later anyway."

"Find out what?" Lexi pulled up a stool and sat down in front of Egg. She could have sworn he had tears in his eyes.

"I should never have gone to the dentist. Now I have to get braces!"

"That's what this is all about?" Todd blurted. "What's the big deal? I thought you were flunking out of school or needed an operation or something, the way you've been acting!"

" 'Big deal'? Braces are the worst thing in the world."

"No they aren't. Practically everybody wears braces sometime or another these days."

"Not me. Not now. Not my senior year in high school. Think about it. I'm a geek anyway. What's a geek who gets braces? A double geek? A quadruple geek? A super geek?" Egg slumped further in the chair. "World-class geek, that's what I'll be. Why me? Why now?"

"Egg, you'll be cute with braces," Lexi assured him. "You'll hardly notice them."

"Hah! I'll lisp and spit. I won't be able to eat popcorn or peanuts. My mouth will shine when I smile—if I ever smile again."

"Oh, quit being such a baby," Binky snorted. She turned to Lexi and Todd. "He's been like this ever since he heard the news. Dad finally told him to go to his room and get a grip and not to come down until he'd decided to quit moaning and groaning."

"It really isn't that bad," Todd assured him. "I had braces when I was in junior high. No big deal."

"Sure. In junior high it might not have been but

it is now. It is to me. I'm not a little kid anymore. I shouldn't have to wear braces. It's going to ruin my looks completely!"

Lexi stuffed back a smile. "Ruin" his looks? Egg was an odd-looking guy anyway, and people loved him just as he was.

"Egg, I think the braces will help. When they come off, you'll have a beautiful smile. It will make you *more* handsome, not less."

He looked hopeful for a moment before dismissing Lexi's comment. "It will wreck everything."

"Now that he's manager of the School Store, people have started to notice him. He's afraid the braces will make everyone forget what a good job he's doing here and remind them that he's a geek."

"Thanks for keeping my innermost secrets private, Binky," Egg growled. "Remind me never to confide in you again."

"Todd and Lexi are our best friends. They deserve to know why you're acting so strangely. Besides, maybe they can help me convince you that your worries are silly."

"Dad has already called me 'metal mouth' and told me I can't go through the metal detector at the airport anymore."

"You could start wearing a pillowcase over your head," Binky suggested unsympathetically, "or a grocery sack. Maybe no one would notice you then."

"Ease up, Bink," Todd scolded softly. "He's really hurting right now." Egg's pride and vanity were at stake, no matter how silly or trivial his friends and sister considered it to be.

"I had braces once before, you know. When I was really young. The dentist thought the problem was solved but I . . . uh . . ." Egg looked embarrassed.

" . . . he didn't wear his retainer and now they have to go back on again," Binky finished for him.

"Egg! Then you did this to yourself!" Lexi gasped.

"I know the dentist told me to wear it, but I never thought . . ."

"And now you expect us to feel sorry for you?"

Egg gave a deep sigh. "Well, *I* feel sorry for me!"

Still, all the sympathy had gone from the room.

Before Todd or Lexi could scold their friend, Angela peeked her head around the door. "Mary Beth and I have to go to class early. Can you and Binky take over until the next shift comes?"

Wearily, Egg nodded. He unfolded from the chair and stood up, not daring to look his friends in the eye.

Chapter Seven

To Egg's obvious relief, they could not continue the conversation after Angela and Mary Beth left the store. A middle-aged lady entered and began to look at the variety of sweat shirts displayed along one wall.

"May I help you?" Egg asked the woman.

Binky hurried to the cash register and tried to look busy and important. She didn't do very well at either.

The woman lifted the bag she carried into Egg's view. "I have a complaint."

Egg grew pale. Todd and Lexi, who were leaving, stopped short. Only two young men who had entered after the woman seemed ignorant of what was happening.

"A complaint? We haven't covered complaints in class yet," Binky muttered. "Now what?"

"I bought this sweat shirt here last spring as a gift for my niece. I didn't give it to her until August and look at it!" She drew the shirt from the bag. It was shapeless and faded. The seam on one sleeve was gaping open.

"Wow," Egg said unhelpfully.

"I paid good money for this sweater and it

started to fall apart the moment she washed it. I'd like a refund."

"Refund?" Egg echoed. No doubt that hadn't been covered in class either.

"We could do an exchange," Binky offered. She pointed at the colorful sweat shirts. "Anything you like."

"They're probably all pieces of junk," the woman crabbed. "Besides, my niece doesn't want this anymore. I'm very embarrassed. I made a special trip to this store and ended up giving her a gift that fell apart."

Binky took the shirt out of the woman's hands. "Do you know if she followed the laundering instructions carefully?"

"Are you saying this is my niece's fault? Who's in charge here? I want to talk to the manager!"

"Binky didn't mean to blame your niece," Egg hastened to say. "We want you to be happy with your purchase here at the School Store. It's important that people in the community know they can come here to shop. We'd be happy to give you credit for the price of the shirt."

"Credit? So I can buy more defective garments? Hardly. Who is the manager? I must talk to . . ."

It was painful for Todd and Lexi to watch Egg and Binky's humiliation. Even though they had not been the ones to order last year's defective merchandise, they were paying the price for someone else's mistakes. Egg's face was red and beaded with sweat. Binky looked as though she were about to cry. Neither was looking anywhere but at the angry woman.

"Let's get out of here," Lexi began when she saw

an odd movement out of the corner of her eye. One of the two guys who had entered was standing over a small display of cassette tapes. She thought she'd seen his hand reach out for one of the tapes and draw it into the pocket of his jeans, but it had happened so quickly that she wasn't one hundred percent sure.

"Todd, I think that guy just put a cassette tape into his pocket!"

"Shoplifting?"

Lexi nodded. "If he did, he picked a good time. Egg and Binky are totally focused on that woman. We were trying to leave. Do you think I imagined it?"

"There's one way to find out." Todd sauntered over to them.

"What have you got in your pocket?" he asked casually.

The guy looked up, startled. Much to Todd and Lexi's surprise, he bolted around them and out the door of the store.

"Shoplifter!" Todd yelled, drawing Egg's attention to what was transpiring. Then Todd darted out the door in hot pursuit.

The woman Egg had been talking to drew herself up to her full height. "Well," she huffed, "I can see that I'll get no satisfaction here."

"Pick out a sweat shirt," Binky pleaded. "Pick out *two*."

At that moment, the new work shift entered the store. "Tim," Binky barked. "Help this lady. She gets two free sweat shirts."

"Free?"

"Don't argue, just do it." And Binky spun out of

the store after Todd and Egg. Lexi followed close on her heels.

Egg and Todd had gone down the hallway to the right. Down that hall was the chorus room, the *Cedar River Review* offices, the typing and computer rooms, and one of two entries to the vocational department where woodworking, basic auto mechanics, and other skills were taught. At the end of the hall was an exit.

"Stop. Stop, thief," Egg yelled as he ran, making it easy for Lexi and Binky to follow. Doors began to open on either side of the hallway as curious teachers wondered what sort of fracas was occurring. Unfortunately, no one stepped out to stop the agile figure racing away from Egg and Todd.

Lexi felt someone grab hold of her arm. It was Mrs. Waverly, the choir director and music teacher. "Lexi? You know better than to be running."

"Someone was shoplifting in the School Store. Todd and I saw him. Now the guys are trying to catch him."

"Oh, dear." Mrs. Waverly's expression changed. "I'll call the office right away."

It would have been too late if the janitor hadn't been scrubbing the tile floor in front of the exit. His large bucket on wheels and selection of mops blocked the doorway. As the young thief's feet touched the wet tile, they slipped out from under him. He skidded, his arms and legs flailing wildly, into the janitor's contraption. With a loud *thunk* his feet hit the door as his head hit the floor.

Todd and Egg were on top of him in a moment. Each was doing some bizarre rendition of a wrestling hold, Egg pinning the feet, Todd the head and shoulders. The janitor stood over the squirming mass of humanity, scratching his head.

"What's going on down here?" Coach Derek demanded to know. Quickly Todd explained the situation and enlisted the coach's help.

After Coach Derek and another teacher had whisked the young offender away to the school offices, Todd and Lexi were left to the hardest job of all—calming the McNaughtons.

———

"This has been the worst day of my life!" Egg moaned as he reached for his sixth slice of pepperoni pizza. "I'm so upset I can hardly eat."

"I can see that," Matt said mildly. "Bummer."

Peggy and Jennifer began to giggle but Lexi gave them a silencing glare. It had taken nearly an hour—and two large pizzas—to settle Egg and Binky after the police had come to the school to question the shoplifters. Egg had been so nervous while the police officers talked to him that one might have thought *he* was the one in trouble.

Now the McNaughtons slouched in their chairs looking more relaxed but no happier than they had an hour ago. In fact, Binky looked as though she were about to cry.

"I just don't understand it!" she finally blurted. "Why would anyone want to steal from us like that? What did we ever do to that guy? I don't even know him."

"He didn't steal from you personally, Bink," Lexi reminded her. "He stole from the store."

"That's just like stealing from me, as far as I can see. Egg and I have been working our hearts out to make the store successful. Everybody knows it. You even did a story on it in the *Cedar River Review*. We've been hanging posters all over school and handing out flyers. Somebody would have to have been hibernating on Mars for the last few weeks to miss it."

"He didn't look like the kind of guy who read all the handouts that come from the school," Todd said. "Besides, you said yourself that you didn't know him. Why should he know *you*?"

"Don't take this theft personally," Peggy said. "You're behaving as though that guy went into your house and took something from your bedroom!"

Binky's lip wobbled. "That's how I feel—like he was intentionally stealing from me or my brother. It's stupid, I know, but I can't get the idea out of my mind. I feel so *hurt*!"

"Get over it, Bink. Logically you have to know that shoplifters are thieves. They don't care who they steal from, only that the store has merchandise they want."

"I know it in my head," she admitted, "but in my heart . . ."

Egg was growing more and more morose as the conversation continued. His half-eaten slice of pizza lay on the plate in front of him.

Lexi was the first to notice. "Egg? Are you all right? You don't feel the same as Binky, do you? You know that boy didn't have it personally 'in' for you, don't you?"

"Huh?" He looked up. His eyes were watery and unfocused.

"Are you all right?" Peggy reached for his hand.

"Are you *crying*?" Jennifer, blunt as ever, demanded to know.

"No! Oh, I don't know. . . ." Egg looked thoroughly miserable.

"All right, that's it," Jennifer asserted. "Edward McNaughton, tell us what's going on. You look like you lost your best friend, and we know for a fact that you didn't—because your best friends are sitting right here and would like to help you. So spit it out."

Startled by Jennifer's blunt assessment, Egg began to bluster. "Nothing's wrong. What makes you think anything's wrong?" His shoulders sank. "Except of course that we had that big complaint today, a shoplifter, and . . ."

Binky squirmed uncomfortably. "You might as well tell them, Egg. If we can't figure it out soon, everyone in school will know anyway."

"Figure what out?" Jennifer demanded.

"Things are not going well at the store," Egg said in a resigned tone. "Today was just an example of how everything has gotten out of hand. Our advisor is on us constantly."

"Why?" Lexi asked gently.

"We've been having trouble balancing the books ever since we took over," Egg admitted.

"Is it that hard?"

"It shouldn't be 'hard' at all. Still, money keeps coming up short. Some days it's a few pennies, other days much more. Once we even came up long. I don't know what to do."

"He's tried everything," Binky chimed. "I know. I've helped him."

"It's been a mess running the store ever since

the renovations and moving were going on, but other businesses—real ones—manage to do it. Why can't we?"

"Maybe it would help if you put everything on computer," Lexi suggested. "If you had your inventory as well as your credits and debits and daily cash flow all in one place, maybe that would help."

"That's not a bad idea, Egg," Binky said hopefully. She was obviously as upset as Egg about this puzzling situation. "We could even ask the accounting and computer classes to help us."

Egg appeared disinterested in the suggestions. Instead he stared at his chewed-off fingernails and muttered, "But why can't *I* get the books to come out right?"

Chapter Eight

"Hi, Mom. What's up?" Lexi came through the kitchen door with Peggy and Jennifer close behind her.

"Be careful. I've got paper strewn all over the place." Mrs. Leighton looked up from the legal-sized note pad she was writing on. Her reading glasses hung precariously from the tip of her nose and her hair was mussed. There were three half-filled mugs of cold coffee on the counter beside her and a partially eaten sandwich drying on a plate.

Jennifer picked up the nearest large piece of paper. On it was a sketch of two young children and a puppy. They were staring with avid interest at a young man in a wheelchair. "Cool. What's this?"

"Are you working on your book, Mrs. Leighton?" Peggy inquired. "Is that what these sketches are about?"

"Yes. I've been jumping from sketching to working on text and back again all day." Mrs. Leighton tugged her fingers through her hair. "I just can't seem to get anywhere!"

"This looks like somewhere," Jennifer said. "Awesome pictures."

"I'm not having trouble with the artwork. In

fact, it's going so well that I wish I hadn't decided to write the text myself. I had no idea that writing was so difficult."

"What's so hard about it?"

"I know what I want to say, but I'm not quite sure how to say it. This project is very important to me. I want to do it as well as I can. There are people who need this book. When I first learned I had MS, I was terrified. I had little idea how to explain this illness to either my husband or to Lexi. I had even less idea how to explain it to Ben without scaring or confusing him.

"That's when I decided to write and illustrate a children's book for kids whose parents are diagnosed with a serious illness. It's very important to me that I do the very best job I can—for children like Ben."

"Tell us about it," Peggy encouraged. Completely at home in this kitchen, both she and Jennifer had found seats across from Mrs. Leighton while Lexi dished up a plate of brownies and brought a carton of milk from the refrigerator.

"It's about a young brother and sister trying to cope with their mother's illness. They meet several adults and children with similar diseases, and with each encounter their knowledge grows."

"Does it have a happy ending?" Jennifer asked.

"Oh yes."

"Good. There are enough rotten endings in life without having one in your book too."

"True." Lexi's mom sighed. "I just hope this book doesn't experience one of those."

"What do you mean?"

"Writing and illustrating it isn't enough. I have

to find a company that's interested in publishing it or it will never be more than my own private little story. I've sent out query letters but there's been no buyer yet."

"You're kidding! No one wants a wonderful book like this?" Jennifer picked up one of the sketches. "Why would anyone pass up such a great idea?"

"It's not that easy," Mrs. Leighton said. "Publishing a book costs a great deal of money. Publishers want books that will sell a lot of copies. That's how they recover their investment. My little book isn't apt to earn as much as those on other, more popular topics. I can only hope that someone sees the need and the potential for a book like mine and is willing to take the risk. Besides, I am a new writer and illustrator."

"Don't look so down, Mrs. Leighton. I know someone will love your book!"

"Thanks for the vote of confidence, Peggy, but, for now, even getting someone to read it will be a big step."

"If writing and publishing a book is so hard," Jennifer commented, "then why do so many people say that someday they're going to write a book?"

"Because they don't actually know how much hard work it is," Lexi broke in. "Mom didn't know either until she started her project."

"Maybe we'd better leave so you can get back to work, Mrs. Leighton," Peggy offered.

But Lexi's mom was already deeply engrossed in the words on the pages in front of her. She didn't even hear the girls leave.

———

"When was the last time you cleaned this thing?" Lexi asked as she maneuvered a vacuum brush attachment over the fuzzy fabric seat of Todd's 1949 Ford.

He looked up sharply. A frown creased his even features. The car was Todd's pride and joy. He kept it in mint condition.

"I found two specks of dust and a dog hair in here. The thing is filthy!"

His concerned expression turned into a smile. "Don't scare me like that. I thought you found mud or something."

"How could I? You clean this thing every day."

"Not quite. And I never clean it on Sundays."

They were bantering as Egg and Binky pulled into the driveway in their parents' car.

"Must be a special day. The McNaughtons usually don't get the car."

"Would *you* be willing to let either one of them drive your car?"

"I get your point."

They would have extended their teasing to Egg and Binky, but the grim expression on Egg's face prevented either of them from saying a word. His eyes were glazed, his face slightly puffy, and his attitude morose.

"Hi," Binky greeted them. "Cleaning again?"

"What's wrong with Egg?" Todd waved a chamois rag in his tall friend's direction.

Binky rolled her eyes. "Let him tell you."

They all turned to Egg.

Slowly, he ventured a pitiful smile. Light caught on the fine metal wires in his mouth and for a moment Egg looked as though his teeth were shooting sparks of electricity. "Bwaces," he said.

"Huh?"

"Bwaces. I got bwaces." His dry lips caught on the wires as he spoke.

"He can't talk very well yet because he's not used to his braces," Binky explained. "The dentist told him that would come with time. He said Egg had to be patient."

"Cool, Egg. Let's see." Lexi peered into Egg's mouth. "Do they hurt?"

He didn't speak, but a single tear leaking down one cheek answered for him.

"That much, huh?"

"He's supposed to take some pain medication for a couple days. The dentist also gave him some wax to put on the sharpest wires to protect the inside of his mouth."

Egg's lips began to work. He obviously wanted to add to this but was having difficulty forming the words. "My teeth hurt, I have a headache, and the inside of my mouth is raw."

The word "teeth"—as Egg pronounced it— sounded more like "teef."

"I can't even eat!" That sounded even worse.

"Have you tried a milkshake?" Todd suggested. "They're soft. Maybe cold ice cream would feel good inside your mouth too."

Egg brightened. He tried to nod but groaned when the motion hurt his head.

"Come inside. We'll make them for everyone."

With the efficiency that comes with experience, Todd found the blender and a five-quart bucket of ice cream. He spooned ice cream into the blender while Lexi added chocolate and milk. They gave Egg the first shake.

After a few tentative spoonsful, Egg began to wiggle his lips and jaw, testing his limits. "I think it helps."

"You mean you'll be able to talk after all? Maybe we should have left you the way you were, with your mouth frozen in pain," Binky teased.

Egg took another spoonful of the concoction before speaking. "I guess it wouldn't matter much. Life as I know it is over anyway."

"What do you mean by that?" Todd handed glasses to Lexi and Binky and took the last for himself.

"What do you think? With this mouthful of metal, I look like a loser."

"You look like a loser anyway," Binky said cheerfully. "Why don't you tell them what's *really* bothering you? Tell them what you really think it will ruin."

"Be quiet, Binky."

"I've *been* quiet and you won't quit whining. Lexi and Todd will tell you the same thing I did— that you're worrying over nothing."

"What will braces ruin?" Todd asked.

"His love life! That's why he's so depressed."

"Girls don't like guys with braces," Egg said.

"How do you know?" Lexi challenged.

Egg blushed. It crept up his neck and across his cheeks like a prairie fire.

"He's worried that *Angela* won't like him with braces!" Lexi deduced. "Oh, Egg, you're so vain."

"That's not it . . . is it?" Todd asked.

"I've heard other guys talk," Egg said. Even his

ears had turned red. "They say braces can . . . get in the way."

"Of what?" Binky asked innocently. Then she, too, began to blush.

"Let's just say they're bad for guy/girl relationships."

"You mean *kissing*!" Binky nearly fell off the kitchen stool giggling. Egg's color was beginning to resemble that of a boiled lobster.

"You don't have to worry," she went on to console her brother. "I'd bet money you aren't a very good kisser anyway, and Angela wouldn't even miss it— if, that is, you've even kissed her yet!"

The concept appealed to Binky and she wanted to explore it. "The dentist says he has to wear them for eighteen months to two years. That's a long time to wait for a kiss, Egg!"

Even in his painful state, Egg had the strength to snarl at Binky. He bared his teeth and gave a gutteral growl.

Unchastized, Binky squinted and stared into her brother's mouth. "Have you been eating broccoli? Or spinach, maybe?"

Egg clamped a hand over his mouth and garbled a muffled "Why?"

"There's green stuff hanging all over your teeth. Gross! Don't you ever brush?"

"How could I eat broccoli? I can't even chew soup."

"Well, you ate something disgusting. Lettuce? Kiwi fruit?"

"I did not!"

"Then what's the green stuff?"

Egg hurried to a mirror to study his teeth.

"Those are the rubber bands on my braces."

"Green ones?"

"I had a choice—pink, black, gray, green, red, orange. . . . I'm going to do red, white, and blue for the Fourth of July and black and orange for Halloween."

"Whatever," Binky said. She turned to Todd and Lexi. "It still looks like broccoli to me."

Chapter Nine

"Look at that." Todd nudged Lexi as they walked toward the high school.

Lexi saw Egg and Angela, deep in conversation, in a shadowed doorway. "Probably discussing Egg's braces."

Todd laughed out loud. "Maybe we were too hard on him."

"He's a good sport," Lexi said absently, still studying the pair in the doorway. "They are an odd couple, aren't they?"

"Egg and just about anyone make an odd couple," Todd commented.

"I'm glad they found each other."

As they approached, Egg waved and Angela gave them a high-wattage smile.

"We were just talking about you," Angela said.

"Would you like to go out with us tonight?" Egg added. "A double date. We're going to play laser tag. There are usually several people wanting to make up a team. We can find someone when we get to the game."

"Let's do it, Todd," Lexi prodded. "Jennifer says it's a lot of fun."

"Wear black clothes," Egg said. "You're a lot

harder to find if you're in black."

———

They met promptly at six. Egg and Angela looked as though they were launching a secret spy mission in their black shoes, socks, jeans, and long-sleeved shirts. Egg even had a black hat pulled down over his hair.

"Don't say a word," was Angela's greeting. "Egg insists we dress this way. I had a hard time convincing him that he didn't need to put black face paint on his cheeks and forehead too."

"I didn't realize how into this you were," Todd commented.

"He's not the only one." Lexi pointed to the lobby. "There's Minda, Tressa, and Mary Beth. They're wearing black too."

"The game room is lit with black lights," Egg explained. "If you wear light colors, you glow in the dark. You make a great target for the opposing team, but it's no fun getting hit all the time. Every time you get hit, you have to recharge your weapon at the power station."

Just then the High Fives spotted their little group. Minda and Mary Beth walked toward them. "Would you like to be on our team?" Mary Beth asked. "We can play with seven."

"Sure," Angela said. "If it's all right with Todd and Lexi."

"Why not?" Lexi's idea of a great date was not spending it with the High Fives. Still, Mary Beth was the most pleasant of the group and there was no point in angering either Minda or the Williams sisters.

They paid their entry fees and lined up for equipment and instructions about the game. By the time everyone was wearing headgear and a small laser gun attached to a power pack over one shoulder by what looked like a telephone cord, they were all laughing.

"You are the green team," the attendant said. "Your goal is to hit the target on your opponents' headgear and to avoid being hit yourselves. You can hide behind the flexible walls suspended from the ceiling or crawl on the floor. Every time you are hit, you'll get a signal in your earphones to re-energize your weapon. Once you do that, you'll be in the game again. When the game is over, come to the front desk and pick up your computer printouts. This will tell you how many times you fired, how many targets you hit, and who the most valuable player on your team is. It will also give you your shooting percentages. Have fun!"

Stealthily the green team crept into the big playroom. Loud instrumental music played and strobe lights flashed. The opposing team entered from the other side of the room.

"This is too funny!" Lexi giggled.

"Shhhhh. Don't let them know where you are."

In seconds Lexi understood what they meant. Her headgear buzzed and a mechanical voice ordered, "Re-energize, re-energize."

"You're hit," Mary Beth whispered as she tiptoed by. "Go to the power station and re-energize your laser weapon."

Recharged, Lexi dropped to her stomach just as she had seen Egg do and squirmed her way to the front line. As she fired at the opponents, she felt a foot in the middle of her back.

"Is that you on the floor, Leighton?" Minda querulously asked. "What are you trying to do, trip me . . . oh, I've been hit!"

The game lasted twenty minutes. The digital sign over the exit door showed a definitive win by the green team. Egg was so pumped by the victory, he actually threw his arms around Tressa Williams, risking more bodily harm than he ever had crawling around on the floor in the dark.

"What's that in your mouth, McNaughton? Swamp slime? It's hanging all over your teeth." Tressa squinted into the interior of Egg's mouth.

Egg clamped his hand over his lips. "Braces. Green rubber bands. And I hate broccoli."

———

They were still laughing over Egg's response when they reached the pizza place.

"Did you see the look on Tressa's face when you said 'And I hate broccoli'? She didn't have a clue what you were talking about."

"At least she didn't yell at you anymore. You surprised her too much."

"Mary Beth is the nicest of the High Fives, isn't she?" Angela observed.

"She's a hard worker at the School Store," Egg agreed. "And not so crabby as Minda. She doesn't say much at all, actually. Sometimes I wonder what she's thinking."

"I don't even know where she lives."

"Over by the Hannafords. I think they have a big house but I heard they might be moving. Her dad got laid off at work."

"Do you mind? Todd interrupted. "I'm starved. What are you going to have?"

Egg looked longingly at the menu. "Soup."

"No pizza?"

"With this mouth? Are you kidding? Soup will be hard enough. I've got wires that keep sticking me in the side of the mouth." Egg pulled a little white case out of his pocket. "I have to wax the ends of the wires to make them less painful, but that's weird too. Every tooth in my head feels loose."

Egg winced and his dry lips stuck on his teeth until he pulled them off with his fingers. "I need water!"

As they ate, Egg stared longingly at everyone's plates and stirred unhappily at the soup of the day—cream of broccoli.

———

"Let's go back to my place," Egg suggested when everyone had finished. "We can hang out there, and I can open a can of *real* soup."

"I have to let Mom know where I'll be," Angela said. "She's not working tonight. She'll worry if I don't come home soon."

"I thought your mother worked during the day," Todd said.

"She found a second job. She's a waitress at a greasy spoon near the mission three nights a week. She's looking for something better, but this is okay for now."

"Your mom works hard, doesn't she?" Lexi observed.

"She says she's never going to be homeless again. That was the scariest time in my life—hers too. School. Work. She'll do whatever it takes."

Egg squeezed Angela's shoulders and gave her a warm smile. Returning the smile, she added, "Good things came out of that bad time too. I know I have to do well in school so I can support myself once I graduate. I don't want to feel as though I can't buy a candy bar or use a pay phone ever again. Being poor is hard."

Then she looked at Egg with a soft expression. "Of course, I was poor when I met Egg. I guess that means that good things can happen when you least expect them."

"You two are very lucky," Lexi murmured.

"I know." Egg's smile was so wide his braces fairly danced in the light.

———

"What are you doing here?"

"Don't act so happy to see us, Binky," Todd retorted as they walked through the McNaughton door. Binky and Harry were sitting on the couch reading magazines. "Harry, how are you doing?"

Harry Cramer unfolded his long body from the couch and smiled good-naturedly. The familiar chip in his front tooth was still there, as was the mop of naturally curly hair.

"I'd almost forgotten how tall you are," Lexi said as she gave him a hug.

His hazel eyes twinkled. "Binky says I've grown."

"And he'd better quit pretty soon, because I haven't. I feel like a peanut next to him."

"You *are* a peanut, Binky."

While Binky was pouting, the others pumped

Harry for information about college.

"Are the girls at college as cute as we've heard?" Todd asked mischievously.

Harry's expression was one of wonder. "Girls? There are girls at college? I guess I didn't notice."

Todd and Egg hooted with laughter as Binky's frown dissolved into a satisfied smile.

"With Binky around who needs other girls?"

"It's that physical fitness program she's been on," Egg added. "Have you noticed her muscles?"

"Quit it," Binky huffed. "You're being silly. Besides, we were busy when you interrupted us. Harry's helping me with merchandise ideas for the store."

"We've already been through these." Harry's eyes glazed as he pointed to a stack of thirty catalogs. "Every single page."

"So far we haven't found much we can afford, but I'm sure there's something."

"Binky, don't bore Harry with our problems," Egg ordered.

"Actually, I'd like to hear a little more about the store," Harry said. "Who's working there?"

"Angela." Binky nodded toward the girl on the couch. "And Tim Anders and Mary Beth Adamson. The kids from marketing class also take turns working there in pairs during the hour class is held. There aren't many of us, so we really need the other employees."

"Tell Harry about the shoplifters."

Lexi glanced at Egg. He seemed detached and quiet, having slipped into that strange, sad mood again.

Lexi was about to ask him what was wrong when the telephone rang.

"Angela, it's for you. Your mom."

Angela rose to take the call. When she returned from the other room, she picked up her jacket. "I have to go. Mom is needed in the office at the mission. They are missing some files and she's the only one who knows where they are."

"Can't she just go?" Binky asked.

"No. She's waiting for a call on a new job. She told them that she'd be home this evening if they needed her. She wants me there to take a message if she's not back before the call comes."

"I'll give you a ride," Egg offered.

"Let me." Harry jumped to his feet. "Binky and I ordered Chinese takeout. I have to pick it up anyway. I'll get a few more egg rolls and fortune cookies while I'm there."

———

After Harry and Angela had been gone awhile, Lexi turned to Egg. "Okay, what's going on?"

"Who says anything is going on?"

"I saw you sitting there, drifting away from our conversation, looking really depressed. You do it a lot lately."

"It was Harry asking about the store that got to me."

"You're taking your job as manager much too seriously, Egg."

"Being manager isn't the hard part. It's the books that are driving me crazy."

"Still can't make them balance, huh?"

"Not even close. Oh, some days I'm still right on, but others . . ."

"Admit it, Egg, you just can't add." Binky dismissed the problems with a wave of her hand. "And you're scared to tell Mr. Kahler that you're having trouble."

"There's a leak somewhere. . . ."

But Binky wasn't interested in what was bothering her brother. Money and the books were Egg's problems. Merchandising was hers.

"Hats. Now *there* is a problem."

Everyone stared at Binky. "What?"

"Hats. For the store. Haven't any of you been listening to me? If we don't order the right merchandise, the store will lose more money than the nickels and dimes Egg lost."

"But it's not just nickels," Egg said dejectedly.

"I talked Mr. Kahler into letting us order two dozen cowboy hats with the school logo on them. I thought they'd be perfect for the Western-themed academic 'roundup' they have during third quarter. The hats cost the store more than anything else we've ever ordered, even more than the sweat shirts. We didn't want to sell chintzy products and the hats are really high quality. I thought the store should have something really special and distinctive. The hats seemed to be the best choice."

"So what's the problem?" Todd asked.

Binky's forehead furrowed. "They were delivered yesterday. They're beautiful, but we're going to have to ask a lot of money for them. What if they don't sell?"

"Didn't you think of that before you ordered them?"

"It didn't seem like such a big deal then. Now we have twenty-four hats lined up in the back room waiting for heads. If I can't sell them, I'll get a lousy grade in marketing class."

"I think *you* need a new head, Binky," Egg said grumpily. "We discussed this in class and you wouldn't listen."

"I just need to know how to advertise and sell them, that's all."

At that moment, Harry came through the door with a bag of Chinese food. "Sell what?"

Binky related her story.

"How about commercials?" Harry asked.

"We can't afford television advertising!"

"You could work something up for a pep rally. I'm sure the cheerleaders wouldn't mind an occasional 'word from their sponsors.' "

"I like it!" Binky jumped to her feet. "Let me get some paper and write that down."

"Why don't you display all twenty-four hats in the window? Tell people that these are the only hats like it in the world and when they're sold, there will be no more. Make people think it's really cool to have one."

"How can I do that?"

"Flyers!" Harry suggested. "I'll help you write up a flyer saying how special and unique these hats are. Send one home with every student."

Binky's head was bobbing eagerly. "Any other ideas?"

"You could ask Minda to endorse them in her fashion column for the *Cedar River Review*."

Binky's nose wrinkled disdainfully. "I don't want her involved in this." Minda and Binky had never gotten along, and Binky wasn't about to share her special position at the School Store with anyone she didn't like.

"Think about it. Everybody reads Minda's column. It would be great advertising. If she said those hats were the thing to have, I'll bet every one of the High Fives would buy one tomorrow."

"Lexi's got a point. Besides, if the High Fives decide the hats are stupid looking, a lot of people who might have bought them will think twice about it."

"That's dumb!"

"I think Binky should work *with* the High Fives, not against them," Harry said. "Ask Minda and her friends to wear them for a day, show them off, even give them a discount on their own hats if they sell one to somebody else."

"I don't know if Mr. Kahler would approve. . . ."

"Face it. Minda and the High Fives can wreck your business if they start poking fun at somebody wearing one of your hats. But if *they* look like the ones who started the fad—"

"Actually, Binky, it sounds like smart marketing. Find an audience and . . ." Egg brightened at the thought of making Minda do some of his selling for him.

" . . . And we've had enough conversation about the School Store for one evening," Todd finished for him. "You are both too focused on the store. It's getting old—fast."

"Todd's right. Let's try to forget it for a while," Binky agreed.

She and Egg sat quietly for a moment before asking in unison, "But *how*?"

"Easy," Todd said. "There's a traveling carnival at the fairgrounds. Want to go?"

Chapter Ten

"I'm glad you suggested this, Todd." Egg breathed deeply of the smells of popcorn and caramel apples. "I needed a break."

Egg, Todd, Lexi, Binky, and Harry meandered down the midway of the bustling carnival. A group of small boys ran screaming and yelling in front of them. Somewhere a baby cried and a dog barked.

"Hey, Mister, win your pretty lady a teddy bear?" a carnival barker yelled at Harry. "Be a hero, win the lady a bear!"

Harry paused but Binky pulled on his arm. "Don't waste your money. We can *buy* a teddy bear for less money than you'd spend trying to win one."

"Toss the ball, hit the bottles, win a prize!"

"Three tries for a dollar. Show the lady you can do it!"

Binky ignored the carnival barkers but pointed to a small booth nearby. "That's the game I want to try."

"Picking ducks? That's stupid. There's no skill involved in that!"

"There's no skill in any of these. We're doomed to lose. At least if I pick a duck, I'll have the fun of doing it." She headed for the tent with a stride that indicated that there would be no changing her mind.

She peered into the moving pool on which hundreds of small yellow ducks floated. "What do I win?"

"A prize every time, little lady."

"Big prizes?"

The barker waved toward a huge panda bear on the wall. "Some like this."

"And the rest worth a penny or two," Egg muttered.

"Shhh. I need to concentrate." Binky studied the ducks as if she were seeing right through them to the numbers on their undersides. Finally she plucked a plastic duck from the water.

The man behind the counter read the number and reached into a bucket behind him. "Here's your prize, little lady."

"A fingernail clipper? What kind of prize is that?"

"The kind of prize you won." Egg pulled on his sister's arm. "Let's get out of here before you waste any more money."

"What a rip-off! I wanted that bear!"

"Who wants to go on the Ferris wheel?" Harry attempted to divert Binky.

"Not me," Egg said. "I get sick on that thing. I'll look around till you're off."

———

They found Egg at the cotton candy stand when the ride was done.

"You should have come with us, Egg. It was great."

"Maybe next time." Egg gave them a wide smile.

"Ewww . . . what's wrong with your teeth?" Binky looked horrified. "Gross."

Egg's smile quickly disappeared. "What?"

"Open up." Todd looked into Egg's mouth. "It looks like caramel corn stuck in your braces. Are you sure you're supposed to be eating that stuff?"

"It looks like mouth rot to me," Binky said. "And you deserve it. The dentist said *no popcorn*."

He'd been caught. Egg looked crestfallen. "How do I get it out?"

"With a toothbrush, I suppose. You're just lucky you didn't break any brackets."

"The caramel corn smelled so good."

"Close your mouth, Egg," Binky ordered. "It makes me sick."

"There's got to be a water fountain around here. I can rinse my mouth. Does anyone carry a toothbrush?" Egg was talking through the hand covering his mouth.

"I have a hairbrush," Binky offered sweetly. "Your mouth is big enough for that."

Egg would have grabbed his sister to shake her, but he was too busy covering his mouth with one hand and clutching the cotton candy with the other.

"Could we have a glass of water?" Todd asked of the concession stand operators.

Egg disappeared around the corner of a tent for a moment. The others could hear him gargling and sloshing water around in his mouth. When he reappeared, he flashed his metal grin. "Better?"

"Now can you do something about your face?" Binky asked.

Egg drew himself to his full height. He might

have looked imposing if he weren't so thin. "You don't respect me, Binky. You should, you know. I'm your brother."

"I was just teasing. Don't get so uptight."

"I guess I'll just have to do something to make you respect me."

"I respect you. I also like to tease you."

"You just wait," Egg blustered. "I'll think of something. I'll *make* you respect me. Just you wait and see."

They strolled through the carnival looking at the colorful sideshows and watching the fascinating mix of people. At the far end of the midway, the trouble began.

"That's it!" Egg shouted, pointing in the direction of a big crane. It looked like something used in erecting a high-rise building. Suddenly, a body fell from the very top of the crane, and a scream went up from the people on the ground.

"Bungee jumping. What a rush that must be," Egg breathed.

The jumper dangled head down from the springy bungee cord.

"Why would anyone want to do that?" Lexi asked with a shudder.

"To gain a little respect, probably." Egg stared thoughtfully at the contraption.

"You aren't thinking . . ." Harry began, but Egg was already moving toward the ticket booth.

He'd laid money on the counter and was reading the release forms by the time the others reached him.

"You can't do this! It's crazy. Do you see how high that platform is? Do you want to kill yourself? You wouldn't even ride on the Ferris wheel."

"I didn't mean what I said about your face, Egg," Binky pleaded, "and I love your braces. Even the green ones."

"Too late. I know what you think. But you'll change your mind once I do this. Nobody's going to think Egg McNaughton is a geek anymore!"

Nothing they could say would dissuade him. Lexi and Binky watched in horror as Egg stepped up to the little car which, attached to the arched side of the contraption, would take him to the top of the crane.

"He'll be fine. Don't worry," Harry consoled. "I've had friends at college bungee jump. Nothing happened to them."

"It's all my fault. I should never have teased him about his braces. He doesn't pay any attention to what I say. Why did he start now?" Binky gnawed at her fingernails. "I'm responsible for this. My parents are going to have a fit."

"He'll be fine. Look at the net beneath the drop. It's nice and sturdy."

"Do you see how high that platform is?" Binky wailed. "Oh, Egg, if you live through this I'm going to strangle you!"

"What are they doing?" Lexi asked as a man bent to attach something to Egg's shirt.

"Putting a mike on him. This is going to be funny. Now we'll all hear what Egg says on the way up to the platform." Harry slapped his thigh. "I've heard guys scream for their mothers all the way up and down again."

"I'm going to throw up," Binky moaned.

92

The little car began to roll up the track to the top of the arch.

Suddenly Egg's voice broke onto the microphone. "Isn't this thing going kind of fast?" They could practically hear Egg swallow and imagine his Adam's apple bobbing wildly in his neck. "Maybe I should think about this a little more . . . if you could just back this thing down again . . ."

The man traveling in the car with him murmured something.

"What do you mean I can't go back? *You're* going back! I want my money returned now!"

The crowd on the ground began to laugh.

"Get me out of here. Turn around. I'm getting sick. I can't look down. Oh. . . ."

Still the little trolley edged upward. At nearly one hundred and twenty feet in the air, Egg emerged onto a platform, hands covering his eyes.

Obviously, the bungee jump operators were accustomed to last-minute mind changes from their customers. They ignored Egg as they hooked the cord to his ankles.

"If he gets killed my parents are going to get really mad," Binky muttered. "And they'll blame me."

"He's not going to get killed. The net is strong. So is the cord." Harry chuckled. "But he *is* going to be scared."

Todd glanced upward. "There he goes."

Egg came diving off the platform with his arms flailing, screaming at the top of his lungs.

"He's not very graceful, is he?" a heavyset lady nearby observed.

That was an understatement. Egg looked as

though he were being flung to the ground by a disgruntled giant.

"He's coming close!" someone yelled. Over the top of the crowd, Egg literally reached the end of his rope. As his body sprang back into the air, he gave a bloodcurdling scream. Binky matched it with one of her own.

By the time her brother was retrieved and helped toward them on unsteady legs, Binky had quit hyperventilating and some of her color had returned.

"You big goof," were her first words. "You nearly gave me a heart attack."

"No sweat," Egg said weakly. His skin was a pale green color. "It was fun."

"You didn't *sound* like you were having fun."

"But I was. Now do you respect me?"

Binky stared at him. "Of course I do. I always have. You're my big brother. You didn't have to jump off a crane to earn my respect!"

"Really? Why didn't you tell me that sooner?" And Egg fainted dead away.

———

"Now what?" Todd asked wearily as Binky raced into the *Cedar River Review* room and skidded to a halt in front of the table where he and Lexi were working.

"Lexi, you have to fix my hair."

"It looks fine to me."

"Not fine enough. Mr. Kahler just told Egg and me that we have to have our pictures taken in a few minutes. The student managers' photos always hang in the School Store for the duration of their management period. The photo also goes into the yearbook."

"Great! You'll be famous."

"Not great. Look at me! Mr. Kahler forgot to tell us about the picture. I didn't work on my hair or wear the right clothes."

Just then Egg entered the room. Binky pointed his way. "And look at *him*."

Egg bared his teeth and flashed a fearsome mouthful of metal. "They could have taken the picture earlier. I don't even want to be seen like this, and certainly not recorded in the yearbook!"

It was a pretty scary sight.

"Just don't smile," Lexi suggested.

"That's not going to help. See?" Egg closed his mouth. His lips did look stretched, as if the undersides were stuffed with dental cotton.

"You have to help us decide if Egg should smile or not. Fix my hair while we're deciding." Binky thrust a comb and hair spray at Lexi.

Todd cleared his throat. "In case anyone didn't notice, Lexi and I have a deadline for some photos for the *Review* that we're working on here."

Binky brightened. "Do you think you could take some photos of Egg both smiling and serious? If we could get them developed before the photographer got here, he'd know whether to smile or not."

"*Binky*," Todd and Lexi said together. "You're obsessing!"

"I'll just keep my mouth shut," Egg said. "It's easier for me than it is for you, sis."

As Binky was about to retort, Mr. Kahler and the photographer entered the room.

Todd and Lexi watched the photographer

briskly organize Egg and Binky and snap their picture. Binky's hair was in a whirl and Egg's expression pained.

"It's not going to matter, you know," Todd whispered to Lexi. "Whatever Egg does with his mouth, this picture will be bizarre!"

Chapter Eleven

After they had finished their work in the *Cedar River Review* room, Lexi and Todd left together.

"Are you on your way home?" Lexi asked.

"I'm going to stop at the School Store to see Egg."

"Do you think he's still there? The store closed half an hour ago."

"I'm sure. Egg rarely leaves early. I've been worried about him."

"Why? Because he's been working too hard?" Lexi asked.

"No, that's not it. Egg always throws himself into projects with too much enthusiasm. It's something else. He's been acting strange lately."

"How can you tell? Egg always acts strange."

"There's something on his mind that he's not telling us. Have you noticed how distracted and worried he is lately?"

"Now that you mention it, he has been acting odd, even for Egg. That little episode with the bungee jump was very strange."

"That's exactly what I mean. Sometimes he acts as though he's running away from something—even his own thoughts."

"Egg would talk about it if something was really bothering him. You're one of his best friends."

"That's what I've always assumed," Todd said, "but it's certainly not like that now. Either this responsibility for the School Store is too much for him or something else is going on."

"Maybe," Lexi said doubtfully. "Egg and Binky tell each other just about everything. I think she would have said something if Egg were having trouble."

"Maybe Binky's in on it," Todd suggested. "After all, she's a manager for the School Store too."

"She has a hard time keeping a secret. I think your imagination is working overtime where Egg is concerned."

"Maybe," Todd said vaguely, "but I'm still going to stop at the store to check on him."

The door to the School Store was locked. When Todd tapped on the glass, Binky hurried to let them in.

"You've got to help me," she said dramatically. "I'm having a crisis." She towed Todd and Lexi toward the back room, where in the midst of a clutter of packing boxes sat several ugly plastic heads, the kind beauty parlors use to display wigs and hairpieces. Some of the heads were empty, others were wearing cowboy hats.

"I'm trying to put together a window display," Binky explained. "I'm going to put one hat at a time in the window. The first person to buy a hat is going to get a special price. One by one the hats will be sold until there's only one left. The person who buys the last hat wins a prize."

"Sounds pretty inventive," Lexi said.

"Not only that," Todd added, "it looks like the Tower of London in here."

Binky looked at him blankly.

"That's a place in London where many beheadings took place," Lexi explained. "Weren't you in history class when we discussed it?"

"Oh, please. I can't talk about that now. I'll be the one beheaded if these hats don't sell. We haven't gotten rid of one of them yet. Our money is tied up in these things. Do you think the countdown idea will work?" She lifted several sheets of paper from the desk by the cash register. "I've also drawn some ads to hang around the school that say 'Hats off to you.' What do you think?"

Todd and Lexi stared at the design with its large lopsided cowboy hats.

"I think you should take this to an art class and have them spruce it up a little bit."

"Maybe. I'm not a very good artist, am I?"

Lexi laughed out loud. "Binky, whoever looks at these ads isn't going to know whether you're trying to sell cowboy hats or mushrooms."

"I'm running out of time, that's all. There's so much to do when you run a business. If these hats don't sell within the next three weeks, we're going to have to have a sale and discount them. That would be just like admitting failure. It would be like going from an A to a C," she snapped her fingers, "just like that."

"Binky, they aren't even in the window yet. How can you expect them to sell if you don't display them?"

Before Binky could respond, Egg came bounding through the door of the shop. He appeared pale and agitated as he closed and locked the doors behind him. "Are we the only ones here?" he asked in a half whisper.

"Of course, the store closed a long time ago. Why?"

"I want to make sure we're alone."

"What's going on, Egg?" Todd demanded. "You look terrible." Egg sank onto a nearby stool. "I worked on the store's books last night and again today. Just now I asked one of the accounting teachers to help me. Still, I haven't been able to balance the store's books."

"So?"

"Someone is stealing from this store."

"Are you kidding?"

"Egg, have you lost your mind?" Binky demanded.

"I've been worried about this for days, but I didn't dare say anything. At first I thought it was my fault, but now I know it's not. I've been tracking the cash every single day. I know how much money is in the till when I open it and how much is there when I close it. I have the schedule of who's worked and who has had the opportunity to lift cash from the till."

"You think someone is stealing from us?" Binky said shakily. "I thought everyone who worked for us were our friends! We can get into a lot of trouble if money is missing. How are we going to pay our bills?"

She looked in horror at the disembodied heads lying about. "How are we going to pay for those?" Binky slammed her hands on the slim shelf of her hips. "Who do you think is stealing from us?"

"I'd rather not say right now."

"If you know when the money was stolen and have a list of the people who worked those days, it should be pretty easy to figure out."

"Don't ask me, Binky. I need to think first."

"Give us a break. You always act first and think later."

"Stop it, Binky." Egg's voice was stern.

Still Binky would not relent. "I'm a store manager too, Egg. I have a right to know who you suspect is stealing from us."

Egg took a deep breath. "I think it's Angela."

Everyone stared at Egg in disbelief. He was not kidding. There were tears in his eyes and his hands were shaking.

"Not your *girlfriend*," Binky finally said. "There must be some mistake."

"She is the only one who's worked every single day that money has been missing."

"Not Angela," Lexi gasped. "It couldn't be."

"What else am I supposed to believe?" Egg pleaded. "I've gone over this dozens of times. You and I are usually there when the other members of the marketing class work. Angela is in and out of the store more than any of the others. She works a lot of hours, some alone. What's more, she's the only common link, the only person who was in the store every single day that money was missing." Egg dropped his head into his hands and his shoulders sagged.

"It's my fault that she's here so much," he admitted. "I gave the hours to her because she is my girlfriend. I showed her where the cash bags were kept and everything about the till. It would be very easy for her to help herself to money and not have anyone else notice. Angela and her mom don't have much money. Maybe it was just too tempting for her to be working around all this cash."

"There has to be someone else who could have stolen the money besides Angela."

"As much as I've thought about this I can't imagine that anyone else could have pulled this off—or would have needed the money that badly." Egg sounded sick at heart.

Lexi, Todd, and Binky were stunned.

"You aren't in the store every minute that it's open," Lexi pointed out. "Students wander in and out all day. Why couldn't it be one of them?"

"How would they get past the person at the cash register?" Egg challenged. "They couldn't just walk in and help themselves. It has to be someone who works here. There's no other explanation."

"Are you sure that Angela would leave a trail like that?"

"Maybe she doesn't think I'm smart enough to figure it out," Egg said bitterly. Hurt and confusion surrounded him like a dense fog. "Two weeks ago, if you'd asked me if Angela could steal anything, I would have said absolutely not. Now, with all the evidence mounting against her . . ." He looked at his friends forlornly. "What am I going to do?"

Binky, Todd, and Lexi stared at Egg in mute horror. He actually believed what he'd just said about his own girlfriend. Egg's face was pale, but his jaw firm with determination. "I have to confront her."

"Please don't," Binky pleaded. "I know Angela couldn't have done this. There's got to be an explanation. Maybe somebody at the till is a lousy mathematician and gave the wrong change. Let's get everyone together and tell them to count out their change more carefully from now on."

"No." Egg's answer was short and sad. "Don't you think I've thought about this, Binky? Do you think there's anything else I *have* thought about in the last few days? Every time I look at Angela, I feel like running the other way. Yet, I want to tell her my problem and ask her to help me solve it. She's so important to me . . . but if I were that important to her, she wouldn't have done this."

"You've got to be wrong. What's her motive?"

"I've asked the same question," Egg said softly, "and I don't like the answer."

"What do you mean?"

"Angela has had a very hard life. You know she and her mother have never had much money. They were penniless when they came to Cedar River.

"Maybe there is something about her past that drives her to do this. Angela never acts like it hurts not to have a lot of money to spend, but perhaps she keeps it inside. Maybe it's too hard for her to work at the till, and the temptation is too great. Who knows? Maybe she and her mom need money for food and clothing."

Binky looked as though she were about to cry. Everything Egg had said was true. Angela's life was hard and money always seemed to be in short supply. Was the cash in the till something she couldn't resist?

"I won't believe that about Angela," Lexi said defiantly. "There's got to be another explanation."

"Even if there is," Todd said, "I agree with Egg. He is the store manager and he has to deal with the situation. That's his job. It's just like real life. Running a business isn't easy. Employers have trouble with employees all the time. Egg has to face it head on. He has to do something about it. And soon."

"I've told myself that over and over," Egg admitted, tears forming in his eyes. "But Angela cares for me. I'm afraid I'm going to hurt her so badly that she'll probably never want to have anything to do with me again." He looked pleadingly at his friends. "What else can I do? I have to tell her what I think is going on."

Todd cleared his throat and tipped his head toward the front of the store. "Well, here's your chance."

They all looked up to see Angela knocking softly on the door, waiting to come in.

Chapter Twelve

Binky gasped. Lexi reached to take her hand. Todd's expression was grim as Egg moved slowly toward the door.

"Hi!" Angela breezed into the store and dropped her book bag on the floor near the cash register. "I thought I saw lights in here. Are you still working? I hope Mr. Kahler appreciates all you've done for . . . what's wrong? You all look like you're about to cry."

"I need to talk to you, Angela," Egg said. "Alone."

"Why?"

"I'll tell you when we're alone."

Angela looked puzzled. "What's going on? Is it something about us? As a couple, I mean?"

"No, not that."

"Then you can say whatever you have to say in front of our friends."

"I think we'll leave now." Todd took Lexi's hand.

Angela stopped them. "Don't go. I didn't mean to chase you away."

"I don't want to do this, Angela," Egg pleaded.

"You're acting weird. Tell me what's wrong!"

Egg took a deep breath. "I've been having trouble with the store's books. Money has been missing from the till on several occasions."

"No kidding? That's serious." Angela frowned. "Do you have any idea what happened?"

"I've kept records of the days we came up short. I compared that to the employee work schedule. I wanted to see if any sort of pattern emerged."

"And?"

"And you are the only one who worked every single time money disappeared."

Angela stared at him. "Me?"

"Yes."

"And money was *always* missing?" There was a catch in her voice that sounded very close to tears.

"I'm sorry, but that's the way it is."

"Are you accusing *me* of stealing, Egg McNaughton?" She pulled her shoulders back and glared at him.

"I don't know what I'm doing. That's why I wanted to talk to you alone, to tell you what I've discovered, to give you a chance to explain."

"Me? A 'chance to explain'? Like you actually thought I stole that money and would want to tell you why? Give me a break, Egg! Who do you think I am? *What* do you think I am? I believed I was your girlfriend and all the time you suspected me of being a *thief*!"

"You're the only connection to the days the money was gone."

"So that makes me a sneaky robber? And I thought you were my friend."

"You are my friend." Egg reached out to her, but Angela pulled away.

"You don't even know me. If you did, you'd know that I could never ever steal anything from anyone.

My mother and I were homeless when I met you, Egg. We didn't even have a place to sleep until we found the mission. If I were going to steal something, don't you think I would have done it then? When I didn't have money to buy a can of pop or a candy bar? When we cleaned up in public restrooms and waited at the back doors of restaurants for leftover food? If I didn't steal then—and I didn't—I certainly don't know why I should start now."

"The money is missing and I . . . Mr. Kahler . . . the store—"

"You care more about that store and your money than you do about people! All you're thinking of is a good grade. You want people to recognize you as the guy who made a big success of that store. And you don't care how much you hurt me in the process."

"But I-I'm—" Egg stammered, too upset to speak.

"Maybe someone else took the money. There are people wandering in and out of that store all the time. Why couldn't someone else open the till? Or did you suspect me first because I used to be homeless? I don't come from a stable family, right? Therefore I must be dishonest. Thanks a bunch."

"Egg is just trying to do his job. . . ." Todd began.

"Don't you start with me too!" Angela spun to face him. "You and Lexi knew about this, didn't you? Why didn't you defend me? Don't you trust me either?"

"Talk to Egg. Help him figure out who *is* doing this!" Lexi pleaded.

Angela was crying now, deep body-wracking sobs that seemed to come from deep within her.

"Please, let me . . ." Egg reached out to her but she pushed him away.

"Don't touch me. Don't even come near me. When you're trying to be a businessman you make a lousy boyfriend."

Egg looked frustrated and hurt.

"But don't worry, you can spend all your time being a businessman now, because you certainly aren't my boyfriend anymore."

Todd and Lexi helplessly watched the friendship which had meant so much to both of them being destroyed. Binky sobbed quietly.

With a quick movement, Angela retrieved her book bag and flung it over her shoulder. "I have to go. There's nothing for me here."

"Angela . . ." Egg pleaded.

But she was gone.

Egg crumpled slowly to the floor, a slow, painful decompression of his limbs.

"What could I do?" he whispered. "What else could I do?"

———

"Still working on that book, Mrs. Leighton?" Todd picked up a cookie and walked to the kitchen table where Lexi's mother was camped with a sketch pad and a sheaf of papers.

"It's going slowly. Writing for children is far more complex than most people realize."

"Why?" Todd dropped into a chair across from Lexi.

"Because of the economy of words."

"What does that mean?"

"Children don't have vocabularies as large as

those of adults. Also, their attention spans are much shorter. I have to tell a riveting story in a short form and with simpler words."

Marilyn Leighton ran her fingers through her hair. "I'm glad I'm doing the artwork. Sometimes as I draw, I come up with new ideas."

"Do other authors do that?"

"Most don't do their own illustrations. I'm fortunate that I can." She leaned back in her chair and stretched. "But, in spite of all that, the book is finally coming together."

"Ben has Mom read it to him at least twice a day," Lexi added. "He's crazy about the dog in the book."

Mrs. Leighton pushed a sketch toward Todd.

"That looks like Wiggles."

"It is. I used our dog as a model."

Just then the real Wiggles ran into the kitchen, his toenails making a clicking sound on the linoleum.

"There he is, 'Wiggles the Soon-To-Be Famous Wonder Dog.' " Todd scratched the squirming animal behind the ear. Wiggles wagged so enthusiastically that his feet slipped out from beneath him and he landed on his hind end on the floor.

"Here, Wigs. Come, boy."

At the sound of Ben's voice, Wiggles forgot all about Todd and darted out of the kitchen.

Mrs. Leighton stared openly at Todd and Lexi for a moment. Todd was crumbling the cookie into bits and Lexi was staring off into space. "Which one of you wants to tell me what's wrong?"

"Did we say that something was wrong."

"Don't give me that, Todd. I know you both

pretty well. Something is *very* wrong. It might help to talk about it."

"I don't know if anything can help. It may be too late."

"For who?"

"For Egg and Angela. For all our friends. Our gang has pretty much broken up and none of us knows how to pull it back together."

"What do Egg and Angela have to do with this?"

When they'd told Mrs. Leighton the whole story, she asked, "But Egg still cares for Angela?"

"Yes. He's so upset that he can hardly function. Binky cries and cries. She says Egg paces back and forth in his room every night. He doesn't eat and has been losing weight. Angela won't look at him in school. She barely talks to us, or anyone, for that matter. The gang is a mess. We don't know what to do."

"Egg didn't want to believe that Angela might have been the one stealing from the till, but the facts told him otherwise. He's had to choose between his head and his heart."

"Binky told me that she and Egg tried to drop out of the marketing class," Lexi said. "They didn't want anything more to do with the store, but it was too late in the quarter. If they dropped the class they couldn't pick up another and would also have to take an F for a grade."

"Egg said he'd be glad to flunk if it would repair the damage done between him and Angela," Todd continued, unconsciously knotting and unknotting his hands as he spoke. "He's slipping into a depression. He sits in his room and stares at pictures of Angela and won't speak."

"I forgot to tell you this, Todd," Lexi said, "but he saw Angela tearing up his picture, the one she'd kept in her locker."

"Great. That will help his mood a lot."

"This sounds rather serious to me," Mrs. Leighton said.

"I know." Todd looked grim. "As I watch Egg, I think about Chad Allen and wonder if we should go to the school counselor to tell him that Egg's depressed."

Todd was referring to Peggy Madison's former boyfriend. Chad had also been depressed and had ultimately committed suicide. None of the gang would ever take depression or its symptoms lightly again.

"He's lost one of his best friends. He feels responsible and guilty and confused. It might not hurt to get him some help."

"Anything to make him quit reminiscing about his times with Angela."

Before Mrs. Leighton could comment, the telephone rang. Lexi punched the speaker phone and answered.

Egg's voice sounded on the line. He was brisk and businesslike—and almost normal. "Lexi, is Todd there?"

"Yes. Right here at the table. Do you want to talk to him?"

"No. Just come over to my place. Now."

"Why?"

"I'll explain when you get here."

"Are you all right?"

"No, but I'm working on it. Can't talk. Come now." And the line went dead.

Chapter Thirteen

The McNaughtons' ramshackled house was bright with light. Bicycles littered the driveway and a forlorn basketball hoop with a tattered net hung lopsided over the garage door. Lexi rang the bell and then, without waiting, walked inside.

Binky was there, as were Jennifer, Peggy, and Matt Windsor. Egg ordered Todd and Lexi onto the couch next to Matt and called his meeting to order.

"I wanted all of you to come today because I need help. You're the only people who know what's been going on at the store. Now, something has happened that changes everything."

"What's happened?" Jennifer asked, her curiosity aroused.

"More money has been stolen!" Egg beamed. "Isn't that wonderful?"

"It is?"

"Yes. It's fantastic news!"

"Why?"

"Because Angela hasn't been anywhere near the School Store in days! There's *no way* she could have stolen this money. The thief has to be someone else. Now all we have to do is find out who it is. Then maybe Angela will speak to me again."

"That might be easier said than done, Egg," Matt said. "Maybe Angela was set up. She might have been the unlucky one picked by your thief to take the blame, and that's why she was always around when the money was stolen."

"I know. I've thought of that." Egg's face fell. "It didn't occur to me until I'd already talked to Angela, though. Otherwise, I might have kept my big mouth shut and we wouldn't have had all this trouble between us."

He was trying hard to be brave. "But I don't think it's too late. The first thing I need to do is find out who's guilty. Then I'll apologize to Angela and hope she'll forgive me."

"If not Angela, who?" Peggy asked.

"I don't know. Two or three times yesterday I had to leave the counter and go into the back for something a customer wanted. Since I was working alone, that left them with the cash register. I thought I'd hear it if anyone tried to open it but . . ."

Binky picked up the story. "But Egg had me open the till while he was in the back and he *didn't* hear it. That means just about anyone who came into the store could have taken the money."

"It wouldn't take more than a couple of seconds to open the till, lift out a little money, and close it again."

"Wouldn't someone see that? Aren't there windows into the hallway?" Jennifer asked.

"Who watches? When people are moving through the hall, they're usually hurrying to get somewhere or talking to a friend."

"It still seems like it would be easier for someone with plenty of access to the store."

"Is that why Tim Anders isn't here?" Matt's eyes narrowed. He was street smart and had figured out quickly what Egg was up to.

"Yes. Even though he's a friend of mine, he still works at the store. I'm not going to risk losing his friendship too. But you must all promise to keep this a secret. If there's any chance at all for me and Angela, it will be that we find out who really stole the money." Egg paced up and down the floor.

"If Matt is right and the thief used Angela to throw me off the track, he or she is really smart. I'm going to need more brains than mine to solve this. Will you help me?"

The response was quick and enthusiastic. And they wanted to start immediately.

"We need a plan," Todd said. "Unless you've already figured something out."

"I thought maybe one of you could come up with something. I miss Angela and I want her back."

"Do you keep a schedule of who works at the store?" Matt asked. "Proof of who's been working?"

"I have a notebook. Every two weeks I assign staff hours and post them in the back room. I also made notes on the books and on my deposit slips on the days the money turned up missing. I've got everything in my room."

"Then we should compare the two. If we cross Angela off the list, we can tell who the next most likely suspect might be."

The evidence against Angela was condemning all right as the gang discovered while they pored over Egg's books. It was understandable that Egg was suspicious. He would have to have been blind not to notice the connection.

"I think it looks *too* suspicious," Lexi finally said. "Angela's not dumb. If she were stealing, she'd be more careful than this. This is very incriminating. She's been set up."

"Who would do that?"

Lexi looked at the list of students who worked at the store.

"It's too bad no one else was in the store with as much consistency as Angela," Todd sighed. "She probably wanted to be near you."

Egg looked as though he wanted to cry. "And I didn't trust her."

"You had a job to do, that's all. She really does look guilty. It's here in black and white."

"But she's *not* guilty. We know that now."

"Then there has to be another explanation," Matt said bluntly, "and we have to find it. Who else was in and out of the store a lot who wouldn't be noticed?"

"Everybody who goes to high school," Egg moaned. "Dozens of kids. Lots of people stop at noon to buy candy bars, cappuccino, or sodas from the machines inside the store."

"Then we need to talk to Angela."

"Matt's right. She's the only one who can tell us who came to the store every day while she was there. Also, she's the only one who'd know who was alone with the till while she went into the back room."

"Good luck," Binky muttered. "Angela won't even *look* at Egg or me. She certainly won't *talk* to us!"

"Then Todd and Lexi can do it." Matt turned to them. "She'll talk to you, won't she?"

"We'll try." Lexi didn't sound hopeful.

"Egg, you and Binky will have to reconstruct the day you had yesterday. Think of every person who came through the store. Who worked, their hours, everything. The guilty party has to be somewhere on that list.

"Also," Matt continued, "those of us in this room will have to watch the store."

"Like a 'stakeout'?" Binky's eyes gleamed.

"There are tables and chairs in the common area in front of the store. Kids sit there and study or visit all the time. It won't be noticeable if we take turns hanging around out there. Everybody has a free period. We'll make a schedule so we can cover the entire day. Write down the names of every person who enters the store. Sit so you can watch the cash register just in case they try something while we're there. It can't hurt. Who knows? Maybe one of us will witness a robbery."

"You're good, Matt. I should have asked you to help me before now," Egg said. "My idea doesn't sound very good anymore, but I'm going to do it anyway."

"What idea?"

"When I was in grade school, I used to pretend to be a detective. My parents gave me a fingerprinting kit for Christmas. I still have it. I thought it might come in handy someday. I'm going to start going to school early and scrubbing the till. Then every night I'll dust it for fingerprints. If I know who should have their fingerprints on the till, then the extra set will belong to the thief!"

"How will you find out who those prints belong to? You aren't the FBI." Jennifer began to laugh.

Egg ignored her. "I don't know. I just know that I'll do anything to prove Angela's innocent. I've hurt her and I need to make it up to her. I don't care how foolish I look or how hard I have to work. I just want her to speak to me again."

Chapter Fourteen

"Anybody home?" Lexi tapped on the half-open door and poked her head into the living room of the apartment Angela and her mother shared.

A light burned on a table near the couch and music played from a small radio on the kitchen counter. The apartment was small and plain but immaculately clean. The furniture had all seen better days, but the room was cozy and inviting.

Lexi turned to Todd. "No answer. They couldn't be far away, though, or the light wouldn't be on or the radio playing. What should we do now—wait or leave?"

Before Todd could answer, a sharp question cut through the air. "What are you doing here?"

Angela was standing behind them, a clothes basket loaded with freshly dried towels under one arm.

"I don't want to talk to you." She walked by them into the apartment. They followed her inside before she could shut the door.

"We need to talk to you."

"Not now."

"We know how angry you are at Egg," Todd began.

"You can't even begin to imagine how I feel." Angela's eyes narrowed and a high color came into her cheeks. "Unless, of course, you've also been betrayed by the person you thought was your best friend."

She set the hamper on the floor. "And I really don't want to talk about it right now. If I do, I'll start to cry—as if I haven't already done enough of that lately."

"Egg would have come himself if he'd thought you'd talk to him."

"Well, he was right. I *won't* talk to him. Not now. Not ever."

"He's sorry he accused you of stealing. He realizes now that he was wrong."

"Too late."

Lexi took Angela's arm. "Listen to us, won't you? We need to explain to you what Egg's discovered."

"The real thief, I hope?"

"Not quite, but we're trying."

Angela became curious. "What do you mean?"

Todd and Lexi explained that more money had been stolen from the store and that Egg knew it *couldn't* have been Angela. They told her how eager Egg was to catch the culprit and that he had involved them all in a new plan.

"It doesn't matter anymore." Angela's expression grew hard.

"It matters a lot!" Lexi protested.

"Not to me. Egg should have *known* that I would never steal anything from anyone. He should have trusted me."

"He did what he thought was right. We saw the schedule. Every time you worked, money did disappear. Egg didn't know what else to do."

"But other people worked too! And the store is always busy. Why did it have to be me?"

"Matt thinks you were set up."

Angela stared at them. "What?"

"He believes someone wanted to pin the blame on you. When he stopped to think about it, Egg realized that no one would leave such an obvious trail—money stolen every day they were on the schedule. Whoever did this planned all along to make Egg think it was you, to keep suspicion away from themselves."

Angela was interested in spite of herself. "What is he doing about it?"

"We're taking turns watching the store from the atrium area. Someone is always there during store hours. And Egg," Todd said with a wince, "is determined to wipe down the cash register every morning and dust it with fingerprint powder every night."

Angela finally laughed. "Does he even know *how* to do that?"

"Don't ask us. You know Egg. Once he gets an idea, he goes with it. If it makes him happy, I don't see how it can hurt."

"Poor Egg." Angela sat down on the couch and motioned Todd and Lexi toward the chairs across from her. "What a goof."

"He's also trying to reconstruct yesterday, to list everyone who came into the store. That will give us a place to start."

"Dozens of people are in and out! Besides, what if somebody forgets—or lies?"

"What else can we do?" Lexi sighed.

"You can help us," Todd said. "Try to remember who you saw *every single time* you worked. It has to be someone who could walk in and out without really being noticed."

"Think about it," Lexi encouraged. "Maybe something will come to you."

"I will, but I don't think it's going to help. I saw too many people every time I worked."

"There's one more thing," Todd said. "Egg wants you to come back to the store and start working there again."

"No way! Is he crazy?"

"Maybe. We never know about Egg. But I agree with him this time. Egg wants to set a trap," Todd explained. "He thinks that if you come back to work, whoever set you up will try to make it look like you stole money again. We'll be watching this time and catch the thief in the act. Whoever spent all that time setting you up needs you back in the store. You're the thief's 'cover.'"

"Why didn't Egg figure this out before he accused me of stealing?" Angela's eyes filled with tears. "I can't face anyone now, especially him."

"Nobody knows outside the gang," Lexi said. "Egg didn't even tell Mr. Kahler. He wanted to handle it himself, especially when he thought it was you doing the stealing. He thought you could pay back the money and no one else would have to know."

"He did? Even though he thought I was guilty?"

"He wanted to protect you. He cares about you, you know."

"Mr. Kahler will have to be told, but Egg wanted to wait until we try to catch the thief first. He's afraid that Mr. Kahler will feel he failed as manager otherwise."

"But it's not Egg's fault!"

"True, but he really wanted to be successful at this project. So many things Egg tries turn out . . . strangely."

"Will you help?"

"I don't know." Angela pondered the question. "I don't think so. Even though I understand what happened now, I don't want to be around Egg. It would hurt too much."

"It's not just Egg. Somebody set *you* up. It was you who got hurt the most. Don't you want to do anything about that?"

Angela considered Todd's question. "At first I wanted to hurt everybody. I felt like that Bible verse, 'An eye for an eye, a tooth for a tooth.' I wanted to hurt Egg as much as he'd hurt me. But now . . ." When she looked up, there were tears on her cheeks. "When I didn't know what else to do, I prayed. That's what you do, isn't it, Lexi?"

Lexi nodded. "You know it is."

"I'm not sure if I got through or not, but I felt better—and I didn't feel like hurting Egg anymore. I felt like forgiving him. Maybe I can learn to forgive whoever did this to me too."

"And you should," Lexi said. "But that doesn't mean this person shouldn't be caught and punished. Stealing money is serious. If he or she isn't caught now, will the stealing continue? I think you have a responsibility to stop it here if you can."

"I never thought about it that way." Angela gave a deep sigh. "Oh, all right, I'll help. But tell Egg that I'm doing this to catch the thief, not for him."

_____

"It doesn't look good for Egg and Angela, does it?" Todd said gloomily as they drove home.

"She's still very hurt. She feels betrayed."

"Our friend Egg is going to have to do some pretty fancy detective work if he wants to get Angela back," Todd added darkly. "Frankly, I'm not very optimistic."

Chapter Fifteen

"There! Do you like it?" Egg hung his photograph on the wall behind the cash register and eyed it proudly. Binky's picture hung next to his above the small sign which read "Student Managers." Egg's braces gleamed wickedly from the photo.

"Very nice," Peggy said.

"Especially if you like metal," Jennifer added.

"Don't get him started," Matt advised. "We have work to do. Is everything ready?"

"We're all set. Everybody knows when they are on surveillance, right?" Egg looked stern and businesslike.

"All the study halls are covered. There will be someone in the atrium as well as someone behind the door in the back room. Nobody will get *near* the till without being caught."

"I hope it happens today," Peggy said. "It's going to be hard to convince the study hall teachers to let us out of class for very many days."

"It will work," Egg said. "It *has* to."

Just then Angela arrived. She hesitated for a moment at the door, then squared her shoulders and walked inside.

"Hello, Angela," Egg said.

Angela nodded but didn't answer. Todd and Lexi exchanged a worried glance. Maybe this was going to be a disaster after all.

Egg chose to ignore the icy greeting. "I've told everybody that you're working today and as much as you can in the next couple of weeks to make up for the time you missed. That should give our crook plenty of time to make a move. I've started posting the work schedule in the window. That way our thief will know when you're working."

Jennifer sighed and put her hand out to steady herself against the till.

"Don't touch that!" Egg barked.

Jennifer jumped.

"I wiped the till. The only fingerprints we want on it are Angela's and whoever tries to get inside."

"Egg, you are too weird for words," Jennifer muttered. "But I won't touch it," she added. Egg breathed a sigh of relief.

They *all* thought the fingerprints were a goofy idea, but Egg was trying so hard that none of them wanted to discourage him.

"It's time," Egg said as the bell rang. Quietly they filed to their classes.

———

At two o'clock Todd found Lexi in the atrium and sat down beside her. "Anything?"

"Scads of people going in and out. I never realized how much time the High Fives spent goofing off. Minda, Tressa, Gina, and Mary Beth have each been in and out three or four times. And the basketball guys drink soda like it's going out of style.

Angela's been really busy. Nobody's touched the till, though."

"Who's in the back room?"

"Jennifer. Egg's been in and out. He's nervous as a cat at a dog show."

Todd looked at the clock.

"I have to go to class. I'm taking the after-school shift. There's a parent-teacher meeting at four o'clock, so Egg is keeping the store open. Matt will be out here, and I'll be in the back room. See you then."

At four-fifteen, Lexi and Binky found Matt lounging in the atrium. His feet were stretched out and crossed at the ankles. He was pretending to read, but his eyes never left the door of the store. From where he sat, he could see the cash register.

"What's happened?"

"Nothing. Angela's looking pretty pale though."

"She's probably scared stiff. She wants to catch whoever has done this, but facing that person will be awful. This has to be hard on her."

"Angela has been intentionally giving people the opportunity to steal money. She's been going into the store room and turning her back to the till at every opportunity, but no one's taken the bait." He looked at his watch. "She's supposed to close in a few minutes. I guess we could give up for today."

"Wait!" Lexi hissed. "Someone's coming."

"That's just Mary Beth Adamson. She works in the store too."

"I know, but we should watch everybody. We

promised Egg. Let's pretend we're studying together."

As they watched, Mary Beth stopped at the door
to the store. She glanced around as if looking for
someone, then went inside.

Angela greeted her with a smile and they visited
a few moments. Mary Beth studied a display of
pens near the cash register. From where Matt and
Lexi sat, they could see her ask Angela a question.
Angela nodded and turned to enter the back room,
leaving Mary Beth alone in the front.

Mary Beth looked around. Then, with a swift-
ness which startled both Matt and Lexi, she
punched the "Open" key and extracted a couple of
bills. Quickly she closed the till and stuffed the
money into her pocket.

"Let's go." Matt bolted to his feet and strode toward the store with Lexi in his wake.

At the same moment, Egg and Todd appeared in
the doorway of the back room. Egg's face was furious.

"We saw that!" he blurted.

"Saw what?" Mary Beth said coolly.

"Saw you open the till and take out some
money."

"Are you nuts? Why would I do that? Besides,
even if I had, you weren't here. You were in the
back."

"Todd and I were looking through the crack in
the door."

"And you think *I* was doing something wrong? I
wasn't *spying*. You're creepy, Egg." Mary Beth was
disdainful.

Egg's face suffused with color. "Matt and Lexi saw you too."

Mary Beth was unconcerned. "Get over it, Egg. They were outside. They couldn't see in here."

"But we did. You opened the cash register."

Mary Beth's expression altered slightly. "Oh, *that*. I had a pocket full of quarters. I dumped them in and took out a couple one-dollar bills, that's all. See? Here they are." She reached into her pocket."

"You stole that money," Egg accused.

"I did not. And you'd better not go around saying that I did. It's my word against yours and I know you're lying."

Egg sputtered and stammered helplessly. What was he going to do now?

Without warning, Egg whipped out his dusting powder. "I'm going to fingerprint this register! You and Angela are the only people who've touched the till today."

Mary Beth looked at him pityingly. "I just *told* you I touched the till! I got change. There's no crime in that. If you're so suspicious, why don't you accuse Angela?"

"But I've already counted money for the day and balanced the till for tomorrow! Angela couldn't have touched it because she was talking to me through the door until you came in. She had no chance to touch the money. All I have to do is count it again. If money is missing, then *you* took it."

"I'm leaving," Mary Beth announced. "You can't blame this on me!"

"We saw you," Matt said quietly. "Four of us."

"Well, you were wrong! You're all too dumb to know anything. I'm a High Five. My friends will vouch for me. I didn't take money from the till any of those times."

"But we didn't say money was missing any other time," Egg said softly. "We were only talking about *today*."

"So was I. I just got mixed up, that's all." Mary Beth's bravado was fading fast. A look of fear came into her eyes. "I want to go now."

"Not just yet." Mr. Kahler stepped out of the back room.

Mary Beth gasped.

"Egg didn't mention that I, too, was watching. He came to me today to tell me what he had planned. While I don't approve of playing cloak and dagger on school time, I agreed to let him try this. Mr. McNaughton was correct. We seem to have captured our thief."

"But I didn't . . ." Mary Beth backed toward the door, extending a pointed finger toward Angela. "*She* did!"

"How could you know that? Unless, of course, you're the one who set her up."

All the color left Mary Beth's face then and she sagged weakly against the doorjamb. "I can explain. I can. I just need a little time. My dad's getting a new job soon. I can pay it back then."

She was still pleading as Mr. Kahler led her toward the principal's office. It was silent in the store.

Lexi sighed. "I feel guilty."

"You? Why?"

"She was in trouble and we never figured it out. We'd heard her dad lost his job but we never put two and two together."

"Just because her family was short on money is

no reason to steal," Todd pointed out. He looked at Angela. "You're proof of that."

"What's wrong?" Binky asked. "You look sad. Aren't you glad we found out who did it?"

"I suppose I am." Angela sat down on the stool behind the counter and propped her chin in her hand. "But I'm sad that someone would care so little about me that she would be willing to get me into that kind of trouble. I thought Mary Beth and I were friends. She could have talked to me. I would have understood her problem—better than anyone else possibly could have."

"You can't tell about those High Fives," Binky said huffily. "They aren't friendly with anyone outside their little group."

"I doubt Mary Beth admitted her problems to anyone, even the High Fives. Instead, she tried to solve her money problems herself—by stealing. Besides, friends aren't always honest with each other. They don't tell each other everything. Our group is proof of that."

"Aw, Angela . . ."

"It's true, Egg. You believed bad things about me. You didn't tell me what was going on in your head. You didn't trust or believe in me."

Chastised, Egg drooped like a wilted flower. When his head came up, his cheeks were flushed. "You're right. I did believe some pretty rotten things about you, Angela. It wasn't because I wanted to, but because all the facts pointed in your direction. That was the way Mary Beth had planned it to be. I'd never felt so torn—between my loyalty to you and to doing what was right for the store.

"One thing is for sure," Egg said with a wan smile. "I'll never doubt you again. You're honest through and through."

Angela listened without speaking, her eyes cast downward. No one could guess what she was thinking.

"I understand why you are mad at me," Egg continued. "I'd be *furious* with me, if I were you. I deserve it. I just want you to know I was trying to do what I thought was right. You can be mad at me for as long as you like, Angela, but I'll never quit caring for you."

"Maybe we should all leave," Todd suggested, uncomfortable with the personal nature of the conversation.

"No. Stay. You've been in this with me from the beginning. I don't want you to leave now," Egg said.

"At least you cleared up any doubts about Angela's innocence," Todd pointed out. "You kept trying, Egg, for a long time after anyone else might have given up. Mary Beth didn't count on that."

"That's not much of a reward," Egg said softly. "I'd rather have Angela's forgiveness."

There were tears in her eyes. "There's a sign that hangs on the wall in the mission. Every time I go there, I read it. It's a verse from Matthew 6 that says, 'If you forgive men when they sin against you, your heavenly Father will also forgive you.' We've all goofed up. It's pretty nice to know that we can be forgiven. I'd hate to have you feel that you couldn't be, Egg." She drew an unsteady breath. "This is going to take a while to *forget*, but I want to forgive you."

Egg looked hopeful for the first time in days.

"Can we seal it with a malt?"

Angela nodded and slid off the stool. They walked out the door together without looking back.

"I guess that leaves me to close up shop and talk to Mr. Kahler," Binky observed. "Egg's certainly in no condition to do it."

"Do you think they'll make up?" Lexi asked hopefully.

"If Egg has anything to do with it, they will. And their relationship will be stronger than ever."

"I agree with Binky," Matt said. "Angela's heart is big and Egg's is even bigger."

It would take some time to pick up the pieces of their lives, but Lexi knew her friends could do it. They'd all faced problems before. Egg and Angela were going to make it.

Lexi and her friends thought they'd outgrown bullies with grade school, but when Egg becomes the target of harrassment by a football player who claims he's just "having fun," they realize that bullying can take on all kinds of shapes and forms—none of them much fun.

Will the Cedar River friends find a way to put an end to the bullying before Egg really gets hurt? Find out in CEDAR RIVER DAYDREAMS #25.

A Note From Judy

I'm glad you're reading *Cedar River Daydreams*! I hope I've given you something to think about as well as a story to entertain you. If you feel you have any of the problems that Lexi and her friends experience, I encourage you to talk with your parents, a pastor, or a trusted adult friend. There are many people who care about you!

I love to hear from my readers, so if you'd like to receive my newsletter and a bookmark, please send a self-addressed, stamped envelope to:

Judy Baer
Bethany House Publishers
11300 Hampshire Avenue South
Minneapolis, MN 55438

Be sure to watch for my *Dear Judy . . .* books at your local bookstore. These books are full of questions that you, my readers, have asked in your letters, along with my response. Just about every topic is covered—from dating and romance to friendships and parents. Hope to hear from you soon!

Dear Judy, What's It Like at Your House?
Dear Judy, Did You Ever Like a Boy
    (Who Didn't Like You?)

Live! From Brentwood High

1 • Risky Assignment
2 • Price of Silence
3 • Double Danger
4 • Sarah's Dilemma
5 • Undercover Artists

Other Books by Judy Baer

• Paige
• Adrienne
• Dear Judy, What's It Like at Your House?
• Dear Judy, Did You Ever Like a Boy
  (who didn't like you?)

Teen Series From
Bethany House Publishers

‒∞‒

Early Teen Fiction (11–14)

HIGH HURDLES by Lauraine Snelling
Show jumper DJ Randall strives to defy the odds and achieve her dream of winning Olympic Gold.

SUMMERHILL SECRETS by Beverly Lewis
Fun-loving Merry Hanson encounters mystery and excitement in Pennsylvania's Amish country.

THE TIME NAVIGATORS by Gilbert Morris
Travel back in time with Danny and Dixie as they explore unforgettable moments in history.

Young Adult Fiction (12 and up)

CEDAR RIVER DAYDREAMS by Judy Baer
Experience the challenges and excitement of high school life with Lexi Leighton and her friends—over one million books sold!

GOLDEN FILLY SERIES by Lauraine Snelling
Readers are in for an exhilarating ride as Tricia Evanston races to become the first female jockey to win the sought-after Triple Crown.

JENNIE McGRADY MYSTERIES by Patricia Rushford
A contemporary Nancy Drew, Jennie McGrady's sleuthing talents promise to keep readers on the edge of their seats.

LIVE! FROM BRENTWOOD HIGH by Judy Baer
When eight teenagers invade the newsroom, the result is an action-packed teen-run news show exploring the love, laughter, and tears of high school life.

THE SPECTRUM CHRONICLES by Thomas Locke
Adventure and romance await readers in this fantasy series set in another place and time.

SPRINGSONG BOOKS by various authors
Compelling love stories and contemporary themes promise to capture the hearts of readers.

WHITE DOVE ROMANCES by Yvonne Lehman
Romance, suspense, and fast-paced action for teens committed to finding pure love.